With his work  **stepped out on realized he was**

He'd never held a baby before—not even when he'd been a godfather, attending his nephew's fancy christening in a Sydney cathedral. Now—tonight—he'd assisted in a total stranger's birth. The little creature had slipped from her mother into the world.

Into his hands.

He'd looked down into her little face, all red and wrinkled. He'd watched her open her slate-grey eyes for the very first time, and he'd seen the tiny quivering tremble of her lip a heartbeat before she opened her mouth to give her first cry.

And he'd lost his heart.

Completely.

Now, as he stood at the veranda railing, trying to get a grip on his galloping emotions, he told himself to man up. He felt as if his life had changed in some significant way, but the reality was it hadn't changed at all.

THE CATTLEMAN'S SPECIAL DELIVERY

BY
BARBARA HANNAY

Reading and writing have always been a big part of **Barbara Hannay**'s life. She wrote her first short story at the age of eight for the Brownies' writer's badge. It was about a girl who was devastated when her family had to move from the city to the Australian Outback.

Since then, a love of both city and country lifestyles has been a continuing theme in Barbara's books and in her life. Although she has mostly lived in cities, now that her family has grown up and she's a full-time writer she's enjoying a country lifestyle.

Barbara and her husband live on a misty hillside in Far North Queensland's Atherton Tableland. When she's not lost in the world of her stories, she's enjoying farmers' markets, gardening clubs and writing groups, or preparing for visits from family and friends.

Barbara records her country life in her blog, *Barbwired*, and her website is www.barbarahannay.com.

CHAPTER ONE

Jess squirmed in the passenger seat as the car sped along the lonely outback road, windscreen wipers thrashing madly. At thirty-seven weeks pregnant, she would have found this journey tedious under any circumstances.

Tonight, in the inky, rain-filled darkness, with the wrong music playing and the monotonously annoying *swish*, *swish* of the wipers, the journey was definitely too late and too long and *far* too uncomfortable.

Beside Jess, her husband contentedly chewed gum and tapped the steering wheel, matching his rhythm to the latest hit from his favourite band. Alan was pleased with himself. Today he'd landed a new job managing an outback pub—a chance, at last, to earn regular wages. Jess had to admit she was pleased about this fresh start, away from the city temptations that had caused them so much trouble.

This morning, they'd travelled out to Gidgee Springs to view the pub and to settle the agreement, and in a few months, when their baby was old enough, Jess would probably work in the kitchen, so they'd both be earning again. Fabulous.

Admittedly, life in a tiny outback town wasn't quite what Jess had envisaged when she'd made her wedding vows, but she'd been pretty naïve the day she'd married Alan Cassidy on a romantic tropical beach at sunset. Now, three years older and wiser, she saw this new job as a much-needed chance to start over, to get things right. Finally.

As the car sped on Jess peered ahead, worried that the headlights seemed too feeble to fight with the rain. They barely picked up the white dividing lines on the narrow road and she was grateful that the traffic in the lonely outback was so sparse.

She closed her eyes, hoping she might nod off, found herself, instead, remembering the terrible day she'd almost walked out on Alan after he lost the last of their money on yet another hopeless business scheme. Jess had made the tough decision even though she'd known firsthand that single-motherhood was a truly difficult option.

She'd never known her own father, instead had grown up with her mother and serial 'uncles', and it wasn't the life she wanted. But she'd realised she had to leave Alan even though it would mean the death of her dreams of a proper, two-parent family. Those dreams had already crumbled to dust on the day Alan lost their entire savings.

Single, she would at least regain control over her income, and she would have found a way to keep a roof over her baby's head. Then, at the last minute, Alan had seen an ad for this job as manager of a pub. It was another chance. And Jess had stayed.

Years ago, her mother had warned that marriage was a gamble, that very, very few lucky souls could ever hope for a happy ending. Now Jess was taking one last gamble, praying that after today things would be different.

Surely they should be different.

Oh, please, let him be different.

They would finish this interminable drive back to Cairns. Their baby would be born in a few weeks' time and then the three of them would start their new life in Gidgee Springs.

She would give her marriage one last chance.

Reece Weston almost missed seeing the car in the ditch. He was about to turn into his cattle property when the headlights picked up the rounded hump of a dead kangaroo lying in the rain at the edge of the bitumen, and then skid marks veering off the road. Driving closer, he caught the gleam of white metal.

Dread settled uncomfortably in his gut as he pulled over. A small sedan had plunged nose-down into a rocky gully.

He knew the vehicle hadn't been there an hour or two earlier, and chances were he was the first person to come across it. Grim-faced, he grabbed a torch from the glovebox and slipped his satellite phone into his coat pocket.

The night was moonless and black and wind threw rain into his face as he negotiated the slippery bank. The car's front passenger door hung open, the seat empty. Flashing the torch over the sides and bottom of the gully, Reece hoped he wasn't about to find a body flung from the crash. He couldn't see anyone outside the car, but when he edged closer to the wreckage he found the figure of a man slumped over the steering wheel.

Scrambling around the vehicle, he dragged the driver's door open, released the seat belt and felt for a pulse in the man's neck.

No luck.

He tried the wrist. Still no sign of life.

Sickened, he wrenched open the back passenger door, shoved a suitcase from the back seat into the rain, leaned in and lowered the driver's seat backwards into a reclining position. It would be hours before help could arrive, so saving this guy was up to him. Struggling to get beside the body in the cramped space, he began to apply CPR.

Come on, mate, let's get this heart of yours firing.

Reece had only done this on dummies before, so he was by no means experienced, but he was glad the training came back to him now as he repeated the cycle over and over—fifteen compressions and two slow breaths.

He wasn't sure how long he worked before he heard the woman's cry coming from some distance away. The thin sound floated faintly through the rain, and for a split second he thought that perhaps he'd imagined the sound, a trick of the wind. But then he heard it again. Louder.

'Help, someone, please!'

Definitely a woman. She had to be the passenger, surely.

He grabbed his sat phone and punched in numbers for the district's one and only cop, praying there'd be an answer. To his relief the response was instant and he'd never been more pleased to hear the sergeant's gravel-rough voice.

'Mick, Reece Weston here. There's been an accident out near the turn off to my place—Warringa. A small sedan's hit a kangaroo and gone off the road. I've been trying CPR on the driver, but I'm not having much luck, I'm afraid. No signs of life. And now there's someone else calling for help. I'm going to check it out.'

'OK, Reece. I'll alert the ambulance at Dirranbilla, and come straight out. But you know it'll take me a couple of hours. And the ambos could be even longer. Actually, with all this rain, they might have trouble getting through. The creeks are rising.'

Reece let out a soft curse as he disconnected. Times like this, he had to ask why his forebears had settled in one of the remotest parts of Australia. He flashed his torch up and down the gully again, then scrambled onto the road and cupped his hands to his mouth. 'Where are you?' he called.

'On a track off the road. *Please...help!*'

The only track around here led into his homestead. The woman must have scrambled from the car in a bid to reach help for the driver. She sounded both scared and in pain.

Rain needled his face as he started to run, the beam of his torch bouncing ahead down the track, lighting muddy puddles and drenched grass and the slim trunks of gum trees. Rounding a bend, he found the woman huddled in the rain, sagged against a timber fencepost.

He flashed the torch over her and caught her pale, frightened face in its beam. Her hair was long and hanging in wet strings to her shoulders. Her arms were slender and as pale as her face, and she was holding something...

A step or two closer, he realised she was supporting the huge bulge of her heavily pregnant belly.

He was shocked to a standstill.

The man arrived just as the pain came again, huge and cruel, gripping Jess with a vice-like force. She tried to breathe with it, the way she'd been taught at antenatal classes, but no amount of breathing could bring her relief. She was too horrified and too scared. She wasn't supposed to be in labour now. Not three weeks early, not on the edge of a bush track in the rain and in the middle of nowhere. Not with Alan scarily unconscious and unable to help her.

The man stepped closer. She couldn't see him very well, but he seemed to be tall and dark-haired. Not old. 'Are you hurt?'

She shook her head, but had to wait till the contraction eased before she could answer. 'I don't think so,' she said at last. 'But I'm afraid my labour's started.'

He made a despairing sound. No doubt he wondered what the hell she was doing out here in an advanced state of pregnancy. She felt obliged to justify her predicament. 'My husband needs help. I was trying to find a homestead.'

By now his hand was at her elbow supporting her. Despite the rain, his skin was warm and she could feel the roughness of his work-toughened palm. She sensed she could trust him. She had no choice really.

'Alan's unconscious,' she said. 'I couldn't revive him, and then the pains started when I had to climb up the rocks to the road.' She gave a dazed shake of her head. 'I couldn't use my mobile. There's no network. But he needs an ambulance.'

'I saw him,' her rescuer said gently. He had brown eyes, as dark as black coffee, and he was watching her now with a worried frown. 'I've rung the local police and help is on the way. But, for the moment, I think you need to look after yourself and your little one.'

Jess's response was swallowed by a gasp as another contraction gripped her, then consumed her, driving every other thought from her head.

'Here, lean on me.' The stranger slipped his arm around her shoulders, steadying her against his solid chest.

Just having him there seemed to help.

'Thanks,' she said shyly when the pain was over.

'Look, you can't stay here.' Her good Samaritan slipped off his canvas coat and put it around her shoulders. 'This will at least keep the rain off you until I get you into the truck.' His voice was deep and kind. 'Can you wait here while I fetch it? I'll be as quick as I can.'

'Yes, of course.' She remembered to add, 'Thank you.'

He was gone then, but he was as good as his word, and in no time the truck's headlights lit up the track. The door creaked a little as he opened it and swung down, his long legs seeming to stretch for ever. Before Jess knew quite what was happening, he'd scooped her up into his arms.

At first she was too overawed by his strength to protest, but she quickly came to her senses. 'For heaven's sake. I'm the size of a whale. I'll break your back.'

'Don't fuss. I'm not letting you climb up into this truck. There you go.' With a grunt he deposited her carefully on the front seat. 'We won't worry about the seat belt. I'll be careful and it's not far.'

'But we're not leaving, are we? What about Alan?'

'The ambulance and the police are on their way.' His voice was quiet, but commanding.

Jess gaped at him. Was he suggesting she should just abandon her husband? 'We can't leave him,' she protested. 'The poor man's unconscious. He's all alone.'

She began to tremble as she remembered how still and pale Alan had looked.

Watching her, Reece drew a sharp breath. Her eyes filled with tears and he had to turn away as he wrestled with this new dilemma. It would be too cruel to tell her bluntly that her husband was beyond help. Somehow, he had to keep her focused on her own needs.

'Seems you're about to have a baby,' he said as gently as he could. 'I'm guessing you wouldn't want to have it in a dirty truck's cabin.'

'Well...no.'

'I can give you a bed at the homestead. It's not much of a choice, I know, but, under the circumstances, I'm sure it's what your husband would want for you.'

Jess felt too confused and uncomfortable to argue. Now, sitting upright in the truck, she could feel her baby's head pushing down.

She felt terrible about leaving Alan, but she guessed she didn't really have a choice. Her priority now was their baby's safety, and almost as soon as the truck started up another contraction began. She dragged in a deep breath as the pain cut harder, deeper, lower, and she began to pant, staring out into the dark, rainy night, trying frantically not to moan and to concentrate instead on her breathing and the skinny trunks of gum trees flashing past.

No one had warned her that the pain would get this bad.

When it finally eased, her rescuer asked, 'Is this your first baby?'

Jess nodded. ''Fraid so. What about you? Has your wife been through this?'

'I don't have a wife,' he said quietly.

'Is there a woman at the homestead?'

'Unfortunately, no.'

Somehow, she managed to suppress a groan of disappointment. She'd been hoping to find a woman who'd been through this. Someone who could, at the very least, reassure her.

'By the way, my name's Reece.' He flashed a shy smile and for a moment his rather stern face looked incredibly appealing. 'Reece Weston.'

'Jess Cassidy. And I should have said—I'm so grateful to you.'

He shrugged. 'I'm glad I found you.'

'So am I, believe me.' She wondered if she ever would have made it, stumbling down this long, rough track in the rain on her own.

'Do you know if the baby's a boy or a girl?'

She supposed Reece was trying to take her mind off Alan.

'No,' she confessed. 'I didn't ask. I told the doctors I didn't want to know. I wanted a surprise.'

The sad truth was, she hadn't wanted Alan to know. He would have been so cocky and possessive if the baby was a boy, and at the time she'd still been undecided about whether she should stay with him.

And now… Oh, God, she felt another stab of guilt as she remembered how terribly pale and still Alan had been.

Was there a chance she'd panicked and overreacted? Maybe he was going to be OK. She was feeling so dazed, so sideswiped by the sudden onset of pain coming right on top of the accident.

Ahead of her now, through the rain, she could see a homestead at last. It was a typically North Queensland, timber dwelling, and ever so welcoming tonight with the golden glow of lights on the veranda. As they drew up at the front steps she saw two striped canvas squatter's chairs and a row of pegs holding battered Akubras and coats.

A stooped, elderly man appeared, squinting out at them like a short-sighted, bow-legged gnome.

In a blink, Reece was out of the truck and at Jess's door.

'I'm OK, thanks. Really, you don't have to lift me down.'

Once again he ignored her. 'Don't want you falling. I've got you.' He lifted her easily, and set her down lightly.

'Who you got there, son?'

'There's been an accident,' Reece told the old man. 'And this young lady needs to lie down. I'm going to put her in my room.'

'One of your fancy tarts, is she?'

Reece ignored this. 'Can you bring us some towels, Dad?' he asked instead.

With a strong arm around Jess, he steered her up a short flight of steps, and across the wooden veranda boards, not to the main front doorway, but to white-framed French doors. The rain hammered on the tin roof as Reece opened the doors and flicked on a light to reveal a large bed with an old-fashioned, blue chenille spread.

'Lean against the bedpost if you need to,' he said. 'I'll get rid of this bedspread.'

'You don't—' Jess's words were cut off as yet another contraction arrived.

Surely they weren't supposed to be so close together? She had no choice but to hang on to the bedpost and cope as best she could.

By the time the pain had eased, Reece had lit bedside lamps and turned the main light off, as well as pulling back the bedcovers. Now he was at her side, ready to help her out of the coat, just as his father arrived in the doorway, bearing towels.

The old man stared at her belly.

'This is Jess Cassidy, Dad.'

'Did you get her into trouble?'

Jess admired Reece's self-restraint as he simply shook his head and said, 'I told you. There was an accident out on the main road.'

'Looks like she's about to drop.'

'Yes, Jess is in labour,' Reece said firmly as he took the towels. 'It would be helpful if you could fetch the Flying Doctors' medical chest. It's at the back of the pantry.'

The old man seemed reluctant to leave, but his son made a shooing gesture and, finally, he hobbled away.

Reece turned to Jess. 'You need to get out of these wet clothes.'

She was wearing a loose top over maternity trousers and, yes, they were wet, but the rest of her clothes were in a suitcase in the back of the car. 'I don't have anything else to change into.'

'You can wear one of my shirts.' Already he was opening a wardrobe, slipping a pale blue cotton shirt from a hanger. It looked almost big enough to serve as a nightgown.

His dark eyes were warm as he held it out to her. 'Can you manage?'

'Yes, thanks.' She would have to manage. She certainly didn't want a handsome stranger helping her to undress, thank you very much. She knew very well that it would be a bachelor's worst nightmare to help a strange woman in an advanced state of pregnancy out of her clothes.

'I'll be fine,' she said to make sure he understood. But the words were no sooner out than she felt as if the bottom half of her were being wrenched away from her with massive force. She only just had time to grab to the bedpost before her knees gave way.

'Oh, God!' Seized by an overwhelming urge to bear down, she slumped against the post and clung for dear life. 'I'm so sorry,' she moaned. 'I think the baby's coming!'

And then her waters broke.

CHAPTER TWO

THE baby couldn't be coming already.

Reece stared at Jess in dismay. If she'd looked scared before, she now looked terrified, and he couldn't blame her. He was terrified too. This was way outside his experience. Weren't first babies supposed to take hours and hours to arrive?

He'd been confident that his job was to keep Jess comfortable until the Flying Doctor or the ambulance arrived—assuming that at least one of them could make it in this weather.

The poor girl.

Reece remembered her husband slumped over the steering wheel. If ever Jess Cassidy had needed her husband's support it was now.

'How can I stop this?' she moaned.

You can't, he wanted to tell her, and he wished he weren't so clueless. He'd only delivered calves—mostly with a rope tied around the calf's hoof and his boot planted squarely on the mother's hindquarter to gain leverage. That sure as hell wasn't going to work here.

'Maybe, if you lie down there'll be less pressure,' he suggested.

'That makes sense. I'll try anything.'

In this light, she looked little more than a girl, with her slender, pale limbs and long, dark hair hanging in limp, damp strands. Her thickly lashed eyes were green or grey—he couldn't be sure of their exact colour—and her nose was fine and slim, in contrast with the pink roundness of her soft mouth. In her wet, bedraggled clothes, she looked frail and helpless.

A wayside waif. In desperate need of his help.

He'd never felt more inadequate.

'You'll have to get out of these wet clothes,' he suggested.

This time Jess seemed ready to submit to his assistance and Reece held his breath as he helped her out of her shirt. It wasn't the first time he'd undressed a woman, although most of the women in his experience were very adept at slipping out of their gear.

This time was *so very* different, and he had to perform the delicate task with the dispassionate detachment of a medical practitioner.

Not so easy when Jess's skin was moon pale and smooth as sifted flour and when her body was lush and ripe with the fullness of her pregnancy. She was lovely. Earthy. Madonna-like. With an unexpected fragile beauty that could catch a man totally unprepared.

He was aware of her distress, however, and he worked quickly as, between them, they eased her maternity slacks down. He rubbed her back and legs dry with a fresh towel while she took care of her front. Then he squeezed moisture from her hair and rubbed at it with the towel.

Her bra was wet too, and he undid it gently, conscious that her full, round breasts might be tender.

When he helped her into his shirt, it came down almost to her knees and he had to roll the sleeves back several times to free her wrists. She kept her eyes downcast, no doubt embarrassed.

'Let's get you comfortable,' he said, helping her onto the bed.

His bed.

According to his mother, whom he hadn't seen in a decade, he'd been born in this room, although his younger brother, Tony, had been delivered in a hospital in Cairns, many hours' drive away.

Now, Jess lay on her side, an expression of fixed concentration on her face, her hand gently massaging her tense abdomen.

'I'm going to ring the Flying Doctor,' he said.

If they couldn't land in this rain, they could at least give him medical advice. He'd take all the advice he could get. This was his worst fear—a dependent woman on his isolated property, with no help for miles. His mother had been right. This was no place for women.

'Can I get you something from the kitchen, Jess? Would you like water?'

She gave a faint nod. 'Maybe a sip.'

He went quickly to the kitchen where he found his father cursing as he fiddled with the knobs on the radio.

'Can't get this damn thing to work.'

Reece sighed. 'Did you find the medical chest?'

His dad looked churlish. 'Forgot.'

'Can you get it now?' Reece gave another despairing sigh. This was a new problem that had arrived just lately—these signs that his father's short-term memory was deteriorating, along with his temper. But tonight he didn't have time to worry about it. 'I'm going to make some calls.'

His dad's face broke into a rare grin. 'At least I remembered to put the kettle on. You'll need boiling water, won't you?'

When Reece came back into the room with a medical chest, extra towels and a glass of water, Jess was fighting another urge to push, blowing frantically as she'd been taught in antenatal classes.

She heard the clink of the glass as Reece set it down on a bedside table.

'How are you doing?' he asked as the contraction finally loosened its grip.

'Awful,' she grunted. 'I'll tell you one thing. I'm never, *ever* having sex again.'

She saw him swallow a smile and she sent him a hefty scowl. It was all very well for guys. They got it easy—a night of fun and, nine months later, someone else endured giving birth to their child.

Perhaps it was just as well Alan wasn't here right now. She'd have given him a piece of her mind.

Oh, dear Lord, the poor man. Jess was instantly ashamed. How could she be angry with her husband when he might be seriously hurt, or even—?

No, she wouldn't allow herself to think the worst, but tears stung her eyes. Tears for Alan. Tears of self-pity.

Hoping Reece hadn't noticed them, she dashed at her face with the sleeve of the shirt he'd given her.

'Would you like your drink?'

She shook her head. She was past needing a drink. What she needed now was a miracle. She needed to be magically whisked away from this isolated, outback homestead. She knew Reece was doing his best and she was grateful. Truly. But how could a lonely bachelor cattleman deliver her baby? She wanted to be safely in

Cairns with a midwife and a ward full of nurses…doctors on standby…

'Did you get through to the Flying Doctor?'

'Yes.'

'Is he on his way?'

Sympathy shone in Reece's dark eyes. 'With all this rain, they can't risk trying to land on our boggy airstrip.'

A surge of hot panic ripped through her now. 'What does that mean? I'll have to wait for an ambulance?'

He dropped his gaze and looked uncomfortable.

'Tell me there's an ambulance on its way,' Jess pleaded.

'Yes,' he said at last. 'A policeman is coming from Gidgee Springs and the ambulance from Dirranbilla.'

She sensed there was more bad news. 'But…what are you not telling me?'

Reece grimaced. 'The creeks are coming up fast.'

'So they might not make it?'

'It's…possible…'

This time, when Jess felt her face crumple, she didn't even try to be brave. What was the point? Everything was stacked against her. First a terrible accident, then her labour starting in the middle of nowhere. And now, no chance of help.

She and her baby were going to die.

All alone out here.

'Hey, Jess.'

She felt Reece's hand on her arm.

'It's OK,' he soothed. 'You're going to be OK.'

'I'm not,' she wailed. 'I don't know how to do this and neither do you.'

'I know how to deliver calves.' He gave a shrugging smile. 'And there's no need to panic. I've talked to a telehealth on-call doctor and he's told me what to do. He's on standby to talk me through step by step if I need help.'

'Oh, terrific. So I can have my baby by remote control and a tele—'

Her words were cut off as the urge to push crashed back with a vengeance. She screwed up her face and clenched her teeth to stop herself from screaming. She so-o-o wanted to push, but she couldn't forget the dire warnings from the antenatal teacher about not pushing too soon. Oh, God, how could she *not* push?

It was too hard to hold back.

'Can you see the baby's head?' she groaned.

'Would you like me to check?'

Exhausted already, Jess nodded, all pretence at modesty gone. If Reece could see the head she wouldn't keep fighting. She'd give in to the urge to push.

She watched his face as he cautiously lifted the shirt, saw his dark eyes widen and his Adam's apple ripple in his throat.

'What?' she demanded. 'What's happening down there?'

'Your baby has dark hair.'

Really?

In spite of everything, Jess felt her mouth tilt in a tremulous smile. The baby was a real little person. It had dark hair. She felt an unexpected spurt of excitement.

She looked at Reece, surprised by the emotion shimmering behind his smile. The poor man hadn't asked to be thrown into this situation, and he was doing his best. She realised he'd spread a waterproof on the bed and he'd set up a tray with items from the medicine chest. He was a stranger, doing everything he could for her and for her baby.

She felt a rush of gratitude. 'Thanks for being here,

Reece. If the baby's a boy I'll name him after you. And I'll—'

Once again, she was overtaken by an incredible force and every cell in her body urged her to give in to it. She was dimly aware that Reece was spreading more towels on the bed and taking something out of the medical chest. She heard the snap of sterile gloves.

There was nothing she could do but push.

And push.

And pu-u-u-sh.

'You're doing brilliantly,' Reece coaxed. 'The baby's shoulders are almost there now. Everything's happening just the way it's supposed to. Good girl. You're fabulous. That's it. Another push.'

'I can't.'

Exhausted, Jess sank back against the pillows. She couldn't push again. She didn't have the strength.

'Honestly, your baby's almost here,' Reece said again. 'Don't give up now, Jess. I can see its face. It's a real little cutie.'

'That's nice,' she said wearily.

But next moment, she was gripping her knees and pushing again, assisted, thank heavens, by another contraction.

'That's it, Jess. Here it comes. Good girl!'

Face screwed tight with the effort of another huge push, Jess felt the baby slip from her and she heard Reece's shout of triumph.

She fell back, panting, hardly daring to believe it was over so soon. Two breaths later, she asked, 'Boy or girl?'

'Well… I'm not sure about calling her Reece.'

'A girl?'

He was grinning from ear to ear. 'A perfectly beautiful baby girl.'

A girl. In the sudden lull, Jess felt exhausted and strangely devoid of emotion. Secretly, she'd hoped for a girl, but she'd been so sure she was having a boy. It took a moment or two to adjust.

She closed her eyes, suddenly weary and drifting towards sleep.

'Waaaa!'

At that tiny, lusty yell, Jess's eyes whipped open and her heart gave a leap of joy, her exhaustion vanished in a blink. She struggled to sit. 'How is she? Is she all right?'

'She has all her fingers and toes. I'm no doctor, but she looks perfect to me.'

Jess wanted to see her, but before she could dig her elbows into the mattress and hoist herself upright Reece was at her side.

'Here,' he said gently.

She felt a warm weight on her chest and looked down. And discovered a miracle. Her baby daughter. Red and perfect, with a scrunched-up face. 'Hey, little girl.'

Her baby's skin was still shiny and wet, but she was so cute. She had tiny little fingers and toes with the sweetest little transparent nails. And she had the most exquisite, perfect, tiny ears. And her nose was tiny and perfect too, and so was her mouth. And her eyes. And her hair.

'Reece, she's utterly gorgeous.'

Looking up, she saw the silver sheen of tears in his eyes. He gave her an embarrassed, lopsided smile. 'Congratulations.'

'Congratulations to you too. You were brilliant.' Jess felt suddenly overwhelmed with gratitude. Everything had happened so quickly and, if it hadn't been for

Reece, her baby might have been born on the edge of a dirt track out in the rain.

Now, this simple room, miles from anywhere, felt like the most wonderfully safe and comforting haven in the world.

'Thank you,' she said softly.

Somehow, just saying 'thank you' felt totally inadequate, but she was scared that she might start to cry if she tried to express how she really felt.

'Let's get this around her to keep her warm.' Businesslike again, Reece tucked a mauve crocheted blanket around the baby's tiny body. 'Do you want to see if she's hungry?'

'I'll try, I guess.'

'Do you know what to do?'

'I think so.'

With his work finally done, Reece stepped out onto the veranda, and realised he was shaking. He'd never held a baby before, not even when he was a godfather attending his nephew's fancy christening in a Sydney cathedral. Now, tonight, he'd assisted in a total stranger's birth. The little creature had slipped from her mother into the world.

Into his hands.

He'd looked down into her little face, all red and wrinkled. He'd watched her open her eyes for the very first time, and he'd seen the tiny quivering tremble of her lip, a heartbeat before she opened her mouth to give her first cry.

And he'd lost his heart.

Completely.

Now, as he stood at the veranda railing, trying to get a grip on his galloping emotions, he told himself to man up. He felt as if his life had changed in some significant way, but the reality was, it hadn't changed at all.

In an hour or two, the police or the ambulance would probably get through. If not tonight, tomorrow, or the next day… Then, this mother and baby would be gone. Out of his life. He'd be back to living alone with his ageing father as he had for almost thirty years. Back to carrying out his duty on this vast, back-breaking cattle property. Back to worrying about his father's health. Back to visiting lonely spinsters if he wanted female company.

'What's happening in there?'

Reece turned as his father appeared at his elbow and cocked his head to the French doors, now discreetly shut with the curtains drawn.

'Jess had a baby girl.' Reece's voice was choked as he said this.

'Crikey. She doesn't muck around, does she? Is she going to stay?'

'Of course not. She'll want to get back to the coast as fast as she can.'

'Yeah. They never want to stay.' His dad released an unexpectedly heavy sigh. After a bit, he brightened. 'Can I see her?'

'She needs a little time alone. She's feeding the baby. It's late, Dad. Why don't you go to bed?'

'What about the Flying Doc?'

'I'm going to ring them again now.' Reece had followed the doctor's instructions faithfully, using sterile gloves and scissors from the specially supplied medical chest, and the placenta had come away easily—*thank God*—but he wanted to double-check that he hadn't overlooked anything.

'You want to put lights out on the landing strip?' his father asked. 'I'll get the tins from the shed.'

Reece blinked. This was the first cooperative gesture his dad had made in ages. Unfortunately, he couldn't make use of it. He shook his head. 'It's too wet for the plane to land.' He smiled. 'But I'm sure we could all use a cup of tea.'

Jess was too stirred to sleep. Part of her mind was constantly worrying about Alan, while the rest of her thoughts were leaping with excitement. And she couldn't close her eyes because she didn't want to stop gazing in awe at the tiny sleeping beauty beside her. Reece had helped her to bath the baby. She'd been nervous of the tiny body, as slippery as a frog, but he'd been calm and gentle and sure.

Jess had dried her then, and wrapped her in strips of sheeting, because they had no nappies, while Reece fashioned a makeshift cot by padding a drawer with blankets and setting it on two chairs beside Jess's bed.

So now the baby was right there, at eye level and touching close, which was perfect. And Jess had chosen her name—Rosie Millicent Cassidy.

'Millicent after my grandmother. And Rosie because it's a bit like Reece,' she'd announced as she'd sat, propped by a bank of pillows and sipping hot, sweet tea.

A dark red stain crept up Reece's neck. 'You know, you don't have to name her after me.'

'I don't feel obliged, but you did save us from the worst possible nightmare. And anyway, Rosie is a pretty name.'

Reece looked down at the sleeping baby. 'Actually, she looks a bit like a half-opened rose.'

Jess grinned. 'That's a very poetic comment. Not

quite what I expected from a cattleman. But it's true. She's pink and a little bit crumpled still, and sort of folded like rose petals.'

He smiled and shook his head at her and their gazes linked for a shade too long. He had the loveliest dark chocolate eyes, and Jess thought, momentarily, *If only...* And then she was ashamed of herself.

Perhaps Reece noticed. He moved to the door. 'I'll say goodnight.'

'Goodnight, and thanks again. For everything.'

'If you need me, call. I won't be far away and I'm a light sleeper.'

Jess felt strangely alone after he'd left. Outside the rain had slowed to a fine, dripping drizzle. She finished her tea, set the mug aside and settled down in the bed. Her body was exhausted. She really should try to get some sleep before Rosie woke again.

She closed her eyes. The house was very quiet and outside there was just a background whisper of rain. She hoped Alan was safely in an ambulance, speeding to a hospital. She had no idea where the nearest hospital might be. She wondered if he would need to be airlifted to the coast...and she wondered when she would be able to tell him about Rosie...

Perhaps she drifted off to sleep, but she roused quickly when she heard the swish of tyres in puddles, and then a vehicle pulling up outside. Footsteps and voices. Men speaking quietly and at some length.

Jess wondered if it was the police, or an ambulance. Had they come for her? She sat up and switched on a bedside lamp and, of course, she checked on Rosie, pressing her hand gently to the baby's back to make sure she was still warm and breathing. Rosie wriggled and made a snuffling protest.

'Sorry,' Jess whispered. 'Didn't mean to disturb you.'

Footsteps approached from down the hallway. A soft tap sounded on her door.

'Come in,' she called.

Reece appeared, wearing an unbuttoned shirt that hung loose over his jeans, giving a hint of his broad chest with a smattering of dark hair, and a finely tapered waist. 'Sergeant Bryant is here, Jess. He apologises for the late hour, but he'd like to speak to you.'

She was suddenly scared and she felt a little sick as the policeman stepped into the room. He didn't look threatening, however. He was middle-aged, balding and thickset and his expression was one of almost fatherly concern.

'Good evening, Mrs Cassidy.'

'Hello, Sergeant.'

He nodded towards the cot and smiled. 'I believe congratulations are in order.'

'Thank you.'

He stepped closer. 'She's a little sweetie, isn't she? It's been a big night for you.'

'It has rather.' Jess swallowed a nervous lump in her throat. 'Have—have you seen my husband?'

Sergeant Bryant dropped his gaze and cleared his throat and in that moment Jess knew, even before he spoke.

'I'm so sorry,' he said.

'He's d-dead?'

'I'm afraid he is.'

At some primitive level, she had probably known all along, but until now she'd never allowed herself to think it was actually possible. But faced with the horrible truth, Jess felt strangely numb. She'd run the full gamut of her emotions tonight and it was almost as if there was nothing left to feel right at this moment…

She couldn't even squeeze out a tear, but she knew the grief would come…later…

'At some stage I'll need to talk to you about the accident,' the sergeant said. 'But I won't bother you tonight.'

She nodded.

'The rain's almost stopped, so I'm hoping that the ambulance will be able to get through in another few hours,' he went on. 'It will bring you back to Dirranbilla. You'll be able to see a doctor. And then we can talk.'

He looked into the cot again and his face creased in a soft smile and then he left her.

Jess lay dazed, unable to focus on anything except the news that in another few hours…she would be leaving. She would be starting a new life.

How strange… For a short space of time this simply furnished room had been a little sanctuary for her and for Rosie…a safe haven from the wild night…and from the real world where all her savings were lost and accidents happened and husbands died…

Reece had been so kind. He'd delivered Rosie so beautifully. But in another few hours…

She would be gone…and the cruel irony was, she would be a single mum, after all.

CHAPTER THREE

2/56 Mary Street,
Edmonton, Cairns
3rd March
Dear Reece,

Once again, thank you, although I know thanks aren't enough. Rosie and I owe you our lives. I will write again properly when I have more time, but I wanted you to know that Alan's funeral was yesterday and I'm managing OK.

I thought you might like this photo of Rosie. She's growing already, isn't she?
Warmest wishes and masses of gratitude,
Jess.

2/56 Mary Street,
Edmonton, Cairns
25th April
Dear Reece,

Thank you so much for the pink teddy bear and the little sleep suit dotted with roses. They are so cute—and such a kind thought. I cried when they arrived. I should be sending you gifts. I owe you so much. One day, I promise I'll repay you.

At least I can tell you that Rosie is thriving.

She's filling out nicely and she doesn't wake too often, although she sometimes takes a bit of settling, especially in the evenings. Still, I can't complain.

She's started smiling. You've no idea how cute her smiles are. Once she starts, she just keeps on smiling as if she thinks the whole world is hilarious.

Thanks again and warmest wishes,
Jess

4a/89 Potts Street,
Redlynch, Cairns
16th June
Dear Reece,

Another big thank you from Rosie and me. What a lovely surprise to open your parcel and to find your note and the gorgeous board books. Rosie loves picture books and these are perfect.

I showed her the cows and the pigs and the turkeys and told her all about your farm—not that I saw much. She squealed and crowed and bashed at the pages with her fat little fingers, which is her way of showing how much she loves something.

You're probably sick of seeing photos of her, but here's one more. You can see she's quite roly-poly now. Please ignore how I look. I was a bit tired that day and I hadn't washed my hair, but then, you've seen me at my worst, haven't you?

Reece, I hope all is well with you. You didn't actually say much in your concise and slightly cryptic note. Mind you, that's not a criticism.
For ever in your debt,
Jess

REECE opened the door to his father's room—just a crack—and made sure the old man was sleeping peacefully. Satisfied, he went back to the kitchen, grabbed a beer from the fridge and snapped its lid. Tipping his head, he took a draught, letting the icy lager slide down his throat.

He pushed the flyscreen door and went through to the veranda, propped his elbows on the railing and stared out at the paddocks that stretched long and flat to the distant line of trees. He thought again about Jess.

She made out that she was fine in her letters, but something wasn't right—he was sure of it. To begin with, she had no computer or phone for sending emails, and now she'd changed her street address. On the surface, that was probably no big deal—although a single mum moving house with a young baby couldn't be a picnic—but it was the photo that really bothered him.

He took it again from his shirt pocket and stepped into a circle of light to examine it carefully. The baby Rosie was as roly-poly and cute as Jess claimed. Reece found himself smiling as he recognised the same features he'd first witnessed on the night she was born, now filling out.

But he was shocked by the change in the young mother. Jess was so thin, with dark shadows under her eyes, and no sparkle to her smile. She'd claimed she was just tired, but to him she looked ill, or worried. Or both.

You've seen me at my worst.

Not so, Reece thought, remembering her flushed cheeks and bright eyes as she greeted her baby for the first time.

Admittedly, becoming a widow and a mother on the very same night would be a terrible strain for any woman, but he couldn't shake off the feeling that Jess Cassidy was carrying an extra burden.

On top of his worries about his father, it was enough to keep him awake long into the night.

At the first lull in the café's morning chaos, Jess gave in to her fear. Ducking out of her boss's line of sight, behind the big commercial refrigerator in the back kitchen, she rang the day-care centre.

'Alana, it's Jess Cassidy. I'm just ringing to check if Rosie is still OK?'

'She seems fine,' the young attendant assured her.

'Are you sure there's no sign of a temperature?' Rosie had been fretful all night and Jess was terrified she was getting sick.

'No, Jess. I knew you were worried so I've kept an especially close eye on her. She's had a nice nap and she woke up quite happy.'

'Well, that's good to hear. She was so upset last night. All night.'

'Perhaps she's teething. I noticed she's been chewing on her fists.'

'That's probably it. I guess it's about time.'

'Jess!' roared a male voice. 'What the hell are you up to?'

Jess spun around to find Joel Fink, her boss, glaring at her. Last time she'd looked, he'd been at the far end of the café busily chatting up his favourite female customer. 'I—I had to make a quick phone call.'

'Not on my time and not on my phone.'

'It wasn't a social call,' Jess told him coldly, refusing to be cowed. 'I needed to ring the day-care centre.'

'My customers' needs come first. And *they* need you to stop chatting and to feed them.' Snatching the phone from her, he slapped an order onto the bench. 'Two serves of strawberry pancakes. Cream, no ice cream. Get cracking.'

Lips tightly compressed, Jess got to work. Pancakes. Again. She was heartily sick of cooking breakfasts and lunches. As a fully qualified chef, she found it a breeze to produce light fluffy pancakes, or perfectly scrambled eggs and crisply fried bacon. But after almost six months of this she was bored. Just the same, this part-time job, working four days a week from six-thirty till two, was keeping a roof over her head and it was keeping Rosie fed. With Cairns's growing unemployment problems, she knew she'd been lucky to get the work and she should be grateful.

It would help if her boss wasn't such a cranky tight-fist. Privately, Jess called him The Cell Warder—even the menus he chose were as unimaginative as prison food. But at least this café was in walking distance of her flat, and working on Cairns's seafront gave her occasional glimpses of palm trees and sparkling water. More importantly, the daytime working hours left her with afternoons and evenings free.

She needed to be with Rosie in the evenings. It was horrendously expensive having to put her into day-care for four days a week, but she couldn't bear to hand her over to strangers at night.

Flipping pancakes, she promised herself she'd go to extra trouble with her own dinner tonight.

Reece was frowning as he knocked on the door of flat No 4a. The frown was partly because he was unexpectedly nervous about seeing Jess again, but also because he didn't like the idea of her living in this shabby, almost squalid building with peeling paint and rusted down-pipes and rubbish bins littering the footpath.

His spirits sank lower when no one answered his knock.

A neighbour leaned out of a grimy window to stare at him. He walked over to her. 'I'm looking for Jess Cassidy.'

The young woman blew cigarette smoke. 'She's at work.'

'Where does she work?'

'No idea.' She narrowed her eyes at Reece, showing her distrust of him and making it patently clear that she wouldn't tell him even if she knew. 'She's gone most weekdays, though.'

'Thank you,' he said with excessive politeness, but as he walked away his worries about Jess multiplied.

Why was she working nearly every day? And where was Rosie? When Jess had written that she was 'managing OK', he'd wondered if perhaps she had to be frugal, but he'd still pictured her at home with her baby, living comfortably, if carefully, on her husband's insurance money.

Of course, Jess's living conditions were none of his business. Truth was, he hardly knew Jess Cassidy, and yet he'd been present at an intensely personal, pivotal moment in her life. They'd been through an emotionally charged ordeal together, and when Rosie was born they'd shared an exhilarating triumph. He'd *felt* connected.

Four months later, he still felt connected. It was a big deal for a man with precious few connections.

When he came back at six-thirty he saw, to his relief, that a light was on in Jess's flat. He could hear music playing a soothing, bluesy tune, and tempting cooking aromas wafted through an open window.

The tension inside him loosened a notch. Seemed Jess was all right, after all.

When he knocked, the door opened slowly and Jess stood before him with Rosie balanced on her hip. He was conscious of her slim, pale arms wrapped around the baby. She was wearing faded jeans and a soft pink T-shirt, and her dark hair was twisted into a loose knot. She was definitely thinner than before and she looked tired. On the other hand, her daughter looked plump and thriving.

At first, Jess's expression was guarded, almost defensive, but then she recognised him and her mouth formed an O of surprise.

'Hello, Jess.'

Rosie cooed at him and Jess smiled cautiously.

'I was in town,' Reece explained. 'I had to bring my father to the hospital for tests. He's being kept in overnight and I thought I'd drop by, to say hello.'

'It good to see you.' Jess hitched the baby a little higher. 'I hope your dad's going to be all right.'

'Thanks. It's hard to say at this stage.' Reece was holding a bunch of flowers wrapped in lavender tissue, but he felt suddenly uncertain about the appropriateness of bringing flowers. They had looked so bright and appealing, sitting in a bucket on the footpath, but now he wondered if Jess would think he was trying to be romantic.

'Rosie looks well,' he said, proffering, instead, the brightly wrapped gift he'd bought for the baby. 'I thought she might like this.'

'Reece, you've already been so kind.' With an embarrassed, almost wincing smile, Jess stepped back. 'You'd better come in.'

It wasn't the most welcoming invitation, but he went in, anyway. The flat was small and simply furnished with a tiny, rudimentary kitchen, a small table, two chairs and a single blue sofa. A door led to what he assumed was a bedroom. Everything was very clean.

'Take a seat.' Jess pointed to the sofa.

Uncertain what to do with the flowers, Reece set them on the table and sat at one end of the couch while Jess sat at the other end with Rosie, balancing the baby and the gift in her lap.

'Look what Reece has brought for you,' she said in a deliberately cheery voice, and the baby's hands swiped and patted at the wrapping paper as Jess peeled it away.

'Oh, wow!' she exclaimed as the brightly coloured toy was revealed.

'I'm told it's a chime garden,' Reece said and almost immediately Rosie banged a bright purple flower and was rewarded by a few tinkling bars of a nursery rhyme.

The baby grinned, and banged another flower, releasing more music, and Jess's face broke into a lovely smile. 'How clever. It's absolutely gorgeous, Reece. And the perfect toy for her age.'

Her green eyes sparkled—yes, her eyes were definitely green—and Reece realised that this was why he'd come: to reassure himself that she hadn't forgotten how to smile. She looked so heart-stoppingly pretty when her eyes lit up.

There was an awkward silence as they sat a metre apart and watched Rosie play with her new toy.

'How have you been, Jess?'

'Fine, thanks.' She tweaked a curl on her baby's head. 'Honestly. I hope you haven't been worrying about me.'

'No, not at all.'

Another awkward silence.

'Where are you staying?' Jess asked. 'Do you have friends in Cairns?'

'Not really. I'm booked into a pub down on the waterfront.'

'Nice.'

'Yes, it's fine. Close to the hospital.'

Rosie grabbed at her mother's nose and squealed with glee. Jess laughed, and then, suddenly, she asked, 'Would you like to stay for dinner?'

'No, no. I just dropped in for a quick hello. I don't want to impose on you.'

'I've made a chicken casserole.' Before he could answer, she hurried on. 'You must allow me to feed you, Reece, after everything you've done for me.'

He remembered her letters. *I owe you so much. One day, I promise I'll repay you.*

'Your cooking certainly smells very good,' he said.

'That's settled, then. It's all ready.' Jess smiled again and then she stood and set the baby down on a rug on the floor, putting the chime garden beside her, as well as the teddy bear he'd sent and a rattle. But as soon as she was down Rosie complained, waving her arms and throwing herself down and crying.

Jess sighed. 'I'm afraid she's always super grizzly and needy at this time of day.'

'Would she let me hold her?'

'I'm sure she'd love it. I'll check the dinner.' As Jess headed for the stove her pink mouth tilted into yet another smile.

Reece swallowed nervously as he looked down at the small, angry infant. His offer to pick her up had felt like the right thing to do, but now he was somewhat in awe of this writing, small creature. He knew zilch about babies. He guessed they were probably like dogs, able to sense a person's fear. Sure enough, when he picked Rosie up, she stiffened as she stared at him.

At the same moment, a knock sounded on the door.

'Gosh,' Jess exclaimed as she set the hot casserole dish on a cane mat. 'I hardly ever have visitors, and now I have two in one night.'

What lousy timing, she thought as she slipped off the oven gloves. Now that she'd recovered from the shock of finding Reece on her doorstep, she'd even managed to shove aside the awkwardness she'd felt remembering her labour and everything poor Reece had been exposed to that night. With those thoughts carefully blocked, she was actually looking forward to sharing her dinner with him.

Apart from the fact that she owed him so much, the past four months had been lonely, with hardly any time for catching up with her friends. Then again, her friends were mostly childless and always on the go at parties, or yachting weekends, or working overtime to 'get ahead'. But although Jess missed them, another visitor now would upset her dinner plans—there were only two chairs.

Someone would have to sit on the sofa.

She sent Reece an apologetic eye-roll as she went to answer the door, and her stomach tightened when she saw two strange, beefy and unsmiling men.

'He-hello,' she said uncertainly.

'Mrs Cassidy?'

'Yes.'

'Is your husband home?'

'No.' A cold shiver snaked over Jess's skin. 'My husband passed away several months ago.'

'I'm sorry to hear that.' The speaker was bald with bushy eyebrows and he looked momentarily wrong-footed. Recovering quickly, he shot a suspicious glance past Jess to Reece, who was standing a few feet behind her, holding Rosie.

Jess noticed, irrelevantly, that the baby looked amazingly tiny in Reece's strong, manly arms.

Facing her visitors again, she held her head higher. The fact that she was a widow alone with a handsome male guest was none of this stranger's business.

'I'm here to represent Tighe's Electrics,' he said.

Jess frowned. 'Electrics? My electricity's fine, thanks. Everything's fine.'

'I'm referring to your electrical white goods.' The man's tone held a hint of menace and he leaned forward to peer through the doorway into her tiny kitchen. 'You have a fridge and a washing machine and dryer and you've received communications from us regarding them.'

'No, I haven't.' Jess felt suddenly sick. 'I haven't heard anything about white goods. But I've moved quite a few times this year, and my mail has been messed around.'

'If you have a problem with the Post Office, that's nothing to do with me.' The man on her doorstep looked unsympathetic and waved an official-looking document under her nose. 'I've been authorised to repossess these items.'

Jess swayed against the door frame. 'You can't. I—I don't understand. My husband paid cash for them.'

He shook his head.

'Alan was absolutely definite. There must be a mistake.' Jess hoped she sounded convincing, but she sensed this was another battle she was almost certainly going to lose.

She'd had so much bad news in the past few months. So many things that Alan had kept hidden from her, including huge debts on two credit cards. She'd even discovered that he'd cashed in his life insurance, leaving her with nothing but a massive debt.

Until now, she'd been grateful that she'd at least found a job to pay for rent and food and the minimum repayments on all these other debts. Beyond that, her prize possessions were her transistor radio and her bed, plus the refrigerator and washing machine.

'Excuse me,' rumbled a deep voice behind her.

Jess jumped. She'd momentarily forgotten about Reece, and now she was flooded with wincing embarrassment. What must he think?

'There seems to be a problem,' he said. 'Perhaps I can help.'

Instinctively, Jess shook her head. Reece had already gone above and beyond the call of duty for her.

'Too late,' the man on the doorstep said, totally unconcerned. 'I have orders to repossess. Today. No more chances.'

'I can write a cheque,' Reece replied firmly.

A bushy eyebrow lifted. 'Sorry, mate. As I said, time's run out.' Switching his attention to Jess, he said, 'We can do this the easy way or the hard way. You let me take these items now, or I can come back with the police.'

'I have no intention of fighting you.'

Chin high, with as much dignity as she could muster, Jess stepped back as the fellow barged through the doorway.

'Come on, Fred,' he said over his shoulder. 'Let's get this lot into the truck.'

'Hang on,' Jess protested. 'There's food in the fridge.'

'I'll empty it out.'

'No, you won't.' With sudden, fierce determination, she pushed past him. She was humiliated and devastated, but she sure as hell wasn't going to let this bullying oaf walk all over her. 'I'll take my food out, thank you very much.'

Lips compressed, she wrenched the fridge door open and began to remove its contents, setting the items neatly and efficiently on the draining board. Eggs, butter, milk, cheese…a plastic container of home-made stewed apple, another of chicken stock…

Watching her, Reece wanted to roar with rage. He'd never felt so furious and so helpless. It was probably just as well he was holding the baby, or he might have shoved an angry fist in these guys' smug faces. He was so maddened to see Jess treated like this. He couldn't imagine the circumstances the poor girl had been left in.

When the refrigerator was emptied, Jess came over to him, her face tight and pink, but composed. 'Thanks for looking after Rosie.'

'No problem.'

She took her baby from him and hugged her close. 'At least no one can take you,' she murmured, dropping a kiss on the little girl's downy head.

Out in the street her refrigerator was being loaded into a truck and for the first time her eyes brimmed with tears.

Reece's throat tightened on a painful rock. 'Will you be able to manage?'

'Oh, sure. I'll have this sorted tomorrow.'

He knew she was covering a host of worries, and she didn't want to admit she was in trouble, which made it hard for him to help.

'I'll duck out and get some ice,' he suggested. 'Then you can keep things cold in the sink overnight.'

She nodded without quite meeting his gaze. 'That's a good idea. Thanks.' Then she looked up at him, her green eyes shimmering, and she gave him a brave but tremulous smile.

Reece felt as if he'd swallowed razor blades.

The truck was gone by the time he arrived back with a bag of ice. He couldn't see Jess, but there was a soft light coming from behind the bedroom curtains and she'd left the front door open. He guessed she was settling the baby to sleep, so he entered the flat quietly and glared at the dusty gap in the corner where the fridge had been. Then he placed the ice in the sink and packed the fridge items in with it.

He noticed that the casserole dish was back in the oven and the radio had been turned down low.

Jess came tiptoeing into the room, a finger to her lips. 'I think she's down for the count,' she whispered, and then she picked up the flowers he'd brought. 'I haven't even thanked you for these gerberas. They're lovely, Reece. So bright and cheerful.'

Once again, he felt sure the flowers were totally wrong.

'I don't think I have a vase,' Jess said. 'I might have to put them in a jug.'

He held up a bottle of wine. 'While I was out, I decided we could use a drop of vino to go with the chicken.'

Jess brightened. 'So you still want to stay?'

'You invited me, didn't you?'

'Of course.' Her smile lingered as she quickly found tumblers for the wine, put the flowers in a green glass jug and set the table with cheery red mats. The bright colours made the fridge-less kitchen seem less depressing.

Jess served up the fragrant meal and they sat, just a little self-consciously.

'This is sensational,' Reece said as he tasted the chicken.

'Yes, it's one of my favourites.'

'So you like cooking?'

'Sure. It's my job.'

'Really?'

'I'm a chef.'

He knew so little about her. She was the girl he'd found on the side of the road. A girl in trouble, a girl still in trouble. He ate in silence, caught up in his thoughts.

'You're not huge on conversation, are you?'

He looked up to find Jess watching him, her eyes dancing with private amusement.

'Sorry. I was thinking.'

'About your father?'

'Partly.' He couldn't deny that he was haunted by the image of his dad looking lost and intimidated in the big city hospital. He would duck back there soon to make sure the old man was settled for the night. 'I was also thinking about you.'

'Don't worry about me.' She picked up her glass. 'This is a very fine wine.'

Reece couldn't let her change the subject so easily. 'Sorry, Jess, but I can't help being concerned. You're not in trouble, are you?'

'No, I'm absolutely fine. I have a job, and I'm managing. Honestly.'

'Are you in a position to buy a new fridge and washing machine?'

'Of course.'

He was sure she was lying.

'Look,' Jess said tightly. 'I don't want to talk about money tonight. I'm sick of thinking about money and bills. I'll deal with that tomorrow. I want to channel Scarlett O'Hara. Another day and all that, and I'll work something out. But tonight, my baby's asleep, I have adult company, and we're drinking a very good wine. I'd very much like to enjoy it.'

With a wave of her glass, she gestured to the table and then to him and her mouth quirked into a shy smile. 'Believe me, this is an unexpected but gratefully appreciated luxury.'

Reece found himself returning her smile. Truth was, this was a luxury for him too. Dining with a pretty girl who happened to also be a fabulous cook made a brilliant change from his own bland cooking and his father's increasingly dour company.

Just the same... Jess hadn't just lost a husband—she'd lost a life partner, a support base. 'I know you don't want to talk about it, but this must have been hard for you, managing on your own. Do you have support? Friends? Family?'

'Yes, Reece.'

Her reply was too quick, but he knew she'd hate it if he pushed her any further.

She smiled again as she sipped her wine. 'So tell me... If you could be absolutely anywhere in the world right now, where would you like to be?'

Here, he almost said, and then checked himself just in time. She would be shocked if she knew how much he was enjoying this meal and her company.

'Come on,' Jess prompted. 'Where would you choose? City or country?'

Reece shrugged. 'City, I guess. I wouldn't mind a city break.'

'In summer or winter?'

'Maybe winter. A total change from the tropics. Possibly with snow.'

'Manhattan in January,' she suggested, her green eyes alight.

'Sounds about perfect.' He pictured her on a crowded Manhattan street. Saw her against a background of yellow taxis and skyscrapers. She would be wearing a long coat with a bright scarf at her throat and there'd be snowflakes in her dark hair. The image was entrancing.

'What about you?' he remembered to ask. 'Where would you like to be?'

Jess's eyes were lit by a gratifying sparkle. 'I wouldn't say no to Manhattan. As long as I could afford to buy really trendy clothes. But…' she cocked her head to one side '…I guess it depends… If I had Rosie with me, I might choose the beach. Not a North Queensland beach. I wouldn't want stingers or crocodiles. Somewhere with surf and sandcastles and wading pools.'

Now, he was picturing Jess in a bikini.

Damn, he was a fool.

Later…Jess washed the dinner dishes in the laundry tub, because the kitchen sink was now packed with ice and the contents of her fridge. Of course, she wouldn't let Reece help her with the dishes, but after she'd sent him away, she felt depressed.

She missed him already, which was crazy. He wasn't hers to miss. He was an out-of-town cattleman passing through, but now that he was gone she couldn't hold off facing her problems. She had absolutely no money to spare. As it was, sharing her dinner with Reece meant that she'd be eating baked beans on toast by the end of the week. But how on earth could she manage without a fridge and a washing machine?

She'd been trying so hard to keep her head above water, but now she felt overwhelmed by debt and black despair. She was drowning.

It had been so hard to hide her desolation from Reece, but she'd been determined. She couldn't fall apart in front of him. Not again.

On the upside, they'd shared a very pleasant evening. Sitting across the dinner table from him, she'd found herself mesmerised by his dark brown eyes and the clean lines of his cheekbones. But, of course, she had to stop any hint of dreamy thoughts.

To begin with, Reece hadn't shown the slightest hint that he was in any way romantically interested in her, and even if he had she couldn't allow herself to become involved with another man. Not for ages, quite possibly not ever.

Not with these debts hanging over her head. She could never go into another relationship so encumbered. Her goal now was a stable, happy life for Rosie, and it was up to her to provide it. It was going to take years to get her finances back on track, and till then she couldn't allow herself to be distracted by another guy, no matter how kind, or heroic, or attractive.

Anyway, besides her debt worries, falling for Alan had taught her many lessons—enough to make her doubt men and to doubt her own judgement when it came to making romantic choices.

She'd been totally taken in by Alan's good looks and charming manner, and, after they'd married, he'd talked her into setting up her dream restaurant. He'd had it all planned. He would help to finance the venture. Jess would be head chef and he would be manager and together they'd attract fame and fortune.

In reality, Jess had worked her butt off in the kitchen, while Alan swanned about in the dining room, greeting their customers like bosom buddies, regaling them with stories they didn't want to hear and drinking their wine. As a business manager, he'd been utterly hopeless. After six months, Jess had been so worried, she'd sat up one night until dawn trying to make sense of their finances.

What she'd found had appalled her. Alan had never invested his own money, and now they weren't keeping up with repayments on the loan, and other bills had also gone unpaid. Their business had gone under three months later.

It was the beginning of a disastrous pattern. Looking back, it was hard to believe that Alan had twice managed to convince her that they'd get it right the next time.

Remembering it all now, Jess felt such a mix of sorrow and regret, *and* anger, but a good swag of the anger was directed at herself. She'd been too easily sucked in by Alan's charm and his hollow promises.

She'd spent three years trying to believe in him.

In the future, she *had* to be wiser, and her safest bet was to rely on no one. Go it alone. She'd watched her mother limp from one disastrous relationship to another, and she'd vowed she'd never follow her example.

Now, she tiptoed into the bedroom she shared with Rosie. The old second-hand cot didn't look as scratched and ugly in the soft pink glow of the rabbit-shaped night lamp. She could see Rosie lying on her side, her hair, lighter now, and soft as a cloud, her little hands loose and relaxed, a bubble of milk on her lower lip. As always, Jess felt her heart swell with love. Love sweet and painful and more powerful than anything she'd imagined.

We'll be OK, she silently promised her daughter. *I can do this. I'm a hard worker and in time, I'll clear these debts and I'll make a wonderful life for us.*

Without a man.

CHAPTER FOUR

AFTER the doctor left, Michael and Reece Weston eyed each other uncertainly.

There'd been good news and not so good. At least, the results of the tests were better than Reece had feared. His father didn't need invasive procedures and he didn't have to stay in hospital. But there were signs of congestive heart failure and, chances were, problems like fatigue, shortness of breath and swelling of his legs would get worse in the not too distant future.

The doctor had increased the blood-pressure medication, and he'd suggested lifestyle modifications. He'd also strongly advised that Michael should consider moving from Warringa to a retirement village in Cairns.

'There's a very good place with a nursing home attached,' the doctor had said, and he'd asked a social worker to provide them with pamphlets.

Now, with a disgusted grunt, Reece's father flicked the pamphlet off his bedspread, letting it flutter to the floor. 'If they think I'm going into one of those damn places, they've another think coming.'

'You'd be able to see a doctor regularly,' Reece suggested carefully.

His father simply scowled. 'I couldn't stand being

holed up with a lot of dreary old folk, all of them losing their marbles together.'

Bending down, Reece picked up the pamphlet. It showed pictures of healthy, happy seniors all neatly dressed and smiling, and enjoying a range of activities—art classes, walking groups, golf, gardening...

'If anything happens...' Reece frowned as he chose his words carefully. 'If there's a medical emergency, you'd be looked after straight away. Think how long it would take a doctor to get out to Warringa.'

'I don't care. I'm happy to die there,' his father announced emphatically. 'I've lived there all my flaming life and I don't plan to leave my home now.'

It was hard for Reece to hear his father speak so casually about death. But they'd lived together, just the two of them, for so long that, of course, he wasn't surprised. His dad had only ever known the red dust and wide open skies and the isolation that came with outback life. He couldn't honestly imagine Michael Weston settling into an art class or going for a walk in the Cairns Botanical Gardens with a bunch of chattering old folk.

His dad's life had been tough and lonely—driving mobs of cattle across vast tracks of wild country, coping with droughts and floods and fires. His father's one attempt at marriage had been an abject failure, and after the divorce Michael Weston had stubbornly turned his back on society.

Reflecting on this now, Reece found himself remembering another time, when he was five years old, when his dad had brought him here to this same hospital in Cairns to visit his mother and to meet his new baby brother. His heart still ached when he remembered his

mother in bed, looking pale and lovely in a frilly pink
bed jacket.

'Your little brother's called Anthony,' she'd told
Reece as he'd peeped shyly into the cot.

'But we'll call him Tony,' his dad had added.

His mother had snapped. 'No, we won't.'

Reece could still remember the fear that had gripped
him as he'd become aware, yet again, of his parents'
tight-lipped animosity. Tension had bristled in the air
around him as he'd stared into the cot at his brother.
He'd been hoping for a playmate—he'd seen baby calves
that could stagger onto four legs within minutes of
birth—and he was disappointed that his brother was
so tiny and helpless. Anthony—or Tony—did nothing but sleep.

'Will Anthony be able to play with me when he
wakes up?'

His mother had laughed at this, and then she'd cried.
She'd cried hard and long.

In the end, Reece had never played with his little
brother, not unless he counted their awkward attempts
to kick a football around a backyard, during his infre-
quent visits south. His mother had never brought the
new baby home to Warringa. She'd stayed in Cairns.

In later years, Reece learned that she'd had post-natal
depression, but even when the depression lifted she hadn't
come home. She'd moved back to Sydney, keeping Tony
with her, and leaving Reece with his father.

So…apart from his years away at boarding school,
Reece had shared his father's solitary life, and he understood how a man could reach a point where he accepted isolation and loneliness as his destiny.

He was pretty damn near that point himself. It was
certainly too late to expect his old man to change.

But accepting this didn't ease Reece's current dilemma. If he was to manage Warringa, including this year's cattle muster, he couldn't also look after his father. He was going to need help, and he was going to have to find that help fast.

To Jess's surprise, Reece was waiting outside the café when she finished work. He was on the footpath, standing with his hands sunk in his jeans pockets and a bulky shoulder propped against the trunk of a coconut palm. Filtered sunlight lent his black hair the sheen of crow's feathers. With the additional bonus of his coal-dark eyes, his craggy cheekbones and a faint shadow of beard, he looked frighteningly attractive.

She didn't want an attractive man in her life, so it was perverse of her to care that this hunky guy always seemed to catch her looking her worst. This time, she was in her chef's gear with her hair yanked back off her face, unattractive trousers, a smeared white jacket and sensible lace-up shoes.

'G'day,' Reece said with a slow smile.

'Hello, Reece.'

His smile lingered. 'Has anyone told you, you make a mean steak sandwich?'

Jess's jaw dropped. 'When did you eat at this café?'

'My father and I had lunch here.'

She remembered now—in the middle of the lunchtime rush, her boss had grudgingly passed on a customer's compliments.

'Best steak sandwich he's ever had,' Joel had grunted, but Jess had been mega busy at the time and hadn't given it another thought.

Now, she couldn't help wondering why Reece was still hanging around. He wasn't stalking her, surely?

'So I guess that means your dad's out of hospital,' she said quickly. 'How is he?'

'Not too bad, thanks. Right now, he's relaxing at the motel, enjoying the air-conditioning and the pay TV.'

'I can imagine. I'm glad he's OK.'

'Well, he's not totally OK.' Reece switched his gaze to the distant horizon where the calm waters of the Coral Sea met the sky. Blue on blue. He turned back to her. 'Were you heading somewhere now?'

'I'm off to the day-care centre to collect Rosie.'

'Walking?'

Jess hesitated. She liked Reece—probably liked him too much—and she certainly appreciated everything he'd done for her and for Rosie, but she had to be careful. She wasn't sure if he was trying to chat her up, and she couldn't afford to give him the wrong idea.

To her surprise, his dark eyes took on a nervous flicker. His throat worked and he shrugged awkwardly. 'If that sounded like a pick-up line, it wasn't what I meant.'

Gosh, had he read her mind? Feeling just a little confused, she smiled. 'The day-care's this way. Let's go.'

Reece fell in beside her and, after a short stretch of silence, he said, 'I was wondering if you planned to shop for the white goods today.'

Ah…so his interest was purely practical. Jess squashed a ridiculous ripple of disappointment. 'No, I won't be shopping for those things today.' The sad truth was that, for the time being, she would have to make do with a picnic ice chest and hand washing or the Laundromat, but she was too proud to admit this to Reece.

Now, however, he stopped abruptly, and once again he shoved his hands deep into his pockets.

They were standing near the fence of a vividly tropical garden, and afterwards, whenever Jess remembered this occasion, she could recall every detail as if the moment had been imprinted on her.

The hum of traffic half a block away…

The heady scent of jasmine…

The industrious buzzing of bees…

Reece's nervousness and the way his face pulled into an awkward grimace…

'Is something the matter, Reece?'

His funny-sad smile should not have sent her insides tumbling.

'I've a suggestion I'd like to put to you,' he said. 'I think it could help you, but I don't know if you'll like it.'

Immediately, Jess was shaking her head. 'If you're thinking about lending me money, forget it. I couldn't possibly accept.'

'It's not a loan.'

She frowned. 'What's your suggestion, then?'

'A job.'

'But…I've got a job.'

'I know, so this may not suit, but maybe if I explain…'

Jess nodded, as curious as a fish rising to the bait. 'OK.'

Reece swallowed. 'The thing is, I need someone to keep an eye on my father, so I'm going to have to hire some help.'

'A nurse?'

'No, not really a nurse. More like a housekeeper. Someone to cook and look after the house and just be there at the homestead. If I can't find anyone suitable, my only alternative is to hire a contract mustering team and let them take care of the cattle business while I look after Dad. I can't possibly manage both jobs.'

'I—I see.' Jess certainly sympathised with his dilemma.

Reece cleared his throat. 'I'd pay you well.'

Her insides were fluttering like leaves in a high wind. 'And this—this housekeeper—would she live at the homestead?'

'Yes, but it's a big house. If you came, you'd have your own room and bathroom and a sleep-out right beside you that could be Rosie's nursery.'

Obviously, he'd thought it all out.

And Jess couldn't deny she was sorely tempted. Wow…if she took this job, she wouldn't have to pay for her food and rent, *and* she'd still be earning money. She could make inroads on those awful debts…

It was incredibly tempting.

Too tempting.

Surely, it had to be a tempting trap.

Her mind raced, weighing up pros and cons. The financial benefits were very clear, and she would quite enjoy the housekeeping and cooking, and she wouldn't mind keeping an eye on Reece's dad.

On the downside, she would be living with Reece—and while she felt an unwise thrum of excitement at that thought, she knew she had to be sensible. Reece was so muscly and tantalisingly good-looking, *and* he was thoroughly nice, but his combined attributes presented a dangerous package.

Only last night, she'd reminded herself that she had to avoid this kind of man-trap. Going out there with Reece, living miles from anywhere, more or less alone with him, could be great fun, but it would also create all kinds of relationship dangers. She had to be sensible. Had to remember her plan to get on top of her problems before she risked another romance.

Reluctantly, Jess shook her head. 'I'm sorry, Reece. I think I'd rather stick to working in Cairns.'

'Of course.' Apart from the tightening of his jaw, she saw no hint of a negative reaction. So that was a good thing.

'It was a long shot.' His quick smile didn't quite reach his eyes. 'Worth a try.'

'Thanks for thinking of me.'

He shrugged. 'No problem.'

Jess glanced down the street. The day-care centre was only three doors away and she nodded towards its sign, complete with pictures of teddy bears and wide-eyed dolls. 'I'd better collect Rosie.'

'Sure.'

'Reece, I hope everything works out for you. With your father and everything.'

'Oh, it'll be fine. Don't worry.'

'Please give him my regards.' Feeling inexplicably depressed, Jess stepped closer, lifted her face and pressed a hasty kiss to his jaw. Her lips met his masculine stubble and she had to fight a longing to linger. 'I'd better go, but I'll keep in touch.'

'Yes, do that. Give Rosie a cuddle from me.'

'I will.'

As she turned and hurried away her eyes filled with tears. How crazy was that? She knew she'd made a wise decision.

And yet…

If I was working in a homestead, Rosie wouldn't have

*to be in day-care. I could have her with me every day,
all the time.*

But no...she couldn't give in to immediate regrets.
She had to be strong, had to stick to her goals of independence and eventual security.

*Then again...taking that job would be a way of re-
paying Reece.*

This thought brought Jess up with an appalled jolt.

Was she being horribly selfish? Reece was facing a
dilemma. He needed help with caring for his father, in
the same way that she'd needed his help on the night
Rosie was born.

He hadn't hesitated to help them, and yet she'd dis-
missed him so coolly...

Poised in the doorway of the day-care centre, Jess
turned and looked back down the street. Reece was
striding away on long legs and he'd almost reached the
corner.

She started to run.

It was for the best, Reece told himself as he walked
away and valiantly ignored the gutted hollowness inside him.

Hiring Jess to work at Warringa was a crazy thought
anyway. Sure, she was a great cook, and she almost certainly needed a chance to save money, but taking her
to Warringa was a risk. Already, after she'd spent one
night in his home, he'd found himself caring about her
and her little daughter. He could become too attached
if they stayed for six months or a year or more before
they left.

And Jess and Rosie *would* leave.

Reece had absolutely no doubts about that. He'd

learned lessons from his mother's desertion as well as a few failed attempts when girlfriends had found his home too isolated. He knew Jess had been sensible when she knocked back the offer, and, despite the lingering imprint of her soft lips on his skin, he was grateful.

He'd go straight to an employment agency and find a sensible woman with good credentials. Failing that, he'd hire a contract mustering team and he'd take care of his dad himself. One way or another he'd get around this problem and—

'Reece!'

Jess's call zapped through him like an electric charge. He turned to find her running down the footpath and, to his dismay, his heart began to pound.

He began to run too. 'Is something wrong?' he called as he neared her. 'Is Rosie OK?'

Jess shook her head and stood panting and breathless. 'This isn't about Rosie,' she said, eventually. 'I—I've had second thoughts. About the job. I'd like to help you out.'

Reece willed himself to remain outwardly calm while his heart thrashed.

'I'm sorry I turned you down,' she said. 'I don't know why I hesitated.'

'Warringa is very isolated.'

'I know that, but I wouldn't mind. Alan and I were planning to live in Gidgee Springs, so Rosie and I would have been in the outback anyhow. And—' She flashed a shy smile. 'And I owe you.'

'No, you don't.'

'I do, Reece. You've done so much for me.'

'This isn't about gratitude. It's a practical job offer.'

'Yes…' Jess nodded. 'And I'd be very pleased to accept the offer.'

Was she sure about this? Reece didn't dare to ask. She might change her mind.

Ignoring the loud pealing of warning bells, he said, 'That's wonderful.'

'Jess Cassidy?' scowled Reece's father. 'Isn't that the girl who had the baby?'

'Yes. She's also an excellent cook and housekeeper.'

His father's eyes narrowed shrewdly. 'So you're keen on her, after all. I thought you were.'

'Course I'm not. I'm hiring her to take care of you.'

'I don't need taking care of.'

Reece sighed. 'OK. I'm not going to argue about this. You know I'll have to start mustering soon and I'll be a darned sight more relaxed if there's someone at the homestead with you.'

'A prison warder.'

'Hardly.'

'What about her baby?'

'Her name's Rosie and she'll be coming too, of course.'

'She'll be crying all night.'

'I don't think she cries much, but, anyway, I'll put her and Jess at the far end of the house, away from you. And I'll buy you ear plugs, or you can turn the television up. I'm sure Jess and Rosie won't bother you. You might even enjoy having a baby about the place.'

'I doubt it.' His father pulled a face. 'You were a terrible baby. Cried all the time.'

Reece sighed again. 'I'm sure Rosie's much better behaved than I was.'

'Gran, it's Jess. How are you?'

'I'm very well, dear. How are you? How's Rosie?'

'We're fine, thanks. Rosie's growing so fast. I wish you could see her.'

'I have the lovely photo you sent on my dressing table.'

Yes, it would be there along with the rest of her seven grandchildren. Sometimes it was hard for Jess to remember that she had to share her grandmother. Since her mum died, Gran was the only member of her close family still alive. But Gran had three sons Jess had only met once or twice and six grandchildren besides Jess. Gran and her sons' families all lived at the Gold Coast at the opposite end of Queensland from Cairns.

After Alan died, Jess had considered moving there, but she couldn't afford the travel and removal costs.

'I'm ringing to tell you that I have a new job,' Jess said.

'Oh. Is it a good one? Are you happy?'

'I think it's perfect, actually. I'm going to be working on a cattle property, as a housekeeper and cook.'

'A cattle property? In the outback?'

'Yes, it's the property where Rosie was born, actually.'

'I see. So you'll be working for that wonderful young man who helped you?'

'Yes. But I'm sure I didn't tell you he was wonderful.'

'But you really liked him.'

'Not in the way you're thinking.' She'd never been a very good liar. 'This new job is just that, Gran—a job.'

She wasn't like her mother, starting a new relationship with each new man she met, but she couldn't explain that to her grandmother without implying criticism of her mum, Gran's daughter.

At least her terms of employment were crystal clear in her own mind.

Jess was pleased about that.

Travelling down the track to Reece's homestead in broad daylight was very different from the other panicky trip through a rainy night. Today Jess had clear views of rolling grassy paddocks dotted with Brahman cattle, as well as the white egrets that so often accompanied them. She could see the dark lines of trees that marked the creek's winding progress, and there were red rocky ridges, long sloping plains and the smudge of blue hills in the distance.

It all felt like an adventure and she took in the views with fresh interest. Reece's ute had a dual cabin, so she was sitting in the back seat beside her dozing daughter, while Reece's father, Michael, was in the front, also napping, with his head lolling sideways.

In the very rear of the truck, along with Jess's gear, they carried a brand-new white cot and a matching white chest of drawers, as well as a high chair, a mosquito net and several packages of baby clothes.

'It gets cold out at Warringa in the winter,' Reece had warned as he piled extra sleep suits and several pairs of fluffy socks into the trolley.

Jess had protested, but he'd insisted on buying these things. 'Rosie has to be warm enough.' He'd also insisted on buying a lovely mobile to hang above the cot—animals made of brightly coloured felt: a purple and pink owl, a black and white zebra with a fiery red mane, a golden and brown lion and a bright pink pig. Jess was grateful for these lovely things, but she hoped she could eventually pay Reece for them. She was determined to hang on to her independence and she didn't want to be beholden.

As they approached the homestead, however, her excitement mounted. Outbuildings appeared—tractor sheds, stables, a windmill. Jess found herself sitting straighter, peering ahead, keen for another glimpse of the homestead.

They rounded a final bend and there was the house, a sprawling, low-set, timber Queenslander, painted white, with a faded red iron roof that was almost completely shaded by two massive old Moreton Bay fig trees.

Jess remembered the other time she'd arrived here—peering at the house through the rain, and seeing the lights shining on the veranda, then the semi-dark sanctuary of Reece's bedroom. Today, sheltered from the blazing sun, this house looked a little shabbier perhaps—certainly in need of new coats of paint—but unexpectedly welcoming just the same. In fact, to Jess, who'd spent her entire life living in cramped rented flats, arriving at Warringa felt like a dream come true. Dangerously so.

But she'd been planning to make a new start with Alan in the outback, and now she was doing it alone. This was her chance to get ahead and she had to get it right.

CHAPTER FIVE

'You'll sleep in my room again tonight.'

Jess stared at Reece in puzzlement and prayed that she wasn't blushing.

'Just for one night,' he elaborated. 'The other rooms aren't quite ready for you and Rosie.'

'But—but—' *Far out.* She should be able to handle this simple situation without stammering, but the day's close proximity to Reece had apparently downsized her brain.

'But?' A dark eyebrow lifted as his mildly amused gaze seared her. 'Are you worried about where I plan to sleep?'

'Not really.' It was a lie. Where he planned to sleep was exactly what she needed to know.

'I'll swag down on the veranda. Same as last time.'

Of course. She should have known that. *Cringe.* She hadn't really thought that Reece was angling for them to sleep together. He showed no sign that he found her attractive, and that was totally understandable after the way they met when she was as wet as a drowned rat and groaning in labour.

But should her employer be sleeping on the floor? It seemed wrong.

'Don't look so shocked, Jess.' His eyes flashed again. 'I've spent a good part of my life sleeping in swags out in the bush.'

'Yes, yes, of course you have.'

'Anyway,' he went on smoothly. 'Before we sort the bedrooms, let me show you the kitchen. We can put the kettle on.'

With Rosie chirping happily in her arms, she followed Reece's easy stride across a covered walkway lined with hanging baskets of rather bedraggled ferns to a smaller wooden building, which proved to be the kitchen.

'The separate kitchen is a hangover from the old days,' Reece explained as he filled a kettle and lit the gas. 'Everyone had wood stoves back then, and the theory was that if the kitchen caught fire, the rest of the house could still be saved.'

'It makes very good sense.' Jess looked about her. She wouldn't mind working in a separate domain. The room was rather plain, with no feminine decorative touches, but it was light and airy, with a bank of deep casement windows to catch the breezes. There was also a huge stove with two ovens, and masses of bench space, as well as a scrubbed pine table and chairs for everyday dining.

Once Rosie's high chair was in place with a few toys scattered about and various ingredients dotted about the work surfaces, it would look very homely. Jess could hardly wait to start work.

'And the pantry's through here,' Reece said.

Wide-eyed, she followed him into another room lined with shelves stacked with enough provisions to stock a small grocery store.

'Oh, wow!' she exclaimed with a huge grin. 'I. Am. In. Heaven.'

Reece gave a shocked laugh. 'You're easy to please.'

'Every cook dreams of having storage space like this.'

'You haven't seen the cold room yet.'

She gaped at him. 'There's a cold room too?'

'Right here.' He pushed open a heavy door.

'Oh, my God.'

'I know it's a bit confronting to meet half a beast hanging from a hook.'

But Jess had no qualms at all about the butcher-shop scenario. 'It's amazing. It's fabulous, Reece.' She was grinning. 'I think I'm in love.'

He switched his gaze to a far corner and scowled.

'With your kitchen setup,' she added hastily, cheeks burning.

'The baby will get cold if we stay in here too long,' he said, but he didn't meet her gaze as he opened the door for her.

Reece's father sat at the dining table, waiting for his dinner, a napkin already tucked into his shirt as he watched Jess mix Rosie's formula.

'What's wrong with mother's milk?' he asked, his jaw at a belligerent angle.

Jess winced, instantly defensive. The old man might have had a hard life, but he had no idea how hard it had been for her in those early weeks. She'd been so scared trying to care for her tiny newborn daughter on her own, and at the same time grappling with the shock of losing Alan while acquiring his mountainous debts.

She took a deep breath before she answered. 'I'm afraid I was too stressed after my husband died, and I just wasn't able to breastfeed.'

As Michael shook his head, unimpressed, Reece turned from the stove—he'd insisted on fixing dinner on this first night. 'Give the girl a break, Dad. What would you know about babies?'

Jess could have hugged him. Michael glared at them both, but after a while his face lost its sneer and he gave a sheepish shrug. 'Well…maybe you'll have better luck next time.'

'Oh, I very much doubt there'll be a next time.'

'Rubbish. You're bound to have a tribe of ankle biters, isn't she, Reece?'

Reece didn't grace this question with an answer, but continued stirring savoury mince at the stove, adding extra Worcestershire sauce. Jess was used to working with men in the kitchen, but she found it incredible that Reece managed to look even more intensely masculine and outdoorsy while he was working at the stove. She was beginning to suspect that his muscles and low-riding jeans were an indoor health hazard.

Her breathing would certainly be a whole lot steadier when this kitchen was her sole territory.

It was shortly after midnight when Rosie started crying.

Reece heard her wailing as he lay in his swag on the veranda, and then he heard the creak of a floorboard as Jess stepped out of bed. He heard Jess's soft whispers as she tried to hush the baby, and he pictured her lifting Rosie onto her shoulder, kissing the baby's soft pink cheek and jogging her lightly up and down, trying to rock her back to sleep.

Problem was, he'd spent far too much time today watching Jess with Rosie. He'd been entranced by the way her face softened whenever she looked at her baby, by the way her voice grew gentle and loving. He could have spent ages watching the way she cuddled Rosie close, showering her with soft, sweet kisses. It touched him deeply to witness such tender intimacy and self-less love…

No doubt a shrink would connect his newfound fix-ation with buried feelings of abandonment by his own mother.

Yeah…

Whatever…

When Rosie's crying continued, he left the swag and tiptoed through the house to make sure his father's bed-room door was closed, and for good measure, he closed the doors at the ends of the hallway as well.

He thought about knocking on Jess's door and offer-ing to heat up a bottle. Imagined encountering Jess in her nightgown and thought better of it.

By the time he was back in his swag, lying with his hands stacked under his head and staring out at the starry sky, the house was silent again. He heard the board creak as Jess climbed back into bed.

So that was that…time for sleep. Only one problem. When he closed his eyes, he was plagued by images of Jess in her nightgown, of the soft see-through fabric and moonlight outlining her slim, pale curves…fantasies of her leaving her room and coming to him…

Damn. It was too late now to admit he'd made a major mistake when he'd invited her here—into his home, his life.

The next morning Jess cooked breakfast.

'You might be all right,' Michael told her with an un-smiling nod as he made short work of bacon and eggs and hot buttered toast. 'Don't get too fancy, mind you. Just serve up good plain tucker and you won't hear any complaints from me.'

Reece rolled his eyes and Jess suppressed a smile.

'Well, I'm afraid you won't be able to have bacon and eggs every day,' she warned Michael.

'I've given Jess the list of foods your doctor recom-mends,' added Reece.

Michael scowled. 'Bloody doctors.'

'Oh, I wouldn't worry too much. There are ways and means,' Jess said airily. Already, she was getting used to Michael's grumbles. She could see they were more a habit than genuine gripes and she was actually looking forward to the challenge of winning him around with tasty, healthy offerings.

Once the breakfast dishes were done and Rosie was down for a morning nap, Reece offered to show her the rooms where she and Rosie would sleep. 'I'm afraid they haven't been used for quite a while.'

In fact they were in a part of the house that was locked up and Reece had to wrestle with old-fashioned heavy keys to open a door at the end of the passage that led to them. This done, he hurried forward and opened shutters and windows, letting sunlight stream in to reveal a vast space as well as plenty of dust and cobwebs.

'Hmm…it's worse than I feared,' he said, grimacing.

'But the room's huge.' Jess didn't care about the mess. It would be gone after a day's hard work. More importantly, this bedroom was as large as the entire living area in her previous flat and it had wonderfully high ceilings that made it feel even more luxurious and spacious. Against one wall stood an old-fashioned iron and brass double bed with a mattress swathed in dust sheets, and along another wall stood a matching pair of old-fashioned wardrobes with long oval mirrors on the doors.

Reece pushed open white-shuttered doors. 'And this area needs a thorough clean too, but I thought it might be suitable for Rosie.'

Jess followed him to find a section of veranda that had been closed in with floor-to-ceiling shutters. It was a perfect spot for catching a cooling breeze, or blocking out the sun, and it was also fully fly-screened, which meant she wouldn't have to worry about flies or mosquitoes or nasty creepy-crawlies.

She grinned with delight. 'It's perfect. Actually, it's better than perfect. It's like something out of my deepest fantasy.'

'And the bathroom's this way,' Reece said, leading the way into an old-fashioned bathroom with black and white tiles on the floor, a separate shower cubicle and a claw-foot bath. Here, sunlight made green and rose window panes glow despite their grime, and there was also a deep cream washbasin set into a marble-topped silky oak dresser.

By now, Jess was practically turning inside out with excitement. 'I can't believe this, Reece. I love it all. Love, love, *love* it.'

She skipped towards him. There was only one thing to do when she was this excited—give the man a great big hug of gratitude. But as she flung out her arms, she heard the sharp intake of his breath, and she stiffened, snatched her hands back just in time.

Yikes. What was I thinking? Reece was her boss and she was a recently bereaved widow. There were boundaries to be kept. Reece had invited her here because he felt sorry for her, not to start something. No wonder he was looking grim and tense, almost angry.

'This is very exciting,' she said instead, and she felt a pang as she wondered what Alan would think if he could see her now. 'When everything's cleaned, these rooms will be gorgeous—like something out of a magazine. I can't wait to get started.' Then she laughed. 'And that's saying something. I'm not usually fond of cleaning.'

'I'll help you.'

'Oh, no, you mustn't.' She wouldn't dream of asking for Reece's help. 'You're far too busy. You have all your cattle to look after.'

His eyes glinted as he sent her a wry smile. 'The cattle can wait for one more day, and the two of us will knock this over in half the time.'

'But you—'

'I'll show you where the vacuum cleaner is,' he said, ignoring her protest. 'And then I'll collect mops and buckets.'

Cleaning walls and windows didn't normally rank high in Reece's favourite activities, but, funnily enough, working with Jess changed his perspective.

He told himself her enthusiasm was catching, and in a way this was true. It was rewarding to work together and to see the honey-gold timber floorboards emerge from beneath layers of grey dust, or to see white walls and window sills looking fresh and cobweb-free.

But it was equally rewarding to look up every so

often to catch Jess's smile…or to see the colour of her eyes…the deep green of a tree-shaded creek.

He didn't mind catching her in profile either. Seeing the curving sweep of her dark lashes was a minor miracle…or the soft curving jut of her breasts…or the tempting inches of bare, pale skin that appeared when her T-shirt lifted.

The thing was…he'd sensed an echoing interest from Jess. A certain look, a breathless awareness…small, innocent signals that drove him wild.

Too many times he was tempted to do something about it. To step closer, certain he'd expire if he didn't let her know that he was desperate to touch her…to kiss her.

But such a move would stuff their plans completely.

This was her first full day here. How hard was it to remember he'd offered her a job, not a relationship?

The poor woman was still mourning her husband. How could he have deluded himself into thinking she was interested?

Proximity was his problem. He wasn't used to having a young woman so close at hand, but that would soon be solved once he started mustering.

Grimy and tired, but exultant, Jess stood back to admire the results of their hard work. 'These are lovely rooms.'

'It'll be good to see them being used again.'

'Have they been shut up for a long time?'

'We've had no use for them,' Reece said, answering her question obliquely. 'Too much housework.'

Jess wondered if his mother had lived in these rooms, but she didn't like to ask, knowing from experience that mothers could be complicated, hurtful creatures.

But thinking about Reece as a little boy made her heart yearn in a soft, achy way, which was so *not* how she wanted to feel around him.

Especially not after the day she'd just spent, surreptitiously sneaking peeks at his behind and his muscles and his handsome jaw line—and generally suffering from lust meltdown.

She was ashamed of herself. She was here to earn and to save and to do a good job of caring for Reece's home and his father. She would be grateful when he started on his outdoor work—mustering cattle, or mending fences, or whatever it was that cattlemen did.

Unfortunately…once Reece was distracted by outdoor work, Jess's gratitude was short-lived.

He rose early, just before dawn, so Jess, as cook, rose early too, but there wasn't much conversation as Reece downed a hasty breakfast, grabbed a sandwich and an apple for his saddlebag and disappeared on horseback with two blue-speckled cattle dogs trotting behind him.

Jess knew he was joined on the muster by a couple of men from a neighbouring property, who then returned to their place each night, but even with their help Reece didn't get back to the homestead till after sundown, which meant he was gone for more than twelve hours.

And she missed him.

Which was crazy considering that her life now surpassed her wildest dreams. The cooking and the housework tasks were dead easy compared with working in a busy restaurant. Her accommodation was divine and it was still a daily miracle that she didn't have to pay rent. On top of that, she loved being a full-time, stay-at-home mum with Rosie, and her little girl was really happy and thriving, having at last settled into a good routine.

To Jess's surprise, she even liked the outback. Many mornings she hung out the washing to the accompaniment of the smile-inducing sounds of a kookaburra's laughter. From the kitchen she had lovely views across grassy paddocks and gum trees beneath the blue, blue arch of the sky. She could enjoy the sight of kangaroos sleeping in the shade at noon, or creeping out to graze in the lengthening afternoon shadows. She loved to watch flocks of corellas dive and wheel like fluttering autumn leaves.

It was very peaceful and restorative to be surrounded by nature, far away from the stresses and hassles of the coast. Out here, she could finally begin to forgive Alan for being such a fool with their money. And she didn't even mind Michael's grumpiness. They were rubbing along OK.

All in all, she was happy.

Her life really did seem to be taking a turn for the better. She wished she could trust that it would stay that way, but it was hard to trust the universe when you'd been brought up by a mega-wary pessimist. Jess could still hear her mum's warnings loud and clear.

'Don't get too contented, Jess. Life won't let you, you know. Just when you think you're on top, the universe will pull the rug from under you.'

Her mum's series of temporary 'life partners' had certainly proved that gloomy theory. Men had arrived in her mum's life, apparently doting and caring. And all had gone well for six months or so, but things always took a turn for the worse and they left. By the time Jess was twenty or so, she'd realised that her mum never really got to know the men she lived with. She seemed to keep them at an emotional distance, as if she was actually terrified she might fall in love.

Jess had been determined to be different. She wanted to love wholeheartedly. When she met Alan, she was ready to give her *all* to their relationship. Over and over, actually.

Each time Alan had disappointed her, she'd forgiven him and was prepared to start again. But her mother was right. The rug had constantly been pulled from beneath her. And it happened again on the night of the accident.

Even now…when her life seemed to be turning out OK, she had to fight off that inner fear that something would go wrong.

In the fading light of dusk, Reece perched on the top rail of the stockyard fence, entering details of the mob he'd brought in that day. In one pen there were branded cattle he would truck to a fattening block near Rockhampton. In another were cleanskins he'd found in wild scrub in Warringa's outer extremities.

These beasts would need to be vaccinated and eartagged, a job Reece would normally leave till morning, but this evening he was contemplating tackling the task now…before darkness fell.

At least it would give him another excuse to stay clear of Jess.

Reece grimaced as he recognised this unattractive new trend in his thinking. He wasn't proud of his avoidance tactics. He knew it made no sense to invite a woman here to the lonely outback and then ensure she was even lonelier by keeping his distance from her.

Problem was, his invitation for Jess to live with him had been fine in theory. And it was dead easy to justify—he'd offered her security and a chance to be with her daughter while she helped care for his father and looked after the homestead.

But, damn it, this beautifully simple plan was incredibly complicated when he put it into practice.

With a soft curse, Reece swung down from his perch on the rail. By now the sun was slanting low, sending long shadows across the paddocks. A cool breeze made his short collar flap as he pondered his new problem.

Or rather, a new twist to his old problem.

He knew well that it was crazy to imagine a long-term future at Warringa with a girl like Jess. Eventually, she would need to leave. She would want to head back to Cairns where she and Rosie could join a playgroup and interact with other mothers and kids. Jess would want cinemas and parties, girlfriends—all the things women missed when they came out here. She deserved an easier life. She deserved happiness, not hardship.

In other words…there was nothing wrong with his original plan, but they couldn't afford to complicate it with attraction issues. He certainly couldn't let on how badly he was attracted to her.

And the only way he knew to handle this was to stay well out of her way.

'So what's Reece up to today?' Jess asked Michael over their mid-morning cuppa. It was a question she asked most days, at morning or afternoon tea, or at lunch.

'Same as yesterday.' He rolled his eyes. 'Rounding up cattle, leadin' them into the yards, drafting out the weaners from the mothers, branding, yarding the beasts he plans to sell.'

'I guess he's going to be pretty busy every day, then.'

'Damn busy.' Michael's eyebrows knitted as he watched Jess spooning mashed vegetables into Rosie's mouth. 'She's not too noisy, after all, is she?'

'Does that mean she's not bothering you?'

'Not yet.'

Jess smiled. 'Glad to hear it.'

Everything was fine, actually. Jess had absolutely no reason to feel twinges of disappointment.

Just the same…there were many nights when Reece didn't get back until after she and Michael had already eaten, and she'd had to leave his dinner on a covered plate in the warming oven. She knew it was probably a paranoid thought, but she'd begun to suspect that he was deliberately avoiding her.

The day in the saddle was long and hot and dusty. Reece showered and changed and ate alone in the kitchen, enjoying corned beef with tomato relish and tender vegetables with a delicious white onion sauce. He had to hand it to Jess. She could turn even the simplest dishes into a gourmet meal.

'Enjoying your tucker?'

'Very much,' Reece agreed as his dad shuffled into the kitchen in his pyjamas and slippers.

'She's a good cook.' Michael was squinting without his glasses.

'Yeah. And I take it you and Jess are getting on OK?'

Michael nodded, pulled out a chair and sat slowly, wincing a little as his old bones creaked.

Reece continued eating. He never minded his father's company, but, from years of living with the guy, he sensed that he was about to find himself on the receiving end of a lecture.

Michael leaned forward. 'Are you going to say goodnight to her?'

'To Rosie?'

The old man snorted. 'To Jess.'

This was a shock. The last thing Reece had expected. Then again, his father had periods of vagueness and weirdness these days. 'She's already in bed, Dad.'

'She's in her room, but she likes to read. She's working her way through the books in the lounge room. I'm sure she's not asleep.'

Frowning, Reece speared a carrot with his fork. 'I don't think I'll bother her.'

'She's lonely, Reece.'

A chill slinked through Reece's veins. His thoughts flashed, without his volition, to boyhood memories of his mother. With unnecessary care, he set his knife and fork on his plate. 'What makes you think Jess is lonely?'

'She asks about you all the time. What's Reece doing today? How long does the mustering last?'

He swallowed as his heart began to pump. 'Jess sees me at breakfast. She could ask me those questions.'

'Maybe.' His dad shrugged. 'She doesn't strike me as the timid type, but I reckon you've got her spooked.'

'That's rubbish.'

For long seconds his father stared at him. His once sharp eyes were now cloudy with age and diminishing health but they hadn't lost their inner steel.

Reece sighed. 'All right. I'll talk to her. I'll make sure she's OK.'

Jess slid a bookmark between the pages of her book and set it on the bedside table. The story, set during the

Great Depression, was about a lonely guy whose wife had left him. As a result, the man had to care for their little daughter on his own. Life was tough in the cities during the depression and he'd come to the bush, trudging from farm to farm, looking for work and bringing the little girl with him.

It was really well written, funny in places, but also gripping and touching, and for some reason that didn't quite make sense it kept making her think of Reece. Now, the story was probably going to keep her awake when what she needed was something boring that would put her to sleep.

Resigned to at least try to sleep, she reached for the switch on the bedside lamp. On the point of plunging the room into darkness, she heard Reece's footsteps in the hall. Her fingers stilled.

He stopped outside her door and she sat up straighter, her heart suddenly thumping madly. Did he want to speak to her? She wouldn't mind if he came in—if he knocked and just popped his head in to say hello.

Her nightie was practically neck to knee. No worries there. If only she'd left the door ajar so he'd feel more inclined to communicate.

Hell, why was she waiting?

Flinging off the bedclothes, she swung her legs out of the bed. Her feet hit the floor as she heard his footsteps again. Moving away.

Away…

OK. She knew it was silly, but she went to the door anyway, and opened it. Of course, the passage outside was dark and empty.

Ridiculously disappointed, she closed the door and went back to bed, flopped onto the pillows. Stupid tears stung her eyes.

God, I'm a fool.

Rolling over, she snapped off the light. For a minute there, she'd thought that Reece might be lonely or longing for company. But why would he be lonely? He had thousands of cows and his neighbours for company, as well as his father and the men who drove the big road trains that came to take his cattle to the sale yards.

He was a man of the land and no doubt he had women friends he could visit when he wanted female companionship.

Jess, in the meantime, had Michael and Rosie and this homestead, which grew more beautiful every day from all her polishing and cleaning. She was an ungrateful idiot for thinking she needed more.

Well...she was, wasn't she?

The sun hadn't yet risen when Reece came into the kitchen next morning. Jess was at the stove, stirring pieces of smoky bacon through a pot of baked beans, and she looked up briefly, the merest ghost of a smile tilting her lips. But almost immediately the smile vanished and she quickly dropped her gaze.

'Morning, Reece.' She spoke without looking at him, nodding instead to the teapot on the table. 'I've made the tea.'

'Thanks.'

'These beans are almost ready.'

Normally, he headed for the table. This morning he walked to the stove.

Jess's dark hair was tied up in a loose knot, leaving her pale neck bare.

He forced his gaze from her to the pot on the stove. 'That smells sensational.'

He was referring to the bacon and the beans, although in truth he was even more entranced by the hint of soap or perfume on Jess's skin. She turned to him, her green eyes wide with surprise, her lips parted.

He longed to lean in, to feel the softness of her lips against his, to taste their rosy sweetness. Damn. This was why he stayed away. He was becoming obsessed.

'Is everything OK?' he asked her.

'I think so.' She frowned. 'Why?'

He tried for an offhand shrug. 'Just wanted to make sure you're not getting too bored with life here.'

'Oh, no.' She answered quickly and moved with haste to retrieve two slices from the toaster. 'Rosie's so much more settled,' she said as she buttered the toast. 'I think she adores having me at her beck and call.'

Reece nodded. 'The house is looking amazing. I can't remember the last time the windows were so sparkling. You don't have to go to too much trouble, you know.'

'I don't mind.' She spooned beans onto the toast and handed the laden plate to him. 'You're working very hard, aren't you?'

'Yeah…' He accepted the plate with a brief nod. 'I know I haven't been around much.'

Her eyes narrowed and when she looked up, her smile was shrewd. 'Has Michael been talking to you?'

'That's a strange question. Of course he talks to me. He's very taken with you, by the way. And I reckon he's happier than he's been in a long time.'

'That's good to know.' Jess reached for the teapot, pouring herself a mugful of hot, strong tea. 'I like your dad.' She added milk to the tea and leaned against a cupboard, sipping, while Reece started his breakfast.

'He's good company.' She looked as if she might have

said something more, but then she pressed her lips together as if to stop herself.

Turning to the bench, she reached for the bread packet and said over her shoulder, 'Roast beef and pickle sandwiches OK for your lunch?'

'Yes, thanks.' Reece knew the conversation had been inadequate. At least he'd tried.

Rosie was cutting another tooth and her afternoons were increasingly miserable, but to Jess's surprise Michael found ways to keep her entertained with old-fashioned games with fingers and toes. "Round and round the garden like a teddy bear..." and "This little piggie went to market" were favourites. And the old man was transformed when he smiled and laughed with the baby.

Jess could see that he'd once been as handsome as his son.

'I wonder if you'd mind keeping an eye on Rosie for me while I grab the washing from the line,' she said. Usually, she sat Rosie on the grass with a few pegs to play with, but there were a few clouds rolling in, possibly bringing rain, and she could unpeg the clothes so much faster if she wasn't trying to keep an eye on where the little girl had rolled to or what she was putting in her mouth.

Michael looked delighted. 'We'll be fine here, won't we, Rosie?'

Jess crossed the stretch of grass to the lines strung between two old mango trees. After living in flats that only had dryers or tiny pull-out lines over the bath, she loved the luxury of hanging washing to dry in fresh, clean air and sunshine. And whenever she took them in from the line, the fabrics smelled good enough to bury her nose in.

This simple little pleasure was one of the many things she treasured about her new life. She was humming to herself as she came back to the veranda.

Michael and Rosie were no longer there.

CHAPTER SIX

Jess stifled her instant flare of panic. Michael had gone inside, taking Rosie with him. No big deal.

'Michael?' she called lightly as she went into the house, expecting to see him in his favourite armchair in the lounge room.

The room was empty.

'Michael, are you there?'

When there was still no answer, Jess felt the first stab of hot fear.

'Michael? Rosie?'

She dropped the washing basket and began to hurry through the house, pushing open doors and calling. There was no sign of them anywhere.

Stop panicking. They'll be in the kitchen.

She ran.

They weren't in the kitchen, or the pantry, or the cold room, and a shot of pure terror ripped through Jess. She tried to tell herself she was overreacting. Michael was a responsible adult—a bit vague at times, perhaps, but not foolish. He'd raised Reece on his own, and he was very fond of Rosie. He wouldn't harm her.

Not intentionally.

Oh, God.

After scouring the house from end to end, Jess raced

outside again, checked all the verandas, the broom cupboard, the laundry, the outside loo. She stood at the top of the front steps, scanning the endless paddocks for a sign of the man and her baby. *Please, just a glimpse.*

How on earth could an old man have got so far away so quickly?

She cupped her hands to her mouth and yelled, 'Michael!' at the top of her voice.

The only response was the harsh cry of a distant crow.

Now, Jess's mounting panic exploded. All the love she'd ever felt for Rosie rushed through her like a geyser, filling her with fierce longing and dread. From the moment she'd first seen her baby, she'd been smitten, and each day since then Rosie's cute, sweet little personality had blossomed, twining strong, deep-rooted tendrils around Jess's heart.

Her little girl was such a loving, chuckling, gorgeous, perfect thing.

Please, please let her be all right.

Crack!

At the sound of a stockwhip, Jess's heart jolted. Cattlemen used stockwhips—which meant Reece mustn't be too far away.

The thought had barely formed before she was flying down the steps and over the grass. The gate in the fence was too complicated to stop and try to open. She scrambled over it, poised precariously for a moment on the top as it wobbled, and then jumped down and continued racing across the paddock of grazing cattle.

I hope there aren't any bulls in this paddock.

A stockwhip sounded again.

The sound was coming from beyond a stand of gum trees at the far end of the paddock. Jess's heart was pounding as she ran. She couldn't find a gate at the far end, so she dived through the barbed-wire fence, ripping her T-shirt and flinching as sharp barbs pierced her skin. Too bad. She had to find Rosie and she needed Reece to help her.

She staggered on, gasping now, and with a painful stitch in her side, but at last, rounding the clump of trees, she saw a mob of cattle in a cloud of dust. And stockyards. Men on horseback.

'Reece,' she yelled, but of course he couldn't hear her. He was too busy prancing about, steering his horse back and forth, turning it this way and that as he guided the jostling cattle through a narrow opening into the yard.

She waved her arms frantically above her head, praying it was enough to catch his attention—anyone's attention. And then, as she drew closer to the yards she saw a quad bike near the fence line and she recognised Michael's snowy hair and stooped shoulders as he sat astride the bike.

Charging towards him, she finally saw that his arm was around a small pink and white figure on his lap.

'Rosie!'

Jess sobbed, staggering to them on legs so suddenly shaky they could barely support her.

By the time she reached Michael, tears were streaming down her cheeks.

'Da!' Rosie beamed a happy, one-toothed grin at her.

'Oh, baby!' Jess scooped the little girl from Michael's lap and hugged her tight. Still sobbing, she breathed in the sweet baby smell of her just as huge beasts filled the yard, mere inches away on the other side of the wooden fence, pushing and snorting and stirring up dust with their hard, dangerous hooves.

Horrified, Jess backed away, clutching Rosie tightly to her. 'How could you?' she screamed at Michael above the noise.

With a rev of the bike he rode over to her.

'What on earth possessed you to bring a baby out here?' she cried.

He shook his head, bewildered and frowning. 'What's the matter, Jess?'

'What's the *matter*? You took off with my baby without telling me. You brought her down here where she could have been trampled!' Jess shot another horrified glance to the snuffling, snorting beasts, now metres away, rather than mere centimetres.

'Rubbish,' responded Michael. 'Rosie's all right. I wanted to show her the stockyards.'

'But she's only a *baby*.'

One stamp of those horrible hooves could have crushed her...

'And you didn't *tell* me you were taking her!' Jess was still shaking with anger and fear. 'I had no idea where you'd gone. Didn't you *think*? Didn't you realise I'd be worried sick?'

Hugging Rosie close, she glared at the old man and he glared back at her, but before either of them spoke there was a drumming of hooves close by. Startled, Jess jumped, and saw to her relief that it wasn't a cattle stampede, but Reece on an enormous black horse.

He frowned down at them from a great height as he reined the horse in. 'What's going on?' He scowled at Jess. 'Why have you brought the baby down here?'

'Ask your father,' Jess cried, but even as the words left her lips she felt bad about dobbing the old man in, especially as the creases in Reece's brow deepened as he swung easily, fluidly, down from his horse.

'Dad?'

Michael bristled. 'You used to love the stockyards when you were little.'

'But Rosie?' Reece was shaking his head. 'What were you thinking?'

'Nothing happened to you, Reece.'

For long seconds, Reece stared at his father, then he sighed and shook his head. His dark, serious eyes rested on Jess. 'Are you OK?' he asked gently.

'Yes, I'm fine.' Her shoulder was stinging a little from the barbed wire, but already she was beginning to calm down.

'I'll walk you back to the homestead.'

'There's no need, thanks. I can manage.'

'No, you're bleeding.' He was looking at her shoulder and when she craned her neck, she saw a dark red stain on her ripped T-shirt.

'I did that on the barbed wire, but it doesn't hurt too much.'

'You'll need to get disinfectant onto it. I'll help you through the fences,' he said sternly. 'You don't want to scratch Rosie.'

This was true. Jess looked again at the stockyard filling with cattle. There were two men on horseback manning the gate. 'Can you be spared?'

'Sure. The others can manage now.'

A deviant quarter of her brain was actually noting that Reece looked devastatingly sexy in his Akubra and battered jeans. Under other circumstances, she might have loved to linger and watch him at his work.

However, as he tied his horse's reins to a fence post he frowned at Michael. 'You should come back too, Dad.'

'I'll come when I'm good and ready.' Michael still

sounded belligerent, but he was looking a bit shame-faced as well.

Watching him, Jess found herself taking fresh note of his thinning white hair and his rheumy eyes, his five-day-old beard, as white as hoar frost. She saw his gnarled, arthritic hands scarred with sunspots, such a cruel contrast to the peach-smooth, perfect skin of the baby in her arms.

In truth, the old man was almost as helpless as Rosie, and, with his unreliable memory, he was almost as in-nocent. Already, Jess was beginning to wish she hadn't yelled at him.

'See you back at the homestead, Michael,' she said gently as they left.

The shadows from the grove of trees were already stretching across the paddock as Reece and Jess walked back. A flock of galahs had been feeding on grass seeds and now the birds rose, revealing deep pink breasts as they circled overhead, grey and white wings flapping.

'I'm sorry this happened,' Reece said. 'I'm afraid my father's "senior moments" seem to be increasing.'

'You don't have to apologise. It's actually my fault. I shouldn't have expected Michael to keep an eye on Rosie. After all, you hired me to keep an eye on *him*.'

Reece shrugged. 'It's a bit of a balancing act, isn't it? One minute he's fine, the next he's—'

He didn't finish the sentence. Instead, he nodded to Rosie. 'I haven't seen her for a while. I'm sure she's grown.'

'She's rocking on her hands and knees these days. I'm sure she's almost ready to crawl.'

'Really?'

'You're missing the fun. She's nearly always asleep when you're around.'

'Yeah, well...'

Another unfinished sentence.

At the fence Reece placed a booted foot on the bottom strand of barbed wire and lifted the other strands high, so Jess could easily climb through unscathed, with Rosie in her arms.

'Thanks,' she said. 'Shall I hold it for you now?'

'I'm fine.' He made it look effortless as he held the rough strands down with one hand and vaulted over them.

Rosie laughed at him and cried, 'Da!'

'Da?' Reece shot a questioning glance to Jess.

'Don't worry, she's calling me Da too. It's her first word, though, so it's cause for celebration.'

'I reckon.' Reece grinned at her and his dark eyes flashed, and it was a lovely moment as the three of them walked together towards the homestead. Jess felt far happier and more *connected* than she had in almost seven long months.

Once again, she felt her old yearnings surface, the dream of an ideal marriage and a home that was more than a rented flat. It was a romantic dream she'd cherished throughout her teenage years, but it had lost its sparkle during her marriage and it had finally died with Alan. It was crazy, *crazy* to let it resurface now.

Reece had employed her for her housekeeping skills. Nothing romantic about that. And how could she forget that she had too many debts to clear before she could even contemplate another relationship? She would never go to a new man burdened by the debts from a previous husband.

Perhaps it was just as well they'd reached the gate at the other end of the paddock.

'Thanks for walking me home.' Jess sent Reece a quick smile.

'I'll come up to the homestead with you. I want to check out that cut on your shoulder.'

Jess knew she must have looked surprised—he'd been so distant lately—and she was sure she could manage the cut on her own. But she didn't want to send him away. *No way.*

'That would be great,' she said. 'Thanks.'

They went to the kitchen and Jess put Rosie in her high chair with a baked crust dipped in Vegemite, the baby's favourite snack.

'The first-aid gear's in the pantry,' Reece said, but as he collected cotton wool and antiseptic Jess realised she faced a new dilemma.

'Um… I'll have to take off my T-shirt, won't I?'

There was momentary silence as Reece turned to her, his dark eyes sharp and bright. She could feel her heart picking up pace.

'Turn the chair and sit with your back to me,' he said quietly, and then a playful smile twitched his lips. 'I won't look.'

She knew she shouldn't feel prudish after everything he'd seen on the night Rosie was born. Back then, however, she'd been too distracted by pain to care. Now, ridiculous flames shot under her skin.

But she had to shake off such nonsense. She was here at Warringa as Reece's employee. Nothing more.

Surely that wasn't too hard to remember?

'This is really going to hurt if you try to get the shirt off by yourself,' he said. 'You'll have to let me help you.'

'Um…no. It's OK. I'll…be OK.'

'Jess, there are bits of fabric caught in the cut.'

'Oh.'

She was almost certainly blushing as he lifted the shirt, gently, gently easing the ripped fabric away. Then she sat, as directed, with her back to him and he began to bathe her skin, but, although he was incredibly careful, every time his hands brushed her she felt fire.

'I think you missed your calling.' She tried to make her voice light. 'First you delivered my baby, now you're tending my wounds. You should have been a doctor.'

She couldn't see Reece's reaction and he made no comment as he continued to dab at her cut. It shouldn't have been sexy, but rivers of heat spread all over her. She was imagining him touching her intimately.

She *wanted* him to touch her intimately.

Wanted it so badly.

'Am I hurting you?'

Jess was too breathless to answer and she had to shake her head, and then she realised she was breathing in rather frantic little gasps. No wonder Reece thought he'd hurt her.

'That should be OK now,' he said at last, with a final dab, and she was practically in mourning as he stepped away.

A wicked imp inside her urged her to turn to him, wearing only her bra, to see how he'd react.

Fortunately, her common sense returned just in time and she remembered that Reece was simply being helpful. He was helping her again, as he'd helped her so many times in the past.

Any romance existed only in her head.

She reached for a tea towel from the back of another chair and held it demurely in front of her as she stood.

She looked up and met his gaze.

Oh.

Longing shimmered like fire in his lovely dark eyes—the same longing she was feeling. Longing mixed with agonising uncertainty.

For ages, neither of them spoke.

She had no idea what to say. Her head was crammed with unhelpful, lustful thoughts. Thoughts of Reece's lips exploring her... Thoughts and yearnings so strong she was bursting.

And Reece looked as spellbound as she felt.

Maybe it was time to admit what was happening? Their chemistry was obvious. Screaming to be voiced.

But this idea had barely formed before Rosie dropped her baked crust and began to cry.

Gripping the tea towel against her, Jess hurried to pick up the soggy crust. 'There you are,' she said, quickly handing it back to her sobbing daughter.

Then she glanced back to Reece. He frowned, looked away and cleared his throat.

The spell was broken.

'I'll get back to the stockyards now.'

He was already heading for the door.

And he was gone before Jess remembered that she hadn't even thanked him.

She felt a little dazed after that, as if she'd stepped off a fast-spinning merry-go-round. But things got back to normal as she turned her attention to mending bridges with Michael. Fortunately, a hearty beef stew followed by baked chocolate pudding seemed to do the trick. Not so fortunately, his fading memory finished the process.

Although Michael surprised Jess a few days later...

'Guess what day it is today?' he asked with a challenging grin at morning tea.

Jess smiled. 'Well, I know it's Thursday.'

'Thursday the sixteenth.'

'Yes. Is that significant?'

'It's Reece's birthday.'

'Really?' Jess remembered her brief exchange with Reece at breakfast this morning. There'd been no hint. They were back to being super cautious around each other.

'I thought maybe you could bake him a cake,' Michael said.

She tried to ignore the sudden flash of excitement, and she concentrated on watching Rosie as she sat unaided on the floor and banged two blocks together.

'I guess I could make a cake,' she said carefully, trying to pretend that she wasn't already in love with the idea of surprising Reece.

'Only if you feel like it.'

'It's no trouble. Does Reece have a favourite kind of cake?'

Michael pulled a face. 'Dunno. I guess everyone likes chocolate cake.'

'I'll see what ingredients we have.'

'Maybe we could have a bit of a party?' The old man's face was lit by a rare smile.

'Well… I guess…' Given the short notice, Jess thought this was going a bit far. She couldn't really imagine herself, an old man and a baby throwing a party.

But Michael looked so hopeful, and who knew how many years he'd be around to celebrate his son's birthday?

'Of course, we can make it a party,' she said quickly. 'Why not?'

There was something different about the house.

When Reece arrived home, dusty and tired as usual, he couldn't quite put his finger on the change. Was it something about the lights?

He took his boots and shirt off in the laundry and padded through to the shower. Under the pleasing hot pressure he rinsed away the day's grime and ran through the tasks he needed to see to tonight. Paperwork, bills... There was a big bill due on the nineteenth and today was the—

Today was the sixteenth of September—*his freaking birthday*—and he hadn't given it a thought. He was thirty-three. Not that it mattered. Birthdays had never mattered at Warringa. Not since—

Abruptly, he snapped off the taps, stepped out of the shower and snagged a towel. In his room he changed into clean jeans and a shirt, and with the shirt hanging open he went down the hallway, noting that the lights were already out beneath Jess's and Rosie's doors. Nothing unusual there, but he was disappointed.

At least he could look forward to finding a delightful meal waiting for him in the warming oven. Jess had produced some pretty amazing dishes, and he fancied he could smell something quite delicious.

But now, as well, that sense of *difference* returned...

Were the lights in the kitchen flickering? The door was ajar. He pushed it.

'Surprise!'

Whack!

Reece staggered backwards, stunned to find the room full of grinning faces. Ryan and Jim, the neighbours he'd been working with all day. Cath and Bill Anderson from Half Moon station. His dad, grinning from ear to ear. Jess, looking sensational in what had to be, hands down, the most attractive little black dress he'd ever seen.

Candles, stuck in bottles or in tin lids, flickered from every bench top. The table was set with a snowy white cloth and decorated with coloured streamers and the best dinnerware and silver.

'Happy Birthday!' everyone shouted, and before he could react they broke into rowdy rendition of the birthday song.

He felt suddenly weak as a kitten, and he wasn't sure if his knees were still working. A rock the size of Uluru filled his throat and the backs of his eyes stung.

The last time this had been sung for him he'd been five years old.

Halfway through singing, Jess's throat felt too tight to go on. She'd been so excited, waiting for this moment. All day her excitement had mounted as she'd worked hard and fast to pull the party together—making phone calls, cooking, cleaning, hunting through the house for everything she needed. Then, there'd been the tension of getting Rosie to sleep and keeping everyone else quiet when Reece arrived home.

And now—

Now, he looked so shocked and incredulous and downright emotional Jess wanted to cry. No one should be *that* surprised by a birthday party. Surely?

The song came to an end. Everyone cheered and clapped and moved forward to shake Reece's hand or, in Cath Anderson's case, to give him a kiss and a hug.

At least he was grinning now—the grin was a bit shaky and he was looking a little flushed perhaps, but his smile held as he returned backslaps and greetings.

He even hugged Michael, which was nice. And then it was Jess's turn.

Reece stepped towards her and she was suddenly super aware of him. His dark hair, damp and sexily rumpled after he'd towelled it dry. His shirt hanging open to reveal the shadow of more dark hair on his chest.

She must have been staring and he must have noticed, for he quickly did up his shirt buttons.

'Happy Birthday, Reece.' She dropped a quick peck on his cheek and she smelled lemon-scented soap on his skin.

His deep brown eyes were a little too shiny. 'Did you do all this?'

'It was Michael's idea.' This time she didn't feel so bad about dobbing in his father.

'But you organised it. You did the legwork.'

'It was fun.'

His gaze travelled over her and his eyes were so appreciative he made her shiver. 'Thanks,' he said softly.

'Can we eat?' chimed in Michael. 'I'm starving.'

It wasn't a late night. Being country folk, everyone had to face early rises in the morning, but the dinner was a lively affair, the conversation convivial. The Andersons had brought wine, which went well with the baked chicken breasts, smashed garlic potatoes and a side dish of broccoli with pine nuts. The rich chocolate layer cake was a hit.

As soon as he'd eaten Michael retired to bed, and, after coffees, Reece went out onto the veranda to farewell his guests while Jess started rinsing plates and stacking the dishwasher. She was almost finished when she heard the vehicles driving away. She closed the dishwasher, turned it on. With the first soft swish of the water filling the machine, Reece came back into the kitchen.

'That was amazing,' he said quietly.

'I'm glad you enjoyed it.'

'I did. Everyone had a great time. The food was sensational.'

'If I'd had more warning, we could have invited more people.'

'Jess, it was brilliant. The best birthday party I've ever had.'

'Really?' It was hardly a party.

Reece was smiling as he shook his head. 'Believe me. It was a stand out.'

She caught a flash of sadness in his eyes. It was as quick as the flick of a horse's tail, but she knew she hadn't been mistaken. It made her wonder about all the birthdays Reece had spent alone here with Michael and she felt the strongest urge to reach out and hug him.

Just thinking about it, she felt her skin heat again. To cover the moment, she said, 'Would you like another piece of cake?'

He laughed. 'Why not? Will you join me?'

It was deliciously intimate, sitting alone in the candlelight with happy memories of the party warming them as they ate second helpings of the luscious layer cake.

'So, how long is it since you had a party?' Jess couldn't resist asking.

'Twenty-eight years.'

'Really?'

'My last birthday party was when I was five.'

'Oh, my gosh.'

Reece shrugged, sliced a chunk of cake with his fork.

'Dad never managed to produce cakes or parties. Each year he'd put money in my bank account instead. I guess he hoped it would make up for the lack of a present.'

He gave a smiling roll of his eyes, as if he was trying to make light of it. 'I wanted toys, though.'

'Of course you wanted toys.' Jess's heart ached for the lonely boy he'd been. Her own childhood hadn't been too flash with a cash-strapped single mum and the itinerant 'uncles', but at least she'd always had presents on her birthday. Dolls, books, a bike, perfume.

'What about your mum?' Jess *had* to ask. 'Did she remember you?'

'Sure. She used to send me clothes. I'd make Dad take a photo of me. To send back to her.'

'Oh.'

Clothes, not toys. So not what a boy wanted.

Once again Reece smiled, but Jess could feel the pain behind his smile. She was so glad they'd made an effort today and she vowed there and then that she would always make a big fuss of Rosie's birthdays. She wouldn't spoil her little girl, but she definitely wanted her to grow up feeling loved and special and secure.

They put their cake plates and forks in the sink. Went down the silent passage to their rooms.

In the hallway they paused, inches apart, and Jess could feel her blood pumping. Thundering. She was sure Reece swayed towards her, and once again she could sense the same killing tension in him that was torturing her. Tonight, her emotions were brimming over. If he wanted to kiss her, she was ready.

So ready and waiting.

More than ready, truth be told.

'Goodnight, Jess,' he said gruffly as he pushed his bedroom door open.

'Goodnight, Reece.'

She was talking to the door.

Perhaps it was just as well, Jess decided much later after she'd finally, *finally* cooled down. If Reece had made a move to kiss her, she might have climbed all over him and made a fool of herself. Much better to have retreated back into their corners.

Their caution was sensible. They'd become closer friends this evening without tipping the delicate balance and finding themselves in a complicated relationship. This was good, Jess told herself, although deep down she was torn between needing to know how Reece really felt about her and knowing they shouldn't and mustn't change anything.

Everything had changed tonight.

Reece stood in his room, looking at the familiar furniture he'd known all his life and knowing that he would never be quite the same again.

Jess probably had no idea how much she'd touched him. For her, the party was a small gesture of kindness, but she'd held out a true hand of friendship. He felt unbelievably happy, as if she'd magically erased the decades of disappointment that had blighted this dubious anniversary.

And Jess had done more than simply throw a party tonight. She'd made entertaining at Warringa look miraculously easy. This evening's simple dinner had been so much fun, and Reece found himself wondering why he and his father hadn't made a bigger effort to socialise. The last thing he wanted was to become a surly recluse like his dad.

But perhaps the biggest thing he'd learned tonight was that keeping his distance from Jess was not only crazy. It was impossible.

CHAPTER SEVEN

THINGS changed a little for Jess after the birthday. Reece wasn't in quite such a rush to get away in the mornings. She usually had the radio playing softly in the background and they got into the habit of listening to the six a.m. news and then chatting about it afterwards.

And Reece seemed to make it back earlier in the evenings too. Many nights now, he was home in time for dinner, and a new pattern emerged. Sometimes, they played a game of five hundred with Michael after the meal. Other nights they watched television, which arrived at Warringa via a satellite dish. Or if Michael retired early, Reece and Jess would read for a bit—in the lounge room together, rather than separately in their bedrooms.

Jess genuinely appreciated his company, loved his quiet humour, his surprising wit, his calmness.

Two weeks later, the last of the cattle were branded and included into the herd, or shipped away to fattening blocks further south. The muster on Warringa was over and Reece spent one entire day lazing, shirtless, in a hammock on the back veranda, drinking icy beer, dozing, reading and cheering Rosie, who'd now started crawling and was turning into quite a little show-off.

Reece announced that Jess had earned a day off too, or at least a break from her normal routine.

'Why don't we go out to the gorge tomorrow,' he suggested. 'Take a picnic lunch and swimming gear.'

'I didn't know you had a gorge. That sounds interesting.'

The gorge was quite spectacular, actually. In many ways it was too good to keep hidden. More than once, Reece had considered reducing the cattle herd and starting up a tourist venture. Michael was dead set against it, though.

At least Jess's reaction to the scenery was gratifying. Her jaw dropped next day when they arrived at the head of the gorge and she saw the rocky escarpments falling away beneath her to the deep aqua-green cavern of water below.

'It's beautiful. But I'll have to hang on to Rosie.'

'Don't worry. I can drive you to a safer spot where we can swim.'

'Are there crocodiles?'

'Not where we're going.'

She sent him a wary smile.

'You can trust me, Jess.'

'Of course I can,' she said softly. 'You showed me that on the night I first met you.'

The shining look in her eyes made Reece want to leap high mountains, fight off wild beasts, light protective fires at the door to her cave.

Actually, Reece did light a small fire when they reached the rock pool where he planned to swim. He made billy tea and they drank from tin mugs, sitting on a rocky ledge and dangling their feet in the cool water, and he enjoyed holding Rosie, who seemed super excited about her new surroundings.

After their tea, Jess changed into her swimsuit behind a rock. She knew she shouldn't feel super self-conscious about appearing semi-naked in front of Reece, but she did, of course. At least the costume was a one-piece in figure-slimming, stretch-mark-hiding black. She stripped Rosie down too and carried her to the water.

This would be her baby's first swim.

It helped to concentrate on Rosie, rather than on the tall, broad-shouldered figure nearby. Reece in bathers was a distraction Jess tried to ignore. With little success.

The water was surprisingly cool and at first Rosie squawked with terror, but she soon adapted, and her cries changed to delighted chortles as she splashed madly, thrilled with this new game.

It wasn't long before Reece appeared at Jess's side, all strapping muscles and sleek satin skin, glistening with water. Jess tried not to stare. She really tried.

'You should have a swim,' he said. 'I can hold Rosie for a while.'

'That'd be great. Thanks.'

It wasn't actually possible to hand the baby over without touching him and, of course, the connection sent a live current shooting through her. So maddening when she was trying extra hard these days to remain immune. But just being with Reece, she felt restless and edgy, as if she'd swallowed fireflies, and there was a permanent, yearning ache low inside her. It was so unhelpful to be constantly attracted to her boss.

As soon as Reece had a safe hold of the wriggling babe, Jess dived quickly away, and she stayed underwater, skimming over the sandy bottom, over the pebbles and reedy clumps to eventually surface, lungs bursting, at the far end of the pool. At a safe distance.

Rolling onto her back, she floated, looking up at the

red rocky walls and the cobalt-blue sky. There was an occasional tree growing out of the wall, miraculously rooted, despite the heavy rains and winds that came with the wet season.

It was a typically picturesque outback scene, the sort of postcard-perfect image many people overseas associated with Australia.

Concentrate on the scenery. Forget Reece. You're lucky to be seeing this place.

So much was different about her life now—the lovely big homestead, the wide open spaces and now this spectacular gorge. She couldn't imagine going back to living in a tiny flat in the city. But that day would come, of course.

For now, she had to make the most of this fabulous opportunity. Not only was she a full-time mum, but her latest bank statements had arrived, and the horrible amounts that she owed were finally beginning to creep a tiny bit downwards.

Everything could be perfect here.

All she had to do now was swim back to the other end of the pool and take no notice of Reece's spectacular muscles.

Which was impossible, of course, but at least she could busy herself with towels, and with getting herself and Rosie dry.

Michael rolled up the bottoms of his trousers and waded in the shallows. They ate their lunch in the dappled sunlight of an overhanging paperbark, and after lunch Michael curled in the shade and had a nap. Reece took off his shirt—Jess prayed for strength—and he made a sling to carry Rosie and then persuaded Jess to join him on a hike.

'The walking will put her to sleep,' he suggested.

And it will wind me into a fever, Jess thought. But she went anyhow, and it was actually very enjoyable to walk along the rocky floor of the gorge, listening to Reece's laid-back drawl as he talked about the first inhabitants of this country, and showed her some wonderful Aboriginal handprints on a cave wall.

'I often think I'd like to open this place up and let more visitors in,' he said.

'Tourists?'

He nodded. 'I've fantasised about building accommodation with views down the gorge. People could use canoes or dinghies to explore.'

'Would you really want strangers tramping all over your land?'

'Under supervision. It could add a new dimension to life out here.'

It certainly could, and it would counter the loneliness factor. Jess's head was already running away, imagining exciting possibilities. 'You'd need a decent cook,' she said.

Reece's eyes flashed. 'I would. Do you know one?'

She was sure he didn't expect her to answer this. His shirtless state was causing her enough problems without discussing impossible fantasy futures with him.

She hoped she'd calm down again once they were back at the homestead, once she was busy with dinner and the nightly rituals of Rosie's bath and bedtime. To her dismay, she was still on edge at ten p.m., and she was still thinking far too much about Reece.

She found it impossible to sleep.

Well after ten, Reece was on the veranda, elbows on the railing, staring out at the moon-dappled paddocks too stirred for sleep. It was impossible when every time he closed his eyes he saw Jess in her bathers, saw her slim, shapely figure, her pale arms and legs, her hair, sleek and wet, the lovely curve of her bum, such a tempting handful.

He'd come out here to switch those thoughts off, but when he heard soft footsteps in the hallway he whirled around, saw a flash of white.

And there she was.

In her nightdress.

Bloody hell.

Ignoring his body's unhelpful reaction, he took a step towards her. 'Is everything OK, Jess?'

'Yes, I'm fine. I couldn't sleep. I was about to tiptoe down to the kitchen to make a cup of tea.'

But now, instead of continuing sensibly on to the kitchen, she came onto the veranda. Her dark hair was loose and flowing about her shoulders and her long nightdress was made from T-shirt material. In the pale moonlight, her skin looked softer than ever. He could see the lush outline of her breasts, their teasing peaks pushing against the fabric.

Desire thundered through him in rolling waves. He'd been going mad all day, ever since the rock pool. He wasn't sure he had the strength to resist Jess now. If she came any closer…

She stepped closer.

She lifted her face, and in the moonlight her lips were soft and full and the palest pink. 'What are you doing out here?'

'I'm not sleepy either,' he admitted reluctantly.

She looked up with a tiny smile, and with something else. An awareness. A challenge in her lovely green eyes.

A challenge he couldn't resist.

When she opened her mouth to say something more, he dipped his head and silenced her with the briefest touch of his lips.

She stilled momentarily, then sighed softly, sweetly, and swayed against him, almost as if her legs had given way. As he increased the pressure and slipped his arms around her she melted into him, her lips opening to him like a flower to the sun.

He couldn't quite believe he was holding Jess. Holding her and kissing her. At last. He knew this shouldn't be happening, but she was so sexy and soft and womanly, and willing. And he was burning up with need, driven wild by the taste and smell of her and the slow, sensuous dance of their tongues.

He deepened the kiss, binding her tightly against him, his hands cupping her bottom, holding her where he needed her, her heat to his hardness. And he sensed the wildness running loose in her. Pushing them both to the brink. Oh, God…

He wanted her. Wanted to lose himself in her, but he knew he had to stop.

He must stop.

He'd started this, but he had to stop.

Now.

Before they fell over the edge into madness.

He was trembling as he released her. And then, as they stepped apart, as cool air touched where her silky warmth had been, sanity returned with a chilling rush.

He shot a wary glance to Jess. 'I apologise. That wasn't supposed to happen.'

To his surprise she was actually smiling, but when he shook his head her smile faded. Abruptly, she turned from him and leaned on the railing, looking out into the endless stretch of the night. 'You're right,' she said softly.

He almost wished Jess would argue, tell him he was crazy to worry.

Her shoulders were hunched, her face tight. 'So I suppose we should pretend it didn't happen.'

He almost snatched her back into his arms. 'We have to. It's common sense.'

'Yes.'

But he also knew that it wasn't sensible to keep dancing around each other, trying to pretend that they weren't attracted. They were adults, not silly teenagers.

'If we were still in Cairns,' he said gruffly. 'Or—or damn New York—or anywhere but here, it would be different.'

Lifting her chin, Jess frowned at the stretch of dark countryside rendered invisible by the night. He supposed she must have been wondering why being out here changed the rules.

'Out here there's no point in starting anything,' he said, knowing how inadequate that probably sounded.

He was digging a hole for himself. He should drop this crazy conversation immediately. Walk away. Go to bed.

But he was captured by the sight of her, staring again, out into the night, her hair rippling about her shoulders like dark water.

'So what are you telling me?' she asked. 'That you live like a monk out here?'

He sighed, closed his mind to the memories of his brief, unsatisfactory encounters in recent years.

Now Jess turned to him, and she looked worried. 'I'm sorry. I assumed you wouldn't have kissed me if you had a girlfriend.'

He glared down at his hands, white knuckled as he gripped the railing. 'There's no girlfriend.' But then, he felt compelled to set the record straight. 'I still shouldn't have kissed you, Jess. I should have shown more respect.'

'Respect?' Her eyes widened as she regarded him with a puzzled smile.

'You're a newly bereaved widow.'

Now she blushed as she whirled away from him. Oh, God.

Her face burst into flames. She hadn't given Alan a thought tonight. She wasn't sure how long bereavement usually lasted. It wasn't that she hadn't grieved for him. Of course, she'd been sad about losing her husband. His death was shocking…and she'd felt a terrible loss, but she'd also been worn down by the reality of their marriage.

Alan had left her with so many problems, and with as many bad memories as good ones. It was hard not to feel resentful now, as if she were still being punished.

She felt a need to explain. 'To be honest, I don't feel guilty. My marriage was pretty rocky. Alan and I had problems.'

Reece's face was grim as he took this in. 'I'm sorry to hear that.'

Jess thought he might leave then, but he remained there, by her side, leaning on the railing, looking out across the dark paddocks. She wondered what he was thinking.

For her own part, she couldn't stop thinking about his kiss—the paralysing moment of anticipation, and then the first thrilling touch of his lips to hers, the bliss of being swept into his arms, of being held against him.

And then the blaze of longing, the wonderful craziness...

She couldn't hold back a wistful sigh and when she turned to him and met his steady, dark gaze, she refused to look away. But his eyes were so fiercely intent that she eventually had to look down again.

There was an awkward silence and her heart picked up pace. She knew very well that they had no choice but to forget the kiss. Reece was right. If they'd been in the city they might have had a fling, a bit of harmless fun. But it was pretty hard to have a light-hearted, casual affair when you were stranded in an isolated outback homestead.

She wasn't sure what she should do now. Stand here bursting with tension? Say goodnight? Go make that cup of tea?

Still uncertain, she pushed away from the railing, but as she did Reece reached for her hand.

His touch sent a streak of fire scorching through her.

And then his fingers closed around hers, sending a second heatwave flashing over her skin.

The tension was electric, but neither of them spoke. It was as if they didn't want to break the spell with anything as dangerous as words. And then, Reece tugged gently at her hand.

And it was too hard to stay sensible. She was powerless to resist.

Any lingering awkwardness melted. His arms tightened around her, crushing her doubts and questions. She was smiling as he kissed her forehead, melting as his mouth found her cheek, her ear lobe, her chin, then everywhere...

She tilted her head back so he could kiss her throat,

and then his lips trailed lower to the neckline of her nightie.

She gasped as his thumbs gently grazed her breasts through the thin fabric.

'Your room?' he whispered.

'Please.'

Of course it was wonderful, and of course they were pleased with themselves. After weeks of suppressing this need, they could at last lie skin to skin, could at last touch and taste to their hearts' content.

Jess's room smelled of cinnamon and vanilla, and they made love on crisp, clean sheets, and she was pleased that she didn't feel the slightest bit awkward or shy. Reece's touch sent a happy charge running through her and everything felt natural and perfectly right.

She loved the giving and the taking, loved the sighing and smiling as they soared together and clung together. Till at last, they plunged from a great height.

Together.

Afterwards.

They lay, limbs loose and relaxed. Sleepy.

'Wow,' Jess said softly.

'Yeah…' Reece drew a deep breath and let it out slowly. 'Wow's the word.'

She smiled broadly in the darkness. 'And thank goodness Rosie didn't wake up.'

It was possibly the wrong thing to say. At the mention of the baby, Reece hitched up on one elbow. 'I guess it's time I got back to my room.'

She considered asking him to stay. She would love to go to sleep beside him, and to wake beside him. But that was probably asking too much. After all, without actually saying the words, they'd more or less agreed this wasn't the beginning of a real relationship. Whatever it was, it was casual.

As he rolled from her bed Jess closed her eyes. 'Goodnight, Reece.'

Even though she knew it must happen, she didn't want to watch him walk away from her.

The warm pressure of his lips on her forehead was a surprise.

''Night, Jess.'

Such a tiny gesture, but after he'd gone she felt so much better.

In his room, Reece sat on the edge of his bed, staring hard at a faint patch of moonlight on the floorboards, as if somehow it could provide him with answers or reassurance.

I swore that wouldn't happen.

But, surely, no man in his right mind could turn away from a girl as lovely and tempting as Jess.

Just the same, he wouldn't allow himself to be totally blown away by tonight. Yes, he was walking on air, but now it was time to throw out an anchor. Time to get real, to accept that nothing that felt this good could last.

Jess might be utterly bewitching, and tonight with her had been far and away the best sex he'd ever known, but now he had to get their fabulous lovemaking into perspective. Had to remember that Jess wasn't here to stay. She was here primarily to care for his father, and if Michael passed away she'd shoot through.

No question.

Reece was regrettably familiar with this pattern of women leaving, although, in his twenties, he'd been more optimistic about his chances of lasting happiness.

Despite the never-forgotten desolation of his mother's desertion, he'd been confident he would be luckier than his dad.

He'd brought girlfriends home to Warringa. Girls he'd met on city-breaks, or on holidays, girls he'd met at parties, at mates' weddings, at the races…

Picking up girls had been the easy part, and they'd arrived here bright-eyed and eager, claiming to be in love with his 'cowboy' lifestyle. Some had begged to stay on, but their rosy expectations had never been close to reality. Averill had become depressed by the isolation. Rachel couldn't get on with his dad. Gemma had been bored by the lack of a cinema, or girlfriends to chat and gossip with.

Reece had realised then that when he eventually chose a wife, he'd have to find one among the girls who'd been born and bred in the bush. His needs were quite clear. She didn't have to be great-looking, but she had to be comfortable around horses and cattle. She had to cope with hard work and isolation, and she had to have a genuine love of the outback life.

In the meantime…

He had to come to terms with having Jess Cassidy here. In his life, close at hand, day in, day out.

And what an enticing but complicated thought that was.

Jess wasn't a girl he'd met at a party or on a beach holiday. He'd met her here, at Warringa, on a night like no other, the night her husband had died and her baby was born.

A night of incredible emotional connection.

And that was his problem. He cared too much about Jess and her cute baby daughter.

Now it was time to remember that when they left,

they would take a sizeable chunk of his heart with them, just as his mother had.

It was a certainty he mustn't lose sight of.

Jess was sure she went to sleep with a smile on her face, still in a happy swoon. She didn't want to overthink this perfect night, so she'd deliberately shut down her thoughts, and she wouldn't let herself ask questions or worry about it. She simply wanted to relax and absorb this new layer that had been added to the happiness that filled her life now.

As she settled into the pillow she felt more secure and serene than she had in years. Perhaps ever.

It was no surprise that she slept soundly until Rosie woke around four. Softly, she tiptoed to the kitchen, heated a bottle and brought the baby back into bed with her.

Snuggled against a pile of pillows, she made Rosie comfortable, then lay looking at her little girl in the faint creamy light that crept through the slatted blinds at dawn. She rubbed her cheek against her soft silky hair and breathed in the pink and white smell of her.

She remembered last night with Reece, and happiness bubbled through her, again. A shiver-sweet delight that had everything to do with Reece. He'd been so flatteringly passionate and yet considerate too. As a lover, he was her secret fantasy come true.

It was tempting to make comparisons with Alan, but she wouldn't allow that. In fact, she was becoming increasingly aware now, in this new light of day, that she needed to get her head sorted.

Yes, last night was a really big deal for her. Huge. Unforgettable. But she had to remember it was a fling, not the start of a new relationship. It had been all about chemistry and it had nothing to do with deeper emotions. She was vulnerable because she'd felt overwhelming gratitude to Reece ever since the night he'd found her on the side of the road.

Looking down at Rosie again, seeing her plump cheeks and the bright concentration in her eyes as she drank, Jess remembered the promise she'd made to her daughter back in Cairns on the night Reece had come to dinner. She'd been sure then that she would get on top of their debts and build a future. Without a man.

She had to stick to that plan. Had to do this alone.

She'd had an unforgettable night with a man who stirred her to her very soul, but it shouldn't happen again.

It was more important than ever to remember that now.

CHAPTER EIGHT

'I've been checking out your garden,' Jess told Reece at breakfast a few days later.

He looked up, amused. 'What garden?'

'Near the back stairs and beside the laundry.'

'You can hardly call that mess a garden.'

'Well, it has potential. I know it's mostly grass and weeds at the moment, but I started clearing a corner and I found brick edges and the start of a pathway. There's been a garden there in the past and it's all just waiting to be uncovered.'

Jess envied people with gardens, and, after a lifetime in rented flats, she'd been really excited by her discovery. It was like finding buried treasure. 'Is it OK with you if I keep clearing?'

'Sure. Be my guest.' Reece's dark eyes glowed with a mixture of amusement and admiration...and something else. 'I'll help you, if you like.'

She turned back to the stove so he couldn't see how pleased she was. Despite her resolution to keep her distance, there'd been a happy vibe between them ever since the night they'd made love.

They hadn't talked about it. Reece had been as careful as she was to get 'back to normal', but another barrier between them had definitely fallen. They couldn't help smiling at each other now, and they were both mega eager to please.

It was a dangerous kind of limbo, a happy bubble that couldn't hold for ever. At some stage they would have to talk about what had happened. Perhaps they were both scared? Perhaps it meant too much? Felt too dangerous, after all?

Even working in the garden with Reece would be perilously like playing Happy Families, although Jess couldn't deny that his muscle power would be invaluable.

'I'd actually love to grow a few vegetables and herbs for the kitchen,' she said.

'Great idea,' he agreed. 'I should have been doing that years ago, but running the cattle business has taken up most of my time. As you know, we tend to live on tinned and frozen veggies.'

'Well, I'm happy to get it started. Pity there's no plant nursery around here.'

Reece shrugged. 'It's easy enough to order seeds over the Internet, and I'll have to take Dad back to the doctor in Cairns again soon. We can buy plants while we're there.'

'We? Are you planning for me and Rosie to come too?'

'Why not? You'd like a break, wouldn't you?'

Jess grinned at him. It was another thing to look forward to. Each day, her life at Warringa seemed to keep getting better, despite the silent, lingering question—

How long could it last?

She shook that menacing thought away. 'Actually, I'm glad Michael is seeing the doctor again,' she said. 'I do feel he's slowed down a bit lately, don't you?'

'Yeah.' Reece sighed softly. 'But he'll never admit it.'

He stood and took his plate and cutlery to the sink. 'We may as well start clearing the garden straight after breakfast, before it gets too hot.' He seemed almost as keen on the garden idea as she was.

It was fun—certainly more fun than a potentially boring job like digging up weeds and grass should have been. After Jess had fixed breakfast for Michael, she set a playpen, a picnic rug and toys under a shady jacaranda tree for Rosie. Reece extracted a wheelbarrow, spades, forks and a hoe from an old garden shed, and together they set to work. Reece wielded the hoe on the tough weeds and clumps of kunai grass, while Jess prised out the roots of the couch grass runners that completely covered the path.

It was rewarding to see the growing mountain of rubbish in the wheelbarrow, while a brick-edged garden emerged beside the house, bordered by a surprisingly beautiful, old-fashioned path made from black and white bricks in a herringbone pattern.

'This is going to be gorgeous, Reece.' Jess was already carried away, imagining clumps of basil and rosemary, and then sage and a ground cover of oregano. Oh, and there'd be parsley, as well, and chillies. And cherry tomatoes. 'We can have a pot of mint under the tap.'

She'd once worked in a restaurant that had its own kitchen garden, and it had become a personal fantasy she'd nursed for years. Until now it had been another pipe dream.

Amazing to think it was coming to life all the way out here. When she'd arrived at Warringa, she'd thought she'd come to the middle of nowhere. Now, this house and the land around it were beginning to feel like the centre of *somewhere*. An increasingly fascinating and alluring somewhere.

Jess realised Reece was smiling at her again. 'Have you any idea how your eyes shine when you're excited?'

'Well, maybe they're a bit like yours?' she suggested shyly and, without warning, the air around them was crackling.

Their clothes and hands were grubby, covered in dirt grass stains, but it didn't seem to matter as Reece closed the space between them and gathered her in. And Jess decided instantly that resistance was futile. She gave herself permission to forget all her questions as he kissed her.

Time stood still. She closed her eyes and his lips worked their magic and the winter sun streamed gently over them.

It was their little bit of heaven until a grouchy *'Harrumph'* from the veranda brought them springing apart.

'What the hell are you two up to?' Michael roared.

To Jess's blushing relief, Reece remained quite calm. Instead of trying to justify their kiss, he sank his hands into his jeans pockets and strolled over to the veranda. 'Hi, Dad.'

She held her breath, waiting for Michael to demand why his son and the housekeeper were madly locking lips.

'What's all this mess?' Michael demanded, with a glare and a sweeping gesture that encompassed their attempts at gardening.

'We're making a vegetable and herb garden.'

'A *what*?'

'A vegetable and herb garden. You know,' Reece said patiently. 'Tomatoes, lettuce, chives—plants we can eat.'

'We don't need to eat plants.'

'Come on, Dad. Don't play games. You know what I'm talking about. Jess wants to grow things for the kitchen. For salads and to use in her cooking.'

Michael continued to scowl. 'This is a cattle station, not a bloody restaurant.' He shot a surprisingly angry glare Jess's way. 'You've been doing something to those hanging baskets near the kitchen too, haven't you?'

'I've been watering them,' she admitted. 'But I haven't wasted tank water, Michael. I've been collecting the grey water from the laundry.' She'd been pleased with her economy and with the lovely green shoots and fronds now sprouting from the ferns' massive, ancient root systems.

'Don't bother,' Michael growled. 'I hate those ferns. They give me the creeps.'

Reece was shaking his head. 'Dad, those hanging baskets have had struggling ferns in them for as long as I can remember. If they gave you the creeps, you could have tossed them out years ago.'

Michael simply growled again and stomped back inside the house. Not a word about their kiss. Perhaps he hadn't noticed?

He was more upset about the garden.

Rosie began to cry then, and Jess went to pick her up. 'You probably need changing, don't you, kitty?'

With the baby in her arms she turned to Reece. 'I might see if she's ready for her nap.'

But he hadn't heard her. He was staring with a puzzled frown at the space where his father had stood.

'Reece?' Jess stepped closer.

He turned and blinked, as if he'd been miles away. 'Is everything OK?'

'Sure.' He sighed. 'I was lost in the past. Trying to

remember. I'm pretty sure my mother planted the ferns in those hanging baskets.'

He hardly ever spoke about his mother, the woman who'd left so many years ago, leaving Michael alone to raise their son.

Jess had no idea what had driven the woman away, and she didn't understand how she could have abandoned her little boy. Just the same, Michael's reaction to the baskets was strange. Why had he kept the plants in a half-dead state? What was he clinging to? Had he never really forgiven his wife? Was he still bitter and angry after twenty-eight years?

These were sobering questions as she went inside. But as she changed Rosie and smoothed lotion onto her soft skin, she realised it was easy enough to wonder about Reece's parents' relationship, but much harder to examine her own behaviour. A few short minutes ago, she'd shared another kiss with Reece in a moment of spontaneous happiness.

Why, when she'd known it was reckless? Why would she risk giving him the wrong idea when she knew she'd eventually have to leave, just as his mother had?

As Reece had predicted, the afternoon sun hit the back of the house and it was too hot to garden after lunch. While Michael and Rosie had naps, he went off to tinker with a tractor's motor in the machinery shed, and Jess turned her attention to housework.

She was dusting bookshelves in the lounge room when she came across a particularly smart-looking photo album. As she picked it up to wipe the thick red leather binding a photo fluttered to the floor. Stooping to collect it, she saw a picture of a serious little boy with dark hair and handsome dark eyes.

He was standing at the bottom of Warringa's front steps, dressed in smart-looking black trousers, a white shirt and a neat little striped waistcoat.

The boy had to be Reece.

Jess slipped the photo back into the front of the album, but she couldn't help taking a peek and she soon realised that every photo in the album was very alike, with Reece standing on the front steps.

Frowning, she looked a little closer. Reece was incrementally taller and older in each photo, and he was wearing a different outfit each time. The clothes looked brand-new.

These had to be the photos of his birthday outfits. He'd told her that his mother used to send clothes for his birthday, and he would ask his father to take a photograph to send back to her with his thank-you notes.

Jess knew she shouldn't be prying, but she couldn't resist taking a closer look. She could see almost immediately that the clothes weren't very suitable for a boy living in the outback. Reece had spent his days helping his dad in the stockyards or riding horses, but there wasn't one pair of jeans or riding boots.

In one photo a young Reece was wearing a long multicoloured T-shirt over cord-style shorts with long tube socks and sneakers. In another he wore a knitted pullover in a totally impractical lemon and white diamond pattern.

There were other photos of Reece in lime-green Hawaiian-print board shorts, or ridiculously oversized jeans with an equally oversized black rock T-shirt. Perhaps worst of all was the photo of Reece in his teens, wearing a pale grey tracksuit with legs that were too short, so that the elasticated cuffs rode halfway up his calves.

What had his mother been thinking when she sent her son garments that were practically useless?

Jess looked intently at Reece's face in each photo, recognising the gradual maturing of his handsome features. His mouth was always curved into a careful smile, but anyone who knew him well could see the questions in his eyes, as if he wondered if his mother really expected him to wear this stuff.

Her heart ached for the little boy who'd longed for toys, not clothes. Poor Reece.

No doubt he'd also longed for a mother who understood him and really cared about him. And yet he'd dutifully sent these photos back to her, no doubt hoping they'd please her.

With trembling fingers, she touched a photo of Reece in pale beige wide-legged trousers and a brown button-down shirt with palm trees printed across the chest. A city boy might have worn these clothes to church or to the movies or a party, but how often could Reece have worn this outfit? Any of these outfits?

Her face crumpled and a tear splashed the page. More tears followed. Tears for a little boy who'd been left behind. A boy who deserved so much more.

Up to his elbows in motor parts, Reece was wrestling with a tractor's innards when he heard a sound behind him. He turned and blinked as a stooped silhouette appeared in the brightly lit doorway.

'Is that you, Dad?'

Instead of answering, his father shuffled forward. 'I thought I might find you in here.'

'You're supposed to be having a rest.'

'I'll rest in a minute. I wanted to talk to you first.'

'Everything OK?' Reece reached for a rag to wipe

the black grease from his hands as his father shambled closer and slowly, stiffly, lowered himself onto an up-turned oil drum.

The old man looked tired and grey, hollow-cheeked.

Reece frowned. 'Are you sure you're OK, Dad? Let me take you back inside. We can talk in there.'

'Stop fussing. I want to talk out here.'

'OK. That's cool. What's on your mind?'

'You, Reece. You and Jess.'

He should have known this would crop up. Their kiss in the garden couldn't have gone unnoticed.

His father's eyes glinted. 'This morning wasn't the first time you've kissed her.' It was a statement, not a question.

'That's my business,' Reece said testily.

'Thought as much.'

'You got a problem with it?'

'I just wanted to warn you to be careful this time.'

'Excuse me?'

'Jess is different, Reece.' The old man raised a shaking finger. 'She's right for you, son. She's a keeper.'

A shocked gasp escaped Reece. 'What the hell are you talking about?'

'You know bloody well. You and Jess, of course.'

'Dad, calm down. You've no idea—'

'No. You listen to me. If you play your cards right with this girl, you could be set for life.'

Reece groaned. The last thing he wanted was his father's endorsement of a possible wife or a life partner. He was hoping to remain sensible about his feelings for Jess. He needed to be fine when he finally saw the end of her time here.

The old man was getting carried away. Just because he enjoyed Jess's cooking. 'You know damn well—if

I was on the hunt for a wife, I wouldn't be looking for a girl from the city.'

'Jess might be a city girl, but she's different,' his father insisted again. 'She likes it out here. She's not pretending.'

Reece stared at him. For a second, the old man almost made sense. Jess did seem to like it here. She'd heaped praise on the place and he'd never heard a word of complaint from her.

Then again, she was being paid to live here and he knew she really needed the money, and she was too smart to bite the hand that fed her.

But he didn't want to stir his father. 'Well...thanks for your advice, Dad. I'll bear it in mind.'

'I hope you do, Reece. I'm dead serious.'

Reece stepped closer, touched his father on the shoulder. 'Now that you've sorted my problems, I'm actually worried about you, old fella. I'm glad you'll be seeing Doc Campbell again next week.'

His father gave a grunt of disapproval. 'Bloody doctors.' But when he tried to stand, he swayed dizzily.

Reece was instantly at his side with an arm around him. 'Easy does it. Lean on me.'

'I'm all right.'

'Yeah, sure you are, but let me walk with you back to the house.'

To Reece's surprise and concern, his father acquiesced, clutching his arm all the way to the house, up the steps and then down the passage to his bedroom. He even let Reece help him to remove his boots, and to assist him onto the bed, accepting the assistance without a word of complaint.

As Reece closed the bedroom door he was recalling the strong, tall hero of his youth. He could so clearly remember his father riding a bucking bronco, or leg-roping a steer, carrying an orphaned calf home on his broad shoulders.

Actually, the day the calf came home was emblazoned on Reece's memory. He'd been so excited as his father put the little fellow down on a bed of hay and then took Reece to the kitchen to mix up a bottle of formula.

'Where's the calf's mother?' Reece had asked.

'She's gone, son. Passed away.'

'Like my mother?'

'Near enough. But don't worry, Reece. The calf will be OK. He's got us.'

As a little kid, Reece had been relieved and reassured to see that the calf had turned out fine, growing big and strong and playful, and eventually joining the herd. He supposed he'd identified with it to an extent. He and the calf could both manage without their mothers. He'd certainly believed in his father's knowledge of how things worked in the world.

Now, he thought again about the message Michael had struggled all the way to the machinery shed to deliver.

If you play your cards right with this girl, you could be set for life.

It was an arresting thought and for an instant Reece felt the possibility glow inside him, filling his head and his heart with brilliant hope. But he had to dismiss it.

He'd lost his naïve faith long ago. He knew that when it came to romance and marriage and happily ever after, his old man didn't have a clue.

Their evenings had fallen into a new pattern. After dinner, if they weren't playing cards with Michael, Jess stretched on the sofa and Reece sat in a nearby armchair. Often they were both reading, as they were this evening—or at least, Reece was reading and Jess was trying to concentrate on her novel. But any minute now, they'd probably go to bed. In their separate rooms.

It was a new form of torture, Jess decided. Each night she wrestled with the stupid fantasy that Reece would make a move again—that she would end up in his lap, or he would tumble onto the couch with her.

Tonight it wasn't just physical yearning. She felt quite emotional too. She couldn't stop thinking about Reece's photo album and she longed to take him in her arms, to give him a thousand kisses and hugs to make up for every one of those unsatisfactory birthday gifts.

As she turned another page of her book she realised she hadn't taken in a single word of the last three pages. She set the book aside with a deliberately noisy sigh.

Reece looked up from his cattlemen's journal. 'Had enough?'

'Just about.' But before he could jump to his feet she quickly asked, 'Do you mind if I ask you a personal question?'

He looked mildly amused. 'I guess that depends on the question.'

'I don't think it's *too* probing. I've been wondering what it must have been like for you when your parents split up. You were only little, weren't you?'

'I was five. Why?'

'That's a long time for you and your father to be living out here on your own.'

'We weren't completely on our own the whole time. We had a succession of housekeeper-governesses until I was twelve. And then I was away at boarding school for six years. After that, agricultural college. But since then it's pretty much been the two of us.'

Jess rolled onto her stomach so she could see Reece properly, and for a moment she simply lay there, admiring his dark hair, his dark brown eyes, the strong lines of his face. 'Can you remember your mother?'

'Sure.' His expression grew serious. 'I've seen her a few times since she left.'

'Do you look like her?'

His eyebrows lifted. 'I doubt it. When she was young, she had long red hair. She was quite beautiful, actually.' His mouth tilted in a rueful smile. 'When I was little I thought she was the most beautiful creature on earth. Beautiful, but unhappy.'

'Did you know she was unhappy even then? When you were only five?'

'Wasn't hard to work out. There were plenty of tears. Especially towards the end, after my brother, Tony, was born.'

Jess hadn't known about a brother. 'Tell me to shut up if I'm getting too nosy, but what happened to Tony? Where is he now?'

'Sydney. My mother took him with her.'

And left you behind?

Could this story get any sadder?

'Don't look so worried, Jess. I was fine here.'

'Of course you were.' She hoped she hadn't looked too appalled, and she tried to cover her reaction with another question. 'Have you seen much of Tony?'

'Once or twice at Christmas. I went to his wedding, and to his son's christening.' Reece had been picking at a loose thread on the arm of his chair, but now he looked up and smiled at her. 'Stop looking at me like that.'

'Like what?'

'Like I'm an orphan out of a Charles Dickens novel.

I'm OK. I'm cool about everything. You don't really miss what you've never had.'

Jess nodded. 'That's certainly very true.'

Perhaps she agreed a little too wholeheartedly. Reece sent her a rather searching look. 'So how about you? What's your family like? Do you have brothers or sisters?'

She shook her head. 'It was only ever me and my mum. Not all that different from you, I guess—except we lived in towns along the coast. Mackay, Townsville, Cairns.'

'What about your father?'

'I've never met him.'

Now it was Reece's turn to look surprised. 'He took off?'

'I guess he must have. That or Mum chased him away. My mum was vague about the full story, but knowing her, there's a good chance she never told him about me.' Before Reece could ask, she added, 'My mum died two years ago.'

'Jess, I'm so sorry.'

For a moment, he looked as if he wanted to leap out of his chair and take her into his arms, and she certainly wouldn't have minded. But if that *was* his intention, he restrained himself.

A small silence passed before he asked, 'Do you know where your father lives now?'

'In New York, apparently.'

Actually, there was no apparently about it. Jess knew *exactly* where her father was. In recent years, she'd kept tabs on him via the Internet. 'His name's Richard Travere and he's a chef.'

Reece grinned. 'So you inherited his talent for cooking.'

'I guess I must have.' She gave a shrug, as if it were

no big deal, but then she felt compelled to confess. 'When I was little, I used to have dreams about him—that he came looking for me—but I can't honestly say that I miss him.'

'At least you'll have photos of Rosie's father to show her.'

'That's true.' Jess grimaced guiltily as she realised how infrequently Alan entered her thoughts these days. But Reece had raised a good point. She must make an album for Rosie with photos of her father, and she should collect and save any other mementos she could find. She knew what it was like to grow up always wondering, and she didn't want those sorts of questions haunting her daughter.

She would leave out the bad bits. Rosie needn't know about the trouble Alan had left behind.

'I'm in the mood for a nightcap,' Reece said out of the blue, and he jumped to his feet, a frown firmly in place. 'Want to join me? There's not a lot of choice, I'm afraid. It's Scotch or Scotch.'

'Oh.' Jess smiled. 'I wouldn't mind a small Scotch.'

He smiled back at her and returned a few moments later, ice cubes clinking in two tumblers, a bottle hooked in one elbow.

To her surprise he came to the sofa. 'Move over.'

A ripple of excitement eddied through her. Sharing Scotch on the sofa was so unlike Reece. Was he letting down his guard again?

Should she be wary?

Hell, no, she decided a second later as he handed her a glass. She wanted to relax and enjoy this close-up view of lamplight on his dark hair and the warm glow in his eyes, not to mention the tempered strength of his body and long, long legs.

By the time she took her first sip of the smooth, fiery liquid, desire was buzzing through her. She was remembering the taste of passion in his kisses, the taut satin of his skin beneath her hands.

Oh, God. She had absolutely no will power. She would be back in his arms in a blink.

CHAPTER NINE

JESS took another, deeper sip of her drink. 'Reece, I hate to ask, but are we ever going to talk about…that night?'

Despite the leap of desire and the warnings clamouring in his head, Reece managed to speak calmly enough. 'I was wondering the same thing. I know it's dangerous ground.'

Jess pursed her lips as she considered this. 'It would only be dangerous if we got too serious.'

'That's a concern, yes.' He couldn't believe how formal he sounded, but discussing this sort of thing was difficult for him. He was a man of action, not semantics.

But while he couldn't allow himself to believe his father's claim that he could have a happy, long-term future with Jess, he knew there were things that needed settling between them.

Right now, she was sitting with her legs curled, keeping her thoughtful gaze fixed on the ice swirling in her glass. She was wearing pale grey trousers and a sleeveless top in a shade of lavender that was perfect for her pale skin and her dark hair. She looked so lovely he was going mad.

'If you're worried about me getting serious, you can

relax,' she said. 'I have no intention of getting in deep with any man. Not for ages. I simply can't afford to get serious.'

She looked up then, and her green eyes were clear as glass. 'And to be totally honest, that's not because I'm grieving, Reece. It's a matter of practicality. I have to plan for the future for Rosie and me, and I can't be sidetracked by relationships.'

'Yes…that's understandable…' He swallowed to relieve the awkward tightness in his throat. 'I need to be practical too. I couldn't get serious about a girl from the city.'

'Of course,' Jess said quickly, perhaps a little too quickly. But then she shrugged. 'Something casual could be another matter. With no strings attached—'

Her self-assurance seemed to desert her suddenly and she dropped her gaze to her glass as colour rose high in her cheeks.

Reece drew a very necessary breath. 'Maybe we're on the same page,' he suggested quietly.

Jess was still staring at her glass, but he knew that her eyes had widened. 'Do you think so?'

'If we both want to keep things casual.'

'No strings.'

'Absolutely no strings. No expectations.'

'So no one will get hurt.'

'I'd hate to hurt you, Jess.'

She looked up again, a small smile shimmering. 'Maybe we *are* on the same page, then.'

Almost in unison they downed the last of their drinks, set the glasses aside. Eyed each other.

Smiled.

Reece reached for her hand, smooth and pale and

fine-fingered, and held it in his splayed, callused palm.
'Look at that.'

'Vive la différence.'

It became amazingly simple then. A matter of being
with the right person in the right moment. When he
leaned in and touched his lips to Jess's, she melted
against him and she kissed him back. She tasted faintly
of Scotch and she smelled fresh as flowers. As she
linked her arms around him he slid his fingers into the
dark silk of her hair.

Need met need.

His need and hers. And everything was OK because
they had it all planned. No one would end up being
hurt. They were OK. And they were so good together.

They kissed with a comfortable kind of urgency,
lips and tongues and hands eagerly exploring, removing clothes, rediscovering.

They made love on the couch and then later, after
gathering their scattered belongings, they retired to
Jess's bedroom where they made love again at a more
leisurely pace this time. Lingering. Slow heat building
to blissful oblivion.

And Reece thought: *This is how it can be.*

This was how it *should* be. No pressure. No expectations. No guilt. He'd felt many emotions after making
love, but never this uncomplicated happiness.

And Jess seemed happy too as she lay beside him,
relaxed and easy, her cheek tucked against his shoulder. Their plan was working.

'Just had a thought,' she said sleepily.

'What's that?'

'Is casual sex usually this good?'

'Does it matter?'

'I hope not.'

A spidery fear crept down his spine. 'Are you actually having second thoughts?'

'No, no.' She nestled against him, pressed a kiss to his shoulder. 'I don't have any doubts. Not about this.'

'Have you finished, Michael?' Jess tried not to sound concerned next evening, when Michael pushed his plate away with half his dinner left uneaten.

'I'm not very hungry tonight.'

She'd cooked a lamb stew, which was one of his favourites, and he usually had a good appetite. When she met Reece's gaze across the table, he looked a bit worried, but he answered her silent question with a faint shake of his head.

'How about a little stewed apple and custard, then?' Jess asked as she removed Michael's plate of stew.

He smiled. 'That'd be nice.' He had quite a sweet tooth.

Jess fixed the dessert with her usual efficiency, pleased that she'd made another of his favourites. Over the weeks she'd spent at Warringa she'd become genuinely fond of Reece's dad, despite the occasional difficult moments. She'd never known her own father or either of her grandfathers, so Michael was the first man from an older generation that she'd spent any amount of time with.

He'd told her stories about his boyhood, spent mostly running wild in the bush in the company of young Aboriginal kids. And he'd told her about his days as a young drover when his team had overlanded a thousand head of wild cattle from Far North Queensland to Rockhampton, spending almost six months on the stock routes.

As a young man he'd even had a stint working on the pampas in Argentina, and Jess had loved hearing about his adventures in a world totally different from anything she'd ever known.

Tonight she was relieved that Michael ate almost all of his dessert. After dinner, Reece carried a cup of tea back to his father's bedroom and settled him comfortably. There was a small television set on his chest of drawers and he liked to sit in bed, propped by a bank of pillows, and watch his favourite TV shows.

Jess was stacking the dishwasher when Reece came back into the kitchen, a line of worry creasing his forehead.

'First thing in the morning, I'm going to ring Doc Campbell's office. I'm going to try to get Dad's appointment brought forward.'

'That might be a good idea.' Jess closed the dishwasher and came to him, touched a hand to his wrist, a gesture of sympathy. She wished she could tell him that Michael would be OK, but they both knew this might not be possible.

'He's always been so strong.' Reece's eyes were extra dark, as if clouded with worry. 'I know he's old and this has to happen, but it's hard to get used to. I haven't seen him this weak since my mother told him she was never coming back.'

'Really?'

Reece glared at a spot on the floor. 'He had a kind of breakdown then. Couldn't get out of bed.'

'Poor man.' Jess frowned. 'But if he didn't get out of bed, I hope there was someone here to look after you.'

Reece shook his head. 'This was before he hired a housekeeper.'

'So how did you cope? Who looked after you?'

'I looked after myself.'

'Reece, you were only five years old.'

It was impossible. Jess couldn't bear to think of it—a little boy alone and a father prostrated by grief.

As much for her own comfort as for his, she slipped her arms around Reece's waist and rested her cheek against his chest. 'How on earth did you manage?'

'Ate whatever I could find. Anything that didn't need cooking. Bread and butter.' He pulled briefly away from her, looked down with a wry smile. 'The butter was so chunky on the bread. I didn't really know how to spread it. But I found apples, oranges, cheese. Ice cream.'

'What about your father?'

'I tried to feed him, but he would only drink water—and not much of that.'

Jess hugged him close, but then she had to step back, needing air. She felt a little dazed and sick at the thought of Michael becoming so completely gutted by his wife's desertion. He must have suffered the worst possible heartbreak.

'What happened in the end?' she asked. 'Did Michael snap out of it?'

'The Pearsons, our neighbours, called in. Actually, I think my memories are based on their story, rather than the true details. They called the Flying Doctor and Mary Pearson cooked up a big pile of meat and potatoes, and then they took me back to their place. I stayed with them while Dad spent some time in Cairns Hospital.'

'Reece, that's terrible. The poor man.' She shivered, feeling chilled as she remembered the pain she'd seen in the eyes of one or two of her mother's cast-off lovers. 'I didn't realise rejection could hit a man so hard.'

She caught a change in Reece's eyes, a momentary bleakness before his gaze steadied again. 'Dad's never talked about it. He's actually tough as nails. I shouldn't have told you. He'd hate it.'

'I'll never repeat a word. I promise.'

Reece nodded. 'Anyway, he got over it, Jess. He had to. He had no alternative.'

Another shiver sluiced through her and she rubbed at her arms. Reece closed the gap between them and pulled her to him. But to her surprise she couldn't relax. She still felt tense, inexpressibly disturbed by his story.

'I'll make coffee,' she said.

His arms tightened around her. 'I want you, not coffee.'

She smiled, relishing his words, and anything might have happened then, if a small wail hadn't come from a distant bedroom.

'That's Rosie.' Jess sighed. 'She's teething again.'

'I'll see to her.'

'No, Reece. You've got enough worries with your father.'

'I don't mind. Honest. You make better coffee than I do. You see to the coffee. I'll check on Rosie.'

He was already on his way.

'The teething gel's on the cupboard in her room,' Jess called after him.

A pink rabbit-shaped night light glowed in the corner of the baby's room. As Reece pushed the door open he could see Rosie gripping the bars of her cot as she tried to stand on wobbly, bowed legs.

'You're stuck, aren't you, mischief? You tried to stand up, and you don't know how to sit down again.'

As he gently lifted her she was already grinning at him and chuckling.

'Hey, this isn't a game. You're supposed to go straight back to sleep.'

Rosie had other ideas. With a gleeful shriek she clutched at his nose and squeezed and tugged.

'Ouch, ouch, ouch,' he joked, eliciting another chuckle from her.

'Dad-da.'

'No, poppet, I'm not your Dad-da.' But even as Reece said this he felt a pang, as if the baby had fired a pygmy dart straight to his heart.

He wasn't sure if he would ever be a father, and tonight that thought seemed to highlight an emptiness inside him that he'd tried his best to ignore. For years.

Rosie made another grab for his nose, and he caught her tiny hand in his and cradled it against his chest. 'Shh,' he whispered. 'Just as soon as I rub this gel on your sore gums, you're going back to sleep.'

He kissed her soft, golden brown hair. 'Shh.'

She smelled amazing. He supposed it was the scents of baby soap and talcum powder, but she smelled so clean and fresh he could practically eat her. And she felt so soft and tiny in his arms as she let him apply the gel, then snuggled into him like a small koala.

Holding her close, he paced the room, rocking her gently as he'd seen Jess do many times, amazed by how much Rosie seemed to love it, how she cuddled into him, utterly trusting.

Man. This feeling was something else. New and totally unexpected. He was gripped by an urge to protect,

and by an astonishing surge of fierce, strange posses-
siveness. How could any parent ever willingly walk
away from a cute little person like this?

With the coffee made, Jess came looking for Reece, but
as she reached the door to Rosie's room she hesitated.

He was standing in the soft pink glow of the night
light, cuddling her daughter, and the baby girl looked
so peaceful and tiny in his powerful arms.

Moments earlier, he'd been assisting his frail, ageing father and now here he was with her baby. This
same man galloped on horseback at breakneck speed,
rounded up thundering great beasts, wrestled wild and
angry bullocks and wielded a dangerous branding iron.

It choked Jess up to watch him now, with his eyes
closed, gently rocking her baby daughter and making
soft hushing sounds.

Anyone who didn't know him might assume he was
Rosie's father. It was so easy to imagine that he actually loved her baby girl...

Perhaps he did?

The thought caused a sharp pang in Jess's throat.
Reece had delivered Rosie. His hands were the first
hands to touch her and he'd guided her safely into this
world. Without Reece, Rosie might have born on
the edge of a track in the mud and the rain and, God
knew, it might have ended in tragedy.

As she remembered how wonderful he'd been that
night Jess's throat tightened so painfully she had to
clasp her hand over her mouth to stop a sob from bursting out. Quickly, she hurried away before Reece caught
her spying on him. And blubbing like a fool.

'So you got her back to sleep?' Jess was pleased she was composed by the time Reece came back into the lounge room.

'Yes, Rosie's out to it again, and Dad's asleep too.'

'All's well, then. Here's your coffee.' She handed the mug to Reece as he sat on the sofa. 'I hope it's still hot enough.'

He took a sip. 'Yes, it's fine, thanks.'

Jess drank her coffee, clasping her mug in two hands, as if somehow its warmth would banish the confusion inside her. She wished she could feel happier tonight, wished she could wind back the clock and feel the way she had yesterday evening, when she'd hurled herself into Reece's arms with hardly a care in the world.

It had been so easy then to effortlessly throw up phrases like 'no strings', and to separate her emotions from her lust. Tonight—only twenty-four short hours later—her emotions were unravelling. She hoped it was her hormones—her period was on its way—but she suspected it was way more than that.

Last night she'd been focused inwards when she'd convinced herself that her feelings for Reece were solely about physical attraction. Her desire for him had been all that mattered.

Tonight she was seeing the bigger picture—not just Reece's lonely childhood with a heartbroken father. Not just his alienation from his mother, but also his current worries about his dad's failing health. And now, his inescapable connection to her baby daughter.

It was so clear to her now. She'd only been skimming the surface, not really getting to the bottom of who she and Reece were when they were together. There were so many threads to the ties that bound them, and now she was beginning to understand why sleeping with him had always seemed so much *more* than mere sex.

They'd been fooling themselves if they thought they could have a casual, no-strings affair. They'd both witnessed hard evidence from their parents' lives, and they both knew, deep down, that lovers could damage each other, sometimes without thinking, and sometimes irreparably.

'You're very quiet.'

'I know. I'm sorry, Reece. I'm in a weird mood tonight.'

He made no comment, but he reached over and tucked a strand of hair behind her ear and smiled. It was only a small smile of sympathy, but his eyes were so very dark and clear and compelling, and, despite everything that was troubling her tonight, Jess still wanted him. She knew he could sweep aside her uncertainty and melancholy with a single kiss.

And she let him do exactly that.

Jess woke around dawn, pleased to find Reece still in her bed. She snuggled sleepily against his warm, broad back, draping an arm over his hip, tucking her knees behind the backs of his knees. In her lovely bedroom at the end of the house, with Rosie's little room and their own private bathroom attached, she felt cocooned and safe from the real world.

Beyond these walls, people hurt each other through neglect or selfishness or the making of wrong choices.

She wished they could stay there all day.

Michael was late for breakfast and Reece went to check on him, while Jess sat Rosie in her high chair and fed her rice porridge.

'Cheeky, cheeky girl,' she told her daughter as she scooped blobs of cereal from her chin. 'Stop blowing raspberries.'

Rosie cackled and banged her spoon on the high chair's tray just as Reece came back into the kitchen.

Jess turned and saw that his face was ashen.

'What's happened? What's the matter?'

'It's Dad.' His eyes looked terrible and his throat worked as if he were swallowing sharp stones. 'He's not— I—I can't—'

He couldn't finish the sentence.

A flame of fear engulfed Jess. 'Oh, no, Reece. No.'

He stood, looking utterly bereft. 'He—he's dead, Jess.'

She took a stumbling step towards him, arms ready to hold him, but she was halted by the stark horror in his eyes.

He was already turning away from her. 'I have to ring the ambulance.' He flung this over his shoulder as he hurried out of the room.

It was the most terrible morning, waiting for the ambulance. Reece stayed in his study, pacing the floor, making phone calls, pacing some more. He felt cold and numb and he wanted to stay that way, at least till the ambulance officers arrived and confirmed the worst.

Jess stayed in the kitchen and baked. She needed to keep busy and she was sure there would be visitors, so she baked the simple staples that Michael had loved—a carrot cake, Anzac biscuits, date loaves, an apple tea cake.

She wouldn't let herself think. She couldn't bear to think about poor Michael, so she concentrated on chopping, weighing, stirring, wiping down floury bench tops. She let Rosie have her way with the pots-and-pans cupboard, bashing saucepan lids together, banging on baking tins with a wooden spoon, and the racket was strangely comforting.

Outside, the sun was very hot and bright, which seemed wrong somehow. Surely, it should have been grey and dreary.

CHAPTER TEN

THE dark clouds rolled in on the day of the funeral, and by the time Jess and Reece arrived back at Warringa the heavy tropical rain was bucketing down.

Jess scooted into the house behind Reece, who was carrying Rosie, doubled over to keep the rain off her, and Jess was reminded of the rainy night she met Reece, when her baby was born. Perhaps it was fitting that it would be raining again now. Before too long, she would have to broach the subject of leaving Warringa.

She and Reece hadn't talked much over the past few days. Reece had retreated again, which was understandable. He'd kept super busy making arrangements for the funeral and notifying people of Michael's passing, attending to his regular jobs around the property, as well as taking long rides on horseback, supposedly checking boundaries.

Jess knew he was hurting way more than he let on. He'd been so close to his father, and he was too caring and sensitive not to hurt. She wasn't surprised that he'd covered his pain with tough armour. And she supposed she didn't really have the right to comfort him, although she wished she could.

To keep occupied she'd cleaned the house from top to bottom. There was always the chance Reece's mother might turn up. After all, Michael was her former husband and the father of her sons.

The funeral was held in a little white wooden church in Gidgee Springs, and a surprising number of people packed into the pews and gathered afterwards in the church hall. Reece's mother had *not* been among the mourners, and as Jess had served afternoon tea she'd battled with murderous thoughts towards the woman who'd caused so much pain.

At least Reece's brother was there to honour his father and to support Reece. A slightly younger, citified version of Reece, Tony Weston declined to stay at the homestead, claiming he had an important court case in Sydney to hurry back to. Jess had spied him briefly chatting with Reece, so that was something at least. And there were plenty of other people wanting to offer their condolences, so Reece was surrounded by friends from all over the district and beyond.

But now, so quickly, it was over.

Jess was on the veranda at Warringa, damp and shivering slightly, as she waited for Reece to unlock the front door.

'I guess you'll need to get Rosie fed and bathed,' he said as he handed her over. 'She was very well behaved today, wasn't she?'

'She had a great time being passed around and having so many people making a fuss of her.'

'While her mum slaved in the church hall's kitchen.'

'I didn't mind.'

'I know you didn't mind, Jess. You never seem to mind and you were fantastic, and I'm really, really grateful.'

He came to her and dropped a quick kiss on her lips. His lips were cool from the rain and the kiss was more courteous than sexy, so it should *not* have made her skin burn, but it was the first physical contact between them in days. Now he shrugged out of his suit coat and tossed it over the back of a lounge chair and began to undo his tie.

As usual, Jess couldn't tear her eyes from him. There was something so very masculine and sigh-worthy about the way he stretched his neck as he loosened the tie's knot and then released the top button on his shirt.

He was, of course, oblivious to her small swoon.

'I'm going to shift a mob of cattle out of the bottom paddock near the creek,' he said.

'Now, Reece? But it's pouring.'

He smiled. 'That's why I have to shift them. If it keeps raining like this all night, the creek might come up and flood that paddock.'

'Can it flood so quickly?'

'It wouldn't be the first time.'

It was completely dark by the time he got back. Jess had bathed and fed Rosie and settled her to sleep to the lullaby sounds of the rain drumming on the iron roof. Tonight it was even louder than on the night Rosie was born.

Then she put a chicken casserole she'd made a couple of days earlier into the oven to reheat, and, while she waited for Reece, she went to her room and opened her wardrobe. She supposed she should start planning the best way to pack up her clothes and all Rosie's things.

She felt sick at the thought. She wasn't sure she had the strength to leave, and she and Reece hadn't talked about it yet, but the depressing fact was, her job here was finished. Reece had only employed her because he'd needed someone to help care for his father.

Now, sadly, there was no valid reason for her to stay. Perhaps, if she hadn't slept with Reece, she might have stayed on as his housekeeper, but they'd complicated things, and he hadn't bothered with a housekeeper before she came. She didn't fancy staying on as some kind of 'kept woman', and she still had her debts hanging over her head. So there was no point in dragging out the inevitable.

Reece arrived in the kitchen, showered and changed, just as Jess was taking the casserole out of the oven.

'That smells sensational. Perfect for a cool, rainy night.'

'It's one of my favourite recipes,' she admitted. 'I'm sure you've had it before.'

He came over and stood close to her. She was conscious of the warmth of him by her shoulder, watching as she lifted the lid, releasing the aromas of chicken and garlic and herbs.

'We had this on that first night in Cairns,' he said. 'Remember?'

'Oh, yes, of course.' It was the night the repossession guys arrived. A night she'd much rather forget, except that Reece's company and their dinner conversation had been so very, very pleasant.

'We fantasised about a holiday in New York,' she said as she ladled food onto plates.

'So we did. Winter in Manhattan.'

Jess didn't return his smile. The fantasy was more alluring than ever now, possibly because she knew with certainty it could never happen. To her dismay, her eyes welled with tears and she was struggling not to cry.

Keeping her face averted, she concentrated fiercely on dishing up their meal, and by the time they were seated she'd managed to resurrect a half-mast smile. 'So how are your cattle?' she asked brightly. 'Are they all safely away from the creek?'

'Yep. I think they should be fine.'

'I still find it hard to believe the creek could come up so quickly.'

'Actually, it's amazing how fast it can happen. It all depends on how much rain has already fallen further to the north.'

'Does the gorge fill up as well?'

'Everything can flood. The roads can be cut.'

'Are you saying that I could be stranded here?'

Reece gave a shrugging smile. 'Why do you think we have such a big pantry and cold room?'

Something in her expression must have alerted him. He put down his knife and fork, his face suddenly wary. 'Are you planning to leave soon?'

Jess's food went down too quickly and she had to swallow again before she could answer. 'I imagine I'll have to go, Reece. You employed me to help keep an eye on Michael.'

'But we both know you've done so much more than that—with the house and—and everything.'

'Well, yes. I've loved working here. In many ways, it's the best job I've ever had. I suppose I could stay on for a week or two.' *If you keep paying me.* Missing so little as a week's wages would cause a dangerous hiccup in her repayments.

'A week or two?'

She didn't like to suggest that she could stay until he was feeling calmer.

'I—I'll need to find another job.'

Reece's jaw tightened. 'Of course.'

She'd never seen such hardness in his face. 'Maybe tonight's not the night to talk about this.'

'Why not?'

His scowl reminded her so much of Michael she wanted to cry. 'Are you angry?'

'Why should I be angry?'

This was going nowhere. Jess knew it was futile to try to discuss how either of them really felt about her leaving. Those issues were emotional and her employment was a business matter. Besides, on the emotional front they'd made promises to each other. No strings. No ties. No expectations.

Her task was clear. She had to convince Reece that she wanted to leave Warringa, even though it would almost destroy her to walk away from him.

Oh, help.

Her fork clattered from her suddenly nerveless fingers as the painful realisation struck home. She *loved* Reece.

She didn't just lust after him. She loved everything about him—who he was, how he behaved, how his mind worked, even where he lived.

Her romance with Alan had been a youthful whirlwind—the whole 'marry in haste and repent at leisure' scenario.

Her relationship with Reece was different in every way. She knew him inside out. She'd lived with him for eight long weeks and she felt intimately connected to him on so many levels. They were linked by all those strings they'd claimed didn't exist.

She loved Reece through and through, but she wasn't in a position to do anything about it.

Reece was frowning at her now. 'I won't try to keep

you here, Jess. Not if you want to leave. I know you said
that you have to go. You have plans…'

Yes…she had plans to find a new job, and to keep
chipping away the debts she'd inherited. She had plans
to one day be free of her most pressing problems and
to eventually find a nice little cottage with a garden for
Rosie to play in, a kindergarten nearby.

'Jess.'

She jumped as Reece's warm hand closed over hers.

'Are you OK?' he asked gently.

Of course she wasn't OK. She was falling apart at
the thought of leaving here. Leaving him.

'Hey.' His harshness had melted, and now the hint of
a smile warmed his eyes as he rubbed his thumb over
the back of her hand.

She stared at his hand covering hers, suntanned and
tough, familiar. His thumbnail was slightly frayed and
she felt an impulse to kiss it, to feel that jagged edge
drag against her lips.

'You know you don't *have* to go.'

This was so hard. She so, *so* wanted to stay. This
man and his home were her versions of paradise. She
would stay in a heartbeat if he wanted her to, and if she
didn't have such a huge mountain of debt.

It killed her that Reece was being gentle and concerned now. She'd found it easier to be strong when he
was angry with her.

'You wouldn't have to stay on as my housekeeper,' he
said next, and his dark eyes shimmered with all kinds
of emotions. 'You could stay here—'

He stopped, and swallowed awkwardly.

What was he trying to say?

'A live-in lover?' Jess suggested, and, despite the

longing that coiled tight and hot inside her, she forced her voice to remain cool.

'As my wife.'

His wife? She gasped as the floor seemed to give way beneath her. This was the last thing she'd expected.

It seemed too big to take in.

Too wonderful.

Too perfect.

If only…

If only she were free. If only she weren't buried beneath those debts. Reece would be shocked if he knew how much she still owed. She couldn't possibly ask him to take on her financial burden.

Her mouth twisted out of shape as she tried to find a way to answer him. 'I—I'm so sorry, Reece.'

His chair scraped on the floor as he rose abruptly. 'Of course,' he said tightly. 'Don't worry. I understand.'

But you don't.

He looked terrible and raw and Jess's throat burned with welling tears. She knew Reece would assume she didn't love him or his lifestyle. He couldn't trust any woman to like it out here.

Oh, God. If only she could explain, but how could she tell him about the debts without implying that she needed his help to pay them? The debts were her problem. She'd inherited them from Alan, and she'd inherited a streak of independence from her mother, and there was no way she could drag the financial troubles from her first husband into a brand-new marriage.

Miserably, she watched the tense angle of Reece's shoulders as he stood at the sink, now with his back stiffly to her.

'If we can get across the creek, you'll want to leave

first thing in the morning.' He spoke matter-of-factly, without emotion.

So soon?

'I'll drive you to Cairns.'

'No, I wouldn't expect you to do that. I'll get a bus from Gidgee Springs.'

He turned, his face unrecognisably stony and cold. 'If that's what you want.'

Jess found it too painful to look at him and she dropped her gaze to his plate where the chicken and sauces were cooling and beginning to congeal.

To her surprise, he sat down again and picked up his knife and fork as if nothing had happened.

Reece ate without tasting the food, determined to hold himself together. He couldn't believe he'd been so freaking stupid as to ask Jess to marry him.

Where the hell had *that* come from?

He'd had no intention of proposing to her. What was the point? He'd known from the start that she'd never planned to stay here, and he had enough history behind him to know better. He and Jess had even talked about it and they'd set boundaries. Nice, clear, safe boundaries with no sentimentality or emotion.

Yet somehow tonight, in a crazy moment of weakness, he'd fooled himself into thinking that his dad's suggestion was possible, that he and Jess could have a happy future here. And he'd misinterpreted the soft warmth in her eyes.

Sympathy, yes.

Love?

No way.

Certainly not enough love to sustain her at Warringa through the long hot summers, through the isolating wet seasons, through the difficulties of School of the Air and every other challenge the outback flung at its women.

Unfortunately, his pride wouldn't allow him to go storming off like a wounded bull. He forced himself to eat.

Jess had no idea life could feel so bad. She'd suffered loss and disappointment, but nothing had left her feeling as empty as she felt this evening when she went back to her room to start packing.

It took a while, and, when the clothes were packed, she went through the house, picking up small toys, stray baby socks and picture books. Reece was in his bedroom with the door closed and she moved quietly, not wanting to disturb him, not wanting to face him again this evening.

When she'd packed everything except clothes for the morning and her toothbrush, she showered and changed into a nightdress, slipped into bed and turned out the lamp, then she lay, stiff as a board, staring into the darkness.

Remembering…

She remembered Reece here in bed with her. Remembered his lips on her skin, the pleasurable weight of him on top of her, beneath her, the power and excitement.

She thought about Reece with Rosie, so gentle and loving. Recalled his patience with his dad. Her excitement when they'd first cleaned up these lovely rooms. Remembered right back to the night he'd found her on the edge of the road.

Now, she was losing everything. Losing the best person she'd ever known. And now, after she'd recalled every precious detail of her time here with Reece and every wonderful reason why she loved him, she tortured herself by reliving his offer of marriage.

You don't have *to go. You could stay here…as my wife.*

Oh, God. She should have said yes. The impulse to leap up now and run to him was so strong, Jess needed every bit of her strength to stay, curled in a tight ball of pain, while her head waged battle with her heart.

If she stayed here she could be happy. If she stayed nothing would have to change. She could marry a good and gorgeous man and live in his fabulous homestead, sharing his life, making him happy. He deserved happiness.

Oh, it was still so-o-o tempting, so enticing to shove aside all those strong reasons why she mustn't stay.

But she knew they would catch up with her in time. The universe would once again pull the rug from under her. After all, Reece hadn't actually said that he loved her. And she couldn't accept his proposal without telling him about the debts—and he'd be so disillusioned. He'd never believe she was marrying him for love.

No, she had to be strong for his sake, had to save him from another bitter disappointment, had to walk away now, before they got in too deep, before she broke his heart, just as his mother had.

But what about my heart?

With a moan, Jess buried her face in her pillow and let the hot tears fall.

She slept deeply, totally drained, emotionally and physically, and woke to a grey and miserable morning. Rosie was already awake and playing happily in her cot, innocently unaware that her life was about to abruptly change.

Dressed, Jess went to the kitchen, planning to make breakfast as usual, but she found Reece was already there with a pot of tea and eggs coming to the boil.

'Good morning, Reece.'

'Morning.' No sign of his usual smile. 'Rosie will have a boiled egg, won't she?'

'Yes, thanks.'

It was awful, so stilted, as if they were strangers. Or enemies. Jess set Rosie in her high chair and the baby banged a spoon and chortled, while Jess concentrated on feeding her with toast soldiers dipped in egg.

'I checked the bus timetables,' Reece said. 'There's one leaving for Cairns at ten. If we leave after breakfast you'll be in Gidgee Springs in plenty of time.'

'OK. That's good, thanks. I'm packed.'

'Good.'

Jess's throat was so tight she could barely swallow her tea, let alone toast. She realised she couldn't even try to eat the egg. Reece made no comment when she left it untouched.

As soon as Rosie was finished, she made her excuses.

'If you leave your bags in the hallway, I'll stow them in the truck,' Reece said.

'Thanks.'

She couldn't bring herself to ask him what he wanted to do about the high chair and the cot. He would probably put them in storage and use them for his own baby one day.

Oh, God. She was fighting tears as she hurried away.

Ten minutes later, she and Rosie emerged from their little suite of rooms for the last time. Reece was waiting on the front veranda and his dark eyes regarded them sternly.

'All set to go?'

No.

Jess nodded, however, and told herself yet again that she mustn't be selfish. She and Rosie were leaving for all the right reasons. She just had to walk down those steps. Get this over.

CHAPTER ELEVEN

RETURNING to Warringa alone was like taking a step back in time for Reece, back to his painful past...

The empty rooms were all too familiar and yet the heartache was worse than anything he'd ever suffered before. Loneliness now was a physical pain, raw and bleeding.

He saddled a horse and took off, riding for hours till he and the horse were exhausted, but when he came home the house was still empty and the pain hadn't eased in the slightest.

It didn't ease over the next few weeks either. He knew Jess and Rosie were gone, but he kept expecting to hear the baby's giggle, to round a corner and encounter the warmth of Jess's smile.

Somehow, some-*crazy*-how, he had to learn to live without them, but all he really wanted was to chase after them, to at least make amends for the hopeless hash he'd made of his marriage proposal.

You could stay here...as my wife...

Bloody hell. Had any man delivered a less romantic proposal?

No wonder Jess turned him down.

He hadn't given himself even *half* a chance. He hadn't told her about the joy she'd brought into his life.

He was so unused to talking about love—the word was barely in his vocabulary. He'd more or less assumed Jess could somehow guess that she and her daughter were precious to him.

It was more than possible that he'd made the same mistake as his dad—never letting the woman he loved understand her true worth. And now history was repeating itself.

There was only one good thing—the expectation of loss was so ingrained in Reece that, despite his despair, he could accept Jess's departure as his fate.

Hadn't he known from the night she arrived in his life that this was how it must end?

It was a long lonely month after Jess left, when the car arrived. The white city sedan was almost completely covered with red dust by the time it pulled up at Warringa's front steps. The driver was paunchy, with thinning hair combed over his bald patch, and he was wheezing and stiff as he climbed out.

He retrieved a bulging laptop bag from the back seat, slammed the door and squinted up at the homestead.

Reece, in his study, dealing with paperwork, had watched the arrival and now he rose slowly, without enthusiasm. He wasn't in the mood for visitors. He was certainly in no mood to be sociable with a stranger from the city. He didn't bother to smile as he went out onto the veranda.

He met the visitor at the top of the front steps. 'G'day.'

'G'day to you, sir.' The fellow's smile was a borderline grimace. 'I'm here to speak to Mrs Jessica Cassidy.'

Reece stiffened. He'd been trying so hard to put Jess

out of his mind, and now everything he'd ever felt for her came back in a painful rush.

'She isn't here,' he said sternly. 'Perhaps I can help you.'

The caller shook his head. 'I need to speak to Mrs Cassidy personally. Will she be back soon?' He frowned at Reece. 'She's a resident here, isn't she?'

Everything about this fellow bothered Reece. Pale and paunchy, he had the air of a guy who spent way too much time perched on a barstool in a smoky pub. 'Sorry, but who are you? What's this about?'

'Ron Harvey from IMP Financial Services.' He flashed a card and Reece's eyes fixed on two words: *Debt Collectors*.

Fine hairs lifted on his skin.

'It's important that I speak to Mrs Cassidy,' the fellow went on, full of brash self-importance. 'If we can't get recovery of her debt, she'll be appearing in court.'

Reece clenched his fists tightly against his thighs to stop himself from grabbing this unpleasant Ron Harvey and shaking him till his nicotine-stained teeth rattled.

'Are you Mrs Cassidy's partner?' Harvey asked.

'I'm not. The name's Reece Weston.' He didn't offer his hand. 'You could say I'm an interested party.'

'Ah.' Harvey's watery grey eyes widened. 'She owes you money too, does she?'

'No, she doesn't. But I'm concerned. This is serious, isn't it? I assume you haven't come all the way out here for a few dollars.'

'Yeah, you're right. The debt is substantial. Obviously, I can't discuss exact amounts with a third party.' Harvey lowered his voice and leaned closer. 'But I can tell you, I don't drive five hundred kilometres for anything under six figures.'

Reece stood stock still, making sure he didn't flinch. But, hell. What was going on with Jess? He'd known she was cash strapped, but she'd never breathed a word of a problem this size.

'Finding her might be difficult,' he said carefully. 'Mrs Cassidy did work here, but she's left.'

The other man's eyes narrowed shrewdly. 'I hope you're not covering for her, Weston. I need to know where she is quickly, or her problems will only get worse.'

'Look,' Reece snarled, his anger boiling over. 'I can't help you, and I can't help Jess, because I don't know where she is.' He took a step back, dragged in a breath, willing himself to stay calm. He couldn't imagine how Jess could get herself into so much debt. She was a struggling widow, for God's sake. A single mum.

Ron Harvey cleared his throat. 'I must admit this is not one of the better aspects of my job, but you'd be surprised how many women end up inheriting their husbands' financial mistakes.' He shrugged. 'I'll bet odds this'll end up in court, but it's my job to find her and give her one last chance.'

Reece held out his hand. 'Give me your card. I'll see what I can do.'

Six-thirty a.m.

Reece was waiting outside the café on the Cairns Esplanade when the owner arrived, bleary-eyed and yawning and scratching at his chest, as if he'd climbed out of bed a mere thirty seconds ago.

'What's your problem?' He scowled when Reece blocked his way.

'I'm looking for Jess Cassidy. Is she working for you?'

Jess's former boss rolled his eyes. 'I s'pose you're another debt collector. Sorry, mate. Can't help you.'

'I'm not collecting debts. I'm a friend of Jess's, and I need to find her. I want to help her. So tell me. Does she work here?'

'No, she doesn't. Why would I take her back? She raced off out west and left me in the lurch. Thought she was too good for this place.'

Reece bit back the comment he wanted to make. 'Do you know where she is now?'

The guy shrugged. 'Maybe she doesn't want to be found.'

'And maybe she doesn't know these debt collectors are after her. I told you. I'm here to help her.'

Precious seconds ticked by as Reece was subjected to narrow-eyed scrutiny. 'You've been here before, haven't you?'

'I've dined here, yes.'

'You're the guy she took off with.'

No, I'm the guy she rejected. Reece didn't grace this with an answer.

The other man shrugged. 'Guess it's no skin off my nose. But all I know is she's at the Lime Tree three nights a week.'

'And do you know where she lives?'

'Wouldn't have a clue.'

Jess placed the bowls of spicy Asian noodles under the warmer, ready for the waiter, then dashed back to the stove to give the gravy for the lamb racks a quick whisk.

Blowing her hair out of her eyes, she grabbed clean plates and set them on the stainless-steel bench, spun around to get fresh herbs from the fridge and bumped into a solid wall of six-feet-plus male.

'Ouch!'

'Sorry, Jess.'

She gasped. 'Reece!'

Her heart slammed hard against her ribs. How had he snuck in here? This was crazy.

Fabulous too. She couldn't believe how good it was to see him again. But he was taking up far too much space in the normally roomy kitchen. She shot a frantic glance to Brian and Gil, on the far side of the workspace.

Fortunately, they had their backs to her as they concentrated on their tasks. Gil was plating up delicate seafood salads, while Brian was cooking his specialty ricotta gnocchi.

'What are you doing here?' Jess muttered to Reece.

'Finding you.'

Her knees threatened to give way and she grabbed at the bench for support. 'You can't come in here. I'm too busy. We're flat out.'

'OK. I'll wait for you. Tell me where.'

There was a sound to her left. A waiter had arrived to collect the bowls of noodles and he was staring through the hatch at them.

'I'm not sure what time I'll be finished.' She shoved him towards the door. 'It could be really late. You have to go, Reece.'

'I'll wait. I'll wait all night. Just tell me where to meet you. It's important, Jess.'

She shook head, completely dazzled by his sudden appearance, by his gorgeousness, by his insistence. She wasn't sure she could deal with this. When she finished work she would be dead on her feet.

'The Night Owl Café,' she said as she pushed Reece through the doorway and closed the door in his face.

It was after midnight and Reece was on his third cup of coffee when Jess appeared, looking tired and pale. The tiredness was expected, but it still cut him to see such obvious signs of weariness in her face and in the slowness of her movements as she made her way to him through the maze of mostly empty tables.

Thank God she'd come. He feasted his eyes on her, loving the familiar mix of her pale skin, dark hair and long, slim limbs. 'Would you like something to eat?' he asked her.

'No, thanks. I've eaten.' Slumping into a seat, she pushed her hair out of her eyes.

'A coffee?'

'It might keep me awake. I'll go for a peppermint tea.'

He went to the counter and paid for her order.

'So…?' she asked when he returned. 'Is everything OK?'

Reece took Ron Harvey's card from his pocket and set it on the table in front of her, watched the flare of fear in her eyes. 'I'm afraid you need to contact this guy.'

'How did he find you? Don't tell me he went to Warringa?'

'He did.'

Jess gave a soft groan and closed her eyes, as if this was one problem too many for her.

'I'm here to help, Jess.'

Her eyes flashed open. 'No.'

She might have said more, but her peppermint tea arrived, and she nodded her thanks and Reece waited patiently while she took a sip.

But he had to ask, 'Why didn't you tell me about this?'

'It's my problem, not yours.'

'But I could have helped you.'

'I didn't want to land my problems on you.'

If he weren't so worried, he might have admired her independence. He could name women who would have chosen a very different option. 'You'll let me help you now, won't you?'

'Reece, I really appreciate that you came all this way. But you can't help me. It's—it's asking too much.'

'You'd rather go to court?'

'Court?' She stared at him in open-mouthed shock.

Reece tapped the card. 'That's what this guy's threatening.'

'Oh, God.'

'Jess, please. At the very least, you're going to need a friend when you have this meeting with Harvey.'

She was pinching nervously at her lower lip. 'Do you have any idea how much I owe?'

'Something in the six-figure range.'

Her eyes widened in surprise, but then she shook her head again. 'See? It's too much. Nobody has that sort of money lying around.'

'Some people do, actually.'

Slow seconds slipped by as she stared at him, his meaning sinking in. 'But even if you have the money, I can't take it from you, Reece. You've already helped me so much. I can't just go on taking and taking.'

'You can pay me back, then. I'm sure we could negotiate friendlier terms than you're saddled with at the moment.'

Jess was still shaking her head, but he knew she was giving this offer serious thought. She was also very close to tears.

She was making her lip quite red from pinching it, and he longed to kiss her, to make her smile. They'd shared so many smiles, so many good times. 'You've got to stop thinking of me as another employer, Jess. Think of me as your friend. We were lovers, for heaven's sake.'

'That's why I hate the idea of you taking on my husband's debts.'

'Listen,' he said, as patiently as he could. 'It's not wise for you to try to handle this on your own. There are all sorts of ways to manage this. But honestly, the loan wouldn't hurt me. We've had some good years with the cattle business. And my father had quite a surprising amount put away. I had no idea he'd made so many shrewd investments over the years.'

She was listening now, drinking her tea and watching him over the rim of her cup, and listening carefully.

'Fate's handed you a raw deal,' Reece went on. 'But Fate has also given *me* a big stake in your life and in Rosie's life. I'll always have an interest in your well-being.'

Tears welled in her eyes, but at least she was no longer protesting.

Reece kept talking. There were other things, painful matters, he needed to set straight. 'I know I blurted out a proposal at absolutely the wrong time, Jess, but it was for all the right reasons.'

Jess tried to answer, but the only sound that emerged was a tiny bleat.

'I totally understand that you wouldn't want to live

out there,' he said. 'So don't let any of that get in the way now. You really should let me help.'

She lifted a shaking hand to her mouth and glistening tears spilled down her cheeks.

Almost simultaneously, they were out of their seats and she was stumbling into his arms.

Jess clung to him, sobbing, her heart breaking for so many reasons. She was so tired and so very stressed, and Reece was every version of wonderful. Actually, he was really just being himself—gorgeous, kind, sexy and generous—and it was killing her.

She wasn't sure how long she took to stop crying. When she lifted her face from Reece's damp shirt, she felt drained and exhausted but a great deal calmer. Looking around them, she saw that the café was completely empty now, which was no doubt a very good thing. Even the guy behind the counter seemed to have disappeared.

'They probably want to close up this place,' she said as she wiped her face on the sleeve of her chef's coat.

'Where are you staying now?'

'Somewhere—' Crumbs, how could she tell him? 'A few streets away. Walking distance.'

'Is Rosie there now?'

'Yes, I pay someone to mind her.'

'Let me drive you.'

She wanted to say no. She was living in a Charity Hostel, and that was information she'd rather not share with Reece, but suddenly she was too tired to argue. 'Thanks, Reece.'

Of course, he was frowning as he pulled up outside. 'What sort of place is this?'

'A hostel. I'm planning to rent a place soon. This is just a stopgap till I've saved enough for a bond on a flat.'

'For heaven's sake, Jess. What about all the money I paid you?' Almost immediately he sighed and answered his own question. 'It all went towards the debts, didn't it?'

She nodded, pushed the door open. 'Thanks for the lift.'

His hand on her arm stopped her, and she remembered they hadn't finalised their plans to meet with the debt collector. She took Ron Harvey's card out of her pocket. 'Is it OK if I ring you about this in the morning?'

Reece was still frowning ahead at the bald concrete building and the bars on the windows. 'I'm sorry. I can't leave you in this place while I trot back to a luxury apartment. Come with me.'

'To your apartment?'

'I'm pretty sure they aren't all booked. I'll ring and check. You can have your own space. Total privacy. Go, get Rosie now and come with me, and at least have a couple of nights of comfort.'

She must have been staring at him as if he'd given her bad news.

'What's the matter?'

'Why are you being so kind? You mustn't, Reece.'

He sighed. 'Just run and get Rosie and whatever you need. Do it for me, please.'

It was the impatience in his voice that sent her hurrying to obey.

The serviced apartments were top-class luxury with a huge expanse of white marble in the foyer, massive urns of tropical flowers, mirrors everywhere.

Reece had made all the necessary arrangements, while Jess was collecting Rosie, and Jess's apartment, with a cot assembled, was ready and waiting as the lift took them silently to the fifteenth floor. The space was fabulous, facing the sea, with a cool breeze blowing in through sliding white, floor-to-ceiling shutters. The rooms smelled faintly of ginger flowers and Jess's aching feet sank into the thick white carpet. The bed was enormous.

And so was the spa bath where she soaked while Reece settled Rosie back to sleep. Luxury with a capital L. What a pity she was too tired to enjoy it.

'Hey, Jess.'

She jumped as she heard Reece's voice and felt a hand on her shoulder. Water splashed and a wave washed over her breasts. Yikes, she was still in the bath.

Reece loomed above her, tall, dark and heartbreaking.

'Was I asleep?'

'Out like a light.' His eyes were fierce and troubled as he held a thick white towel. 'Do you need a hand?' There was no levity in his voice. He wasn't flirting.

'No, thanks.'

She waited till he'd left the room before she climbed out of the bath, painfully aware of those happy times in their recent past, when Reece had been intimately acquainted with every inch of her naked body.

Now as she went through to the bedroom, wrapped in the towel, she was assaulted by memories of him in her bed. So much pleasure and passion and sweet contentment, and all of it lost.

There was no sign of him now. Rosie was cosily tucked up in her cot in the corner, and Jess was bone weary. Slipping beneath the bedcovers, she gratefully sank once again into sleep.

Bright sunlight streamed through the shutters—and there were voices on Jess's balcony. Reece's deep voice rumbling in a low murmur in response to baby chuckles.

'How long have you two been out there?' Jess called.

Reece appeared at her bedroom doorway with her daughter on his hip, her two hands beating the air with excitement when she saw Jess. 'Good afternoon.'

'Afternoon?' Jess shot up quickly and realised she was still naked. Hastily she grabbed at the sheet as Reece came into the room and sat on the end of the bed, letting Rosie crawl over the mattress to her.

Jess greeted her daughter with laughter and a kiss and a cuddle, but she was soon frowning at Reece again. 'Tell me it's not afternoon.'

'OK. I was exaggerating. It's ten.'

Ten? She'd never slept so late. Not since Rosie was born. 'You haven't been here all night, have you?'

'I slept on the sofa.'

'Really? Why didn't you go back to your apartment?'

'I knew Rosie would wake at some stage and I wanted you to have some uninterrupted sleep.'

'That's incredibly thoughtful, Reece.'

He shrugged. 'I won't be here long. You might as well make the most of it.' His dark eyes rested on her briefly, softening in a way that made her heart ache, but then he flicked his gaze away to the view through the open shutters. 'I've ordered a room-service breakfast for you. And as soon as you're dressed, we'd better ring your debt collector.'

'Are you still planning to go to the meeting with me?'

'Of course. Come on, Rosie.' He scooped the giggling baby up into his arms again. 'We'll let your mum get dressed. She has a big day ahead of her.'

Jess felt terrible as she watched Reece leave. He was being magnificent. Unbelievably kind and generous and thoughtful. From the night she'd met him she'd been in his debt. Now he wanted her to add money to the list of everything she owed him.

How could she possibly allow him to do that?

But—how could she not?

If she didn't accept his help, she could end up in court. She had to think of Rosie. But she also had to remember that as soon as their financial agreement was formalised, she'd be saying goodbye to Reece again.

'I thought that went quite well,' Reece said once they were well clear of Ron Harvey's office.

'He was a bit of a softie, really, wasn't he?'

'Hell, no, Jess. Don't let him fool you.'

'I'm sure he wasn't fooling. I swear he was almost reaching in his pocket for a handkerchief at one stage. He was incredibly moved by your generosity, Reece.'

She touched Reece's hand, and he came to an abrupt stop. 'I want to thank you, but it seems so inadequate.'

Reece looked as if he was trying to smile, but couldn't quite manage it. He looked away, his throat working overtime. 'Let's not make a big deal about this. It's something I wanted to do.'

Jess found this so hard. Reece was being so stoical. Again. And any minute now she'd start bawling. 'One thing you simply must let me do is cook dinner for you,' she said.

'Actually... I'm not sure that's a good idea.'

'Don't say no. Please, Reece. Now it's my turn to insist.' She forced a brave smile. 'Think of me as your kitchen genie. Name your favourite dish and I'll produce it.'

He smiled at that, white teeth flashing in his suntanned face. 'OK. You've twisted my arm.'

'And your favourite dish is?'

'How about fish and chips?'

'You're joking,' Jess said, but almost straight away she could see that he wasn't. And it made sense, actually. A man who'd eaten so much beef all his life would hunger for something simple but totally coastal, like fish and chips.

'Well, it won't be any old fish and chips,' she promised, and, true to her word, she cooked coral trout in beer batter with the very best crunchy, salty, potato chips, and sides of wilted greens, slices of lemon and tartare sauce. She hoped it was a straightforward, man-pleasing meal.

And this man did seem to be mightily pleased with it.

There was only one problem. Cooking in the kitchen, preparing a meal they would share, and having Rosie nearby, getting under her feet—was all too familiar. It was like being back in the homestead kitchen, as if they'd returned to a time when they were both ridiculously happy.

Throughout the meal, Reece extravagantly complimented Jess's cooking, but she was aware of underlying pain.

His pain and hers.

And the separation that was now looming so close.

She should have listened to Reece when he said this dinner wasn't a good idea. She could see now that it created a false scenario that was painful for both of them.

They had to pretend they were nothing more than friends. She had to act as if this gorgeous man opposite her hadn't once asked her to marry him, and that she hadn't turned him down for very good reasons. It was so hard to know that he'd misinterpreted those reasons and she hadn't been able to set him straight.

All in all, the night was a terrible ordeal.

By the time they reached after-dinner coffee, Rosie was asleep, but the baby had been a helpful distraction and now Jess could feel the tension between herself and Reece magnifying tenfold.

It was totally understandable that he left early, and Jess knew she shouldn't be miserable as they said good-night at the doorway to her apartment. She should be walking on air, pumped up with relief and gratitude and big plans for her future.

Not a chance.

'That was a memorable meal,' Reece said politely.

'I'm glad you liked it. As you know, it was an important occasion for me.' *Good grief. That sounded so stiff.*

Her face was almost wooden. 'I'm going to miss you and Rosie.' His voice sounded rough.

'We'll miss you.' A sob threatened as she said this.

Reece turned to leave.

This was it. The final goodbye.

In the hallway now, almost gone, Reece turned back to her. 'Before I go,' he said sternly. 'There's one thing I'd really like to know.' His dark eyes were so direct, they burned her.

'What's that?'

'Did you knock me back because of your debt?'

Jess was suddenly shaking as a month's worth of regrets and useless wishes welled inside her. But when she tried to speak, her throat was too full. She nodded, blinking tears. 'Yes,' she sobbed. 'It was only about the money. Never about you.'

In a heartbeat, Reece was back inside her apartment, closing the door behind him, leaning back against it, staring at her with hope and a hint of happiness shining in his eyes.

'I'm sorry,' Jess managed to say. 'You've ended up with my debt anyway.'

'You think I care?'

She swiped at her tears. 'I felt so bad. I knew you thought I'd left because I didn't like living at Warringa. And that's so wrong. I love it, Reece. I love the house, the paddocks, the people I've met. I didn't even mind your cow—'

He silenced her with a finger against her lips. 'That's all I need to know.'

He kissed her then, and, oh, my God, how wonderful it was. Jess's blood was singing as his lips sealed with hers, as she leaned in to the hard, solid strength of him, and felt at last his arms around her, holding her, binding her close against his thudding heart.

When at last, too soon, he loosened the hug, he reached for her hands instead. 'OK. I'm going to try again, Jess, because I love you. So much.'

He looked suddenly terrified. 'I'm very much hoping you'll marry me.'

To her horror, Jess burst into tears. 'I'm so sorry,' she sobbed, swiping at her eyes with the heels of her hands. 'I'm not unhappy.'

Not surprisingly, Reece still looked uncertain.

'I'm deliriously happy.' Tears and all, she slipped her arms around his neck and kissed him.

'I've missed you so much,' she told him and she kissed him again. Kissed his jaw, his throat, his lips. 'I love you, Reece. And it's been agony not telling you.'

He touched a trembling hand to the side of her face.

'I've missed you so much. Life's not much fun without you and your cute little daughter.'

'I've been so miserable without you.'

This time when they kissed again she could feel the relief and happiness flowing through them both. At last they had reached the emotional honesty they'd both craved. At last they were free to *love*.

They lay in bed, pleasantly tired and aching and sated, the shutters open to the sea breeze and the moonlight.

'Give me your hand,' Jess said, and she placed her hand against Reece's, palm to palm. 'I could marry you just for your hands, you know. I love how big and rough and manly they are.'

He chuckled. 'And I'm crazy about yours. They're so small and pale and girly. How do you keep them smooth like that when you work in a kitchen?'

'Industrial-strength hand cream.'

'It works.'

'I'll bring a gallon of the stuff to Warringa.' Jess pressed kisses to his hand, relishing the luxury of having him close, to kiss and to touch whenever and wherever she wanted. She didn't want to close her eyes in case he disappeared. 'You know one thing that amazes me, Reece?'

'What's that?'

'You're such a kind and generous person even though you've had all kinds of reasons to be bitter and resentful.'

'I could say the same about you.'

She thought about this, about her mum and her serial lovers, about Reece's mother remaining in bitter silence in Sydney. 'I really, really want to be a good mother.'

'You will be, Jess. I know it. Rosie's a lucky girl.'

'Her luck began with you. It's all thanks to you.'

'Hey, enough with the gratitude. I get to keep the two of you. I'm the winner here, OK?'

'OK.' Jess was smiling into the darkness as she snuggled against Reece while he gently sifted strands of her hair.

She was almost drifting off to sleep when he said, 'I have the best idea for our honeymoon.'

'Wow, I hadn't even thought about honeymoons. Where would you like to go?'

'New York.'

'Really?'

'Why not? We've talked about it and I've always wanted to go there. It's one of the most exciting cities in the world and it's good to get a total change from the bush.'

'Would Rosie come too?'

'Of course. We could hire a nanny to help.'

'Reece, that would be amazing. There's so much to do there.'

'I know, and we'll do it all. All the sights, the shows. And while we're there, we could try to find your father.'

Thud. Jess had been thinking about Richard Travere from the moment New York was mentioned, but she hadn't expected Reece to remember.

'I don't know if that's a good idea,' she said. 'He doesn't even know I exist.'

'Well, it's worth a thought. It doesn't seem right to me—a father who doesn't know he has a daughter as fabulous as you are. And you never know, he might be the one grandparent Rosie can grow close to.'

'That's—that's a nice thought.' Amazing, actually.

Reece kissed her ear lobe. 'Sleep on it.'

'I will. Thanks for the thought, Reece. I love you, you know.'

'I know.'

EPILOGUE

THE restaurant was magnificent, an expansive space, with beautiful arched windows and high ceilings, as well as an outside terrace that overlooked a snowy, but bustling, Upper East Side street. Jess decided the place was trendy, cosy and romantic without overdoing it. She was glowing with approval as she and Reece removed their coats and were shown to their table.

Since arriving in New York with Rosie and a nanny, they'd enjoyed all the usual tourist treats. Museums and art galleries, shows on Broadway, sightseeing bus rides and ferry rides. It was all fascinating and exciting. Busy, busy, busy. Cosmopolitan. Energetic.

Wonderful.

New York, New York.

They'd walked the famous avenues and they'd spent hours and hours exploring Central Park. They'd eaten hotdogs with mustard on a sidewalk, and they'd break-fasted on scrambled eggs and lox in a diner. And they'd shopped till they dropped.

This evening, Jess was wearing the most divine black and silver twenties-flapper-style dress. Reece had in-sisted on buying it the instant he saw her in it, and, of course, he'd then had to buy a superb Italian suit to match her fine style. Tonight they felt like film stars. This dinner was to be the highlight of their trip.

'You look stunning,' Reece whispered.

'You too.'

Their excitement was fizzing as exquisitely as the French champagne they sipped while they studied the menu. They finally settled on lamb spare ribs and tuna tartare, and when the meals arrived they were mouth-wateringly delicious.

'So you approve?' Reece asked. 'You reckon the chef knows how to throw a meal together?'

Jess smiled archly. 'I'll admit he's not bad.'

They were talking about Richard Travere, of course, the man she believed to be her father, who was both head chef and owner of this fine establishment. They'd discovered during their Internet searches that he usually made an appearance during the evening, and the chance to see him, even from a distance, had been too huge for Jess to resist.

'I won't actually talk to him,' she'd insisted nervously. 'I'll be happy just to see him from the far side of the room.'

They were eating dessert—chocolate semifreddo for Reece and a hazelnut praline for Jess—when the low buzz of conversation in the restaurant dimmed and eyes turned towards the kitchen.

A tall man in chef's whites strolled through the doorway and Jess held her breath. This was the man whose upwardly spiralling career she'd followed from afar. She knew that he'd worked in Brisbane, then Sydney and finally in New York. He was the man she'd wondered about for so long.

Reece reached across the table and his hand on hers

was warm and reassuring. Her heart was galloping, but her husband's touch helped to calm her, momentarily.

Richard Travere was impressive with a tanned, longish, slightly arrogant face and steel-grey hair swept back from a high brow. The arrogance disappeared when he smiled, Jess noted, as she watched him pause to chat with diners.

'Looks like he's talking to everyone,' she hissed in a sudden panic.

'That's what we want,' Reece assured her. 'It's better than coming here and missing out on seeing him.'

She took a deep breath and then another. Seemed there were plenty of chef groupies among the diners tonight. Plenty of beaming smiles as people talked to the famous RT.

He was getting closer. In an attempt to look casual, she lifted her spoon, but she was shaking so badly it clattered against her dessert plate and she had to set it down again, quickly, just as the big man greeted them.

'Good evening,' he said smoothly in a broad Aussie drawl. 'I'm Richard. How's the meal? I hope everything's OK.'

'It's fabulous,' Reece assured him.

'Amazing,' managed Jess.

'Hey, you're Australians.' The chef's eyebrows lifted in obvious delight. 'What part of Oz are you from?'

'North Queensland,' Reece volunteered because Jess's throat was no longer working.

'Nice part of the world. I was there for a time.'

He smiled directly at Jess and she saw that his eyes were the same shade of green as hers. Her heart was almost leaping out of her chest and she was terrified she might cry.

With a supreme effort she forced herself to speak.

'This dessert is truly delicious.' She gestured to the cinnamon gelato, the espresso gelée and the tiny toasted meringue that accompanied her praline. 'All the flavours are so perfectly balanced and complement each other beautifully.'

'Thank you,' he said graciously, clearly pleased. 'Are you a chef?'

'I am, actually.'

He looked at her again, and his smile froze for a split second. He frowned and something stirred in his gaze, but almost immediately his face cleared, and he gave a small, smiling bow and moved on.

Across the table, Reece was grinning at Jess as he reached for her hand again. 'How was that?'

'Scary.'

'You shouldn't be scared. He seems friendly enough.'

'Yes.'

'Are you still determined you won't tell him who you are?'

She nodded. 'It's best like this. I've seen him. That's enough.'

'Are you sure?' Reece's gorgeous face was full of sympathy and understanding. And concern.

Jess knew that look well, and she loved him for caring, but this father business was too iffy. 'I feel better leaving it like this. After all, you have next to no contact with your mother. We have each other and Rosie, and that means everything to me.'

'Well, yes. It means everything to me.'

They shared a smile brimming with all the reasons they loved each other.

'However,' Reece said, looking serious again. 'The big thing I've learnt from you, my sweet Jess, is that it's worth taking emotional risks. I die a thousand deaths every time I remember how I almost lost you. I was almost too scared to try that second proposal.'

'Oh, Reece.' Every time he told her about this, her love for him deepened, widened. Exploded. She blinked away tears before they wrecked her mascara. 'So you really think I should say something?'

'I do.'

'We'd have to get his attention again.'

'Or maybe not,' Reece said, looking over her shoulder.

She turned, stunned to see Richard Travere coming back to their table.

'Excuse me,' he said with an awkward, lopsided smile. 'I know this might sound strange, but I was wondering if you might possibly know someone I used to know in North Queensland.'

It was the early hours of the next morning when Reece and Jess walked arm in arm down Madison Avenue. They'd had the most amazing evening. Richard had taken them to his private apartment on a floor above the restaurant and the three of them had talked for hours, making up for all the years, all the silences, all the mistakes.

They'd wept and laughed and hugged.

Now, snow was falling lightly. People still lingered on the sidewalks. Yellow taxi cabs streamed past, and steam rose through vents in the middle of the road. True to its reputation, this city had no intention of going to sleep.

And on this exciting, unforgettable night, neither did Reece or Jess. They had a future to plan.

* * * * *

Jake was an honest-to-goodness hero, judging by the expression on that young mom's face.

"You were really wonderful with that patient," Hope told him.

His eyes narrowed, but not before going stormy as shadows flitted through the gray. There was desolation there, too. Hope wasn't sure how she knew that, except maybe it took one to know one. She'd experienced despair, and when you've gone through something like that, it wasn't hard to recognize the look in someone else.

"It's easy when the news is good." Jake slid his hands into the lab-coat pockets. "I'm not sure what gave you the impression that my heart is two sizes too small, but I do have one. And I know how it feels to have absolutely nothing."

Surprise didn't come close to describing what Hope felt. He was the golden boy with the magic hands.

Dear Reader,

As I drove to my semiannual plot group, a song came on the radio that always makes me cry. It's the part where Johnny Mathis and Jane Oliver's achingly beautiful voices blend in the refrain, and sing that the last time they felt like this they were falling in love. In *The Surgeon's Favourite Nurse*, that became the core of Hope Carmichael's conflict.

Two years after the loss of her husband, she takes a temporary job in Las Vegas to escape the painful memories. She never wants to hurt like that again, and her instant attraction to surgeon Jake Andrews is not a happy thing. But the doctor is as stubborn as he is charming and refuses to give up on the woman who is quickly becoming his favorite nurse. He teaches her that life is precious and love is a miracle.

These two characters became very special to me. I hope you enjoy spending time with Hope and Jake as much as I did.

Happy reading!

Teresa Southwick

THE SURGEON'S FAVOURITE NURSE

BY
TERESA SOUTHWICK

First published in Great Britain 2013
by Mills & Boon, an imprint of Harlequin (UK) Limited,
Eton House, 18-24 Paradise Road, Richmond, Surrey TW9 1SR

© Teresa Southwick 2010

ISBN: 978 0 263 90077 4
ebook ISBN: 978 1 472 00432 1

23-0113

Harlequin (UK) policy is to use papers that are natural, renewable and
recyclable products and made from wood grown in sustainable forests. The
logging and manufacturing processes conform to the legal environmental
regulations of the country of origin.

Printed and bound in Spain
by Blackprint CPI, Barcelona

Teresa Southwick lives with her husband in Las Vegas, the city that reinvents itself every day. An avid fan of romance novels, she is delighted to be living out her dream of writing for Mills & Boon.

For Gail Chasan, who saw
the emotional depth of this story from the beginning.

Chapter One

Here comes trouble.

Hope Carmichael knew more about trouble than she ever wanted to and recognized it instantly. The man who'd just walked into her office had the big *T* written all over him.

Jake Andrews, M.D. Dr. GQ. That's what the Mercy Medical Center nurses called the hotshot trauma surgeon.

She could see why. The charcoal suit probably had an Armani label. His snappy red tie said follow me home if you're looking for a good time. And the sexy grin aimed straight at her was all about who he intended to have that good time with. Simply put, his fabulous dark hair, chiseled jaw and charismatic career made him a chick magnet.

"Hi. I'm Jake Andrews—Dr. Andrews," he added.

Hope stood behind her desk. Ordinarily she would have walked around it to shake someone's hand. This time she didn't and wasn't sure why. "I know who you are."

"I didn't think we'd met."

"Because your memory is infallible?" she asked, trying to control the nerves tweaked by his shameless scrutiny.

"Because a pretty lady like you is unforgettable."

Oh, please. If she had a nickel for every time she'd heard that line before.

Actually, she'd never heard it before.

Hospital gossip had warned her about him. Two out of the three doctors in his medical practice had recently married and officially resigned from the bachelor ranks. Jake Andrews was the last playboy standing. Her new job meant she'd have to deal with him—whether she wanted to or not.

Two weeks ago she'd arrived in Las Vegas to assume her duties as trauma coordinator of Mercy Medical West, the hospital's third campus which was a few months away from opening its doors. She'd done her employment orientation at the main campus and someone had pointed out Jake Andrews to her, which was why she knew him. Definitely a capital *T* for trouble.

"You're correct," she said. "We haven't been formally introduced."

"A situation I'm here to rectify." He held out his hand. "Let's make this official."

She hesitated to touch him and knew she didn't cover it very well because she was out of practice with men in general and a man like him in particular. Although out of practice would imply that at some point she'd been competent with his type, which was so not the case.

Finally she reached across the desk to place her hand in his. "I'm Hope Carmichael, Dr. Andrews."

"A pleasure. And call me Jake."

Maybe it was his take-no-prisoners smile or his touch, but Hope felt a blast of heat that was nuclear in scope. With good reason she'd hesitated to touch him, but there was no uncertainty when she quickly pulled her fingers from his.

"It's nice to meet you," she said.

"Likewise. So, I'm curious. How did you know who I was?" One corner of his mouth quirked up.

His ego was asking and she resisted the urge to roll her eyes, but on the inside she was groaning. It was a good thing her job was to organize the new hospital's trauma department and not choose the doctor who would run it, the job this surgeon was campaigning for. If she got a vote, it would be firmly in the no column.

"Process of elimination," she finally said.

"Excuse me?" He didn't look puzzled, just amused.

"The other two candidates for trauma medical director have already stopped by to introduce themselves."

"Worthy adversaries both." He moved closer and rested a hip on the corner of her desk, a blatantly masculine pose. "But neither of them is going to get the job."

Hope refused to give in to the very strong urge to put space between herself and Doctor Dashing because she suspected he would notice. There probably wasn't much those piercing gray eyes missed and even the slightest retreat would give him more intimidation quotient than he already thought he had.

She remembered his competition for the position—Dr. Robert Denton and Dr. Carla Sheridan, both in their forties. The former was a small, studious man who reminded her of Albert Einstein. The female doctor was all business. If she had charm or a sense of humor, both had been well concealed. Jake Andrews had set both his charm and humor on stun.

"It's my understanding that the hospital board hasn't made a final decision about who gets the contract." She sat behind the desk and looked at him. "How can you be so sure the position is yours?"

"Because the appointment means more to me than it does to either of them. And I'm the best trauma surgeon in Las Vegas."

The words ignited something in his eyes that hinted at a fire in the belly. A need for victory. Determination to succeed. A passion for power. Hope didn't remember either of the other doctors exhibiting a similar vibe.

"If it's what you want, then I hope the vote goes your way," she said.

"Me, too. Even more now." His eyes gleamed again as he looked her over with an expression of admiration and approval.

"Are you flirting with me?"

"Not very well, if you have to ask."

Almost as soon as the words were out she wanted them back. He might think she was fishing for compliments, but nothing could be farther from the truth. Part of her was surprised that the thought of flirting even entered her mind. She'd thought the ability to detect it had died two years ago with Kevin on their first wedding anniversary.

Dr. Andrews hadn't exactly confirmed or denied flirtatious intentions, but that really didn't matter. The game required two to play and she wasn't interested. More important, this conversation had already taken a different tone and direction from her meetings with the other two doctors in line for the top trauma job. It was time to fix that.

To do it, Hope knew she needed to take control, but the shimmy in her belly and the buzz in her head made thinking a challenge.

"Here's the thing, Doctor—"

"It's Jake. Remember?"

She was trying not to. This encounter and its ripple of

sexual awareness were disturbing, to say the least. The longer he perched on the corner of her desk looking all hot and sinful, the more she wanted to see his bluff, round the desk and raise the temptation factor. That's what the old Hope would have done. There were a lot of reasons it was a bad idea, not the least of which was that she wouldn't take the chance of letting a man close to her.

Flirting led to feelings and that equaled a potential for pain. Losing Kevin had hurt. A lot. She'd rather feel nothing than hurt that much ever again.

"Jake—"

His name on her lips stopped her. Jake—a strong, masculine, heroic name. And wasn't that the stupidest thing that had ever crossed her mind. She didn't want a man and she especially didn't want a hero—although hospital gossip didn't paint Jake Andrews as the type to throw his cloak—or his surgical mask—over a puddle for a lady. He was more rascally rogue than white knight.

"You were saying?" Idly he picked up a supply order list from a stack of papers on her desk and looked it over.

"I'm here to do a job and—"

"You're from out of state, right?"

She nodded. "Texas. Mansfield, a town halfway between Dallas and Fort Worth."

"I thought I heard some Southern comfort in your voice."

Was he flirting again? She couldn't tell. This was no time for her blarney meter to crash.

"Like I said, I was hired to organize the trauma department and have it ready when Mercy Medical West opens its doors to patients."

"Tell me about yourself, Hope." It sounded like he was testing out her name on his lips. "Wait, let me guess. You have sisters named Faith and Charity."

She had to smile. "As a matter of fact…"

His laugh was rich with humor. "Am I good, or what?"

She refused to comment without her own independent confirmation, and pigs would fly before that happened. "Faith is older. Charity younger. I'm in the middle."

"What made you want to be a nurse?" he asked suddenly.

"A strong desire to help people and make a difference. From the time I was a little girl it's all I ever wanted to do."

"So it was a calling of the heart. Not because it's a profession with pretty good pay for a woman who might need to support herself and her family?"

Funny that he should zero in on that because it's exactly what happened. And it was her fault that the man she'd loved had been in the wrong place at the wrong time.

"Nursing is a noble profession," she said, a little more sharply than she intended. "And there's a critical need, like so many other causes."

"Causes? Plural." He looked thoughtful. "Such as?"

"Feeding the hungry. Houses for the homeless. Teen pregnancy. Global warming. Vaccinating children in third world countries."

"Saving the spotted owl?"

"If necessary, to preserve an ecosystem," she said, lifting her chin a notch. "You're making fun of me."

"Heaven forbid." His expression was exaggerated innocence. "Community service isn't just for criminals anymore."

"You don't believe in helping others?"

"I'm a doctor." Again he hadn't answered.

"That's about helping people for money."

"It's my job, yes."

"And what made you want to be a doctor?" she asked, echoing his question.

He glanced at the paper in his hands. "I'm smart. In school I excelled in math and science. And doctors make a lot of money."

"So it's *not* about helping people," she accused.

"By definition what I do helps people. For doing it I'm well compensated," he said, putting a finer point on it.

"Wow," she said wryly. "Let's all pause and feel the love."

He looked up and met her gaze. "Medicine is a business. Surgery is invasive intervention to save or improve a patient's life. But still a business. You know that as well as I do because in addition to your nursing credential and working as a trauma nurse manager, you have a master's degree in healthcare administration."

"How do you know all that?"

"I made it my business to know." He let that sink in, then added, "I checked up on you because we'll be working together. People will be watching when this facility opens. If we fail, it will be very public and with a direct impact on my reputation. I don't take chances with my career."

So a successful launch of this campus was all about him. How was he arrogant? She needed more than the fingers on two hands to count the ways. "There's certainly a lot of bastard in you."

"Thanks." He stood away from the desk and straightened to his full and impressive height. "Coming from a Birkenstock-wearing, granola-munching, bleeding heart liberal like yourself, that's high praise."

"I'm glad you think so." Could they possibly be more philosophically opposed? She hadn't meant to call him names, but it just popped out. The guy pushed her buttons, all the wrong ones. Apparently her diplomacy meter had also crashed. "I have a lot of work to do. If you'll excuse me—"

"About your work—I asked for a particular type of surgical instruments. They're from a German manufacturer and are specifically calibrated. Is there another list?" He pointed to the paper he'd replaced on her desk. "I don't see what I requested on that one."

She knew the brand he meant and it was out of the question. "You don't see them because they weren't ordered."

"Just like that?"

"Too expensive." She blew out a breath. "Every surgeon has a favorite, but it's my job to whittle down the list to the most commonly used."

"Even if the most common ones result in limitations that prevent the patient from getting the best possible results?"

Was this his way of pushing back, being difficult, punishing her for the bastard remark? It had been out of line, but so was his flirting. And it had provoked her own fight-or-flight response. She wasn't running, unless you counted taking this job in Las Vegas to avoid painful memories back home.

"If you're half as good as you think you are, Jake, you can use a potato peeler and a watermelon scoop to get a positive outcome."

"And what if that doesn't fly with me?"

"Then I might have to conclude that you can only make do with one product and suggest that perhaps you need to take another class or something." She stood, but still had to look up at him and knew this wasn't a good time to notice how he towered over her. The silence grew bigger and more awkward until she felt compelled to fill it. "Jake, you're not my boss."

"Yet."

"Even so——"

"I'll see you tonight, Hope." His grin was highlighted with smug self-confidence that was darn sexy. And hot.

The resulting sizzle and burn fried all the electrical impulses in her brain, but she managed to stay on her feet and avoid embarrassment. Then she realized he was waiting for a response and tried to remember what he'd said. "Tonight?"

"The hospital's private open house for state and city officials. Dignitaries on parade. It's where we get to show off. There's a rumor that the governor plans to drop in." He stopped in the doorway and slid his hands into the pockets of his slacks. "You'll be here, right?"

"I'm giving guided tours of the trauma department. But why are you coming?"

"It would be rude to miss the moment when they announce my name as the new trauma medical director."

He flashed a wicked grin before sauntering out of her office. She took a deep cleansing breath, but it didn't help. Her pulse was pounding. Her heart was racing. And she was pretty sure if she looked in a mirror, her face would be flushed. Wasn't it just her luck that the most arrogant, annoying, exasperating man on the planet had put the color back in her cheeks.

Also just her luck that this was the most alive she'd felt in a very long time.

Trouble had definitely paid her a visit and she would do her level best to avoid it tonight.

Jake didn't dislike obligatory hospital functions, but he rarely anticipated one with as much enthusiasm as he did now. And there was only one reason.

Hope.

He'd parked his car in the lot outside Mercy Medical

West on the corner of Warm Springs and Durango roads, then leaned into the cold January wind as he walked toward the brightly lit facility.

The bilevel architectural design combined with artistic touches and made this house of healing pleasing both to the eye and the spirit. On each floor of the building walls were painted a different color—blue, lavender, green or yellow—and the furniture and floors were done in coordinating shades.

Medical equipment was state-of-the art, the latest technology available. This hospital was going to be the jewel in Mercy Medical's crown and it would do the same for his career. Maybe, *finally,* he could silence the voice inside him that warned he would always be that homeless white-trash kid who would never be good enough for the prom queen.

When he got to the facility's double glass doors, they whispered open and released the noise from the crowd inside. Men in dark suits and women in cocktail dresses jammed the usually quiet, serene lobby. Waiters in black pants and crisp white shirts circulated with trays of food and glasses of champagne.

Jake scanned the gathering, searching for a blonde, but not just any blonde. There was a certain shade of honey in Hope's hair and she had the prettiest hazel eyes he'd ever seen.

But it was her mouth that amped up his anticipation. Very defined, full lips curved up at the corners and were just about the most tempting thing he could imagine, and he could imagine a whole lot of temptation. If Hope Carmichael had been as provocative as a potato, he could have put her out of his mind, but his life had never been that simple or uncomplicated.

Jake glanced at his watch. The shindig had been under

way for almost two hours and judging by the crowd concentrated in this area, tours of the facility were complete. So if she wasn't jumping through hoops for dignitaries, where was she? Before he could decide what to do about that question, the president of the hospital's board of directors introduced himself over a microphone. Jake located former Congressman Edward Havens on a dais set up for the occasion.

Ed introduced the governor, senator, mayor—blah, blah, blah. Then he ticked off the names of the campus president, department directors, etcetera. Finally he made eye contact with Jake and smiled, before announcing that the contract for trauma medical director was going to Dr. Jake Andrews.

Jake nodded, waved, smiled politely at everyone applauding around him and mentally high-fived himself. He loved it when a plan came together, and in this case the plan was all about his career and long-term financial security. All the hard work had paid off. He would be able to write his own ticket now. No one would ever again look at him like he was something worse than dirt on their shoes.

Searching faces in the crowd, he still didn't see Hope. Suddenly he had an overwhelming urge to tell her "I told you so." He wandered the facility and was oddly disappointed when his search didn't produce the result he wanted. On his way back to the lobby, he passed the closed door of her office and tried the knob. When it turned, he pushed into the room and saw her there.

"Knock, knock," he said, then softly tapped his knuckles on the door.

She looked startled before her eyes widened in recognition. "Doctor…Jake," she corrected.

He walked inside and closed the door. Her desk was littered with computer equipment and stacks of folders.

Around the perimeter of the room were moving boxes with flaps opened. The office paraphernalia inside looked as if it had been rifled through but not put away. So she was still settling in.

"How about a tour?" he asked.

"Sorry. You're too late."

Her eyes went from surprised to sad and he wondered what would make such a pretty lady unhappy. Then he wondered why he would notice at all. Or why he should care. It could have something to do with her bastard remark earlier. He liked that she didn't scrape, bow and kiss his ass. That kind of crap got old real fast.

Jake slid his hands into the pockets of his slacks. "You're missing the party all locked away in here."

"It's work to me, and I'm taking a five-minute break."

"Want some company? I'd like to talk to you about something."

Her gaze turned suspicious which was better than sad. "You're not here to pester me about getting Bugs Bunny bandages, are you?"

"Something like that." He moved closer, near enough that the sweetly sensuous scent of her perfume nearly made his eyes cross. "I was looking over the names and certifications on the trauma team and wondered why there was no admitting specialist in the group."

She put her hands on her hips and her eyes narrowed. "So you want designer scalpels, Bugs Bunny boo-boo covers *and* a personal assistant?"

"Yes."

"Are you aware, Doctor, that it takes a hundred and fifty million dollars of up-front money to open a facility like this?"

"I think I heard that figure somewhere." Although he found her figure in the snug little black dress with almost-not-there straps far more interesting. Mile-high heels made her legs look incredible. One glance was better than a shot of adrenaline to get his heart pumping.

"Did you also hear that a new facility is expected to lose money at first, because there's no revenue stream?"

"Makes sense." Unlike the fact that he couldn't seem to take his eyes off her mouth.

He knew she was attracted to him because he knew women and this one wasn't very good at hiding her feelings. Her tone was full of Southern fried deference. She was trying to bow and scrape, but it was more about establishing a safe zone for herself.

She hadn't wanted to shake his hand earlier and that was to avoid touching him. Because of her attraction. It was incredibly inconvenient that the feeling was mutual.

"My job is to keep expenditures within limits and confine losses to conform to the budget." She let her gaze run over his pricey suit and tie before asking, "You do understand what a budget is?"

Oh, yeah. He'd learned the hard way, although having money was a prerequisite for learning how to spend it wisely. His mother hadn't had enough to pay the mortgage after his dad left them. Their house was foreclosed on. A rented roof over your head takes first and last month fees and a security deposit. If his mom had had a chunk of cash like that she'd have been able to make the loan payment. So they ended up homeless. He'd been thirteen.

Memories of that long-ago fear and humiliation rippled through him. "My point is that an admitting specialist will more than make up for the initial salary and benefit costs in revenue recovered."

"Really?"

"Yes, really."

He figured she knew her stuff or she wouldn't have been

hired for this job. So this attitude of hers must be about him personally. He wasn't sure what he'd done to tick her off, but apparently annoyance was contagious because he was feeling it, too. He'd caught it from her. Now was the time to let her know that she wasn't the only one who knew their stuff.

"Care to explain how an admitting specialist earns their keep?" she said.

"I'm glad you asked." He took a step forward, close enough to feel the heat from her body. "I'm sure *you're* aware that per diem charges mount up fast. And I'm also certain that you've heard of DRGs."

"Of course. Diagnosis-related groups."

"Give the lady a gold star. So you also know that every medical problem, difficulty, malady or disease has a price tag. Just like a bathing suit at the mall."

"What's your point, Doctor?"

"An admitting specialist is necessary to set up protocols for screening every case that comes into the E.R. for insurance information, any secondary financial help the patient might have, anything that will assist in charges. Because without proper billing, codes and patient details, payment can be delayed indefinitely or denied altogether. And that kind of a loss is something your budget can't absorb no matter how it's structured."

"Do you care more about money than medicine?" she challenged.

"And there's the gray area. Best answer? We can't afford to care more about medicine than money. You can't have one without the other. In the end it's a business and if we can't meet our expenses we go out of business. If that happens, we can't help anyone and the people of this community lose a valuable healthcare resource."

"Maybe my short-term memory is on the blink, but

aren't you the same doctor who just hours ago, in this very spot, hit me up for pricey precision instruments?"

Hit her up? No way. She'd know if he hit on her because there'd be no question.

Jake was almost certain there was a vein throbbing in his forehead. "I don't care about that."

"What do you care about?" She shook her head. "Never mind. I don't want to know. I have to go."

She moved too fast when she tried to sidestep him and ended up unsteady on those sexy high heels. He caught her as she stumbled and pulled her into his arms.

He couldn't say that kissing her hadn't crossed his mind, but he'd never planned to act on the impulse. Now here she was with her curves brushing against him and the pulse in her neck fluttering as awareness flashed in her eyes.

At that moment he couldn't think about anything *but* kissing her, and lowered his mouth to hers.

Chapter Two

Hope was pretty sure a kiss had never before made her toes curl, but that changed the moment Jake's lips touched hers. It was insane. She should back away from the heat. The problem was, insanity and heat had never felt so good. There was nothing aggressive or insistent about the way his mouth moved slowly, seductively, deliciously over hers. It was all lazy, luscious sizzle and simmer. She felt oddly safe and wanted to stay exactly where she was for as long as she possibly could.

He pulled back first and let his gaze wander boldly over her face as a small, puzzled smile curved his mouth. Apparently he saw something that made him thread his fingers in her hair and cup her cheek in his palm, brushing his thumb over her bottom lip. Her heart pounded almost painfully and her chest rose and fell rapidly with the need to draw in air. It felt as if she'd caught fire and the flames fed on every last ounce of oxygen in the room.

"Hope, that was…" He shook his head. "I didn't mean for that to happen."

Not what her quivering hormones wanted to hear. She was pretty good with a snappy comeback, a quick retort, witty one-liners. But her senses were in freefall and they'd taken rational thought along for the ride.

"And I didn't mean to kiss you back. This is a bad idea. The worst. Like kissing common sense goodbye."

Amusement turned his eyes silver. "Sometimes common sense is highly overrated."

"That's probably the first thing you've ever said that I agree with."

She wasn't sure, what with the blood rushing to her head, but she thought he groaned softly before taking her mouth again. Her lips parted and his tongue slid inside, thoroughly plundering any reserves of willpower she had left.

Their hands were all over each other as they panted and moaned and turned in circles, the intricate choreography of a sensuous waltz. Hope felt the wall at her back and Jake pressing against her front. Want tightened in her belly as need pooled between her thighs.

It was as if their minds and bodies had melded. Jake cupped the backs of her thighs and lifted at the same time she wrapped her legs around him. The harsh sounds of their breathing filled the room and fueled the fire of her wild abandon.

He kissed her neck and brushed away the skinny strap of her dress in his impatience to get to her bare shoulder. Then he trailed his lips down to the very top of her breast just visible over the neckline. He drew his tongue over her skin before blowing on the moisture. The sensation of cool on her heated flesh drove her crazy and she wanted him inside her more than she could remember wanting anything in her life.

When his cell phone rang, she changed her mind. Now more than anything she wanted to put the heel of her stiletto straight through his SIM card.

He pulled back, breathing hard. "I'm on call."

"Uh-huh."

"I have to answer." His voice was harsh.

"Right."

As she let her legs slide to the floor, he reached to the holster on his belt and retrieved the phone, turning his back as he answered.

"Andrews."

Hope smoothed her palms over the skirt of her dress as she drew in a shuddering breath. This was like stubbing your toe and the too-short span of time before the inevitable unfortunate consequences registered in the brain. It was going to be uncomfortable and she wanted to hang out in limbo for just a while longer. Otherwise she'd have to admit that a cell call was the only thing that had prevented her from having sex with a virtual stranger against the wall of her office.

Her only excuse was that she hadn't had sex for a very, very long time.

"Everything went as expected." Jake's voice was surprisingly normal. "Yeah. Not a single hitch in the plan. Right. Thanks." While listening, he glanced over his shoulder to look at her. Intensity glittered in his eyes as his gaze settled on her shoulder and the dress strap trailing down her arm. "Definitely. Details when I see you."

She slid her thumb under the strap and righted it as he ended the call. "Emergency?"

It hadn't sounded that way. But she could hope. Maybe

he would have to rush off and spare her an awkward conversation.

"No." He raked his fingers through his hair.

She blew out a breath, not quite meeting his gaze. "So…"

"So…"

The corners of his mouth tilted up. Clearly he was amused. Hope was not. Irritation aimed at herself straightened her spine and fueled the need to regroup.

"I take full responsibility for that," she said.

One dark eyebrow arched upward. "That?"

"You know."

"Not so much. The receptors in my brain are fried. Put a finer point on it for me."

He was enjoying this, she realized and started to fume. But she'd be darned if she'd give him the satisfaction of confirming her acute discomfort. Or the fact that he'd majorly turned her on.

"The kiss," she said, deliberately lifting her chin so their gazes locked. "My mistake. I freely own my part in what just happened."

"Very generous of you." He slid his hands into the pockets of his charcoal slacks. The black shirt and tone-on-tone tie fit his trim body perfectly. Dr. GQ wouldn't have to worry about the fashion police.

"Not generous. Honest."

"Still… An admission like that could be construed as encouragement. How do you know I won't stoop to using it to my advantage?"

She refused to give any ground. "That mistake is on me, but the bigger one would be assuming you could use it for your own personal agenda."

"Agenda? Personal?" A wolfish expression settled on

his handsome face making it an uphill battle to get this conversation back on a professional plane.

"Don't miscalculate, Doctor. My slip-up will not give you currency in the workplace."

"Oh?"

"You can't come up with an unrealistic wish list and expect me to smile politely just because I kissed you."

Jake's sinful smile was a clear indication that the message missed its mark. "At the risk of shattering your illusions, Hope, nothing about that kiss was polite, which suits me just fine."

She groaned inwardly, still living in limbo and guarding herself from the guilt. "You're deliberately misunderstanding my point."

He shook his head. "On the contrary. I got it. But you don't have all the facts."

"Which are?"

"I actually came to see you tonight to tell you I told you so."

"I don't get it," she said.

"Okay, here's the deal. My wish list just might carry more weight since earlier tonight I was offered the contract to be the chief trauma surgeon. I'm officially your boss."

And Hope was officially in trouble.

She'd missed sex.

She hadn't realized how much until Jake kissed her. Now she missed it a whole lot more.

The next day Jake sat in on Hope's meeting with the department directors to assess their status regarding the target date for the Mercy Medical West opening. He had the chair to her left and knew she was talking because her lips were moving. The thing was, he was so fascinated by her mouth that he couldn't concentrate on what she was saying.

Only last night he'd tasted her just down the hall from this conference room. If Cal Westen, his medical practice partner, hadn't called to find out whether or not he'd been appointed to oversee trauma services, Jake would have done a whole lot more than just kiss her.

That had never been part of his plan, and he always had one. You didn't go from living on the street to chief trauma surgeon without a disciplined and detailed blueprint of how to get there. Kissing a colleague wasn't so much as a footnote on the blueprint, even if she did have a mouth in desperate need of a kiss.

"I'm sure you all know Dr. Jake Andrews."

The sound of his name yanked him into the moment and he smiled at the directors of radiology, respiratory therapy, the emergency department and the E.R. doc, all gathered around the mahogany conference table. He was acquainted with them all.

"Dr. Andrews was appointed Mercy Medical West's chief trauma surgeon last night." A hint of pink creeping into Hope's cheeks told him she hadn't forgotten what else happened last night.

And what *almost* happened.

Everyone applauded the announcement and seemed genuinely pleased at the news. It was worth the price he'd paid—all work, no play or much pay for more years than he cared to remember. Now that he was at the top, nothing was going to get in the way of his staying there.

"Congratulations, Dr. Andrews," Hope said. She barely met his gaze, then glanced at the agenda on the table in front of her. "Next I'd like a report from each department, in terms of how we stand in supplying trauma personnel."

As the directors took turns getting her up to speed, Jake

studied Hope and knew she was aware of him, too. The pulse at the base of her throat beat just a little too fast. He didn't know whether or not to be pleased about that. The timing of *this*—whatever it was between them—was damn inconvenient.

"All right," she said nodding. "Now I want to make sure we're on the same page with identifying the levels of trauma. Mechanical injury—broken bones—is level one. Penetrating wound is level two. Head or traumatic brain injury is level three. Preliminary paramedic evaluation in the field will determine the trauma level of patients transported by ambulance. And walk-ins will have to be assessed by the E.R. doc who will determine the trauma level."

A murmur of general agreement followed her remarks as the directors took notes.

"Next on the agenda is medical staff. We will apply for a level-three designation since Dr. Gallagher's group signed on for neurosurgery and agreed to be in-house 24/7. That doesn't mean on standby or on call. They will be physically on premises. Dr. Andrews can fill us in on whether or not we have adequate trauma surgeons signed on."

"I'm in the process of interviewing several surgeons right now," Jake said. "I'll be ready before the doors open."

"Good." She was all business, the polar opposite of the tantalizing temptress of just a few hours ago. "Now for Radiology. Dr. Edwards, about the Nighthawk system…"

Jake knew that radiology used the Nighthawk system to send nonemergency tests to Australia via the Internet for interpretation. But the state of Nevada mandated that an interventional radiologist be in-house for invasive procedures that required diagnostic imaging or guidance for tapping blood buildup in the chest cavity or other emergency situations. Edwards was a hard-ass and not receptive to change, making Hope's job a challenge.

The heavyset, balding doctor tried to glare her into submission. "It's cost-effective to use the Nighthawk system."

"In most cases, yes," Hope agreed. "But there isn't a choice about this. We can't be designated a trauma center without an interventional radiologist in house."

"And I need to pay the I.R., Miss Carmichael," he said stubbornly. "They don't come cheap. I have a budget."

"Don't we all." She glanced at Jake, her hazel eyes narrowing slightly. "But there are other ways to trim."

"None of them pretty." He rested his elbows on the table. "What if there are no traumas?"

"It doesn't matter. We're a trauma center and have to staff for what could happen."

"And I still have to pay the staff for doing nothing. My partners will not be happy and neither will I."

"You agreed to the terms of the contract, Dr. Edwards," she reminded him.

"Terms can be amended. I think hospital administration should absorb some of the cost."

Hope stared him down. "I understand that the tendency is for every department to become territorial and insular, but the goal is for all the parts to function as one. Just like the body which can't sustain life without a brain, heart or liver, a trauma response relies on all the departments for a successful outcome." She glanced at each department director in turn before saying, "But I'm sure you're all as aware of that as I am."

Dr. Edwards shook his head. "When I can't justify expenditures, it's my reputation on the line. My ass in a sling."

"As is mine," she said.

Jake glanced in the direction of the body part in question which she was currently sitting on. From what he remembered, it was an excellently curved butt that fit nicely in his hands.

"This is not the time or place to be discussing financial arrangements. I suggest you speak to the administrator regarding your concerns. Bottom line," she said, momentarily glancing at Jake as if she could read his thoughts, "I need your assurance that you'll be prepared with an in-house radiologist around the clock."

The radiologist stared at her for several moments, then finally nodded, albeit reluctantly.

"Good," she said, smiling sweetly. "And last but not least, I'd like to discuss who should respond to a code-trauma page."

Jake knew how he wanted it to go and was acutely interested in how she'd present this.

After glancing at her notes, she looked around the table. "In my opinion there should be someone from the lab, Radiology, Respiratory Therapy, Admitting and an ICU nurse. Just in case."

"How about housekeeping and dietary?" Jake asked. "Or lions and tigers and bears, oh my."

"Excuse me?" She met his gaze.

"You're aware of the limited space in the trauma bays?"

"I am."

"If you get all those people in there, it's like an IV push of adrenaline. Looky-loos show up in droves. It will be a three-ring circus and you might as well sell tickets."

Around the table everyone laughed and Hope narrowed her gaze on him.

"You didn't let me finish, Doctor."

"So you were going to say that the key to an organized trauma team response is…"

"Security," she finished, one eyebrow raised. "Security will be trained to monitor who should and should not respond to a code trauma."

He nodded, more than satisfied with her response. She knew her stuff. She was a smart cookie and sexy as hell. Damn inconvenient this thing arcing between them.

"That's it for me," she said, glancing at everyone around the table. She looked at him. "Dr. Andrews, it's your meeting."

"Gripes anyone?" They all got a chuckle out of that, including the radiologist. It took the edge off the tension of moments before. "Any other business?" Before they could answer, he stood and said, "Hearing none, I call the meeting to an end."

Jake figured that everyone had had enough for today. Especially Hope. The room cleared quickly, as if they were afraid he'd change his mind and bring up something really complicated, like open-heart surgery with a cheese grater.

He remembered Hope telling him if he was as good in surgery as everyone thought, he could get a positive outcome with a potato peeler and a watermelon scoop. That made him smile.

"Something funny, Doctor?"

"Nope. Not a thing," he said. Her frown said she wouldn't find his thoughts amusing.

"Not even throwing me under the bus with the three-ring circus remark?"

"It was an attempt at humor. To keep tempers in check."

"At my expense," she accused.

"Did it occur to you that they were testing your resolve?

That I set you up to show these guys you know what you're doing?"

"Actually, no." She folded her arms over her chest and leaned back against the table. "Did you?"

"Actually, no." He wished that had been his motivation. "I was testing you."

"You didn't think I knew that a free-for-all in the trauma bay is a whole different kind of trauma?"

"I only know what's on your résumé. Not your philosophy on setting hospital protocols." Or anything else for that matter. Part of him wanted to know everything about her and that was bad.

"Apparently I passed."

Oh, yeah. His gaze settled on her mouth and the memories came flooding back. One minute they'd been on opposite sides of the money-versus-medicine debate and she'd skewered his last nerve with her stiletto. The next he had her up against the wall and both of them were breathing hard while he kissed her senseless.

And she kissed him right back.

Another thirty seconds and he'd have been inside her. He'd been almost grateful when his partner's call interrupted what would have been a huge mistake. But he carried around a big fat regret that he would never know what loving Hope would feel like.

"Yes," he finally said. "You passed the test. Obviously you've been through a trauma situation with no one directing traffic."

She nodded. "You do the best you can to think of everything, all the medical consequences. Sometimes you forget to factor in human nature. Basic curiosity."

"Speaking of that—" He was so damn curious about her. If only he had internal security to direct that somewhere it wouldn't bite him in the ass.

"Yes?" She tilted her head and her hair swung sideways, revealing the smooth expanse of sexy skin on her neck.

"Edwards is a pain in the butt. I'll speak to him and make sure he backs off."

"Why would you do that?"

Good question. He hadn't planned to offer his help. Watching his own back had been top priority for a long time. "I know him. It might help."

"Thanks. But it's my job to deal with him."

He nodded. "Okay, then."

She was right; not his responsibility. Since when did he run interference for anyone? That was way too easy to answer. Hope Carmichael had tripped the switch on his protective instincts. There was something fragile about her that made him want to keep her safe when she should be dead last on his priorities list.

He hadn't worked his ass off and scraped out a living all his life just to let sex with a tempting coworker derail his career plan.

"Okay, then," she echoed. She straightened from the table and started to walk away. "I have work to do and I'm pretty sure you do, too."

"Wait, Hope…"

She stopped and looked up. "Yes?"

"We need to talk."

Something flickered in her eyes. Heat? Awareness? Regret? "I really have to go, Jake. You're the one who ended the meeting because there was no other business."

"It's not about the hospital."

She tucked a silky strand of honey blond hair behind her ear. "Then this must be about last night."

She'd blamed herself, but he'd been a more-than-willing participant. He hadn't meant for it to happen. He'd told her common sense was highly overrated, but that was lip service. No pun intended. Common sense had gotten him to where he was now. His career trajectory was right on target.

"Yeah. About last night—" He pushed his suit jacket aside as he rested his hands on his hips. Kissing Hope came under the heading "Seemed Like a Good Idea at the Time." They'd even agreed that kissing common sense goodbye was a very bad idea. Then they'd turned the bad idea on its ear and went for each other again.

It was time to clarify the mistake, clear the air and put the personal behind them. Get back on a professional footing because he had a lot at stake.

"Our priority needs to be getting the hospital open and running smoothly. At a profit," he added, bracing for her reaction.

"You're absolutely right," she said.

"Anything of a personal nature between us would distract attention from that goal."

"I agree completely." She nodded so eagerly that it made his head hurt.

"This is important for the community."

Not to mention himself. Success equaled power and security. Only someone who'd been powerless and insecure could understand how vital those intangibles could be.

"I'm really glad you brought this up," she said seriously. "It's like lifting a heavy load from my shoulders. What happened was a momentary, involuntary, reflexive, impulsive, spontaneous, inconsequential, insignificant—thing."

"Agreed." And yet her qualifying it to the size of something you could only see under a microscope was starting to tick him off. He'd spent a lot of time and energy worrying about how to handle this. "So we'll just forget it ever happened."

"Right. I *so* don't need any problems in my life. Already forgotten. Thanks, Jake."

Could she be any happier to be done with him?

He wanted to stop her when she walked to the door. He wanted to take back his words, but she might claim it was such a nonevent that all memory of their lips touching and sparks flying had been completely removed from her memory bank.

And how perverse that erasing it had been his goal in bringing up the subject. Talking about the elephant in the room was supposed to make it go away. He felt as if the effort had been a complete failure to meet the objective he'd had in mind.

Not only could he *not* forget about kissing her, but he was also annoyed that she could. Being frustrated at the success of his strategy was too stupid for words.

Chapter Three

"How many traumas would you guess come into this E.R. in a month?"

Hope put the question to Dr. Cal Westen, a pediatric trauma specialist, and Dr. Mitch Tenney, the E.R. doc on duty. They were Jake's partners in the trauma practice. Both worked at Mercy Medical Center's main campus and they stood with her in a hallway just outside the emergency room.

Mitch thought about the question for several moments. The dark-haired, blue-eyed hunk was dressed in green scrubs. He was on duty but had taken a few minutes to answer her questions after waiting patients had been triaged and sent to rooms where they'd be seen in the order of symptom severity.

Dr. Tenney had a reputation for passionate intensity, but had been eager to help when she'd explained she had staffing questions regarding the soon-to-open hospital.

"In a month we probably get ten to twelve level threes," Mitch said. "Those are usually head trauma from MVA—motor vehicle accidents. Or GSW—gunshot wounds."

"How many children?" she asked the pediatric specialist.

Cal Westen was no less super-hot than his partner, but his coloring was different. Dark blond hair and blue eyes made him look more relaxed, but his skill and rapport with kids was well-known.

"We probably get twenty-five kids a day," he said, sliding his stethoscope over the back of his neck, letting the ear tips and circular chest piece dangle. "Fever is the most common complaint followed closely by wheezing—a level-one nebulizer."

Hope jotted down a few things in a small notebook. "I'm guessing that those kinds of issues are seasonal?"

Cal nodded. "Spring and fall pick up because of allergies. And we get a surge when kids go back to school. In large groups the germs spread faster. They get colds and flu. Wheezing is a secondary complication."

"As far as staffing we need to take that into consideration." She'd been an E.R. nurse, but every hospital had its way of doing things. It was her job to observe Mercy Medical's procedures and improve on them with the new campus. If possible. "What's the work flow like? What happens when patients hit the door? Where do they go?"

"Sometimes we sit around and twiddle our thumbs. Sometimes it's saturated." Mitch rubbed a hand across the back of his neck. "We assess everyone right away. If we're really busy, the least severe cases see a nurse. Next would be E.R. doc. Me. The level threes are evaluated by the trauma surgeon."

"That would be Jake." When both doctors looked at her she said, "We've met."

Especially their lips and bodies from chest to thigh had *met*. The memory made her hot all over even though she'd enthusiastically agreed with his suggestion, just yesterday, that they forget all about that *meeting*.

"I understand Jake was with you the other night when he was appointed to chief trauma surgeon." There was a gleam in Cal's blue eyes.

"I did see him. Right after Congressman Havens made the public announcement."

She remembered Jake's gruff, curt responses when he'd answered his cell that night. Probably Cal had been on the other end of the call. He'd be curious because the appointment would impact their practice. Did he also know that he'd interrupted an intensely personal moment? If he didn't, she certainly wasn't going to confirm. All business. She and Jake had agreed.

"So," she said, looking from one hot doc to the other. "You both put in a lot of hours here in the hospital?"

"Yeah." Cal checked the pager at the waist of his scrubs. "We're in the process of looking for another pediatric specialist and E.R. intensivist for the practice. Both of us are married and want to spend as much time as possible with our families."

"You have children?" she asked.

"I have a little girl," Cal said, a proud smile curving his mouth. "Almost two."

"And I have a son." Mitch's smile was pleased. "Going on a year."

So hospital gossip was right. Two of the trauma docs were no longer single. All evidence pointed to the fact that they couldn't be happier about losing their playboy position to Jake.

"Is it hard," she said, "seeing sick children when you have little ones of your own?"

"It was hard even before I became a father," Mitch answered. "I went through a cynical phase and had to work through some issues. A lot of patients come in for things that could easily have been avoided. I had little tolerance for that. It was my wife who helped me mellow."

"Really?"

"Yeah," Cal said. "Jake and I are incredibly grateful to Sam for this kinder, gentler Mitch."

"Bite me," his partner said.

"Seriously," Cal continued. "I don't see my daughter in every child I treat. But I do understand now how parents feel and try to be more sensitive to that."

"I see." Hope saw a nurse in the E.R.'s doorway signaling to the doctors. "One last question. Stryker gurney or Hill-Rom? Hospital administration has a contract with the latter. We get a rebate after a certain number ordered. But I like Stryker."

Mitch thought for a moment. "Hill Rom is fine."

"The goal is to see patients as quickly as possible," Cal interjected. "But when it's nuts in the E.R. people have to wait and the Hill-Rom beds are more comfortable. We're so ready for the new campus to open and take a little of the heat off us."

"I bet."

Mitch nodded. "In fact administration is training a sales nurse to channel people in your direction when the hospital's up and running."

"Really?" She hadn't heard about that yet and wasn't sure how she felt. Sales and patient care seemed mutually exclusive—or should be.

"Yeah—"

There were footsteps behind her and she saw recognition in both doctor's expressions.

"Hi, partner," Mitch said.

"Hi." Jake was looking at her.

Hope noticed the green scrubs and knew he'd come from the OR. She'd heard he was working on a young boy. The dashing hero. At the moment he didn't look dashing, just dog-tired and she asked, "How are you?"

"Bushed," he confirmed.

"How's the kid?" Cal asked, worry sliding into his eyes.

Jake looked at his partner, then met her gaze. "Dare-devil boy plus flashy bike equals belly trauma. He won't be taking jumps off the curb at warp speed again anytime soon. But he'll be fine. I just gave the good news to his parents."

"Glad to hear it," Cal said. "Speaking of parents…I have to go."

"Me, too," Mitch agreed.

"Thanks for your time." Hope wanted to beg them to stay and not leave her alone with Jake, but she knew they were busy. "It was a pleasure to meet you both."

"Happy to help." Cal disappeared through the double doors.

"Good luck with the new E.R.," Mitch said, then followed his colleague to where the trauma bays held patients waiting for treatment.

She was about to excuse herself when Jake unexpectedly said, "I need caffeine. Stat."

"Rough day?" The words just popped out.

He nodded and even that small movement seemed an effort. Normally he looked magazine-ad perfect, every hair in place. Not so much right now. Gray eyes were dull with fatigue and his cocky, confident attitude was missing in action.

"Want to join me?"

She found him dangerously endearing, which seemed

an oxymoron, but definitely dangerous because she was unable to tell him no.

"Are you buying?"

He grinned. "I think I can handle a cup of coffee."

She walked with him through the hospital lobby and its high dome that allowed lots of sunlight. They passed the information desk staffed with volunteers, then out-patient admitting and down a hall. Jake opened the door to the doctor's dining room and let her precede him inside where she saw a scattering of tables covered with white cloths.

He took two mugs from a side table, then stuck each in turn beneath the spigot of a large silver coffee urn. After snagging a dessert plate, he filled it with several chocolate chip cookies and a couple of blueberry muffins. Then he sat at a table by a floor-to-ceiling window that looked out on the front parking lot and Mercy Medical Center Parkway. He leaned back and let out a long sigh.

Hope took the chair to his right. "Your partners were filling me in on what to expect when the new hospital opens."

"Patient load is just a guess. Mercy West will be slow at first, just because it's new. Although I understand people are coming in asking if it's open because the outside looks ready. But the type of trauma will be different just because of the location in the southwest valley."

"Oh?"

"Not as many MVAs or shootings."

"I see." She remembered something Mitch said. "Have you heard there's going to be a sales nurse to channel patients to the new hospital?"

"It was my idea." He blew on the wide opening of his steaming mug.

"Why?" she asked, surprised.

"It's human nature to resist change."

Not a news flash. She was a prime example. Her husband died and she'd had no choice but to accept the sudden traumatic differences of having the man she loved ripped away from her. Somehow she'd managed to move on with her life. Now she had a choice and alone was how she planned to stay. That would exclude the possibility of any unexpected and painful changes in her future. Pain was a warning system and she got the message. Alone equaled safe.

So that begged the question—why in the world was she sitting here with the guy whose kiss had reminded her how much she missed being with a man? But they'd agreed that their relationship would be professional only. Back to business.

"Mitch mentioned that there's a real need to take some of the patient load to the new hospital. But a sales nurse?" she asked.

"Patients and family members used to coming here aren't going to want to go somewhere else."

"How can you be so sure?"

"Like I said, people resist change. But the load here is becoming overwhelming." Amusement chased some of the fatigue from his face. "Not long ago a former patient was here complaining about the bill he'd received from the hospital regarding his bed."

"Why?"

"He was billed for an ICU bed. Then he was downgraded to IMC—intermediate medical care. And then lowered to floor status."

"What was his problem?"

"He never left the E.R." The corners of his mouth turned up. "It was explained to him that he still received the same care he would have in the unit, but there wasn't a bed available upstairs for him."

Hope couldn't help smiling, too. "I know it's not funny. That poor man."

"When Mercy Medical West opens, someone in those circumstances here will be offered a bed there. A sales nurse will sweeten the deal with a promise of hot meals, privacy and a computer in every room. All the comforts available."

"I see your point. Maybe it's the 'sales' part that bothers me. Couldn't they call the job Patient Placement coordinator?"

"PPC? Perfectly politically correct?"

"Why not?" she demanded, laughing in spite of herself.

"No reason I know of." He took a cookie and chewed thoughtfully. "So you had a nice chat with Cal and Mitch?"

"Yes. They were very informative. And I'm wondering…"

She stopped herself just in time. Wondering about Jake was another dangerous activity.

"What?" As he blew on the steaming coffee, his gaze never left hers.

Damn. Even tired he didn't miss anything. Ignoring his question would just get more attention. "It just occurred to me that both of them are married and have families. You don't. Why is that?"

"I have different goals."

"Oh?"

"I want other things from my career. Being chief trauma surgeon will get me where I want to be in terms of practicing medicine. After that the sky's the limit. I've thought seriously about politics."

"That seems self-indulgent. A power trip."

"You don't approve." He wasn't asking.

Without confirming, she said, "Medicine is community service in its purest, most basic form. It's a higher calling than self-gratification."

"Without politics, policies don't change and people don't get help."

"But not just anyone can save a boy with belly trauma. You're highly trained to save lives. Let someone else without those skills change policy."

His expression turned stormy. "Someone with my particular skill set has a unique perspective in shaping the future of health care in this country."

"Maybe. But I can't help thinking that it isn't people in general, but you in particular at the top of your priority list. It seems to me that you're all about money and power."

Fire turned his eyes to quicksilver. "Does taking shots at me make you feel better about kissing me back?"

"That's not what this is about." Although she knew his question wasn't far from the truth.

"I'm glad burying your head in the sand is working for you." He looked at the pager at the waist of his scrubs. "I've got patients."

Without another word he stood and walked out. Suddenly she was alone. It's what she wanted and it should have made her happy, but it didn't. And it had everything to do with her damned attraction to that man. It simply refused to go away. What she needed was anger, buckets and buckets of being mad as hell. That's what had gotten her through the first stages of grief after losing her husband.

She needed to get angry and channel her *mad,* use it in any way possible to protect herself.

But she shouldn't have to work so hard. The allocation of that much energy didn't make a whole lot of sense given the fact that she didn't have an especially high opinion of Jake. His medical expertise was exemplary. His moral high ground? Not so much. And yet, her mouth still tingled every time she saw him.

The trick would be *not* seeing him at work as much as possible.

Twenty-four hours after running into Hope, Jake was still intrigued and annoyed in equal parts. He walked into the office he shared with his partners where their billing and paperwork were done. Mitch and Cal's specialty was emergency medicine, which meant no long-term care. Jake had a single exam room for his occasional follow-up on a surgical patient. In the back, their conference room held a classy, mahogany table and three high-backed leather chairs for monthly status meetings. He was hoping that seeing his friends would take his mind off Hope.

She was deliberately trying to piss him off. Really working at it. What the hell had he ever done besides kiss her? He had to admit it was a really great kiss, but still…

"Are you going to stand out here in the hall and day-dream?" Mitch had walked up behind him. His smile was set on screw-with-a-friend. "We were foolishly hoping our fearless leader would come inside and celebrate his shiny new promotion with the peasants."

"It's not daydreaming if one is gathering one's thoughts," Jake defended. Only he knew the lie for what it was.

"You have that look on your face," Mitch said. "The confused-about-a-woman expression."

Just then Cal walked by and made a dramatic show of putting his hands over his ears. "I don't want to hear. I'm an impressionable and sensitive man."

"Sensitive like a water buffalo." Jake was glad his part-ner had given him an excuse to ignore the "woman" com-ment and dodge that bullet.

The three walked in the conference room and took seats

around the table with Jake taking the head and his friends on either side, as usual. They were barely settled when Cal pulled out his wallet. As usual.

"Before we get down to business you have to see this picture."

Mitch took the photo and grinned. "Look at those blond curls Annie's got."

"Looks just like me," Cal said proudly.

Jake studied the photo of Cal, his daughter and wife, Emily. "Annie's really getting big."

"So is Em. At least she will be," Cal answered. "Before I'm accused of being a pig, you should know she's pregnant. We're going to have another baby."

"That's great." Mitch reached across the table for a congratulatory handshake. "How did she pull that off? Surely you didn't have anything to do with it."

"Yeah. Right. Immaculate conception." Cal glared. "Buddy, you need a refresher course in anatomy and the reproductive process."

"Hardly." Mitch wasn't intimidated by the glare. In his glory days he could give lessons on the care, feeding and fringe benefits of a really good glare. "Samantha and I have the whole birds-and-bees thing goin' on just fine." He slid his wallet from the back pocket of his jeans and took out a picture. "Equal time. This is the latest one of *Lucas*."

Cal took it and smiled. "Tall, dark and dandy, just like his dad. Look at those teeth."

"Two on the bottom and he's working on the uppers." Mitch's tone was rueful. "He's waking up a lot at night and Sam thinks it's teething."

"I feel your pain." Cal tucked his picture away. "Annie is getting her two-year molars and it's not pretty."

"Great. More to look forward to. I can hardly wait."

Without comment Jake listened to his two friends go

back and forth about who was losing the most sleep. Once upon a time they'd both resisted love, even after meeting the right woman. Compelling personal reasons had put a fear of commitment into each man until a lonely future was far worse than taking a chance. Now when they gathered to discuss finances, goals, problems and growing their practice, the monthly status meeting started with an update on married life and growing their families.

Jake had always tolerated this part of the monthly meeting, not that he wasn't happy for his friends. It's just that he had career goals and success aspirations different from theirs. But today he was having a strange reaction to news about wives, kids and a new pregnancy. He always cared, but only half listened. Today he was interested. What was that about?

It was definitely new and he wondered what was different since last month. There were only two changes. His appointment to chief trauma surgeon.

And Hope.

He heard his name and realized they'd been talking to him. "What's wrong?"

Mitch's expression was intense. "That's what I'd like to know."

"Yeah." Cal rested his forearms on the table. "You have something against marriage?"

"Not if it's working for you."

"It definitely is," Mitch said. "Marrying Sam was the smartest thing I've ever done."

"So says the man who in this very room swore up and down that he didn't need conflict resolution counseling and it would be a waste of time," Jake reminded him.

"You neglected to tell me that my counselor would be sexy. And smart. And the love of my life," he added.

"My bad." Jake grinned.

He remembered when Mitch's attitude had ticked off most of the Mercy Medical staff, some of the physicians and administration. His behavior had put the trauma practice in jeopardy of not having their contract renewed. That would have dealt his own career trajectory a serious blow. But his friend salvaged the professional relationship with the hospital *and* found personal happiness.

"Darn right your bad," Cal said. "I'm grateful every day that Emily came back into my life and gave me another chance. I don't know what I'd do without her and Annie."

"You sound like girls," Jake teased.

The two looked at each other before Mitch said, "We're okay with that."

"So you guys are blissfully happy and recommend marriage. Good for you."

"Don't knock it till you've tried it," Mitch cautioned.

"I'm not knocking anything," Jake protested. He looked at Cal on his right and Mitch on his left. "I get it. You guys are happy. Can we talk about business now?"

"One question. What's going on with you and what's-her-name? The daughter of the president of the hospital's board of directors?" Mitch settled an intense look on him.

"You mean Blair Havens?" She was definitely Congressman Havens's daughter and he was definitely president of the board of directors. Jake answered, "We're dating."

"Is it serious?" Cal asked.

"What are you? Her father?"

"I have a daughter," he said. "And if any guy messes with Annie he'll have me to deal with. So, I'm just saying…"

"Well, I guess it depends on what you mean by serious." Jake was dodging the question.

"Serious as in settling down. Marriage," Cal spelled out.

"I've thought about it," he admitted. "Blair is beautiful,

smart and connected. Her father was in Congress and still has political influence. It would be a good career move. But…"

"Ah. *But*," Mitch said, a knowing look in his eyes. "A three letter word that means not so fast."

"Something like that," Jake agreed.

His personal life had flatlined a long time ago when he fell in love but didn't pass her family's white-trash test. In their eyes, once you've been homeless the smell of loser never goes away. The experience taught him not to take anything for granted. Hard work alone didn't guarantee success or happiness. So, a relationship should buy you something. A career boost. Connections. The path to power. *Something*.

"Okay, guys." He looked from Cal to Mitch. "Can I start the meeting?"

"Fine." Mitch nodded.

"Okay with me." Cal met his gaze. "The sooner we're done here, the sooner I can get home to the family. Go, bro."

Agendas were passed out and the first item was a status report on hiring new doctors for the practice. While his friends talked, Jake's mind wandered to the memory of a pair of pretty hazel eyes flashing with humor and intelligence. A mouth, with its defined upper lip and full bottom one. A mouth that could be cute and crooked when she smiled. It was just a memory, but still had the power to drive him crazy.

And, dammit! This was his practice. The one he'd started with nothing but determination and guts. His career and the stability of his future was on the line. Everything he'd ever wanted was now his for the taking. This was an incredibly inconvenient time to lose focus.

He and Hope didn't have a relationship, let alone

anything that would guarantee him success. In fact, what was between them had the potential to implode all his plans.

Maybe he needed to talk to her again about keeping things between them purely professional.

Chapter Four

The sports bar across the street from Mercy Medical West was noisy and Hope didn't really want to be there. But a couple of the E.R. nurses had reached out to her and socializing was a good way to generate trauma team spirit. On second thought, maybe a sports bar was the perfect place to be. She sat with her coworkers at a tall bistro table in the far corner of the room to the right of the walk-up bar. Flat-screen TVs were mounted on the walls and visible from every seat in the place.

Karen Richards, a petite strawberry blonde, was a hard worker and experienced E.R. nurse, by all accounts one of the best on staff. When the newest campus opened, her reputation would be put to the test. She held up her long-neck bottle of beer and said, "This is your official welcome to Las Vegas, Hope."

Green-eyed brunette Stacy Porter held up her pink cocktail. "I second that."

"Thanks." Hope touched her glass of white wine to each of theirs. "So, tell me about yourselves. Married? Kids?"

Karen toyed with her beer bottle. "I'm divorced. Two girls, Cassandra and Olivia, ages six and four. We live with my mom who's a nurse at Mercy's main campus. I'm twenty-six and still live with my mother. Is that pathetic, or what?"

There were worse things, Hope thought. "Is it working for you?"

"Yeah. She's my rock and helps with child care."

Hope nodded. "What about you, Stacy?"

The twentysomething held up her left hand and wiggled her fingers, showing off a diamond solitaire. "Just got engaged. Tim works in Human Resources at the hospital."

"Congratulations."

Even as she smiled, Hope tried to suppress the pang of envy. She remembered the huge joy of being with the man she'd loved and the shimmering anticipation of their life together. A life that barely got started before it was gone. Losing Kevin had nearly crushed her.

"When's the big day?" Hope plastered a big, fat, fake smile on her face.

"April," Stacy said. "Before Vegas is hotter than the face of the sun. It will be a church wedding, not in the Garden of Love Chapel with an Elvis impersonator."

"Are you sure?" Hope held her palms up and lifted each in turn as if weighing something. "Elvis? The Chapel of Love? Church could be boring."

The women laughed, but Hope knew from personal experience that boring was a blessing. Just then a cold wind blew into the bar and blasted boring into oblivion because Jake Andrews had walked through the door. It felt as if her heart hit a pocket of turbulence that made boring look even better. Some kind of radar drew his gaze to their secluded corner and he nodded at her before heading in their direction.

"Look who's here," Karen said when he joined them. The tone of familiarity indicated they knew each other. "Hi, Jake. To what do we owe the honor?"

"Ladies." He looked around, then let his gaze linger on Hope. "There was a rumor that the E.R. department was here for happy hour."

"All three of us," Stacy said.

"Is this a ladies-only initiation rite for the new girl in town? Or can anyone join?"

"Have a seat, Doc," Karen said. "This is the first annual Mercy Medical West employee-bonding ritual."

He sat on the empty chair between Stacy and Hope. His shoulder brushed hers, sending a blast of heat through her. The waitress took his drink order and brought him a bottle of beer, as if he were just one of the guys. But he didn't look like just one of them.

Except for scrubs after surgery, she always saw him in a suit and tie, as if he were running for elected office. Tonight was no exception. The charcoal slacks, matching jacket, crisp white shirt and tone-on-tone silver tie made him look *so* good, broad-shouldered and masculine. The pocket of turbulence spread from her chest to her stomach and made her as nervous as a fearful flyer.

She didn't like being aware of him. She didn't like being aware of him in a way she hadn't been aware of a man since her husband. Jake Andrews? Really? It made no sense. He and Kevin were nothing alike. Jake was mercenary and ambitious—not at all her type.

She wanted to get up and leave but felt it would appear rude. Not to mention weird. So she toughed it out until everyone had finished their drinks.

Then she pushed away her wineglass. "I think I'll call it a night."

"So soon?" Karen said.

Hope slid down from the high chair. "Busy day tomorrow. The fire department is inspecting the building and if we don't pass they'll revoke our certificate of occupancy. But you all stay and have fun."

"Don't have to ask me twice. Mom's got the girls." Karen looked at Stacy.

"I'm free. Tim has a late meeting."

"I'll see you both tomorrow. This was really great," she said. "Good night, Jake."

He stood beside her. "I'll walk you to your car."

"I'm parked just across the street." It was an effort to keep her tone light when her heart was beating like crazy. "Don't bother."

"It's no bother." He smiled at the other two women. "See you later."

Then he settled his palm at the small of her back, escorting her through the crowded bar and into the chill air of the late-January night. Hope felt the pressure and heat of his fingers. Just that casual touch made her heart pound and her knees wobble. It wasn't okay and she stepped away from him as they walked side by side across the dark, hardly used street between the strip mall and the recently black-topped hospital lot.

"My car is by the E.R. entrance," she said and walked as fast as she could toward it.

"Do you have somewhere to be?"

Glancing up at his profile, the lean line of his cheek and jaw she said, "No. Why?"

"Then you're cold?"

His touch had gone a long way to taking the chill out of the dark night. "A little. Why?" she asked again.

"Because it feels a lot like you're going for a land speed record. As in running away from me."

"No." It was only a small lie. "But you and I aren't exactly on the same wavelength."

"Really?" He slid his hands into his pockets. "You mean because you accused me of being selfish, self-centered and motivated by power and greed?"

And he'd accused her right back of taking shots at him to ease her guilt about kissing him. There was enough truth in his words to make her squirm.

"It's just been a long day in a series of very long days."

"So you're just anxious to be home," he guessed.

"Something like that." She looked up at him. "Besides, we're being strictly professional. Your words, your idea. And a good one."

"That's possibly the nicest thing you've ever said to me."

Fortunately she didn't have to respond. "Here's my car."

The one with the rental company sticker clearly visible on the bumper. She pressed the button on her keys to unlock it.

"Thanks for walking me," she said, then quickly slid inside before he could even think about kissing her. Not because she thought she was all that, but past history and the way he kept looking at her mouth suggested he might.

He waved once, then disappeared into the dark. Hope sat for several minutes to pull herself together and cursed Jake for the fact that she *had* to pull herself together.

When her hands stopped shaking and her heart slowed to a manageable rhythm, she turned on the car, backed it out of the space and headed toward the exit. After rounding a corner of the hospital, she passed the front entrance where designated doctor parking was located. Her head-lights picked out the only car in the lot and the hood was up.

A guy was leaning over looking at the engine and she knew that guy was Jake. Even if she hadn't recognized the suit, the excellent butt was a giveaway.

In a span of possibly three or four seconds she had a plan and was only surprised her mind could function that fast given its recent workout after exposure to Jake Andrews. He was a perfectly capable male and she sincerely wanted to blow by him, but that just seemed too harsh.

She pulled into the space beside him and pushed the button to roll down her window. "Trouble?"

"What was your first clue?"

She'd known he was trouble the first time he walked into her office and nothing that happened since had changed her opinion. "Is there anything I can do?"

"If you have any experience with explosives, you could put this piece of trash out of its misery."

"So the trouble is chronic."

"In for maintenance or repair every other week," he con-firmed. "I've got the tow company on speed dial. They're en route as we speak."

She hesitated, knowing she'd hate herself, but finally said, "Do you need a ride home?"

"I could call a cab, but…" He walked closer, then leaned down until their eyes met. "I wouldn't have to wait for one. Would you mind?"

In more ways than he could possibly know. But it was too late to take back the offer. "Hop in."

About thirty minutes later his car had been towed. Jake had given her directions to his house in the upscale Lakes area of Las Vegas and she pulled into the semicircular drive.

She admired the front of his sprawling home where flood-lights illuminated the large yard and stately exterior.

"There's enough light out here to do vascular surgery without eyewear enhancement." She slid a wry look at him. "If that was a prison there'd be no chance of escape, what with the way it's lit up."

"I'm glad you like it. Want to come inside and see how the inmates live?" The questioning look in his gray eyes had a challenge around the edges.

Excitement skipped down her spine and for that very reason she should say no. Unfortunately that's not what came out of her mouth. "I've never been in a McMansion before."

"I'm happy to be your first."

The remark was casual, teasing. Was she the only one thinking it had sexual overtones? Adrenaline surged through every last one of her nerve endings. This was a bad idea, but there was no way to retreat that wouldn't show weakness. Jake was the kind of guy who could smell vulnerability and pounce. Quick tour, she told herself, then she was out of there.

After Jake unlocked the door and disabled the security system on the wall just inside, she followed him into the impressive, two-story entryway. The floor was neutral beige travertine that separated the living and dining rooms.

Trailing after him, she found herself in his big kitchen with stainless steel appliances and a granite-covered island big enough for its own zip code.

Adjacent to that was what he called the "media room." It looked a lot like a family room to her, but she wasn't a person who needed gadgets to make it look, feel and sound like a war zone. In her opinion, there was enough real in reality and making it feel more authentic in your own home wasn't entertaining.

Five beautiful bedrooms and four baths later they were standing in the master suite. Through floor-to-ceiling windows she could see the huge backyard with pool and patio area lit up as brightly as the front. A king-size four-poster oak bed sat in the center of the longest wall with nightstands on either side. The doctor didn't make his bed as evidenced by the comforter, blanket and sheet that were bunched at the foot, with pillows tossed haphazardly in the center of the mattress. A matching oak dresser and armoire were arranged around the room.

There was a step-down area with a cozy love seat arranged in front of a fireplace, without a single TV or home entertainment center in sight. She could easily imagine the sexy sort of entertaining he did in here. Part of her envied the woman lucky enough to be involved in that entertainment.

She took a steadying breath before looking at him and saying, "So, other than not making your bed, you have the perfect place to hang your hat and a pricey set of wheels that can't be relied on to get you here. What's up with that?"

"At least I own the clunker in question." He loosened his tie, an incredibly masculine movement. His silver eyes shimmered with teasing, and something more intense that made her shiver. "Can you say the same about your ride?"

"It's a rental."

"I sort of figured that out. What with the name of the leasing company on the back."

"You have no room to talk. At least it reliably gets me from where I hang my hat to work. That's all I care about."

"Where *do* you live?"

"The Residence Inn a couple of miles from the hospital."

"Are you working with a Realtor? If not, I can recommend someone—"

She shook her head. "There's no point. I accepted the assignment on a temporary basis, only until the new campus is up and running."

He looked puzzled. "Surely the job offer was permanent."

"It was. But those weren't the terms I wanted. Human Resources was desperate and the agreement is for me to stay until they can find a long-term replacement."

Moving to the French doors, she stared outside at the lights until her vision blurred. Body heat and her Jake sensors made her hyperaware the instant he came up behind her.

"I don't understand. You're not interested in putting down roots?" he asked.

His breath stirred her hair and she shivered. Longing swelled through her, making her chest ache for what she would never have again. She'd put down roots once and they'd grown deep. When a senseless act of violence pulled them out, her heart came, too. It kept beating and maintained life, but that was all. The part that made her want to live and love had died.

"No," she finally said. "The job, car and housing are all temporary, which is just the way I want it."

Her attempt to keep her tone light and breezy must have failed because Jake touched her shoulders and turned her. His eyes were dark with questions.

"What is it, Hope?"

"Nothing. That's just how I want my life to be."

"You're not like most women, are you?" His gaze went from teasing to intense as it skimmed over her face.

Before she could find the words to explain why temporary worked for her, he'd dipped his head and touched his mouth to hers, proving he'd missed the point. Temporary meant not doing this. Temporary meant no ties. It did not mean the sweet and sexy and soft feel of his lips on hers. Or making her forget what she'd been trying to say because her insides went liquid with longing.

Then heat exploded through her.

It felt as if an invisible switch flipped her mind off because suddenly their mouths were greedily devouring each other. Fumbling hands removed ties, blouse, shirt and pants. They stepped out of their shoes and Jake toed off socks before inching her toward the bed.

When she felt the mattress behind her, he cupped her face in his hands and stared intensely into her eyes. "Hope—"

She didn't want to talk and touched a finger to his lips. He smiled and held her wrist still, then drew each of her fingers into his mouth, sucking until the throbbing between her thighs made her need in a way she'd never needed before.

She settled her other hand on his bare chest and shuddered with desire at the way the dusting of hair tickled and teased. His heart pounded against her palm and it was as if she could hear the thundering sound. Then he pulled her close, reaching behind her to unhook the clasp on her bra. She backed away and kept her gaze on his as she stripped off the small scrap of chaste cotton. His eyes caught fire and turned to molten silver. His breathing was hard and heavy.

She would never be sure whether she consciously sat on the bed or simply collapsed because her legs wouldn't hold her any longer. But there she was with the cool sheets caressing her bare thighs. Jake took the hand she held out and slid beside her on the mattress, pulling her down with him.

He cupped her left breast in his hand and rubbed his thumb across the nipple until it went as hard as a diamond chip. Catching her breath became a challenge when he replaced his hand with his mouth and stroked her with his tongue. She writhed beneath his touch. It had been so very long and felt so very wonderful.

He slid his hand over her belly to the curls between her legs and slipped one finger inside her. A single light, loving touch sent sharp currents to the bundle of nerve endings that wept for him, then she went straight over the edge with a small, strangled cry of pleasure.

Jake held her while she shattered into a million pieces and didn't let go until she came back together again. Then he reached into the nightstand, pulled out a condom and covered himself. She held out her arms and he came to her, his body covering hers, her body welcoming his as he gently pushed inside.

Then he began to move and their hips found a rhythm almost instantly. She arched toward him, instinctively trying to get closer, deeper. He plunged into her again and again. He drove them both higher and higher until he stilled and the lines and angles of his face went rigid with intensity. He groaned out his pleasure and she held him until the spasms rocking his body ended.

He drew in a long breath and kissed her, softly sweetly.

A kiss that made her heart hurt and stirred up guilt because of what she'd done.

Jake made a quick trip to the bathroom, then hurried back to Hope. Who knew car trouble would turn into a close encounter of the horizontal kind? He was looking forward to savoring the softness of her body again. Cuddling on a cold night was just what the doctor ordered. And the naked woman in his arms just moments ago was about as close to heaven as he ever expected to get.

He settled into bed beside her, but when he tried to pull her back into his arms she stiffened and slid out of reach. In his version of heaven a woman's afterglow didn't usually disappear in a nanosecond.

She was holding the sheet over her breasts and up to her neck as if he hadn't just kissed almost every square inch of her skin. And he'd had every intention of repeating the experience to taste the parts he'd missed the first time around.

"What's wrong?" he asked.

"So many things, so little time." Her voice was filled with self-loathing.

Regret had surfaced awfully fast and he felt the need to defend himself.

"I didn't plan for that to happen," he assured her.

"I know. But that doesn't erase it."

"Are you accusing me of something?"

"No. I was just wondering what happened to keeping things between us strictly professional." When she shook her head ruefully, the light from outside turned her hair to spun gold. "Of course I don't blame you. I take full responsibility for my actions."

"That's not what your eyes are saying." There was a bruised look on her face and he wanted to erase it. "Talk to me, Hope."

"Just so you know, I don't make a habit of this."

"Neither do I."

Sleeping with a coworker could be the quickest route to career suicide. This was the first time he'd ever done this. But wanting her the way he had made it impossible to remember why he was driven to succeed. Now those reasons came flooding back with a vengeance. He wasn't sure there was enough career success or money in the world to silence the hungry, homeless kid who still lived inside him. The black, empty, helpless feeling grew, reminding him that he couldn't get complacent.

Not ever.

Without another word, she slid out of bed, then disappeared in the shadows of the room. He could hear her rustling around and figured she was picking up clothes and wouldn't appreciate him grilling her about what the hell had her panties in a twist. When she disappeared into the bathroom, he got up and dressed in a pair of jeans, then yanked on a shirt that he didn't bother to button. She still hadn't emerged, so he went to the media room to wait.

Finally she joined him there and announced, "I have to go."

"Not so fast." He moved in front of her. "Talk to me, Hope."

She turned away and started pacing. "I was married—"

Married? That was a line he didn't cross. He'd been so sure she was single. Then her words sank in. "Was? That means you're not married now?"

"No. Now I'm a widow." She stopped moving and looked up at him. "My husband died two years ago."

"I'm sorry."

That's not what he'd expected to hear, but the words came automatically. Early in his training he'd memorized how to say the correct words to a grieving family. *Although everything possible was done for your friend, brother, sister, wife, husband, or child, the damage was too severe and we were unable to save his/her life. I'm sorry for your loss.*

She was young and odds were that her husband hadn't been very old. He couldn't help wondering. Illness? Accident? "What happened?"

An expression that looked a lot like guilt made the gold in her hazel eyes darker, more brown than green. "That's not really the issue. I just needed you to know that I had a husband. He died. And you're the first man I've slept with—"

Information he wished he'd had a little while ago. He'd have been... What? More tender? Gentler? At least she wasn't a virgin. But in a way she was. Her first experience after a trauma was a different kind of pressure. Had he known...would he have backed off? Maybe. But probably not. He'd wanted her too badly. Now he could be tender and gentle as he reassured her that it was okay for her to move on.

"It's all right, Hope."

"No, it's not." Her mouth tightened with anger. "I don't blame you. I don't blame anyone."

"Then what's the problem?"

"It—" Her cheeks flushed and her gaze dropped. "What we did, it just feels wrong."

"Not to me," he said.

Her gaze lifted to meet his. "How nice for you. I wish it were that easy for me, but it's not. It feels like cheating."

Close, he thought. But not exactly. Not for her.

"Life goes on," he said as gently as possible. "You're a single woman. You have needs and you're allowed to—"

"You asked what was wrong," she interrupted. "I'm sorry I can't explain it any better, but—"

The phone in the kitchen rang and they both jumped. He didn't move, just glanced at it, then looked back at her as it sounded again.

"Aren't you going to pick up?" she asked.

He shook his head. "If it was an emergency they'd have called the pager or cell. Whoever that is can leave a message. Now, you were saying?"

"Actually I was finished. Now I'm leaving. It would be best."

"Best for who?" He dragged his fingers through his hair. "Just seems to me like you're running."

His voice on the machine came on and curtly ordered, "Leave a message."

A familiar female voice said, "Hi, baby, it's Blair. Europe was fabulous. My aunt is in from New York and is dying to meet my boyfriend. That would be you, in case you were wondering. Mother and Daddy are looking forward to seeing you for dinner Sunday. Can't wait to tell you all about my trip. Call me back."

Color drained from Hope's cheeks. A series of emotions kaleidoscoped across her expressive face before she whispered, "You have a girlfriend?"

Chapter Five

"It's not what you think," Jake said.

"It never is," Hope countered.

Sleeping with Jake made her a slimy cheater. Her husband was gone, but she didn't feel single. Death hadn't ended her feelings for him. Kevin was the first, last and only man she would ever let into her heart.

Now that she knew Jake was seeing someone, that made him a slimy cheater, too, not even in the same league with the husband she'd lost. Rampant gossip said Jake was a playboy, and by definition that meant many women and that alone made her choice bad. Stupid, actually, although in all the talk about him, there hadn't been a single hint of a girlfriend or even steadily dating anyone. But there was a woman out there who thought he was her boyfriend. He'd never said squat about that to Hope when there was a chance of *not* sleeping with him.

And *that* was the definition of low.

Hope stared at him and knew she was going to hell for sure when desire simmered through her again. So which one of them was the lowest of the low?

Damn him for standing there in worn jeans that hugged his hips and legs like a sexy second skin and a shirt he hadn't bothered to button. Double damn him for showing off the hair-dusted masculine chest she badly wanted to explore again.

Jake rested his hands on those lean hips. "Look, how about I fix us a drink? We can take a breath and have a civilized conversation—"

"No."

"Which one?" He folded his arms over his chest. "Drink? Or talk?"

"Both."

"You owe me a chance to explain."

"That's a joke, right?" She stared at his expression, not making the mistake of letting her gaze go lower. "You didn't really just say that I'm obliged to give you the opportunity to justify what just happened because you're a guy."

His eyes narrowed dangerously. "I *am* a guy. And I won't apologize for the fact that I want you."

Not past tense, she noted. That meant presently he still wanted her. For the life of her she couldn't figure out why that was so seductive, but it was. The spurt of desire dancing through her was proof. The only weapon she had to fight against it was anger.

She glared at him. "Maybe you should apologize for not telling me you're involved with someone."

"Blair and I are dating," he confirmed. "But there's never been a conversation about being exclusive."

"Actions speak louder than words," she pointed out. "Show, don't tell. The term *dating* implies some sort of relationship and is information worthy of sharing, don't you think?"

"You want information? Here's some. We're friends. Our paths crossed frequently because her father is Congressman Havens—"

"The president of the hospital's board of directors Congressman Havens?"

"Yes."

Hope felt her eyes widen. "The same man who gave you a career-making contract?"

"Yes, but it's not how it looks," he said again.

"You're right. This time it's actually worse, because it looks to me like you used her *and* you're cheating on her."

With me, Hope thought. That made her a cheater times two. The anger coursing through her was invigorating, sort of satisfying as guilt and grief fused, sparked and exploded, blotting out everything else.

"There's no possible way to put a positive spin on that," she added.

"For the record," he said, "before I asked her out, I ran it by her father, because I'd already declared an interest in the position. He assured me that his decision would be based on ability and experience."

"And showing his daughter a good time sure didn't hurt your chances of getting the contract, did it?"

"I'm not a liar, Hope. I've always been up front with Blair. She knows my career comes first and is okay with that."

"How wonderful for you. Such an understanding woman is so rare." She tried to mean that sincerely. Made a valiant attempt to strain the sarcasm from her voice. On both fronts she failed completely and just couldn't be sorry.

"Blair is a politician's daughter. She likes being seen with ambitious, up-and-coming men."

"And isn't that special? What are the odds of finding your female equivalent?" Hope asked. "Wow, a match made in heaven. You both have an agenda."

"That's not what I meant."

"What did you mean?" she asked.

"We have a good time together. There's been no discussion of taking things to the next level."

Hope resisted the longing to believe him. Giving in to that was the last thing she wanted because it would slick the way for her to slide right into caring. Not going there, she thought.

"Again, I say, show don't tell. If you're 'dating'—" Her tone added air quotes to the word. "There's every reason for her to expect loyalty from you."

"I am loyal," he defended. "And so is she. Companionship and respect for each other's goals has defined our friendship." He paused briefly, then added, "Until now."

She barely resisted the urge to ask what had changed now. It was a slippery slope and she didn't want to go back where she'd just been, a place where she might be tempted to think about a future. That was very dangerous. She was living proof that plans had a way of being blown to bits. With the luxury of hindsight she'd learned that it was best not to have expectations.

"Are you saying that all of a sudden you're not getting what you want from Blair? Or that you already got what you wanted and your goals have changed?"

"Neither. And that's a lot like a 'have you stopped beating your wife?' question." He looked frustrated and angry as a muscle in his lean jaw bunched and contracted. "I'm not a player, Hope."

She laughed, but there was no humor in it. The sound

was brittle and harsh. "That's not what hospital gossip says about your trauma group's token bachelor."

"Since I'm the only single doctor in the group, that makes me the bachelor. And hospital gossip is notoriously unreliable. Do you believe everything you hear?"

"Depends on who's saying it. You have a short memory, Doctor. Push the flashing red button on the answering machine. The message confirms the rumor that I heard about you being the last playboy standing."

"For what it's worth, I plan to tell Blair what happened between you and me."

"Good for you. Straighten out that halo. Maybe if you come clean she won't mind. But I do. Being the other woman isn't a role that I want to play."

His eyes flashed with irritation and he blew out a long breath. "Does picking a fight with me really help?"

"I'm not picking a fight. Just clearing the air."

"Then why is your pulse elevated? Respiration rapid and shallow?"

"Because I'm mad, that's why."

"And being deliberately unreasonable. Guilt does that to a person."

"What are you talking about?" she demanded.

"You're painting me with the bastard brush because it makes you feel better."

The jab hit too close to the mark. She lifted her chin slightly and said, "When you have this bare-your-soul conversation with Blair, be sure not to leave out the part about you being a fried Twinkie."

His eyes narrowed. "What are you talking about?"

"You know." She stepped around him and walked to the front door. After opening it she turned to find him right behind her. "A fried Twinkie—fluffy extravagance.

It's okay once in a while, but a steady diet is bad for the heart."

She walked out and slammed the door before he could answer. The chilly air cooled her hot cheeks, but the shivering had nothing to do with weather. Hurrying to her car, she got in and drove away as fast as she could. In case he tried to stop her.

It would only take a single touch.

She wasn't proud of that. She'd loved her husband with all her heart and it shamed her to think about how easily she'd succumbed to Jake's charm.

The "fried Twinkie" warning was just as relevant for her as it was for him. She'd had her taste, her indulgence. Guilty pleasure.

It was only sex; it was out of her system. Now she was going on a diet.

Jake sat across the table from Blair in a steakhouse on the second floor of the Suncoast Hotel in Summerlin. They were next to the drapery-framed windows that overlooked the glittering lights of the Las Vegas Valley. This place was one of his favorites. Good food. Great service. Although price wasn't an issue anymore, the cost was reasonable. The woman staring over the spotless white tablecloth, candles and flowers didn't feel the same way. Blair was into pricey, exclusive places where she could be seen and photographed with the rich and famous. It was a world where perception was everything.

So his choice of venue should have been a big clue that this dinner wasn't about impressing her.

Last night Hope had all but accused him of using Blair to get the hospital appointment. Years ago when he was nearly finished with college and applying to med school, someone else had accused him of using the woman he loved to buy his way into the big time. It wasn't true then, but he'd lost her anyway. There was just a little truth in what Hope had said, enough that he didn't like himself. It was a feeling he was too familiar with. He was here to make things right with Blair.

She was a beautiful, long-legged, blue-eyed brunette. In her lavender cashmere sweater and body-hugging black slacks, she was a stunner who turned men's heads every time she entered a room. He'd been one of those men, once upon a time. Tall women were his type. Until recently. If he were being honest with himself, it had changed when he met Hope. Somehow her compact, curvy little body had snagged his attention and wouldn't let go.

"You're preoccupied." Blair's foot slid up and down his calf as she sipped her white wine. "Is it work?"

If only. That would be less complicated. "No. Work is going fine. Couldn't be better."

"Is there a reason why you brought me to your favorite restaurant?"

He was a little surprised she remembered how much he liked this place. "Yes."

She looked around at the dark wood walls and crystal chandeliers overhead. Fresh flowers topped the snow-white tablecloths on every table. "I suppose it's romantic." Smiling, she reached across the table and touched his hand. "Is there something you want to ask me?"

"We need to talk."

"That's a chick line. Are you getting in touch with your feminine side, Jake?"

"It's more under the heading that confession is good for the soul."

A slight frown puckered the skin of her forehead. "Oh? That sounds ominous."

"I've met someone. A woman," he clarified.

A small smile curved her full lips. "If you'd confessed to meeting a man that would be seriously surprising."

"Actually it's more than that. I slept with her, Blair. Last night." He didn't mean to be quite so blunt, or add details, but there was no point in dragging this out either. He lifted the longneck bottle of beer to his mouth and took a drink, letting the information sink in.

"I see."

Then she was leaps and bounds ahead of him because he didn't see at all. "It wasn't planned. It just happened."

Jake was watching her face, the lack of immediate re-action, knowing what was coming. Wait for it. Wait. And there it was. A slight pursing of the mouth. The head tilt and hair toss followed by the pretty, practiced pout.

"Although we never officially committed to an exclusive arrangement, I have to admit that's not what I expected," she said.

Neither had he. Hope was a predicament he could never have foreseen. "I'm sorry."

"I suppose this is the night for it." She sighed. "I have to confess, too."

"Oh?"

"While I was in Monte Carlo, there was a man. Paolo. But it was just a fling. A very European thing." She reached over and covered his hand with hers. "I hope you're not upset, baby."

He wondered whether she would have confessed on her own if he hadn't. Or quite possibly it was a lie to keep the playing field level. And that was the thing. It never would be level if you compared their backgrounds side by side. She was way out of his league. She'd grown up in a gated estate in Las Vegas and a luxury home in Washington with private schools and tours of Europe. He'd been homeless and hungry. Scholarships and student loans paid for his education.

Whether she'd actually had a fling or was lying to make him jealous, it didn't matter. Unlike the last time he fell for someone out of his league, his heart wasn't damaged. He wasn't the least bit peeved. They'd been over for a while, but neither had taken the steps to officially end the relationship.

"I'm okay with it," he said.

"Really?"

"Really." He met her gaze. "Are you upset?"

"You're a man. I was gone a long time." She shrugged as if that made complete sense. Maybe it did in her world.

The waiter showed up to take their orders—filet mignon medium rare for both of them. Salads with oil and vinegar. Garlic mashed potatoes. He didn't plan on kissing her good-night. And it was as if the "aha" light went on inside him. Cuisine compatibility wasn't enough on which to base a deeper connection. Not that he wanted a deep connection, but there was no point in dragging on the little they had.

When they were alone again, she reached over and rested her hand on his again. "Now that everything is out in the open, we can discuss Senator Gold's fundraiser next month? It's a very high-profile event. Mainstream media will be covering it and Daddy thinks it would be good for us to be seen there."

He shook his head. "This isn't working, Blair."

"You mean us."

"Yes."

Again he waited for a reaction. Some show of genuine emotion. Something like Hope telling him he was the first man she'd been with since her husband died. And the tears glistening in her eyes when she'd said it. She'd cared deeply for the man she'd lost. He was jealous of a dead man, which made him pond scum. He'd wanted to hold Hope, just to offer comfort, but she'd looked as if she'd shatter at another touch, especially his.

"That depends on what you mean by working." Blair lifted one perfectly arched brow. "I think what we have is a mutually beneficial relationship. You have opportunities to meet politically powerful people. And I like being with a man who's going places, a man other women want to be with."

To her he was just another Paolo. A fling. A Las Vegas thing. Blair was unfazed that he'd been with another woman. Unlike Hope. She'd made her feelings about his behavior pretty clear. She'd shown genuine, uninhibited, honest emotion. She'd been clearly upset that there was another woman. Maybe she was jealous. That wouldn't upset him in the least.

On the contrary, her reaction produced a spark of hope that she might be interested in him. Hell, she slept with him, which should be a clue. Now he was comparing Hope to Blair as if he needed more proof that it was in Blair's best interest for him to break things off now. He would never deliberately hurt her and prolonging this had the potential to do that.

He slid his hand from beneath hers. "You're a wonderful woman, Blair. But I'm pretty sure that I'm not the right man for you."

"Daddy thinks you are."

"I have a great deal of respect for Congressman Havens, but a relationship between you and me is not his call to make."

"No, it's mine. And I think we shouldn't be too hasty about calling it quits."

"I don't agree. And in my opinion letting things go on as if nothing's wrong will hurt you in the long run."

"That's your official diagnosis, Doctor?" There was amusement in her tone.

He'd never claim to be an expert on touchy-feely stuff. But one thing he had in spades was street smarts. In his gut he knew he was doing the right thing. "As far as I'm concerned we shouldn't see each other anymore."

"We don't have to be exclusive." She sipped the last of her wine. "And I don't believe you and I are over, Jake."

They were definitely done, but there was no win in hammering home his point. He'd kept his promise to Hope about full disclosure with Blair. It was important that he end this complication even though he and Hope had agreed to a strictly professional association.

So he'd really just cleared the air with Blair because it was the smart thing to do. Pursuing anything personal at this juncture was not part of his career plan.

The problem was still Hope. He'd never met a woman who so completely tempted him to toss his career plan in the trash can.

Chapter Six

Two days after sleeping with Jake, Hope walked into the office of Mercy Medical West's president and tried to act professional. Val Davis was in her fifties, an attractive brown-eyed brunette with a stylishly layered, shoulder-length haircut and a reputation for an anal-retentive, obsessive-compulsive attention to details—in the nicest possible way. The artistic and color-coordinated ambience of this hospital, in addition to the no-expense-spared health care, was all about this woman. This facility was her baby and Hope knew she was as protective of it as any mother lion.

"Hi," she said from the office doorway.

Val glanced up from the paperwork on her desk and looked over the reading glasses on her nose. "Hope. Come in. Have a seat."

"Thanks."

She sat in one of the green tweed chairs in front of

the desk. The pale gold walls held pictures of seascapes and flowers. Family photos of her husband, two adult children—a boy and girl—were prominently displayed beside the computer monitor and coffee mug.

Hope had interviewed with the other two campus presidents and Val before accepting this temporary position. The woman had a friendly warmth that made her approachable, a positive quality in an administrator. She'd canceled their last two scheduled meetings due to building permit and certification issues.

"How are you holding up?" Hope asked, knowing her boss put in fourteen-hour-plus days, like so many of them were doing to open on schedule.

"Hanging in there." Val removed her glasses. "How are *you* doing?"

Hope wondered for half a second if the emphasis and nuance in her tone meant that she'd heard a rumor about her being with Jake. There was a reason every soap opera on TV had a hospital in it. Probably she was just hypersensitive because the guilt of what she'd done was heavy on her heart.

"By that I'm guessing you're asking whether or not I have hearing loss from the fire alarms going off constantly?"

"Oh," Val said wryly. "I was hoping you hadn't heard that."

Hope laughed. "Just a guess, but that high-pitched shrieky sound is kind of designed to get your attention."

"Lord knows it's taken a lot of mine," the other woman said ruefully. "It seems that the manufacturer put in cheap smoke dampers that won't close."

"Not my area of expertise," Hope said. "But by definition aren't they supposed to shut and contain smoke in the event of fire?"

"Yeah. The whole system starts with the alarm which

triggers the dampers. Then the fire doors close automatically and the sprinklers go on."

"The domino effect," Hope said.

"Exactly. But if the damn dampers don't close, we can't pass the fire inspection and the fire marshal won't give us the go-ahead to accept patients. We had to get a special dispensation for that dignitary open house the week before last."

Hope remembered it well and not because of the dignitaries. It was the night Jake had kissed her for the first time. If the alarms weren't functioning properly, that would explain why the heat they'd generated hadn't triggered the high-pitched shrieky noise.

Maybe if the sprinklers had soaked them that first time, she'd have avoided an even bigger mistake. The man was a two-timing cheater. *So* not her type. *So* not noble like her husband. And not even thinking the worst of Jake could get him out of her mind.

That made a mockery of the agreement to make their association all about the work, because even in this meeting thoughts of him had crept in. What were they talking about? Oh, right. Fire.

"So is the system fixed?" she asked Val.

"It is. After much swearing and gnashing of teeth," the woman confirmed. "You'd think we could just replace the dampers, but nothing is ever that easy. Doing that would require ripping out the ceilings."

"Yikes."

"No kidding. So, we had to change the motors. And that did the trick. This morning each section of the hospital was tested."

"I heard." The alarms had gone on for hours. "There were a lot of areas to check."

"The good news is you just passed your employee

hearing test." Val grinned. "And the building passed the fire inspection. We got a gold star."

"Good for you."

"I know more about fire alarms than I ever wanted to." Val took a deep breath. "So how's E.D.?"

"The emergency department is coming along fine."

Val checked her notes. "Good. I wanted to clarify with you the protocols for O.R. availability."

"Okay."

"As I'm sure you're aware, surgeons have a problem when an operating room stands empty. But it's standard trauma procedure to always have one open in the event an E.R. patient needs emergency surgery."

Hope nodded. "Right. If it becomes an issue for the surgeons, I'll remind of the administration directive."

"Another way to say refer them to me. That works. Next on my agenda—reasons to go on trauma divert."

Hope glanced at her notes. "Equipment. CT scan down. Shortage of personnel in the event of trauma saturation."

"Right." Val met her gaze. "Everyone needs to be on the same page as far as evaluating which trauma room to put a patient in. Some are set up specifically for head or belly trauma, others for less serious cases."

"Right." Hope jotted things down on the notepad she'd brought in with her.

"Now E.D. staffing," Val said.

"I imagine it's going to be slow at first," Hope said. "We might have to flex off some of the staff if there's not enough work to support the load. I'll make them aware of that."

"Good. I talked to Dr. Edwards."

Hope remembered the radiology specialist raising his issues at her meeting. "He was upset about paying his doctors for round-the-clock staffing whether or not there were cases."

Val nodded. "I set him straight on that and administration will *not* be kicking in anything. He signed the contract. Doctors *need* to be here so that this hospital can maintain its trauma-level designation. I've gotten the hospital legal department in the loop in case that becomes an issue."

"Good." Hope tapped her lip. "Speaking of staff…"

Val looked up quickly. "Yes?"

"It's come to my attention that Dr. Andrews…" How could she phrase this delicately? "I have a concern about his appointment to chief trauma surgeon."

"In what way?"

"It has to do with who he knows being a factor in why he got the job. That makes me wonder about his qualifications for the position."

And that one word sent her thoughts straight to his bedroom and him hovering over her.

"You're new in town," Val pointed out. "Have you talked to some of the veteran staff members who've been around a while?"

"Yes. But I thought it best to ask you. To separate real from rumor."

She hoped that her behavior wasn't making its way through the Mercy Medical gossip mill. If she could erase what happened that night, she'd do it in a heartbeat.

"Okay. This is off the record." Val leaned back, shaking her head.

"What?"

"I'm aware that Jake is dating Blair Havens."

"The daughter of the hospital's board of directors," Hope confirmed.

"Yes. But you shouldn't hold that against him."

Personally? Or professionally? Because either way she

was doing her level best to constructively use the information and put up barriers.

"Why?" she asked.

"Jake Andrews is a good doctor. And a smart businessman. Most important, he's a brilliant surgeon. Regardless of who he shows the bad judgment to see when he's not on duty, the man's hands are pure magic."

That's something Hope was well aware of. It had nothing to do with surgery, scalpels or sutures, and everything to do with seduction, satisfaction and seeing stars. His hands and mouth had taken her to places she'd never been before. Not ever. And that could very well be the source of her guilt.

She'd loved Kevin and losing him had hurt deeply. It still did. But she'd never experienced need like she had in Jake's arms. That meant there was some kind of connection which was exactly what she was trying to avoid.

Now she knew and had independent confirmation of the fact that he wasn't free. That should help put him out of her mind because so far she'd been unsuccessful. She wished, and not for the first time, that she'd left him stranded that night. Now she was in a complication that proved no good deed goes unpunished.

On the bright side, he was seeing someone. That gave her a level of protection from his specific brand of temptation. He was comfortable juggling women but couldn't if she refused to be juggled.

It was close to 7:00 p.m., past time to leave the hospital, and Hope was still studying the budget spreadsheet on her computer. Keeping the emergency department within the parameters of the allocated funds was going to mean sacrifices, doing more with less. In today's world where individuals were more concerned about themselves and paranoid about being treated unfairly, managing personalities was going to be a challenge. The staff needed a charismatic director who could lead by example.

Kevin had been that way, she remembered sadly. He'd put in more hours than the Department of Children and Families could pay for because he loved kids. If he'd been more selfish and less heroic, he would still be with her.

The sound of voices in the hall outside her office broke up her pity party. She'd forgotten to shut her door and walked around her desk to do that. A few feet away, she stopped, recognizing Jake's deep voice. It always triggered a ball of heat in her belly and did now, even though she couldn't see him.

"This place feels like a hotel. It's really something." The male voice was unfamiliar. "But it's too far away for me to do hospital rounds. You know my office is on Horizon Ridge. That makes seeing patients at this facility problematic."

"What did you think of the MRI and the new cath lab, Dean?"

That was a clue to Hope that he was talking to Dr. Dean Harrison, a busy internist.

"It's very cool, and you know it, Jake."

"How about the gamma knife?" There was just the slightest bit of snake-oil salesman wheedling in Jake's tone.

"Remarkable. No pun intended—cutting-edge."

"Good one. It's state-of-the-art medicine," Jake said. "So it takes you a couple minutes out of your way. Isn't that a small price to pay? Here, your patients won't have to wait for a bed like they do at Mercy Medical's main campus."

Hope remembered his talking about the patient billed for ICU, intermediate care and step-down beds when he never left the E.R. There was certainly a need for more acute-care beds in the Vegas Valley. But change was never easy and people pushed back even if it was good change.

"Tell you what, Jake," the other man said, "I'll think about coming on staff here at Mercy Medical West if you'll agree to speak at the Nevada Hospital Council in Reno next month."

"Happy to do it," Jake said.

"I'm holding you to that." Hope could picture the doctor pointing a finger at Jake. "Thanks for the private tour. This place really is impressive."

She heard retreating footsteps and went back to her desk. The two doctors were gone now, so there was no reason to shut her door.

"Knock, knock." The words were followed by a light tap.

Unlike her heart which was tapping like crazy. She braced herself as best she could and looked up. "Jake."

"Hope."

They stared awkwardly at each other for several moments while she wished he would go away and stop torturing her. Finally she asked, "Was there something you wanted?"

The way his eyes turned to silver told her that was a bad choice of words even as a rebellious little thrill skipped through her.

"You're here late," he said, not answering the question.

"So are you. Blair must be busy." She pressed her lips together and wished it were possible to rewind or delete the previous words.

"I honestly have no idea what her plans are." He leaned a shoulder against the doorjamb, deliberately not moving closer. "I'm laying off sugar and fat. Especially no cream-filled sponge cake."

"No more fried Twinkie?" She picked up a pen and nervously pressed the top, pushing the ballpoint's tip in and out.

"I will neither confirm nor deny engaging in such behavior."

"Okay." Her tone left no doubt about what she believed.

"I'm here touting the merits of Mercy Medical West to one of my colleagues."

"So I heard."

"You were eavesdropping?" One dark eyebrow lifted as a teasing expression slid over his face.

"Not on purpose," she defended. "But I couldn't help overhearing the *deal* you made with Dr. Harrison."

"Deal? Interesting choice of words. If I didn't know better, I'd say you disapproved."

"Not me."

"All evidence to the contrary," he drawled. "What do you have against a speaking engagement?"

"Rumor has it that you're a gifted surgeon."

"Really? Says who?"

She didn't want to inflate his already-inflated ego, *or* admit to asking about him. "Does it matter?"

"Yeah. I need to know who to thank with flowers."

She sighed and gripped the pen tighter. "I had a meeting with Val Davis. We were discussing staffing for the emergency department. Your name came up."

"In reference to fried food?"

"Are you ever going to let that go?" she asked.

"Probably not." He slid his fingers into his dark slacks, lifting the bottom of the expensive matching jacket. "But back to me being good at my job."

"She said—" Hope bit back the words on the tip of her tongue. The exact quote: *No matter who Jake showed the bad judgment to see when he wasn't on duty, the man's hands were pure magic.* She shivered again as a vision flashed through her mind of those strong sensitive hands skimming over her skin as she lay beside him in his bed. The ball of fire in her belly got bigger and hotter. "She said you're a good doctor and a brilliant surgeon."

"So a nice big bouquet of flowers to Val's office for the hospital grand opening." He smiled.

His grin could bring women to their knees and made Hope glad she'd showed the good sense to remain seated.

"Don't you think it's a better use of your time and reputed talent to take those skills out for a spin in the operating room instead of the boardroom?"

"Community engagements put the hospital's name and excellent reputation in front of the public." His teasing tone disappeared and she missed it.

"In Reno?"

"It's not far from Carson City, the capital of the state and seat of government. There's a lot of media attention for the hospital council and part of my job is to spotlight Mercy Medical West for donations and grants to fund health programs."

He had a point, darn it, but she wouldn't say those words out loud. "Okay. And all work no play makes Jake… Well, you get the drift."

His eyes narrowed as he straightened, still in her office doorway. "You've been taking a lot of shots at me. What's really bugging you?"

"Nothing."

He moved into the office, close enough to smell the spicy scent of his aftershave. "This is about sex, isn't it?"

"No."

"This is Vegas, Hope. You need to work on your bluffing skills."

"I'll take that under advisement."

"So we slept together. Big deal. Over and done with."

This was a bad time to wish she'd closed her office door. "It's already forgotten."

He shook his head. "If that were true, you wouldn't be acting like I was the sleazy saloon owner who stole the new schoolmarm's virtue."

"Respect has to be earned." And he hadn't earned hers, she thought.

"If I could take back what happened, I would," he said. "It wasn't the wisest thing I've ever done."

"Oh?"

"The fact is we need to clear the air. Sexual attraction impairs judgment and makes people do stupid things. It jeopardizes the mission and puts the goal at risk." He ran his fingers through his hair. "We need to fix this. Find a way to be cordial. Go back to the way we were."

The way they were? Exactly where was that? Sexual tension snapped between them from the moment their eyes met. Going back there was not a good place to take a stand.

"I have nothing against you, Jake." Except for the fact that her hormones whimpered every time she heard his voice or set eyes on him. That wasn't his fault, but it didn't stop her from resenting him for it. "I guess my behavior is about motivation. You could say that I believe challenge keeps people on their toes."

"You're challenging me?"

"Yes."

"You want a challenge?" He moved and stopped just on the other side of her desk, looking down as intensity snapped in his eyes. "I've got one for you. What have you done for people lately?"

"What?"

"You know. People. The less fortunate. Have you worked with Habitat for Humanity? Built a house? Served meals at a shelter? Do you throw out seed for the spotted owls?"

"They're not people."

She'd gotten on his last nerve, but this was not the best time to notice that he was sexy when he was angry. His eyes darkened and her stomach dropped as if she were on the down loop of a roller coaster. This had definitely backfired. This intense Jake was even more compelling than the easygoing, teasing one. This steely-eyed man made her *want* again.

"You want to talk people? I can do that." He stared down at her. "You're a nurse, right?"

"You know I am."

He glared at the framed Nevada nursing license hanging on the wall behind her. Without warning he took the pen out of her hands, careful not to touch her. He grabbed a square of sticky notes from her desk and wrote something on it, then tossed it back in front of her.

"If you really want to help, be there. Eight o'clock Saturday morning." He punctuated the words with a frown, then walked to the doorway. "And, Hope?"

"What?"

"If you don't chicken out and actually show up, be prepared to use your nursing license for more than wall decoration."

The words were barely out of his mouth and he was gone. It felt as if she'd been caught up in the vortex and power of a tornado, then suddenly dropped to earth. Hard. Jake Andrews had basically told her to put up, or shut up. And she had to hand it to him; the logic was brilliant.

She couldn't back away from the challenge no matter how much she wanted to back away from the man.

Chapter Seven

Eight o'clock Saturday morning Hope showed up at the appointed place, a community center near the downtown Regional Justice Center. It was an old stucco building with small circular marks she swore were bullet holes. She walked inside where there was a large waiting room. About ten or twelve people sat in folding metal chairs. Three young boys were on the floor, playing quietly. In the front of the room there was an oblong table where a woman was doing paperwork.

Hope walked up to her. "Hi. I'd like to—"

"Here you go." She smiled and held out a clipboard. "Just fill these out. The second form is a medical history and we need you to be as thorough as possible."

"I'm not here to see the doctor." That wasn't exactly true, Hope realized. Her heart beat a little faster at the thought of seeing Jake Andrews, but she wouldn't admit that had anything to do with why she'd accepted his challenge and shown up. "I'm Hope Carmichael. A nurse. Dr. Andrews asked me to come by today."

"Nice to meet you." The thirtysomething, jeans-clad brunette was wearing a badge that identified her as an employee at Mercy Medical Women's Wellness Center. "Liz Healy. And I'm happy to see another pair of hands. Although not surprised. Jake has a way of inspiring volunteers."

Inspiring was one way to put it. Hope thought verbal pressure was more accurate. He'd dared her to come. "Can you tell me where to find him?"

The woman nodded. "He's doing outpatient surgical procedures. Around the corner at the end of the hall."

"Thanks."

She followed the directions and noticed computer-generated signs taped to the closed doors starting with "Exam Room 1" and so on down the corridor. In the doorway to the room straight ahead she saw Jake talking to a young blond woman. She stopped, giving him privacy with the patient. But then he glanced her way and smiled before continuing the conversation. His voice drifted to her.

"I aspirated the cyst," he told the woman.

"You're absolutely sure it's not breast cancer?" she asked anxiously.

"No. Tumors are solid. A mass. There's nothing to suck out," he said, simply and firmly.

"I'm so relieved, Doctor. I didn't want to come here. It's very hard for us to take a handout. We lost our health benefits when my husband was laid off. He's so proud and determined to provide for his family. But he insisted I come here. He's in the waiting room with the kids."

"How many do you have?" Jake asked.

"Three. All boys. They keep me pretty busy—" Her

voice caught. "I was so afraid I wasn't going to be around to see them grow up."

"Hey." Jake dropped his hand to her shoulder and gave her a reassuring squeeze. "Boys hate to see their mom cry."

"I'm sorry. But a breast lump is pretty scary."

"Yeah, it is. And now you know there's nothing to worry about. You may have some discomfort from the procedure, but over-the-counter pain medication should take care of it. Don't take more than the recommended dosage. And don't be playing tackle football with the boys."

She laughed. "Can I have a doctor's note to get me out of cooking?"

He patted the side pocket of his white lab coat. "I've got a prescription pad right here. I can write up something about pampering mom and picking up toys. Doctor's orders."

"If only…" She held out her hand. "Thank you again, Doctor. For everything."

Jake took her fingers in his. "You're welcome."

The woman smiled when she passed, then Hope met him in front of the door to Exam Room 8. "Hi."

"Hi, yourself. I see you found the place."

"Yes."

She'd found more than the place. Jake had definitely taken his halo out, dusted it off and settled it securely in a holding pattern above his head. She found out he was an honest-to-goodness hero, judging by the expression on that young mom's face.

"You were really wonderful with that woman."

He shrugged. "It's easy when the news is good."

She glanced down the hall where a door opened and a man walked out with what looked like a prescription in his hand.

She met Jake's gaze. "You're not the only doctor here?"

"No."

"And you do this out of the goodness of your heart?"

He slid his hands into the lab coat pockets. "I'm not sure what gave you the impression that my heart is two sizes too small, but I do have one. This endeavor has nothing to do with business and everything to do with helping people who need it."

She was trying to think of a way to frame a question about his motivation and couldn't come up with anything that didn't sound snarky. After the gentle and reassuring bedside manner she'd just seen, snark was totally inappropriate. So she finally just said, "Why?"

His eyes narrowed, but not before going stormy as shadows flitted through the gray. There was desolation there, too. She wasn't sure how she knew that except maybe it takes one to know one. She'd experienced despair and when you've gone through something like that, it wasn't hard to recognize the look in someone else.

"Why do I do it?" Anger chased away the darkness. "Because I know how it feels to have absolutely nothing."

Surprise didn't come close to describing what Hope felt. He was the golden boy with the magic hands. She'd seen his home and knew the price tag would make the average person as pale as his white coat. It was really hard to comprehend his having nothing. *Absolutely nothing.*

But she realized something else, too. Jake Andrews was one-dimensional only in her mind. She had assumed things about him, made unflattering assumptions that she'd *wanted* to be true. The fact was, she knew hardly anything about him and now very much wanted to change that.

"Jake, I—"

"Dr. Andrews?"

The female voice was laced with alarm and diverted Jake's attention. "What, Liz?"

"There's a little girl here. Pretty bad leg laceration."

"Bring her back right away," he said.

"She's out in the car. Mom's in the waiting room. Borderline hysterical."

"Okay."

He ran down the hall and out the door. Hope followed and it wasn't hard to find the emergency. A small, older compact was right outside the door.

A reed-thin woman straightened from the rear passenger side of the car and waved them over. "Taylor fell off her bike."

"How old is she?" Jake asked, before leaning in to examine the child.

"Ten," the mom answered.

A moment later he looked at Hope. "I'm going to carry Taylor inside. Can you handle the mom?"

"Of course."

He bent into the opening and talked to the child. "Hey, kiddo, I'm going to pick you up. I'll be as careful as I can not to hurt you. I'm a doctor. My name is Jake. I'll have this leg fixed in no time." In spite of his cheerful running commentary, the little girl started to cry.

He gently lifted her out of the car. Her brown hair was coming loose from her ponytail and tears made tracks through the dirt on her face. There was a towel covering the lower half of her leg which she held stiff and straight out in front of her. As if she weighed nothing, Jake carried her through the door Liz held open.

"There was so much blood," the woman said, looking at her hands.

"What's your name?" Hope asked.

"Mary Ferguson. I didn't know what to do. I'm a single

mom. I don't have medical insurance or much money. But she's my baby—"

"You did the right thing." Hope slipped her arm around the woman's shoulders.

"The emergency room costs a lot. My neighbor told me about the clinic."

"Your daughter is in excellent hands. The doctor will take good care of her."

Liz met them inside the door. "Hope, Dr. Andrews took Taylor to Exam Room 2 and wants you to meet him there." She looked at the mother. "He asked if you could fill out the paperwork."

"I don't have insurance," she protested, panic in her voice again. "It's not free?"

"There's no charge," Liz assured her. "But the doctor needs a permission form signed in order to treat your daughter. And a complete medical history—any allergies to food or medications. That sort of thing."

Mary nodded. "Okay."

Hope left her with the volunteer and went to Exam Room 2, then tossed her purse into a corner. The little girl was sitting up on the table, her legs stretched out in front of her.

Jake stood beside the exam table. "Gloves are in the bottom drawer with disposable gowns."

She found the items, washed her hands, then gowned and gloved herself. She joined him beside the table as he cut away the jeans to give him a clear field of vision for treating the laceration.

"Bike one, Taylor nothing," he said grimly.

Hope saw that the wound was deep and would need stitches.

"I want my mommy. I wanna go home," the little girl sobbed.

Hope didn't miss the look he slid her. The mother was too distraught at the moment to help keep this child calm. It was up to them to establish a trusting relationship with her.

"Your mom has to fill out some forms. As soon as she's finished, she'll come and see you."

"My leg hurts," she said, still crying.

"I know. As soon as I fix it up, you'll be out of here," he promised.

"What are you gonna do?" Taylor's brown eyes were wide and tearful. "I don't want stitches."

"I can understand why that would upset you," Jake said. "But here's the thing… If we don't, you're going to have a scar."

"I don't care."

"Okay." He looked thoughtful. "But your boyfriend might have something to say about it."

The girl stopped sniffling. "I don't have a boyfriend."

"But you like boys, right?" He was channeling her attention away from the painful laceration.

"Eww." She scrunched up her freckle-splashed nose.

"Okay." He pressed his lips together to hide a smile. Glancing at Hope, he asked, "Taylor, why don't you like boys?"

"They're mean to me," she said.

"How?" he asked. "What do they do?"

She rubbed a finger beneath her nose. "Laugh."

"There's nothing wrong with laughing, right?"

"They make fun of me," she said. "Some of the girls do, too. My shoes are old. Or Mommy puts patches on my clothes."

"That is mean," he agreed. A muscle jerked in his jaw as he clenched it. "Those boys are dorks. Or dweebs. Or jerks—whatever the current word is that kids use."

"Mommy says it's not nice to call people names."

"Your mom is a nicer person than I am. Kids who make fun of other kids don't deserve any consideration." He looked angry enough to test the limits of the "first do no harm" portion of his Hippocratic oath.

But Hope was pretty sure she knew where he was going with the whole girl/boy issue. Someday this girl was going to grow up and care about how her legs looked. He needed to pull the ragged edges of the gash together to facilitate healing and minimize any scarring.

"Is it possible that some day you *might* like boys?" she asked.

"No," the child said stubbornly.

"Hope likes boys." The tension in Jake's face eased as he looked at her. "Right, Hope?"

"Sometimes." Although not now that he was going down this road, she thought.

"And do boys like you?" There was a gleam in his eyes because he knew she had to give him an answer fit for young ears.

"No."

"You're wrong about that. I'm a boy and I like you very much," he said.

"But you like lots of girls," she shot back.

"I do." He nodded. "But not as much as I like you. And one of the first things I noticed was your legs. In that very pretty black dress you wore the night of the hospital open house."

Her heart was hammering at the same time she wanted to wring his neck. No one could ever say the man didn't know how to multitask. He was teasing her hormones at the same time he talked a little girl into letting him stitch up her leg.

"He didn't laugh at you?" Taylor asked, looking back and forth between them.

"No." She remembered that his mouth had been too busy kissing her for him to laugh.

Jake smiled and the smug expression on his face indicated he was thinking about that kiss, too. "Taylor, I want you to think about something. You may not like boys now, but some day you could. And if you do, there's just a chance that you might care whether or not you have a bad scar on your leg."

Taylor bit her lip, clearly in conflict about what to do. "If you don't do stitches, will it be a gross scar?"

He looked thoughtful and so darn cute. "I wouldn't say gross. But it might make you self-conscious." When she frowned, he added, "You might want to always wear long pants to hide it. Do you like to go swimming?"

She nodded hesitantly. "Mommy takes me to the pool at the park near our apartment on her day off."

"And summers here in Las Vegas are pretty hot." He settled a disposable drape over her leg with a cutout that had a big enough field to work in. "Did you ever fall in the water with your clothes on?"

"Once. At Lake Mead."

"They were pretty heavy, right?" When she nodded he said, "So you don't really want to go swimming with your clothes on, do you?"

"No." She met his gaze with resignation in her own. "Do stitches hurt?"

"I'll tell you the truth. I have to give you medicine to make it not hurt. And it sounds kind of stupid, but that will hurt. Just a little pinch from a tiny needle, I promise." He rested his hands on the table as he met her gaze. "If it hurts more than that, I'll let you punch me as hard as you can."

Taylor giggled. "Okay."

And just like that the glare from his halo was blinding. Against the odds, Jake had managed to secure this child's cooperation. *And* he made her laugh. Granted, she was female, but because she didn't like boys, that canceled out the charm factor. Except, his charm was pretty potent stuff and it didn't much matter how old a girl happened to be. He was absolutely wonderful with children.

Hope felt the familiar sadness trickle through her, but for a different reason. She'd wanted children so much, but that dream died with her husband. She loved kids and missing out on being a mom made her hurt for what would never be.

Oddly enough, watching Jake make this little girl laugh coaxed a smile out of Hope, too. And the warmth of it seeped through her, making the dark places in her soul a little smaller, a little brighter.

"You should have promised Taylor that you'd let *me* sock you if the stitches hurt."

Jake chewed the last bite of his burrito as he studied Hope. They were in a booth at a Mexican restaurant around the corner from the clinic. It still wasn't clear to him how he'd talked her into dinner. Maybe she was just hungry.

He watched her lick a piece of rice off her bottom lip and knew tacos and refried beans wouldn't fill him up in the places he was empty. He was hungry, but not for food and she'd made it clear a friendly dinner was all she could give.

"You think you could hurt me?" he asked, studying her slender shoulders. "I outweigh you by at least eighty or ninety pounds."

"It's not what you've got, but how you use it." When the double meaning sank in, she went still.

And just like that the wanting he usually managed to

control went nuts. If there was a way to go back, to a time before he'd made love to her, he would give anything to find it.

She ate the last of her taquitos and managed to meet his gaze. "I know some self-defense moves."

"Did your husband teach you?" he asked, then wanted to kick himself when the light in her eyes dimmed.

"Yes. He worked for the Department of Children and Families in Texas. That put him in domestic situations that always had the potential to be volatile. He learned how to handle himself and taught me." For a moment she looked as if she was remembering something painful, then the shadows disappeared. "So tell me how you got involved in the clinic."

Way to turn the conversation away from yourself, he thought. Although he wanted to press her for answers, there was a part of him that didn't want to know. More revelations meant more bonding and he'd done that too fast as it was. Just then, the waiter stopped by their table to remove their dinner plates.

When they were alone again, Jake said, "It's been almost a year since one of the nuns at Mercy Medical approached me about volunteering at the clinic. The need really escalated when the economy soured and so many people lost their medical insurance along with their jobs. They couldn't afford treatment."

"Who funds the project?" Hope ran her index finger up and down the condensation on the outside of her glass.

"It's community outreach through Mercy Medical Center. To maintain their tax-exempt status, they can't show a profit on paper. To do that they channel money into projects like the free clinic."

"And now you see patients there on a regular basis."

"Originally I was asked to gather medical supplies and assemble volunteers."

"As Liz said—" Hope's full lips curved upward as she smiled. "You have a way of inspiring people to volunteer."

He shrugged. "It's a gift."

Her amusement vanished as quickly as it appeared. "Who's responsible for the building expenses?"

"The hospital. They pay rent and utilities. As word of mouth spreads, docs have been sending over patients and we treat them at no charge."

"Like Taylor," she pointed out. "Her mom said a neighbor told her about the clinic. But what if a patient needs a prescription? Or labs?"

"I'm glad you asked." And he was. If he talked shop, it took his mind off how much he wanted to kiss her. "I'm in the process of working out a deal with the largest diagnostics company in the valley. I think they'll be on board for doing routine lab work at no charge. And a local pharmaceutical company partnered with the clinic from the beginning so patients could get medications at no cost."

Hope drank the last of her soda and sighed. "I'm so full. How is that possible when I was so hungry only ten minutes ago?"

"That's what happens when you work through lunch." He looked at her in the dim light. He preferred the word dim to romantic, although it was that, too. "You were great today, by the way."

Jake had goaded her into coming because she'd ticked him off, always assuming the worst about him. Technically, he wasn't a bastard; his parents had been married when he was born. His dad left later, when they'd needed him most. But maybe there *was* more of his father in him than he wanted to acknowledge, which could explain why he was the last bachelor standing. He never wanted to do to a woman what his father had done to his mother.

"It's getting late," she said. "I should go."

He almost tried to talk her out of it. Words to that effect were on the tip of his tongue, but he bit them back. Instead he signaled their waiter for the check.

A moment later, the restaurant owner, Jose Castillo, appeared at their table. "Did you save any room for dessert, Doctor?"

When Hope groaned and shook her head, he laughed. "Not tonight. Just the check please."

Jose shook his head. "For you, it is on the house. There is no charge. It is my way of paying it forward. In these difficult times we all do what we can to help."

"Thanks, Jose, but I don't mind—"

"I wouldn't hear of it." The dark-skinned man bowed slightly from the waist. "Come and see us again soon."

"Two weeks," Jake said. "That's when I'll be back to the clinic."

"Thank you so much," Hope said to their host.

"It is my pleasure. I wish you both a pleasant evening."

Jake left a generous tip before they walked outside where the chilly January wind hit them head-on. Hope burrowed into her light sweater which wasn't nearly enough to protect her from the cold. Jake found himself wanting to do that. He wanted to pull her against him, share body heat, but he held back. And the effort cost him.

"That was really nice of him to not charge us for dinner."

"Yes."

"Obviously word of your good deeds has also spread," she said wryly.

"What can I say? They love me."

Unlike Hope, who carefully kept him at arm's length. After he found out she'd lost her husband, that made more sense. But her low opinion of him rankled. Pushing her into coming today was about showing her that he wasn't the greedy, career-focused man she thought. At least not entirely. He wanted her to admit that he had some admirable qualities.

When she didn't, he looked down. "Don't you think it's about time for you to concede that I'm not quite the rogue you thought?"

"No." But the look she sent him was full of laughter. "Not after you put me on the spot in front of that little girl."

"You mean about liking boys?" He slid his hands into his jeans pockets. "I was winging it."

"You really rocked the wings and halo today."

"Careful, that sounded like a compliment."

They'd stopped beside her rental car and she was looking up at him. Staring at her mouth spiked his testosterone levels to the point of crowding out common sense and he simply couldn't help himself. He dipped his head and claimed her lips. He braced his hands on her car, trapping her between his arms as his lower body brushed against hers. She groaned, a throaty reluctant sound that started the blood pounding in his ears.

Jake traced her lips with his tongue and she opened. He swept inside and caressed her mouth, imitating what he so badly wanted to do with her again. Their harsh breathing drowned out the wicked gusts of wind and any rational thought he might have mustered. Not a chance in hell, what with her soft body next to his.

Then he heard her moan, a hesitant, almost unwilling sound as she pressed her palms to his chest. He lifted his mouth from hers, satisfaction swirling through him when he saw that her breathing was as ragged as his own.

"Jake—" There was regret in the single word.

"Don't say it," he warned.

She drew in a deep gulp of air. "One of us has to say it and apparently it's my turn to bring the willpower."

"Self-discipline is not all it's cracked up to be," he said.

"This is a bad idea. We agreed."

"That was before. This is now," he ground out.

"And nothing has changed. I still refuse to be the other woman."

She turned and opened the car door, forcing him to step back. When he did, she slid inside and closed herself off before he could tell her she wasn't the other woman. As she pulled out of the parking lot he thought it was probably for the best. Being alone wasn't the worst thing that could happen to him.

But alone after Blair was very different from being alone after Hope. He didn't like the feeling of cold that seeped deep inside him as he watched her taillights disappear.

Chapter Eight

Jake hated Mondays.

As a medical student, one of the first things he'd learned was that treating the sick and injured was a twenty-four-hour-a-day, seven-days-a-week profession. But the first day of the traditional week always seemed worse.

Friday, Saturday and Sunday you expected traumas. It was the weekend. People were off and out playing, usually too hard. Stuff happened. MVA. GSW. Domestic violence. He and his partners in the trauma practice expected emergencies and were prepared for them. They moved fast, made decisions, saved lives. They worried about the rest later.

Monday was when "the rest" had to be cleaned up. Charges. Billing. Follow-up appointments.

He pulled into the parking lot just off Eastern Avenue, where he and his partners had their office not far from Mercy Medical Center. There was a small reception

area with an adjacent cubicle where the two reception-
ists answered the phone and handled patient charts and
paperwork.

Jake walked in and down the hall, waving to Ashley
Gable, his office manager. He'd hired her even though she
was young and inexperienced, taken a chance when her
sharp intelligence impressed him during her job interview.
With her help, he'd set up the clerical part of the practice—
medical records, insurance and billing. She'd been there
two years and he didn't know what he'd do without her.
With luck he wouldn't have to find out.

"Hey," he said, passing by the doorway to her office.

"You have a visitor," the blue-eyed redhead told him.

He slowed, then backed up and poked his head in.
Ashley was sitting at her desk, looking at the computer
monitor.

"Who is it?" he asked.

"The dragon lady."

He took a wild guess. "You are aware that her name is
Blair?"

Ashley shrugged. "You say potato, I say po-tah-to."

"You don't like her." It wasn't a question.

"Not much, no."

Ashley had never pulled her punches where Blair was
concerned and Jake had never called her on it. Maybe because deep down he'd known Ashley was right.

"Okay."

"Do you need backup?" she asked. "One of those stilet-
tos could put your eye out."

He fought a smile. "I think I can handle her."

"Right." She tilted her head to the side, appraising. "I
think you'd look roguish with a patch over your eye. What
the well-dressed pirate would wear."

"Have a little faith."

"Okay. Just leave my door open so I can hear when you holler for help."

He grinned, nodded, then backed up and continued down the hall. He passed the conference room with the big mahogany table and three high-backed leather chairs, then turned right into his office and saw Blair.

"And Monday it is," he muttered. "Hi, Blair."

"Hi," she answered cheerfully.

Sitting in the leather barrel-back chair in front of his desk, her long legs were crossed. She was wearing pricey jeans tailored to showcase every curve with a crisp white blouse tucked into them. A navy pullover sweater was loosely tied at her neck and a four-inch black leather stiletto sandal dangled from her red-painted toes. Thick, layered brown hair framed her stunning face. She was walking, talking male fantasy material and all he could think was he wished Hope had been sitting there instead.

He walked around the desk and sat, then hit the power switch on his computer. "What's up?"

"You're going to work?" There was a hint of pout in her voice.

"Yes." He met her gaze. "Did you want something?"

She usually did.

"I'd like you to take me to dinner."

"Can't." Aside from the fact that he had a lot of work to take care of, they were no longer together. "I've got stuff to do."

"I know how you hate Monday, so I'm here to take your mind off all that 'stuff' from the weekend."

Good luck with that, he thought. It would take a coma to make him forget kissing Hope. The heat generated by the barest touch of their lips burned promises of professional-ism right out of his mind. Then she had to go and spoil it by bringing in willpower. Restraint was highly overrated, at least until reality had set in.

He looked at Blair and pulled his self-control together. They'd had fun, but it was over now.

Jake shook his head. "It's not a good idea."

"Which part?" She tucked a strand of hair behind her ear. "Dinner? Or taking your mind off work?"

"Both."

"Oh, come on, Jake. You have to eat. It will be fun," she coaxed.

He couldn't blame her for trying. There was a time when she'd been able to distract him for a while, but he'd never had trouble returning his focus to work. Successful careers weren't made by losing focus. And therein was his problem. Hope constantly challenged his focus.

"I can't," he said.

She pressed her full lips together. "Since when?"

"Since we broke things off."

The full-on pout puckering her mouth had lost its appeal. "I didn't think you were really serious about ending it."

"What part of 'this isn't working' wasn't clear?" he asked.

"You're determined to go our separate ways?" She sat up straight, all traces of the laid-back sexy pose disappearing.

"Yes."

"But I found the diamond ring. In your dresser."

She'd gone through his things? "How?"

"After we had sex I was looking for a T-shirt to slip on and there it was." When he didn't return her smile, she looked offended. "Are you accusing me of something?"

"No." There was no point. He didn't care enough to go there. A fight needed heat on both sides and he simply didn't feel it. But honesty was something else. "I'll admit that the idea of proposing crossed my mind."

"Why didn't you?"

A good question and she deserved an honest answer. "Just couldn't bring myself to do it."

"I don't understand."

"Come on, Blair." He leaned forward and rested his forearms on the desk. "You know as well as I do that we're not in love."

"We like each other and have fun." She tossed her hair.

"That's not enough."

"And love isn't the only reason to get married," she snapped.

"What other reason would there be?"

"I can open doors for you that you didn't even know existed. Come on, Jake. You're good-looking. Smart. You save lives. With that background and my contacts, you could go really far. Senator. Maybe even the White House."

"And you could be First Lady?"

"Stranger things have happened," she said. "Why not?"

So many speed bumps. So little time. "What if I don't want that?"

Her eyes narrowed and anger slid into the blue depths. "One of the first things I liked about you was your ambition. It's something we shared. What happened, Jake? Is it the woman you slept with?"

Another good question, but the answer wasn't so straightforward. Hope had certainly challenged his principles and priorities. He liked her. And he couldn't really say that about Blair.

"Nothing happened. The truth is that you and I had a good time while it lasted, but we're over now."

She stood and slid the strap of her sinfully pricey purse on her shoulder and tried to glare him into submission. "It's not over until *I* say it is."

It took two for an argument and he wasn't going to play. "If you're finished, I have work to do."

"Are you throwing me out?"

"No. You're welcome to stay and watch if you'd like." He shrugged. "Makes no difference to me."

"This isn't the end," she said through gritted teeth.

Then she swept out of the room.

Jake let out a long breath as he raked his fingers through his hair. Why had he never seen the witch within? Probably he just hadn't wanted to acknowledge the darkness beneath the beautiful exterior. Blair was all fun and games until she didn't get her way. He couldn't believe he'd actually bought a ring and thought about asking her to marry him. That was a part of the career plan he was glad he hadn't acted on.

And he had Hope to thank for it. Just meeting her, feeling the chemistry that fueled their mutual attraction was the whole reason he knew Blair was all wrong.

Spending time with Hope had been the highlight of his weekend. Kissing her. Holding her. Those moments were serenity in the sea of insanity that was his life. Then she'd left after saying she wouldn't be the other woman.

He reached over and turned off the computer. It was time to tell her he'd broken things off with Blair.

Hope realized something as she walked back to her office from a meeting with the hospital comptroller. For the first time in a long time she was happy.

Her job was going well. The CFO seemed pleased with her work. Management called him David the Devil, but she didn't see him that way. He'd been very nice and said her department was in great shape budget-wise. Everything was falling into place for the new campus opening which was getting closer every day.

There was a spring in her step and a lightness of heart she'd been missing since… She pushed the thought away. Not going there. The feeling of peace, tranquility and balance was one she planned to hang on to.

She walked down the long hall, then turned left into her office and saw Jake. Instantly her heart dropped, her pulse pounded and her palms started to sweat. This was unexpected. She'd been so sure that playing the willpower card to protect herself from that kick-ass kiss would buy her a pass from future attention. Only part of her was doing the dance of joy that she'd been wrong.

"Greetings," he said.

"Hi."

He looked good. Duh. He always did. She'd seen him in jeans, scrubs, suits and nothing. The man didn't have a bad look. Today it was gray slacks several shades darker than his eyes and a white dress shirt with sleeves rolled up to mid-forearm. No tie. Very rugged chic, with lots of masculine flair. The top two buttons of his shirt were undone and she swallowed once, remembering the touch and taste of the chest hidden below. Her slick palms started to tingle.

"How are you, Hope?"

With an effort she lifted her gaze to his face. "Good. You?"

"Never better."

That made one of them. A minute ago she'd been happy. *Happy.* Maybe this visit was fate's way of reminding her yet again how fragile and fleeting that feeling was.

A reminder that the nightmare could happen without warning. You kiss your husband goodbye in the morning, tell him to have a good day and drive safe, not knowing that his commute wasn't the thing to worry about. He calls to say he's been asked to work late, but it's your anniversary and he wants to get home for the big plans.

You encourage his noble streak and tell him to do his job. Kids in the middle of a domestic dispute are in danger and he needs to be there when cops remove them from the home and into children's protective services. A matter of hours later you get another call, this one telling you that he was killed. The details are a merciful blur, but the message is carved into your heart forever.

The man you love is never coming home again.

You try not to breathe because when you do the pain is going to make you implode. But breathing is involuntary, unless a bullet to the heart says otherwise.

"Hope?" There was concern on Jake's face. "You just went white as a sheet. Something wrong?"

"I'm fine," she lied, waving a hand in dismissal. Then she walked behind her desk and sat in the chair. She frowned up at him. "But why are you here? Did we have a meeting I forgot about?"

"It's about a meeting, but has nothing to do with the hospital. And, for the record, my ego will be on life support if you forgot. I'm here to talk about what happened Saturday night."

Ah. That would be the meeting of their mouths. She definitely hadn't forgotten, although a small case of selective amnesia would be incredibly helpful.

"I'm pretty busy, Jake—"

"You can give the chief trauma surgeon a couple of minutes." He settled his hip on the corner of her cluttered desk and the material of his slacks pulled tight across his thigh. It was a breathtakingly masculine pose and one that showed he wasn't leaving until he was good and ready.

"Okay." She leaned back in her chair. "What is it you want to say?"

"I just want you to know you're not the other woman."

"Technically I am. You're seeing Blair and me. She was there first, which, by definition, makes me the other woman."

"Only if I was still going out with her."

The implication of his words sank in and stirred up the happy factor she'd been rocking just moments ago. If she was understanding him right, he was no longer with Blair. Part of her was high-fiving that information. The other part was running for cover and having difficulty finding any.

"*Are* you still going out with her?" Hope asked, well, hopefully.

"No." His gaze locked with hers. "And I wasn't before Saturday night. But you left before I could tell you. I broke things off with her. Twice."

"As in two times?"

"It didn't take the first time," he explained. "But after our conversation a little while ago, I'm confident we're on the same page."

"Oh."

Oh, crap, is what she'd meant to say. If she allowed it, a remark like that could annihilate self-control that was barely hanging on. He'd broken up with Blair Havens to keep her, Hope, from being the other woman?

If possible he stared harder which was a clue that her reaction wasn't what he'd expected. "I wanted you to know that it's okay to go out with me."

Was it? Not in her frame of reference.

"Can I ask you something?" she said.

"Shoot."

"What did you mean when you said at the clinic that you understand how they feel? What it's like to have absolutely nothing?" It was the first thing that popped into her mind and as good a question as any to use for a stall tactic.

He stared at her, looking more intense as the seconds ticked by. She wasn't sure he would answer, but finally, he let out a long breath.

"When I was about thirteen, my father took off. No word, no warning. One day he was there, the next he was gone."

"Do you know where he went?" she asked, astonished.

He shook his head. "We never heard from him again. I have no clue if he's alive or dead. And I don't much care," he added bitterly.

If anyone knew how a shock like that felt, Hope did. Would the pain be worse if an important person in your life was out there somewhere and you had no idea whether or not they were alive, or that they just didn't want to be with you anymore?

"What happened?" she asked. "To you and your mom, I mean."

"She didn't make enough money from her housecleaning business to pay the mortgage. We lost the house."

"Oh, Jake—I'm so sorry." She winced at the pain in his eyes. "Going from a house to an apartment is a big change—"

"That would have been better than what happened."

"I don't understand."

"To get an apartment you need first and last month's rent and a security deposit. If we'd had a chunk of money like that, making a house payment would have been easy. We had nowhere to go. We ended up homeless."

"On the street homeless?" she asked, unable to grasp what he was saying. "No family or friends to take you in?"

"Negative."

Images went through her mind. She'd seen homeless people pushing their belongings along the street in a supermarket cart. The nightly news did stories of tent cities in downtown Las Vegas and law enforcement moving them because of nearby businesses that reported theft and vandalism. Looking at the expensively dressed man lounging on her desk, it was impossible to picture him that way.

"What did you do? Obviously you got an education, unless you're like that character pretending to be a doctor," she said.

One corner of his mouth curved up, but humor never made it to his eyes. If anything he looked more grim, a window into the pain and hopelessness he'd experienced. "It's a particularly challenging scenario to attend school when you don't have a permanent address."

"How did you?"

"My mother is a very determined woman. She made it happen. Starting at the local high school, she eventually ended up talking to the district superintendent."

"Gutsy." That's where he got it, she thought.

"She was pretty mortified, actually," he said, his voice hard, grating. "But it paid off. There were programs and help. We got an apartment, such as it was."

"That's good."

There was irony in his expression. "I had an address, but going to high school was its own particular hell."

"Kids can be selfish and cruel," she said, remembering what he'd said to the little girl at the clinic.

"The staff did their best to keep everyone equal and protect privacy, but kids know who has money and who doesn't." His eyes went hard as a faraway look hinted at the flash of unpleasant memories playing through his mind.

But all he said was, "The have-nots are targets for humiliation."

"So that's why you wanted five minutes alone with the dorks, dweebs and jerks taunting little Taylor?"

This time when his mouth curved up, amusement cut through the painful thoughts. "I didn't think it showed."

"You hid it well." She smiled. "Not. It was clear what she said really pushed your buttons."

"Yeah."

"So you managed to go to college," she nudged, wanting to hear the rest.

"When you work to help keep a roof over your head, that tends to cut down on making friends. That meant more time to study." He shrugged. "My grades were good. I got a scholarship."

"Medical school?"

The flash of pain and anger on his face was unexpected. "Student loans."

"That would explain why you give back to others who need it."

He folded his arms over that impressive chest. "At the risk of having a *Gone with the Wind* moment, I vowed to never be poor again."

"And you're not," she agreed. "But you're also doing a good thing, helping sick people."

"It's selfish, actually. Being there reminds me how far I've come."

"So, you're not altruistic at all. And giving of your time has nothing to do with helping out. It's all about you," she teased.

He grinned. "I'm glad you finally know the truth."

If only. He was being modest, self-effacing and darn it all—noble. She wished like crazy that he was the shallow man she'd so hastily judged him to be. That would give her a shield, something to protect herself from the feelings that threatened.

The last time she'd felt like this, she was falling in love.

And she'd let herself go for it because she didn't know how easily and unexpectedly her whole life could collapse. But now the raw edges of that agonizing wound were coming together. The hurt that had kept her from caring again was disappearing.

And she couldn't let that happen. The prospect of losing control over her personal happiness was terrifying.

He stood and settled his hands on lean hips. "So, now that you know I'm a free man, would you have dinner with me tonight?"

"No."

"No?" He stared at her as if he had no idea what the single-syllable word meant.

"It's not a good idea, Jake."

"That's where you're wrong. It's actually an excellent idea. Just give me a chance to show you I'm right."

She already knew that they had a good time together. What was not to like? He was handsome, witty, smart and the sex had been good, too.

And that's what she was afraid of. It would be so easy to fall for him and she couldn't go there. It wasn't fair to Jake.

"At the risk of crushing your ego," she said, "I just don't want to go out with you."

"Your eyes are telling me something else."

"Oh, please. Like I've never heard that line in a romantic comedy before."

Something that looked a lot like a challenge shifted into his expression when he pointed at her. "This discussion is not over, Hope."

Yes, it was. *They* were over before ever really starting and that was almost fine with her. Right now she had a choice. Right now she could choose to go out with him. See if the chemistry arcing between them could grow into something deeper. She was choosing not to do that. Her life—the one she'd embraced before—had been torn apart by events beyond her control. How many times could a heart be mangled and still be expected to keep beating? Hers had been damaged once and she'd survived. Her heart was still pumping away even though there'd been a time she'd wished it wouldn't. She was at a crossroads and recognized it as the point of no return.

She was choosing control and safety.

The little twist in her chest when Jake walked out the door was *nothing* compared to what might happen if she threw caution to the wind and agreed to go out with him.

Chapter Nine

There was more than one way to get what he wanted.

Jake hadn't figured it would be necessary to throw a party for the emergency department four days after Hope had rejected his dinner offer, but it was the best idea he could come up with.

He'd posted an invitation and spread the word at Mercy Medical West that he was having an employee appreciation party to thank everyone for their hard work in getting the third campus ready to open. How could Hope turn *that* down?

It was now Friday and he stood in his kitchen to observe the employees who'd already arrived. If his luck hadn't sucked, right this minute he'd be at a fancy restaurant with Hope. He still couldn't believe she'd turned him down flat.

It wasn't ego talking either.

Well, maybe a little, if he was being honest.

But Hope was attracted to him. He knew that as surely as he knew there was no life without a beating heart. If she didn't show up tonight, it would make her look bad in the staff's eyes, and he was betting she wouldn't do that. She wouldn't let him take her out, so he'd backed her into a virtual corner and when she arrived, he planned to back her into a corner for real.

Jake grabbed a longneck bottle of beer from the fridge as conversation buzzed in the media room. Twenty or so people were milling around, an exceptional turnout for such short notice. Employees from Respiratory Therapy, nursing staff and clerical. Housekeeping personnel, too. He knew how it felt to clean up after people who chewed you out for missing a dust bunny behind the bedroom door. No one had been excluded. This big house was full but not one of the people filling it was the person he most wanted to see.

He looked down at his watch, then frowned at how late it was getting. When he glanced up, a familiar blonde was headed in his direction. Mitch Tenney's wife was a striking woman. His partner was a lucky guy.

Jake grinned when Samantha Ryan Tenney stopped in front of him. "Hi, Sam."

She grinned right back. "You're looking good, Jake. Was that sweater a Christmas present? It matches your eyes."

He glanced down at his jeans and the gray cashmere she was asking about. "A gift from my mother as a matter of fact."

"It looks very preppy over the white shirt. Your mom has great taste."

"I think so, too." And now his mom had the money to indulge it, he thought, dark memories of their long-ago financial struggle creeping in.

Sam glanced over her shoulder and across the granite-topped island to the crowd in the adjacent room. "Great party."

"It is." Although, so far, the event had failed to reach its target objective. "Are you having a good time?"

"Yes. But I miss Lucas." A wistful look softened her pretty blue eyes at the reference to her baby. "I know what you're thinking."

He folded his arms over his chest. "In addition to being a conflict resolution counselor, you're also a mind reader?"

"That's what makes me so good at what I do."

He couldn't argue with results. "You straightened Mitch out so you'll get no argument from me about your gift. So what am I thinking?" Besides wondering whether or not Hope would show up tonight.

"You're trying to figure out how I can lust after an evening out with my husband, leave a clingy baby with my father to get what I want, then miss that clingy, crying child so much." She looked completely forlorn.

"Definitely a mind reader. That's exactly what I was thinking." Jake slid her a wry look. "What can I say? You're good."

She skimmed her gaze over the crowd in the media room again and spotted her tall husband by the table spread with hot food. "Don't get me wrong. It's a great party. Too bad Cal had to work. But Emily is having morning sickness all the time, so they probably wouldn't have come anyway."

"He mentioned they were expecting."

Sam nodded. "Mitch said you decided just a few days ago to do this."

"Yeah. Gatherings outside of the hospital help coworkers to bond." Although an appearance in person was required to complete the bonding process. And so far Hope hadn't put in an appearance. But when the doorbell rang, his pulse kicked up.

"Are you going to get that?" Sam asked.

"Ashley's doing hostess detail."

"Did your office manager do double duty as party planner, too?" She smiled. "You're a good surgeon, but I'm pretty sure you didn't cook the food and assemble drinks. Not on this scale."

"Busted. Ashley handled everything. And no one cooked. Except maybe the caterer."

He looked over her head to see who had arrived and smiled when Hope joined a group of nurses. With an effort, he pulled his attention back to the conversation. "Before you go into conflict-counselor overdrive, you should know that Ashley received a very generous holiday bonus for all her extra duties."

"She'd do it without a bonus," Sam answered. "You do know your office manager has a crush on you, right?"

"Wrong." He shook his head, but Sam didn't smile. "You're kidding."

"I couldn't be more serious."

"No way." Why was it that when your life was firing on all cylinders someone threw sugar in the gas tank? He needed this like he needed a sucking chest wound. "I've never encouraged her. She's great at her job and I make sure she knows I appreciate all she does. I don't know what we'd do without her."

"I'm not saying you did anything inappropriate. Sometimes the feelings just *are*."

"What am I supposed to do with that information?"

"Let her know that you're interested in someone else," Sam suggested.

"Even if I'm not?"

"Oh, please." Her gaze narrowed. "Didn't we just establish that I'm a mind reader?"

"I was humoring you."

She didn't look humored. "Then tell me you're not oozing testosterone for that beautiful honey-blonde honey who just walked into your family room."

"Media room."

"Whatever," she said dismissively. "You *like* her, Jake."

"What is this? Junior high?"

Sam ignored his attempts to deflect her. She glanced over her shoulder and said, "She's popular with the staff. Seems down-to-earth. And that mouth…" She arched an eyebrow as she asked, "Collagen injections?"

"How should I know?"

"You seriously expect me to believe you haven't kissed her?"

He'd done more than that, none of which was anything he cared to share. But darned if he could maintain an innocent expression under Sam's relentless cross-examination. Mind reading wasn't for real, but this woman had skills that were all about not missing details.

"That's Hope Carmichael, the nurse coordinator for Mercy Medical West."

As he talked, Jake watched the lady in question move from group to group in the other room. She said hello, listened, chatted and laughed, then moved on. She hadn't grabbed a drink or food and only once looked in his direction. It didn't take a mind reader to figure out why she was here. This appearance was nothing more than being politically correct.

When he saw Hope move to a group clustered closer to the entryway and escape, he looked at Sam and said, "I have to—"

"Go talk to Hope before she gets away," Sam guessed.

He didn't bother to deny her speculation. Grinning, he said, "You're good."

"I know."

Jake wished he could get a glimpse into Hope's mind. He met Sam's amused gaze, then grabbed her hand. "You and Hope should meet."

The two of them caught up with her just as she said goodbye to a group of nurses and RT staff before heading to the front door.

"Hope?"

She turned and didn't look happy, then noticed Sam. "Hi, Jake."

"I'm glad you could make it. This is Sam. Samantha Tenney meet Hope Carmichael."

"Dr. Tenney's wife?" she guessed.

"Yes," Sam confirmed. "But don't believe any bad hospital gossip you may have heard about me."

Hope smiled with genuine warmth. "I've only heard good things. But since it all came from your husband—"

"Really?" With gooey, goo-goo eyes she glanced over her shoulder and met Mitch's gaze, then wiggled her fingers. Her husband's responding grin said he was ready to get her home.

"He credits you for bringing out his sensitive side," Hope said.

"Sam's pretty special," Jake agreed. "She can read minds, too. Tell me what Hope is thinking."

He looked from one woman to the other. Both were beautiful and brainy. Sam was a golden blonde and Hope had the soft shades of honey running through her hair. What combination of qualities made it impossible for him to stop thinking about her?

Thoughtfully Sam tapped her lip as she studied the other

woman. "Hope is thinking that she works too hard and getting Mercy Medical West open is sucking the life out of her."

Jake had been hoping for something along the lines of she'd been thinking about him and changing her mind about dinner.

Hope smiled. "You are a mind reader."

"Also," Sam added, "you did your duty here and would like to go home and put your feet up."

Again not what Jake was looking for. "Hope doesn't have a home. She's got a room at the Residence Inn."

"That sounded disapproving." Sam's gaze narrowed on him. "All of a sudden I feel used. Like an interpreter. A go-between. Jake, my advice is to just tell her you like her. Be honest. Direct. Girls like that from a guy. It's refreshing." Impulsively, she hugged Hope. "Nice to meet you."

"You, too."

Sam stood on tiptoe and kissed his cheek, then moved away and joined her husband by the food table. After slipping her arm through his, she stood on tiptoe again and whispered something in his ear. When Mitch looked down at her, there was a gleam along with the love in his eyes.

Jake envied them. When he looked back, Hope was walking away. He caught up to her just as she reached the double door entry. "Leaving so soon?"

Her shoulders stiffened before she turned. "Like Sam said, I'm tired and I want to go put my feet up."

"You could do that here." He slid his hands into the pockets of his jeans. "I'd be happy to rub them for you."

"Thanks. But I have to go."

"If I hadn't brought Sam over to meet you, you'd have been gone before even saying hello to me. Why is that?"

"I didn't want to disturb you while you were talking to her."

Was she jealous? He wanted to believe she might be, but that was a long shot. More likely she was avoiding him.

"Hope, I understand that you've been putting in a lot of hours at the hospital. That's what this party is all about. A chance to relax, let your hair down."

He remembered the last time she'd been here and he'd run his fingers through the silken honey strands. Sex was a whole different level of relaxation, one he'd like to repeat with her.

"I really can't stay."

"Because of your busy social life?" The words slipped out before he could stop them.

"No, because tomorrow is the public open house for the new hospital and I'll be there giving tours of the emergency department. Sam is right. I *am* tired and want to put my feet up."

"Okay." Jake pulled her into a quiet corner of the living room. "But Sam is right about something else, too. I do like you, Hope. I'd really like to spend time with you. Outside of the hospital."

A skeptical expression darkened her hazel eyes. "So you're actually taking her advice?"

"I'm told it's refreshing. Although, I'm basically an honest guy."

"Really?" She slid the strap of her purse more securely on her shoulder. "Or are you one of those guys who wants what he can't have? The kind who loses interest as soon as he gets what he's after."

Jake blew out a long, steadying breath when anger spurted through him. "What is it exactly that you have against me?"

"Other than Blair Havens?"

"That situation has been resolved and you know it."

"Even so," she conceded, "it's just not—"

"No negatives. Go out with me, Hope. Let me screw up before you judge me. Earn the right to say I told you so." He met her gaze. "Or not."

She shook her head. "Not a good idea."

"Why?" Frustration edged into his voice. "Tell me you don't like me and I'll walk away. No harm, no foul. But only if that's how you feel. Guys think honesty is refreshing, too."

"I don't dislike you," she hedged. "But it would be *dishonest* to start something I have no intention of finishing."

"Define finish." He folded his arms over his chest.

"You know." Fear and pain flitted through her eyes. "Marriage."

"I just want to spend some time with you. Get to know you. Who said anything about getting married?" he demanded.

"No one," she admitted. "But there's no point in beginning anything that might go there. Hanging out with you is a waste of time."

"It's my time," he countered. "But for the sake of argument, why is it a waste?"

"Because I've been married and have no intention of ever doing it again. You're a bright guy, Jake. The smart thing would be to walk away from me. Running would be even better."

She brushed past him and let herself out the front door. One of them was running, Jake thought, but it wasn't him. He never had to work this hard for a date and wasn't sure why he was doing it now. Maybe she was right about him wanting what he couldn't have. It wouldn't be the first time.

He'd never forget being dirt poor and not good enough for a rich girl's snooty family, so he made himself good enough. Now he could hold his own in any socioeconomic group.

Hope was right about one thing. A sharp guy *would* give up on her, but maybe he was more stubborn than smart. He wasn't walking away without knowing why she was commitment-phobic.

And nothing kicked up his obstinate streak like rejection.

Jake liked her. Last night he'd told her so and the words had warmed a trail straight to Hope's heart.

It was the best of news.

And the worst.

Mostly it was distracting, Hope thought. She couldn't afford to be distracted while Mercy Medical West was having an open house. The public was invited to tour the soon-to-open facility and she was guiding a group around the emergency department. She'd shown them the MRI room and where heart catheterizations were done. Probably pointing out the surgery table, how it could be lowered and raised to accommodate a taller surgeon had turned her thoughts to Jake.

In her spartan rented room there were no personal reminders of anyone, including him, and no excuses for thinking about him. Although that didn't stop her. But it was time to focus.

She held an arm out, indicating the doorway. "Ladies and gentlemen, if you'll follow me through here, we're going to see the trauma bays. Notice how the flow of traffic and ancillary services such as radiology and lab are all located in a compact area to facilitate emergency treatment. After a trauma there's what we call 'the golden hour,' sixty minutes when what we do can mean the difference between life and death. We can't afford to waste time shuffling equipment or personnel where they're needed."

A murmur of awed agreement hummed through the group as they walked. In the trauma rooms, she pointed out the distinctive features of each bay and what emergency situations could send a patient there.

"What if the room for a particular trauma is already occupied?" a slim, older blonde woman asked.

"We can handle all emergencies in any bay," Hope explained. "But these are set up for functioning in a perfect world. If there was a major disaster, for instance, there are protocols in place to stretch emergency services. All personnel, whether on call or not, are required to report to the hospital. Patients would be triaged so that the most severely injured get attention first. But under normal circumstances, trauma cases are channeled to the bay best suited to deal with it."

"I see," the woman said nodding. "This is quite a beautiful facility."

"Yes, it is."

Right now the lavender walls and color-coordinated countertops were pristine. They wouldn't stay that way long. When the doors opened, and that would be soon, there would be patients and paperwork and paraphernalia everywhere. Hope was sad that she wouldn't be here to help navigate the speed bumps, adjustments and growing pains of the new campus. She'd be leaving as soon as her replacement was hired. That would be for the best because Jake Andrews refused to stay out of her head.

She looked at the six or seven men and women in this tour. "If you haven't already seen the patient rooms upstairs, I highly recommend that you do. There are volunteers in the lobby to form groups for that. I'll be leaving you there."

Everyone followed her, commenting on the exquisite artwork hanging on the walls and the pleasing color scheme that streamed from one department into the next.

When they arrived at the information desk in the sunlit lobby, she said, "Outside under the white tent, representatives from medical companies are set up with information about services from health clubs, vision screenings, orthotics and general wellness. And if you're interested in a cholesterol screening, there are people just around the corner who can help you with that. I hope you enjoyed the presentation."

Everyone thanked her and moved away, all except the blond who'd asked about full trauma bays. She was stylish in crisp jeans, a soft powder blue sweater and a tailored jacket. She stood by the desk glancing around.

"Is there something I can help you find?" Hope asked.

"I'm just looking for my son." Her gray eyes scanned the crowd milling around and the people walking through the double doors.

Because the woman was in her fifties, Hope assumed the son in question wasn't a toddler who'd wandered off.

"Were you supposed to meet him somewhere? At a certain time?"

"No." The woman continued her search. "He works here and I just figured—"

"Mom, there you are."

The voice came from behind them and Hope knew it instantly. She turned and the lurch of her heart confirmed what she already knew. "Jake."

"Hi, sweetheart," the woman said. "It's about time you showed up."

"I've been around." He grinned, then leaned down to give her a hug. "Where were you?"

"Pestering this young woman with questions," she said, glancing at Hope.

He looked from one to the other. "I see you two have met."

"Not really." Hope was still trying to wrap her mind around the fact that this was his mother. She'd never expected to meet the woman who raised him under such difficult circumstances and did quite a remarkable job.

"Susan Andrews," he said, "meet Hope Carmichael, Mercy Medical West's nurse coordinator."

His mother held out her hand. "It's a pleasure to meet you, Hope. Jake has told me about you."

Hope squeezed her fingers and wondered if he'd shared with his mother any of their rocky history. Probably not the story of their one-night stand in his bedroom. Or the sexy close call up against the wall in her office.

A gleam stole into the gray eyes so like his mom's. "I only told her the good stuff."

Hope wondered if he could read her mind, because he was definitely messing with her. "Then it was a short conversation."

The woman laughed. "Good for you, Hope. Don't let him push you around."

"Mom? Whose side are you on?" he asked, his tone teasing.

"Hope's," she answered emphatically. "Women have to stick together. And you can be incredibly annoying sometimes."

"Wow, feel the love. I didn't know that gender tops DNA in the loyalty department."

"We should compare notes," Hope said, liking his mom immediately. "How is he annoying? Let me count the ways."

"For one thing he thinks he's always right," the older woman said.

"I noticed that the first time we met." The second time he'd kissed her and put everything out of her mind except wanting to be with him. That was pretty annoying.

"He's stubborn, too." Susan Andrews slid a teasing glance up at her son.

"Hey, I'm right here," he protested.

Without acknowledging him, she continued. "When he was little, he used to throw temper tantrums if he didn't get his way."

"Really?" Hope could see that he wasn't the least bit upset at this revelation.

Mrs. Andrews nodded. "I kept my sanity by telling myself that determination is a good quality in an adult. In a two-year-old, not so much."

"I can see that about him. The whole stubborn thing," Hope agreed.

One of his dark eyebrows arched. "Has anyone ever told you that two against one is piling on? There are penalties against that in football."

"Football isn't always fair," the older woman said. "And neither is life."

"Words to live by. You should listen to your mother."

"What makes you think I don't?" The pretended affront was reflected in the tilt of his head and made him look too cute. "Everything she says is a pearl—"

His phone must have vibrated because he reached for it, looked at the display, and said, "Stop talking about me."

His mother frowned as he moved a few feet away and answered the call. "He works too hard."

"How do you know the call is about work?" Hope asked.

"The look on his face. Suddenly serious. I worry about him."

Hope studied the concentration on his features where the teasing expression had been only moments before. He was certainly driven to succeed. She'd wrongly judged him as mercenary when they'd first met and felt bad about it.

"Maybe," Hope said, "he can slow down a little now that he's the trauma medical director here."

"That would be nice, but I'm not holding my breath. Failure isn't an option for Jake. Hard work and too many hours are the price he pays."

He replaced his cell in the holster on his belt and rejoined them. "I have to go. Paramedics are bringing in accident victims." He looked sincerely regretful. "Sorry about lunch, Mom. I'm on call."

"No need to apologize." She touched his arm. "I understand."

"I was going to show you stuff not on the public tour, but duty calls—"

"I'll do that," Hope offered. "A special tour rate for the medical director's family. If you're up for it, Mrs. Andrews?"

"Call me Susan. I'd like that, Hope. How very sweet of you."

"Yeah," Jake agreed. "I owe you one."

"No, I'm happy to—"

"Gotta go," he said, checking his phone. He leaned down to kiss his mom's cheek. "I'll call you."

"When you have time, sweetheart."

Hope stood beside the older woman as they watched him hurry through the hospital's automatic double doors to the designated doctor parking just outside. The teasing was fun and she missed him already. That was beyond stupid and fell into pathetic territory.

She pulled her gaze from where he'd disappeared and looked at his mom. "I'll show you the rest of the hospital."

"Wonderful."

They took the elevator upstairs for a look at the cheerful and sunny patient rooms. There were pullout beds tucked away in a window seat to allow a family member to spend the night with a sick loved one. Each bed had a computer where medical information was charted and could be shared in e-mail updates to family and friends. It also functioned as a personal computer.

Susan looked impressed. "You mean I could do online banking while being laid up?"

"Yes." Hope smiled. "While someone is trying to get well, they shouldn't have to feel trapped and worry about the bills getting paid. The hospital looks at healing from a three-pronged approach—mind, body, spirit."

"This is pretty amazing."

When there was nothing left to see in the main building, Hope offered to accompany the woman to the health fair outside under the tent.

"That's not necessary. I've already taken up too much of your time."

Hope told herself that looking after Jake's mom was nothing more than politeness to a nice woman who happened to be related to her boss. It was all about doing a good job because the job was all she had.

"I don't mind," she said.

"You're a sweetie, but I think shepherding an old lady is above and beyond the call of duty."

"No, it's not. And you're not old. I've enjoyed showing off what we're doing."

"It's certainly impressive. And I'd like to thank you for taking me under your wing." She tapped her lip thoughtfully. "Jake tells me you're staying at the Residence Inn, practically living out of a suitcase."

"Well, I—"

The woman continued, "Eating out all the time isn't good for you," she warned. "Too much salt is bad for your blood pressure. I'd like to fix you a home-cooked meal."

"That's too much. I don't want you to go to any trouble," Hope protested.

"Jake can barbecue. It relaxes him. Or so he says. Please say yes, Hope."

This woman's genuine warmth melted the ice inside her and opened up a chasm of emptiness that Hope had only begun to realize was there. Jake had tapped into it first. Just the mention of his name intensified the loneliness until she didn't have the emotional reserves to say no.

Surely two years of soul-deep aloneness atoned for her sin. Just once in the light wasn't a punishable offense, was it? The price for protecting herself was to be by herself and right this minute, that price was too high.

Before she could talk herself out of it, Hope said, "Thank you, Susan. I'd love to join you for dinner."

Chapter Ten

At Mercy Medical Center, Jake walked into the E.R. doctor's lounge and poured himself a cup of coffee from the pot. This small room tucked away from the bustle of the trauma bays was an oasis of serenity with gray-brown Formica countertops and generic linoleum floors. A rectangular table stood in the center of the room with four metal folding chairs around it. Along with the never-ending coffee, there were stale cinnamon rolls on a paper plate. When you were too busy to grab a meal, that rock-hard pastry could taste like the best steak at Delmonico's.

Just as he took a sip from his mug, the cell phone clipped to his scrubs vibrated. He leaned back against the counter and looked at the display before answering.

"Hi, Mom."

"I hope I'm not interrupting you."

"Nope. I just got out of surgery. Repairing a lacerated liver."

"That sounds bad. How did it go?" she asked.

"The patient is young and in exceptional shape so the prognosis is good. He should do fine. And he'll be more careful the next time he rides his skateboard off the curb and pretends it's a half pipe."

"I'm glad it went well," his mother said. "And that I'm not catching you at a bad time."

"I'm between traumas. Paramedics are on the way."

"So you are busy. I should let you go," she protested.

"I've got a few minutes. Mitch will do the initial eval. He'll holler if he needs me. What's up?"

Something was, because when he was on call Susan Andrews didn't bother him unless there was a good reason.

He straightened away from the counter. "Is everything okay, Mom?"

"Hopefully." She laughed a little nervously. "And speaking of Hope, she's like a breath of fresh air, a ray of sunshine. Don't you think?"

"Yeah."

Hearing Hope's name produced an image in his head of her sparkling eyes and the amused, yet mysterious, smile that curved up the corners of her full mouth. That put a hitch in his breathing.

"Yeah?" his mother echoed, uncertainty in her voice. "I was going for a more enthusiastic reaction. You're going to be really upset with me. Don't worry. I can get you out of it. You're on call. I can just say that you got hung up at the hospital. I'm sorry I bothered you—"

"Whoa, Mom." What the heck was she talking about? "Did something happen with you and Hope after I left?"

"Not in a bad way. She was so charming and gracious that I invited her to dinner. And volunteered you to do the grilling," she added. "But it's all right if you don't want to.

I wasn't matchmaking. Honestly. I just had a spontaneous thought and the words came out of my mouth. And I—"

"Take a breath, Mom."

"Okay."

There was silence on the other end of the phone and he assumed she was breathing. He needed to take his own advice because this unexpected good news made him want to pump his arm and holler from the top of the hospital's bell tower. The reaction would seem out of proportion to his mother and he didn't have time for the long, sad, frustrating story. Along with giving him life and unwavering support, she'd just given him the gift of time with Hope. He needed to reassure her that this couldn't be more okay with him.

"Not a problem, Mom. You know I like to grill."

"That's what I told Hope. That it relaxes you."

With Hope in close proximity relaxation was a challenge, unless he had her in his arms.

"What time?" he asked casually.

"She's coming about six-thirty. But you do what you have to at the hospital."

"I'll be there, Mom. Or I'll call," he added, not wanting to sound too eager. Nothing short of a disaster could keep him away.

"Okay. Bye, sweetheart."

Hot damn! If he'd known his mother was the secret weapon to hanging out with Hope, he'd have used her sooner. Before he could take that thought further, the door opened and Mitch walked in.

His partner looked at him, then did a double take. "Good news?"

"What makes you say that?"

"You look—" Mitch's eyes narrowed suspiciously. "I don't know. Happy?"

"What makes you think that?"

"You're smiling."

"I'm always happy."

"And politicians always tell it like it is." Mitch, the world's greatest skeptic, settled his hands on his hips.

"Is there some reason I shouldn't smile?"

A frown darkened Mitch's already-intense blue eyes. "As a matter of fact—"

Jake's trauma-sense started tingling. "What's wrong?"

"Ashley says you dumped Blair Havens."

"Take that out of the rumor column and put it under fact," Jake confirmed. "So what?"

"That's not actually the rumor I meant. All the way home from your party last night Sam couldn't stop talking about you and Hope. There wouldn't be a you and Hope if Blair was still in the picture."

"Thanks for the vote of confidence. But how does Sam know there's a me and Hope?" Besides the fact that she was a mind reader.

"Damned if I know," Mitch answered, shaking his head. "Maybe because she's a woman. Maybe it's her job and she's good at it. Whatever. She's convinced that the last bachelor standing won't be standing very much longer."

"That's a pretty big leap."

"I said the same thing. But my wife was willing to put money on it," Mitch commented.

"A bet on my love life?"

"It's Vegas." Mitch shrugged. "Don't get me wrong. I like Hope. If she makes you happy, I'm happy." But he didn't look it.

Jake's bad feeling went viral. "Quit stalling. What's up?"

"No point in sugarcoating this. There's talk around the hospital that the board of directors is rethinking your appointment to trauma medical director."

"Where did that come from?" Jake demanded.

"Your guess is as good as mine. No one ever knows where the talk starts, but I've got a hunch it's leaked from Havens's office."

Jake felt himself start to do a slow burn. "Ed Havens gave me a contract."

"Signed?"

"It's going through legal now. But there's a verbal agreement. And he announced it publicly." The same night Jake had kissed Hope for the first time. The same night he'd realized that not breaking things off with Blair would be a mistake.

Mitch sighed. "Any lawyer will tell you there's a world of difference between verbal and signed."

"I'm the best candidate for the job. No one wants it more or has worked harder."

"Does that hard work include going out with the guy's daughter to tilt the scales in your favor?"

Jake felt a burst of anger roll through him. "Let's be clear. I didn't date Blair to get the appointment from her father."

"I believe you. I'm just repeating the talk. Forewarned is forearmed." Mitch held up his hands to signal peace. "A word of warning... Ed Havens isn't just a powerful man. He's also vindictive. He won't take his daughter's public breakup well and we both know it."

Jake started to protest when Mitch looked at the pager on his scrubs' waistband. "Paramedics just rolled in. One of the vics has belly trauma. I'll order an MRI."

"I'm right behind you."

When he was alone, Jake took several deep breaths to clear out the anger and frustration. He hadn't asked Blair out to stack the career deck in his favor. She was beautiful and fun. It had seemed like a good idea at the time. And if he was being honest with himself, he'd known the relationship had a short shelf life, although he'd kept hoping he was wrong.

There'd been a part of him reluctant to let go, but he realized now that a lot of it was about the poor boy getting the prom queen. He'd let things go on too long because there was no reason to alter the status quo. He'd had everything to gain, nothing to lose.

Until Hope.

One look at her had changed his life and he was still trying to figure out if that was a good thing.

Susan Andrews lived in a beautiful condominium community in Summerlin, not far from her son. After being buzzed through the gate, Hope followed verbal commands from the rental car's GPS to find her way. The houses in this development were actually duplexes, she realized. They shared a common wall.

The properties she passed were all beautifully landscaped and well-lighted. It made her think of Jake's house, the time she'd ended up in his bed. She couldn't say that was the worst night of her life, but there was no doubt in her mind it had been a mistake.

That unexpected passion had ignited without warning and reminded her of what she was missing. Remembering simply made her regret what she couldn't have, so it was best to forget about it.

She'd come here tonight for two reasons. She hadn't been able to make herself say no and it would be rude not to show up.

Hope parked at the curb when the GPS announced the destination on her right. The stucco was painted chocolate brown, with a cream-colored trim. In front of the house, smooth rocks formed a dry riverbed and flat stone steps created a path from the street to the sidewalk leading to the entrance. Within a few artistically displayed mounds of rocks, lantana bushes protruded.

Right now they were nothing but sticks. She'd been told that these plants looked lifeless in the winter, but spring revived them in brilliant and vivid shades of gold, yellow and purple. Again she was sad that she wouldn't be there to see spring in Las Vegas. It occurred to her that she was the opposite of winter lantana—outwardly alive but dead inside. The difference was that she had no wish to be revived. She didn't want to come back to life and risk hurting so badly that she would die inside again.

Blowing out a deep breath, she walked past two cars in the driveway. One of them she recognized. Apparently repairs had been made to it since the night she'd given Jake a ride home. A night she would take back if she could. The other was a hybrid compact.

She stopped on the covered porch and knocked. Seconds later she heard footsteps inside, just before the door opened.

"Hope," Susan said, smiling. "Welcome. Come in."

"Thank you." She saw Jake, leaning against a railing in the entryway where stairs went up to the second story. He looked casual and handsome in worn jeans and a long-sleeved navy cotton shirt. Her pulse raced as she said, "Hi."

"Did you have any trouble finding the place?" One of his dark eyebrows lifted, probably because he knew she knew he didn't live far and she'd found her way to his place. Twice.

"Olga got me here without a hitch."

"Who?" he asked.

"The GPS. It's voice-directed. Female voice. Sometimes she sounds sort of Ukrainian, so I named her Olga."

He straightened and folded his arms over his chest. "You know, I have some influence at the hospital. A psych evaluation could be arranged."

"Don't pay any attention to him, Hope. He calls his GPS Tiffani with an i." Susan was looking slim and fit in tailored gray slacks and a black cashmere sweater that highlighted her blond hair. "Don't you have steaks to cook?" she asked her son.

"Yes. Big, thick filets. I'll get right on that."

He disappeared around the corner and Hope wanted so badly to follow. Instead she smiled at her hostess. "This is a lovely neighborhood."

"Thanks. I really like it." She slid her hands into the pockets of her slacks. "Would you like to see the place?"

"Very much."

"Follow me."

They walked straight ahead into a room with floor-to-ceiling windows along the back that looked out on the lights of the Las Vegas Strip. It had a fireplace on one wall with a celery green microfiber corner group arranged in front.

"Family room," Susan pointed out. "The kitchen is there."

Hope figured it for the kitchen, what with the granite-topped work island, cook top, oven and refrigerator. The bonus was the unobstructed view of Jake's excellent backside as he bent to retrieve something from inside.

"Don't mind me," he said, without looking at them. "Dinner will be about a half hour. The steaks will take a while, which is good. I have a lot to relax from."

"Take your time, sweetheart. The dining room is through that doorway," Susan said to Hope.

She peeked inside at the beautiful cherrywood hutch, buffet and matching formal table. Three place settings were arranged with simple platinum-trimmed white china and silver. Cloth napkins. The chairs were covered in a chocolate-colored nubby material.

"It's lovely," Hope said.

"Wait until you see the upstairs."

Her hostess showed her into the master bedroom with a walk-in closet big enough to house a family of four. An oak sleigh bed dominated one wall with a matching dresser and armoire arranged around the perimeter. White shutters complemented the crown molding and gave it a simple, clean look.

The bathroom was spacious and bright with its marble countertops and tile floor. Gold fixtures added an elegance and charm that reflected Susan Andrews.

"There are two other bedrooms and my office up here."

Susan guided her through the expertly coordinated rooms and they sat on the hunter green and maroon love seat in the last one. Clearly it was a home office with a desk, computer and file cabinet. The stack of papers and folders told her it was a working office and not just for show.

"May I ask what kind of work do you do?" she said.

"I own a cleaning service business. Maid to Order. I have ten crews of two people who do commercial buildings and residences."

Hope noticed the abundance of paperwork and said, "It looks like business is thriving."

"Yes." Susan glanced at the desk and nodded. "Thank goodness. I'm grateful to keep my people employed."

Hope could tell by the tone that she felt a deep responsibility to her employees. "How did you get into the business?"

"Necessity is the mother of invention. I married too young and had Jake right away. I had no skills or training for any kind of job outside the home. But when my husband walked out on us, I needed to make money. All I knew how to do was clean."

Susan shrugged as if it was that simple, but Hope remembered the look on Jake's face when he told her about being homeless.

"That must have been hard on you," she said. "Jake told me what happened."

"If it was just me—" Susan stopped and swallowed hard. "Jake was about twelve or thirteen when we lost the house. I can't even begin to understand how hard it was on him. But he helped me clean other people's homes and never once complained."

Hope remembered his telling her that when you work to keep a roof over your head it's hard to make friends. That must have been incredibly lonely for him, she thought as her heart squeezed tight. But all he'd said was that there was more time to study and he earned scholarships.

"I can't even imagine what you went through. Jake told me a little about it. He said you went to the high school. To make sure he didn't miss out on an education. Because of your situation," she added.

"It was the lowest point of all. Humiliating to tell strangers that you couldn't take care of your child," Susan said, her mouth pulling tight. "But as bad as it was for me, it was a hundred times worse for Jake."

"He didn't talk much about that," Hope commented.

"To their credit the teachers and administrators tried to be discreet. Every Friday they sent him home with a backpack filled with snacks for the weekend, to make sure he had enough to eat. A child can't learn if he's hungry. But the kids all knew who had money and who didn't."

Hope remembered Jake hinting that kids taunted him. He'd said the have-nots were targets for bullies.

"More than once Jake came home with a black eye or a fat lip when someone made fun of his clothes or his shoes. That just broke my heart." Susan's mouth trembled. "I didn't know how to deal with that, how to raise a boy into a man. So I told him not to start trouble, but if anyone else did he should fight back and finish it. Don't walk away."

"That sounds like wise and practical advice to me," Hope said.

Susan smiled. "Those are the experiences that build character, and my son has more than I'd ever have wished for him."

"And now he's a doctor," Hope said. "You must be so proud of him."

"Yes." Tears glistened in gray eyes so like her son's. She held out her hand, indicating her home. "He bought this place for me, made sure I'd always have a roof over my head. No matter what."

The words tugged at Hope's heart. Now she knew why he'd vowed never to be poor again. He worked hard to fulfill that promise, but he didn't forget to give back to others less fortunate, too.

Her opinion of him had certainly changed since their first meeting. She'd thought him arrogant, ambitious and avaricious. Now she knew that he was gifted, good and sensitive. She wasn't exactly sure what to do with the information.

"It says a lot about you that your son is such a remarkable man." A man it would be far too easy to fall for.

A gleam stole into Susan's eyes. "You know, you can tell a lot about a man by the way he treats his mother."

Hope wasn't going to the matchmaking place. Instead she asked, "Why do you think he's never married and settled down?"

"Part of the reason is about being too busy. He's driven

to establish a solid financial foundation. I worry that after what he went through, he'll never feel secure enough."

"Part of the reason?" Hope prompted.

"He's also concerned about his DNA, that when the going gets tough, he'll take off like his father did."

"Even though you taught him to stand his ground and fight?"

"You're a smart girl." Susan smiled. "That's what I keep telling him."

The revelation made Hope sad for him at the same time it was a relief that he was unwilling to take a chance any more than she was. If that was really true, why was he trying so hard to change her mind about going out with him? The answer was easy. It was because his mother had taught him to stick around and fight. When he won the battle, then he could walk away. In her case, it was a campaign he would never win. She'd be walking away first.

Susan patted her knee and stood. "I didn't mean to talk about that."

"It's all right. I can see why Jake is so proud of you."

"That could change if I don't get the salad made," the other woman teased.

"Can I help you with anything?" Hope offered.

"Yes. You can go out and keep Jake company while he's slaving over a hot barbecue."

Hope knew protesting that assignment wasn't the way to be a good guest, so she dutifully went downstairs and opened the sliding glass door to the patio. The backyard was as immaculately landscaped as the front. A built-in spa was situated in the corner of the yard. Rocks and shrubs covered the area that wasn't patio.

She walked over to where Jake stood by the grill. "Hi."

He looked over his shoulder. "Did you see everything?"

Even more than he knew. "It's a beautiful home. Your mother is a remarkable woman."

"You'll get no argument from me." He looked down at her. "Are you hungry?"

She nodded. "Working open house for the new campus really gives a girl an appetite."

And looking at Jake Andrews gave her ideas that had nothing to do with food. Changing the subject was a good idea.

"So there's a nasty rumor going around that you find grilling relaxing," she said.

"Not a rumor. It's the honest truth." He lifted the barbecue lid and studied the steaks, focused as if it were the most complicated surgery.

"I don't like to cook," she said.

He stared at her, faking surprise. "I'm shocked and appalled."

"Be that as it may, I find the whole ordeal stressful. I'm a frozen entrée kind of girl."

"Dinner from a plastic carton stored in the freezer is just nasty," he said.

"And turning raw meat over an open flame doesn't make you tense?"

"Nope." He looked at his watch, clearly timing the raw meat in question. "And after a day like today, I have a lot of relaxing to do."

"What happened?" she asked.

Something that looked a lot like anger flashed through his eyes, but it was gone quickly. "A couple of surgeries. It was a rough day out on the roads. People in the wrong place at the wrong time. Ruptured spleen. Lacerated liver. But everyone should be good as new."

"Then they were lucky to have the new trauma medical director in the right place at the right time."

"You think so?" There was an edge to his voice.

"Why do you ask?"

"Not so long ago you weren't a fan. I'm just trying to figure out if you're now on my side because of surgical skill. Or maybe my magnetic personality pulled you in."

She groaned at the pun, then said, "I think it was your humility that made the difference."

"Like everything else I do, I'm good at humility, too."

She couldn't help laughing. "You're incorrigible."

"Thank you." He lifted the barbecue lid to check the steaks, then closed it.

She folded her arms over her chest and stared at the view. "I can see the Rio resort from here." The distinctive pink and purple lines were easy to spot. "It's beautiful."

He didn't follow her gaze, but was looking at her when he said, "Yeah."

Her heart started beating too fast and she felt light-headed. That was the only explanation for what she said next. "I'm going to have to do some research on local hotspots. My sisters are coming into town from Texas next weekend."

"I can help you with that," he offered. "I know all the best places and would be happy to show all of you around."

"Thanks. That would be nice."

The words came automatically from her heart, not her head. She wanted them back desperately. This was exactly the reason she'd resisted going out with him. Every time he was around, she got sucked in deeper. The last time she'd felt like this she was falling in love.

She didn't want any part of love.

She also didn't want any part of explaining Jake to her sisters.

Chapter Eleven

Jake wasn't sure what alignment of planets, suns and moons was responsible for Hope's agreeing to let him squire the three sisters around Las Vegas, but he was grateful.

It was a chance to spend time with Hope even if they weren't alone.

He'd hired a limousine for the day and took them first to the new and impressive CityCenter. After that there had been stops at the Hard Rock Café, dinner at Delmonico in The Venetian and a club at Bellagio. Now they were sitting in a wine bar at Red Rock Resort where the two visiting sisters were staying. It wasn't far from Mercy Medical West and Hope's room at the Residence Inn. The four of them were having a nightcap.

The three sisters were all about a year apart in age and couldn't be more different. Honey-blonde Hope sat next to him. Across the small table in a leather club chair was Faith, the oldest, a brunette with turquoise eyes. Beside her was brown-eyed redhead Charity, the youngest. She wasn't the least bit intimidated by being at the bottom of the birth order and gave as good as she got from the older two.

Each was beautiful and would attract male attention wherever she went, but Jake wasn't attracted to Faith or Charity. If he had to pick a feeling toward them, it would be brotherly. Hope was the one he couldn't stop thinking about, the one he wanted to touch. To hold. To bed.

It wasn't rational or smart and he was normally a smart, rational guy. Not this time. If he were, he'd be with Blair Havens even though she wasn't the woman who made his pulse pound and his palms sweat. She wasn't the one who frustrated his need to take her in his arms. The one who kept resisting him. His life would be so much easier if she were *the one*.

Mitch had been right. Jake had done some discreet digging and found there was disturbing talk about his appointment to trauma medical director. More often than not information was deliberately leaked and rumors were based on fact. Former Congressman Ed Havens was probably behind a movement to oust Jake before he could sign on the dotted line, as revenge for Jake not being his daughter's trophy boyfriend and arm candy.

Jake couldn't deny that wanting the job was like a fire in the belly. It wasn't enough that he'd bought his mother a house and had an impressive bank account. He wanted to be so important, so powerful that the embarrassed and humiliated boy he'd once been would cease to exist. And Hope was definitely an inconvenient complication to his plan.

"You're looking awfully serious about something, Jake." Faith tilted her head as she studied him and a silky strand of brown hair brushed the shoulder of her purple sweater. "Is it work?"

"Hospital politics."

The three women groaned in unison before Charity said, "I work at Texas Children's Hospital in the pediatric ICU and if there's one thing you can count on it's politics."

Faith nodded ruefully. "I'm at Baylor in Fort Worth and it's no different there. Why do you think every soap opera on TV has a hospital in it?"

"Do you have time to watch every soap opera on television?" Hope teased.

"I'm just saying." Faith smiled. "I never thought you'd go to the dark side into hospital management."

Hope shrugged. "The job came up and it's temporary."

"So was the last one," Charity pointed out, twisting a strand of red hair around her index finger.

"That works for me." Hope sat up straighter and her arm brushed Jake's. She settled her hands in her lap before meeting his gaze. Her eyes were soft with sympathy. "Is there anything you can do about the problem that's on your mind? Jake?" she prompted, touching his arm when he was lost in thought.

"No," he said. "There's nothing I can do about it."

"Okay, then. No shoptalk," Hope said firmly.

"I'll drink to that." Charity held up her chardonnay and the four of them clinked glasses. After sipping, she set it on the glass table between them. "Can we talk about that adorable hot-pink Michael Kors handbag?"

Faith and Hope groaned.

Jake was clueless. "This is about shopping, right?"

"Crystals. At CityCenter. It's not shopping. It's a religious experience," Charity corrected. She crossed one jeans-clad leg over the other.

"How do you figure?" Hope asked.

"It's as close to heaven as I ever expect to get on earth."

"There's something you should know about Charity." Hope grinned at her sister. "She's only working as a nurse to support her retail habit."

The redhead smiled right back. "It's my duty as a loyal American to stimulate the economy."

Faith sipped her cabernet, then set the wineglass on a cocktail napkin. "If there was an Olympic gold medal for shopping, you'd definitely be a favorite to win."

"Thanks." The baby sister was completely undaunted by the teasing. "But you have to admit that I have standards. Otherwise I wouldn't have thought twice about buying that handbag."

"It was over a thousand dollars," Faith protested.

"But I loved it."

"That was obvious. And you definitely get points for negotiating," Hope said.

Charity nodded. "You're talking about my idea for all of us to chip in and buy it, then share."

"Yeah. That was a creative plan, but doomed from the start." Faith's expression was wry.

"I don't see why you both were against it. A designer bag that you get to use four months of the year. Seems like a sweet deal to me."

Hope shook her head. "Let me say again that you're a klutz who shouldn't spend the equivalent of rent money on any one thing."

"That wasn't my fault," Charity protested.

"What?" Jake asked. He looked at Hope when she touched his arm and barely resisted the urge to take her hand in his and link their fingers.

"You really don't want to hear about that," she said.

"Sure I do. Tell me." With an effort, he dragged his gaze away from Hope's.

"It was a date. The guy was a jerk, but that's another story." Charity shuddered, then continued. "We were at a concert and I had a glass of wine. Technically it was a plastic cup because they don't use glass at that kind of venue. I put mine in the seat holder and when the lights went down for the show, he set his in the same one. The contents overflowed and nailed my purse which was on the floor. Poor baby was never the same again."

"There are so many ways that was your fault," Faith said. "Always pick the cup holder to your right. And don't date anyone with a higher klutz quotient than yourself."

Charity shook her head. "I still say that we could have worked out a purse-sharing plan that would have been mutually beneficial to all of us."

"Even though Hope doesn't live in Texas?" her sister pointed out.

"That's temporary," Hope reminded them.

"See? She's coming home soon." Charity seized the statement to strengthen her bargaining stance. "We should go back to CityCenter before we leave and invest in that handbag."

"You're persistent." Hope sighed. "And before you turn that into another negotiating tactic, I'm going to excuse myself and find the ladies' room."

"I'll go, too," Charity said, standing.

Jake watched the two sisters walk down the two steps to the door, then out of the bar. Hope was shorter than her sister, petite and pretty. If only he could define what it was about her that appealed to him, maybe then, he could get over her.

"Penny for your thoughts."

"Hmm?" Jake looked back at Faith who was watching him watch Hope.

"I'd ask you to tell me what's going on with you and my little sister, but you'd probably tell me to mind my own business."

"On the contrary. I'd be more than happy to clue you in, but I'm not really sure myself."

"Oh?" Faith leaned forward and rested her forearm on her knee.

"Are you asking me my intentions?"

"Kind of." A small smile curved the corners of her mouth.

"My continuing mission is to get your sister alone, but she's not going for it."

"So you want to sleep with her."

"Yes." The word popped out before he thought about it. "I mean no."

"So you don't want to sleep with her?"

He'd already slept with her and wanted to again with every bit of testosterone in his body. But that's not something he would share. "I've asked Hope to dinner and she turned me down flat."

"So she's not interested in you." The conclusion put a puzzled expression on her face. "That doesn't make sense."

"What do you mean?"

"Look, Jake, I could beat around the bush and play coy, but that's not me. I call it as I see it. All day I've been watching the two of you. A blind person could see the connection. You like her and she likes you."

That was something he already knew. But maybe she could tell him the things he didn't know. "How can you tell?"

"The way she looks at you when she thinks no one is watching."

"How's that?" he asked, curious.

"Like you're a designer handbag that she wants more than her next breath." She grinned briefly before concern clouded her eyes.

"Look, Faith, I could play the game, too, but honesty is all I know how to do. And the honest truth is that I've told Hope how I feel and she's not willing to meet me halfway."

"I don't get it. She's happier than I've seen her in a long time."

"How so?"

"There's life in her eyes again. She laughs and it's genuine, not a front to keep us from worrying about her. I think the difference is you."

He'd like to think so, but turning down his every invitation was a funny way of showing happiness. "I was completely up front about wanting to get to know her better and she said it was a waste of time. That she was married before and won't go there again."

"Did she tell you about Kevin? Her husband?"

"I know she's a widow, but that's all."

"She doesn't like to talk about it." Faith sighed. "Her husband was killed in the line of duty."

"A police officer?"

"No. Social worker."

"Domestic dispute," he guessed.

"Yeah. There were children who needed to be removed from an abusive situation and the cops brought in social services to take them from the scene. No one knew there was a gun in the home. Shots were fired and Kevin died."

"I don't know what to say," Jake admitted.

"Horrible. Awful. Sorry." She shook her head. "There

are no words to describe how devastated my sister was." She met his gaze. "You're a trauma surgeon, so you know better than anyone that violence happens. It's your job to repair the damage when it does. Bad things happen to good people and Kevin was one of the best. He was just gone before anyone could intervene. It was horrible and awful. Everyone who loves Hope is sorry because the trauma damaged her in a place where we can't fix it. You have no idea how much I hate that."

Jake didn't doubt what she was saying. He felt it, too. More than she could know. Illness and death were bad enough, but a life taken by violence just sucked because it didn't have to happen.

Hope's sister had just confirmed what he suspected. She kept herself in a protective bubble. A woman like Hope gave nothing less than her whole heart and that kind of shock would crush a sensitive soul like hers.

The revelation explained a lot, but he wasn't sure how much it helped. He could repair bodies, but souls were not in his job description.

Especially when the lady in question didn't want to be repaired.

"So, can we talk about Jake?"

Hope had barely walked into her sisters' room at Red Rock Resort before her youngest sister, Charity, asked the question. There was no easy way to avoid a discussion because she'd planned to spend the night here. If she left in a huff, they'd tattle to her mother, which would cause her parents to worry. It couldn't hurt to try evasive tactics.

There were two queen-size beds pushed up against a wall painted a bold shade of brick. The remaining paint was a soothing shade of pale yellow. In the bathroom, tile covered the floors and the shower had a glass door. All e handles and faucets were gold. If she commented on the accommodations, that might deflect Charity's question about her and Jake.

"Nice room," Hope said, sitting on the rust-colored chair before settling her feet on the matching ottoman.

"Beautiful," Faith commented, sitting on the bed across from her.

"Comfy," Charity added, sitting next to Faith.

They both stared at Hope.

Evasive tactics hadn't ever worked especially well with her sisters. They never let her get away with it. Plan B: Bluff. Maybe she'd lived in this gambling town long enough to pull it off.

"So what did you think of Jake?" She plastered a smile on her face. "Hottie? Right?"

Charity shifted into a cross-legged position on the bed. "He reminds me of that actor on the TV medical show. The character who needed a new heart and died."

"You actually watch that?" Faith asked.

"Yeah. You don't?"

"Too much like being at work. What about you, Hope?"

"I don't have much time for anything *but* work. All my attention is focused on getting the hospital open on time." All the attention not used up by thinking about Jake, that is.

"It's time to move on, Hope." Faith wasn't talking about the job now.

"You've grieved long enough," Charity said, suddenly serious. It was as if they'd planned a coordinated attack.

"How do you know it's been long enough?" she demanded. "Have either of you ever lost the love of your life? Are you experts on the *dos* and *don'ts* of it all? Maybe Emily Post has a chapter in an etiquette book about just the right way to handle the loss of a spouse so that you don't offend your family."

"I wouldn't know about that," Faith said quietly. "But I've heard it said that you always hurt the ones you love, the ones you shouldn't hurt at all."

"We're only trying to help," her little sister added.

"I know." Hope felt like sludge—slimy, black and disgusting. "I'm sorry. If it weren't for you guys, Mom and Dad, I wouldn't have made it this far. It's just—"

"Two years is a long time and—"

"And nothing," Hope said before Faith could finish. "For the record, I'm not grieving anymore. I've made it through all the steps and reached acceptance."

"So what you're trying to say is that you and Jake are hooking up?" Charity asked.

Hope shook her head. "I'm trying to tell you that I'm past the grief. But there is no me and Jake. Or anyone else for that matter. It's the only way I know to keep from hurting like that. I don't want to ever experience that dark pit of despair again."

The silence dragged on as she studied her sisters, hoping the message to stand down had gotten through. They stared back until Faith slanted their younger sister a look.

Charity nodded, then stretched and yawned. It wasn't a great performance. "I'm tired."

"You shower first," Faith directed.

"Roger. We have a plane to catch tomorrow." Charity slid off the bed and stood. "Speaking of tomorrow, there's still time to swing by the Michael Kors store. I bet that evening bag is still there."

"You're probably right," Hope said. "No one can afford it."

"No, really, we can, if we all chip in. I can work out a custody agreement satisfactory to everyone. Trust me."

Hope laughed. "Never trust anyone who says 'Trust me.'"

"I thought you were exhausted," Faith reminded her, nodding toward the bathroom.

"Yeah. Right." Charity moved around the bed. "Lusting after something I'll never have is a giant energy suck."

When the door closed Faith said, "I'm sure you can relate to what she just said. And I don't mean pricey purses."

"You drew the short straw," Hope guessed. "The one who has to talk some sense into me."

Faith shrugged. "So tell me about Jake."

This would be best handled by pretending he was just a friend and that they hadn't had sex. "Jake had a difficult childhood. His dad walked out on the family and he and his mom ended up on the streets."

"Oh, my."

"Yeah." Hope warmed to her subject. "In spite of that, he got an education. Went to college and med school. He's a gifted surgeon and works a couple weekends a month at a free clinic. And he bought a house for his mother."

"Have you met her?" Faith asked.

"Yes. Very nice woman who is understandably proud of her son."

"Now tell me about Jake and *you*."

"There is no Jake and me."

Faith nodded as if she'd expected that answer. "That's because you're building barriers as fast as you can."

"What does that mean?" Hope removed her feet from the ottoman and slid forward in the chair.

"You like him. He likes you." Faith put up a hand to shush the protest. "Don't waste breath. I could see it every time you looked at each other. The electricity coming off you two could light the Vegas Strip for a month."

No way, Hope thought. She'd been careful to hide her emotions. "Your imagination is working overtime."

Faith's eyes narrowed. "You slept with him."

Hope's heart felt like it stopped for two beats, then speeded up double time. "Where in the world did you get that idea?"

"I was fishing, but you just confirmed it. The best defense is a robust offense. You went to bed with him and now you feel guilty."

The bad news was her sister could see through her. It was also the good news even though right this minute she wasn't sure why that was so. "I will neither confirm nor deny that you're right."

"It doesn't matter whether I'm right. The fact is that you're attracted to him. And that's a wonderful thing. It's a sign that you're moving forward."

"Wrong," Hope said. "This job is temporary. I'm not staying in Las Vegas and Jake's practice is here. His mother is here. Staying put is a deal breaker for me. There's nothing now nor will there ever be anything between Jake and me."

"But there could be. And the job could be permanent if you said the word."

"That's true. But this is my life, not a romance novel. There are no happy endings for me and I won't take a permanent position."

Faith's eyes brimmed with sadness. "Hope, honey, I understand why you're protecting yourself. I do. This is me. I held you when you cried after Kevin died. The thing is, if you keep on like this you'll miss the pain, but you'll also miss out on the passion."

She'd had passion and pain. If those were her choices,

I prefer to continue in this holding pattern that was ...her.

"I'm okay with that," Hope said.

"Kevin wouldn't be okay with it. He was all about living and loving."

The words pierced her protective shell and lodged in her heart. He had been all that, Hope remembered sadly and glared at her sister. "That was low."

"I'm okay with that," Faith echoed. "Whatever it takes to get through. You should know better than anyone about this precarious, unexpected fragile thing we call life. Stuff happens. You need to grab every possible moment of happiness and hang on with both hands."

"Tell me how to stop loving Kevin so I can let someone else into my heart."

"Oh, sweetie, you don't have to stop. You'll always love Kevin. No one expects that to go away. But it doesn't mean that you can't fall in love again. There's no reason you can't find another man to build a life with."

"What if my definition of a happy life is to not be hurt again?"

"No one can guarantee that."

"And that's my point."

"Oh, Hope—" Faith's shoulders slumped and there was surrender in her expression. "I had to try and talk some sense into you."

"I love you, too." Hope stood and hugged her sister. "And I appreciate it. Good try. But I've got to navigate this situation the best way for me."

Faith nodded. "But do me a favor. When Charity comes out of the bathroom, just tell her you've seen the light and I saved you."

Hope arched one eyebrow. "So you guys did have a plan."

"Yeah. Me first. She was reinforcements."

"I have the world's best sisters."

"And don't you ever forget that," Faith said with a grin.

As if, Hope thought. The family she'd been born into was all she needed. At least it had been until she'd met Jake.

Part of her wanted him to know the whole story of the night Kevin died. The other part was against that because he would hate her as much as she hated herself.

Chapter Twelve

After four days of dealing with the final county, state and federal building inspections, Jake walked into Hope's office, eager to share the good news.

He stood in the open doorway and indulged himself in just looking at her before she noticed him, before she put the emotional walls up. The way she worried her full bottom lip made his chest ache with yearning. She toyed with a lock of hair and it made him want to bury his fingers in the thick, silky strands. Her tired sigh made him want to hold her. And that was the hell of it.

He needed to get her in his arms or out of his system because living in limbo wasn't working for him.

She glanced up from the computer monitor, saw him and did a double take, and then seemed to withdraw. "Jake. Hi."

"You looked deep in thought about something."

"Just cleaning up e-mail. How long have you been standing there?"

Too long. Not long enough. He couldn't decide. There was no answer to the question of how long it would take to look his fill. "Just a few seconds."

"Please don't tell me that yet another agency is here to inspect something."

"Why would you assume that? Just because we've been under the microscope for the city, county, state and federal governments?"

She glared at him. "If you're here to check out the interior of my desk, I should warn you that it might *look* like I impulsively dumped everything in there so the rest of the office would appear tidy, but I have a system and know where everything is."

He laughed and suddenly it was clear why this was his first stop after a long week. Looking at her didn't make him want to run screaming from the room. In fact, she was a beautiful woman. But it was her sharp wit and sense of humor that made all the tension go away. There was nowhere else he'd rather be and no one else he'd rather be with. Her office was tidier than the first time they'd met, but there was nothing neat about his feelings.

He walked farther into the room and leaned a hip on the corner of her orderly desk. "The inspection is what I'm here to talk about."

"It's the Nevada Department of Health, isn't it? What's wrong?" She looked grim, trying to interpret good news or bad from his expression. "The environment of care stinks? Procedure manuals don't meet the standard? Staff licenses and certifications are not up-to-date? Smoke detectors don't work? The computer system has been taken over by aliens?"

olded his arms over his chest. "Why are you going
e bad place?"

"It's easier to go there first because one doesn't have to
brace for good news."

If anyone knew that it was her. Faith had told him about
the sudden and violent loss of Hope's husband. The man
had just been doing his job. It was impossible to imagine getting that kind of news, the kind that would forever
change a person. Jake had been teasing her, but now he felt
like the planet's lowest and most insensitive life form.

"It's all good," he said quickly. "We passed the final
hurdle. Since we're all about health care it seems appropriate to get the go-ahead from the Department of Health. Val
Davis is flying up to Carson City to pick up the license at
the state capital. Once she has it, Mercy Medical West is
open for business." He grinned down at her. "You've done
a hell of a job, Nurse Carmichael."

"Thank you. That's wonderful news."

Her radiant smile chased the shadows from her eyes and
something twisted inside him. It was all about his need to
keep the carefree expression on her face forever.

"It's the best possible outcome," he said. "I'm doing the
dance of joy."

She leaned back in her chair. "I would never have
guessed."

"Like the chaos in your desk drawers, it doesn't show.
But I guarantee that inside I'm having a victory party."

"As well you should. You're about to get everything
you've worked for, Jake. Everything you want. You deserve this and should be proud. A celebration is in order,
Doctor."

He stood, then leaned closer to her, putting his palms
flat on the desk. "Have dinner with me. We'll have an
expensive bottle of champagne and celebrate together."

The vibration of his words hadn't even died away before she was shaking her head. "Thanks, but I can't."

"Why?"

"I still have work."

"Join the club. But it will be there tomorrow. I guarantee the paperwork elves will not sneak in and do it for you. Now that we're all but open, you can slow down the pace." The adrenaline of a challenge pumped through him. This time he wouldn't take no for an answer.

"It's been a brutal week and that's not going to change when the hospital opens."

"All the more reason to kick up our heels now."

She looked surprised that he hadn't backed down. "Well, you could round up some of the others whose blood, sweat and tears helped make this moment possible."

"No. This time I just want to take you to dinner. A quiet, romantic place with flowers on the tablecloths, candles and very expensive champagne. Somewhere the two of us can savor the satisfaction of goals met, obstacles overcome."

"I can't do that, Jake."

"Why not?"

When pain trickled into her eyes he wanted to back off, make it go away. But maybe the time had come to get it all out in the open. Sometimes the body needed invasive therapy to get rid of damaged or diseased tissue. Maybe intervention was good for the soul, too.

"Are you afraid to be alone with me?" he asked.

"Of course not. Why would I be?"

"You tell me. We had dinner with my mom and went sightseeing with your sisters. All evidence points to the fact that you'll hang out with me if there are chaperones, but not just the two of us. So I must have failed inspection. Somehow I'm deficient."

t you." She shook her head. "There's something
with me."

That's not true, Hope."

"I beg to differ."

"This is about losing your husband. Faith told me how
he died. And I know what you said about not leading me
on, but sooner or later you—"

"I bet she didn't tell you that it's my fault Kevin is dead."
There was anger and recrimination in her voice.

Startled, he straightened away from her. "It can't
be—"

"Yeah, it can. I'm the reason he was there that night."

He shook his head. "Your husband was doing his job.
He was in the wrong place at the wrong time."

"Because I encouraged him." Her eyes were bleak.
"Technically he was off the clock, but a call came in to
the office. The cops needed a social worker to ride along
when they removed a child from an abusive situation. Everyone else was tied up and he didn't want a kid in danger
any longer than necessary."

Jake didn't think he could ever measure up to that kind
of noble memory, but he couldn't throw in the towel either.
Not when she looked the way she did.

"Okay. So he was on overtime. That doesn't make you
to blame for what happened."

"He called me because it was our first wedding anniversary. I had a special dinner planned. Flowers. Table
linens. Candles. Romantic. We'd decided it was time to
start trying for the baby we both wanted so badly."

He didn't know what to say. If he was in surgery there'd
be no question. Scalpel, suction, skill and sutures would
repair the damage. Words were his only tool and the right
ones deserted him.

"The timing sucks," he finally said. "But it was still his job."

"You don't understand." She stood and started pacing.

"Explain it to me."

"All I had to say was let someone else go. If I had encouraged him to come home and celebrate our anniversary he would have. But that's not what I did. I told him to go do his job. That he was the best one to be there for a scared child. Dinner would keep and I'd be waiting for him when he came home."

He never came home, Jake realized. Someone had called her with the bad news. "It's not your fault, Hope. Taking the blame is all about trying to control an uncontrollable situation. It's not possible—"

"You think I don't know that?" she said. "We'd been together since college. We made plans, worked and saved for a wedding. A house with enough bedrooms for two kids. We got married and planned so things would be perfect when the time was right to have a baby. And that night, in a split second, everything went horribly wrong. He said he'd come home if I said the word, but I didn't say it."

He moved to block her path, then put his hands on her shoulders. "And you didn't point a gun at him or pull the trigger. It's time to stop punishing yourself. You're a good person. You deserve happiness."

She shook her head. "I don't ever want to go through that again."

"There's no reason to believe you will."

"I'm not willing to take that chance. You don't know what it's like to lose someone."

Not entirely true. He'd lost his father. Technically the bastard had walked out, but he was still gone. Would it be worse if he knew for sure that the guy was no longer on the face of the earth? He'd never know and it was still different from what she was going through.

"You can't give up," was all he could think of to say.

"I already have." Her eyes were bleak. "After the shock wore off, I had an emotional meltdown every day. Sometimes it was private, but not always. I couldn't control the grief. In public it was humiliating and horrible." She met his gaze. "One minute I'd be laughing. The next I'd hear a song that reminded me of him and end up on the floor sobbing."

He'd never wanted to hold her more than he did right then. If wrapping her in his arms would assure her that nothing bad would ever happen again, he'd do it. But no one could promise that.

"Hope…"

She met his gaze. "Then I began to realize something. After every episode there was more time until the next one. A couple of days would go by before I fell apart again. Pretty soon the memory of losing him wasn't the first thing that popped into my mind when I woke up in the morning. Weeks would pass without remembering he was gone."

"It's called healing. You go on living your life as before."

Her eyes blazed with anger. "After falling off a cliff, if it's survivable you heal. That doesn't mean you do it again. If there's enough pain, you stop climbing mountains."

"Listen to me, Hope." Gently he squeezed her arms, just enough to get her attention. "If anyone understands dedication to the job it's me. Did you ever consider the possibility that your husband would have gone on that call even if you'd asked him to come home?"

"No—" She shook her head.

"Be honest. Sometimes the job has to come first. Kevin sounds like he was a really good man. There was a kid who needed him. It never occurred to him that he couldn't do what had to be done and still get home to you."

Her eyes widened as she let out a long sigh. "Maybe he'd have gone anyway. Maybe I knew that—"

"It's not your fault, Hope." If he repeated it enough, she might start to believe.

She nodded, but the tears welling in her eyes slid down her cheeks. Jake gathered her against him and held her, just to comfort her, but the quiet crying didn't stop.

One minute Hope was in Jake's arms, the next he'd hustled her out into the parking lot without anyone seeing the humiliating meltdown. He didn't let go of her until he'd unlocked the car door and handed her into the passenger seat. The leather was soft but cold and she missed the warmth of his body.

He got in beside her and started the car, then pulled out onto Warm Springs Road. After making a right on Durango Road, he made a left onto the 215 Beltway and headed… Somewhere. She didn't even care.

Hope leaned back against the seat and closed her eyes, but that didn't stop the tears from leaking out. Part of her wondered where Jake was taking her and the other part didn't give a damn.

She didn't know how much time passed before he drove through a familiar gated entry and a minute later into his driveway. The front of the house looked exactly as it had the two times she'd been there, bright with strategic lighting. She liked his place. It was a reflection of him—brilliant and noble. Fighting against that hadn't worked out very well and the battle was wearing on her.

Jake shut off the car, then exited and came around to her side. When he opened the door and held out his hand, she put her fingers into his wide, warm palm and let him help her out. The chill wind blew, making her shiver.

He pulled her against him and said, "Let's get you inside."

She'd barely nodded before he was moving forward. After unlocking the door and disarming the security system, he led her into the media room.

"Have a seat. I'm going to turn the heat up and get a fire going."

She sat on the leather corner group and watched him press the igniter on the wall beside the fireplace where flames instantly appeared. A small smile curved her mouth when she thought he probably wouldn't win any wilderness badges, but she was grateful for not having to wait long for the heat.

Right after he disappeared down the hall she heard the hum of the furnace. When he came back, his suit coat and silk tie were gone and he was carrying a brown-, beige- and peach-colored afghan. He bent in front of her and took off her shoes, then met her gaze, a worried look in his eyes before tucking the blanket around her.

"I'm going to get you a brandy."

"No. It's okay, I don't need—"

"How long do you want to fight it before you give in and listen to me?" He rested his forearm on his thigh and studied her.

Her eyes hurt from crying and she was just plain tired of fighting. His fiercely protective expression had already started to warm her, but she said, "Brandy would be nice. Thank you."

He nodded, then stood and disappeared somewhere beyond where she was sitting, mesmerized by the dancing flames. A clink of glass told her he was making good on the promise, then he reappeared with a snifter in his hand and held it out.

"Thanks." Their fingers brushed when she took the glass and electricity arced from the point of contact all the way to her toes.

"I'm going to fix something to eat," he said.

So there she sat looking at a cheerful fire and holding a glass of brandy. After taking a sip, she shuddered at the taste, then closed her eyes and let the warmth roll clear through her.

Behind her she heard the rattle of silverware and the refrigerator door slamming. She wasn't particularly hungry but figured this was less about food preparation and more about giving her space.

Suddenly space seemed highly overrated. She'd been alone for a long time and could hardly remember what it felt like to have someone take care of her. It was nice. A pathetic word for the care, support and attention Jake had just given her, but the best she could come up with. For reasons unclear to her, the words and scene a short while ago in her office had lifted the burden of regret and sorrow from her heart.

The problem was that fear had moved in and taken its place. Letting go of the guilt felt a lot like flying, but a crash landing could follow and the thought of that was terrifying. Loneliness was sad, but safe. She just wasn't sure she could pick herself up and go on if fate smacked her down again.

"Are you a fan of mustard?" Jake called from the kitchen.

She shifted on the couch and tucked her bare feet up beside her as she turned toward his deep voice. Her heart skipped and twisted at the sight of him. His dress shirt was unbuttoned at the neck and the long sleeves rolled up to midforearm. A lock of dark hair fell over his forehead and the gleam in his eyes lit a fire inside her as real as the trail of heat from the brandy. He was looking at her expectantly, clearly waiting for an answer to the question.

For the life of her, she couldn't remember what he'd asked.

"Mustard?" he said.

Right. A yellow condiment. Huh? "For what?"

"Ham sandwich."

"Do you need some help? I've just been sitting here like a lump. Someone could use me for third base."

He shook his head. "You've been regrouping."

"Is that your official diagnosis?"

"It is. And brandy is the official prescription. Have you finished?"

She looked at the small amount in the snifter and drained it, then looked at him as fire spread through her for an entirely different reason. "Yes."

"A model patient." He rested his palms on the kitchen granite as he looked at her. "So...mustard or mayonnaise?"

"Mayo."

"Cheese?"

"No."

He finished up in the kitchen, then carried two paper plates into the room and handed both of them to her. Then he went back for napkins and a beer before joining her again. When he sat close to her, his thigh somehow ended up beneath her knees. She craved the closeness but also feared it.

She gave back one of the plates after he set his drink on the coffee table. "Thanks for cooking."

"Yeah, a regular gourmet feast."

She took one of the triangles and bit into it, then realized how hungry she was. It didn't take her long to finish.

One of Jake's dark eyebrows arched. "Do you want another one?"

"I'm not ruling it out until after the first one hits bottom."

He chewed thoughtfully and finished his sandwich before saying, "I'm sorry it's not champagne and celebration."

"That was my fault," she said.

"Honest emotion isn't something to apologize for."

"Still, I'm sorry you had to see that."

"I'm not," he said, all hint of teasing gone. "In fact I've been trying to figure out what to say to get through to you."

"About?"

"The fact that you didn't die and it's okay to be alive."

She sucked in a breath at the blunt statement. "You don't think I know that?"

"You have a room at the Residence Inn and drive a rented car."

"My job is temporary."

"Because you won't let it be permanent. All the better to run away from life."

"That's not what I'm doing," she protested.

"You think I don't know what living looks like?" He stared at her, intensity crackling in his gray eyes. "I'm a surgeon. I do invasive procedures to fix people fighting for as many days on this earth as they can get. Quite literally I hold life and death in my hands. Sometimes a patient slips through my fingers for no apparent reason, even though I've done everything right, everything in my power to save them. You think that doesn't piss me off?"

"I'm not your patient," she snapped. "This isn't surgery. It's my life—"

"And I'm trying like hell to save it. Because I know that the patients I lose would have given anything for just one more shot at a life. And you're wasting yours. I hate waste. It pisses me off, too."

She threw the afghan aside, slid her legs off the couch and shot to her feet. "How dare you? Why do you care?"

He stood, too, staring down at her. "I just do."

"Not my problem." She started to turn away, not sure where she'd go, anywhere away from him. But he stopped her with a hand on her arm.

"You're wrong about that. When are you going to get it that your problem *is* my problem?"

Hope glared at him. "Why did you bring me here?"

"That's a good question." He raked his fingers through his hair. "To talk this through. Privacy."

"What do you want from me?"

"What do you think I want?" he shot back.

She searched his eyes and her soul. A shudder ran through her. "A chance," she whispered.

"What are you afraid of?"

She dragged in a breath. "I'm afraid that taking the next step means that I care more than I want to. If I let myself go there, it could destroy me. Because if I get knocked down again, I'm not sure I'll be able to get back up."

Jake slid his fingers into her hair and cupped her face in his hands. She tilted her cheek into his palm, unable to pull away from his touch.

"No one knows what's going to happen tomorrow. I can't promise to make your future perfect. But I want to make you see what I see."

"What?"

"You're stronger than you can possibly know. Hope—" The single word vibrated with intensity. "It means belief in something with the expectation of fulfillment. Even your name is about moving on."

His gaze skipped over her face for several moments before he dipped his head and gently kissed her. The soft, sweet touch was like an explosive charge that punched a hole in the dam of her feelings and brought them surging out. She cupped his face in her hands, savoring the scruffy roughness on his cheeks and jaw. He needed a shave and she didn't care if he scraped her raw. She wanted to laugh at the sheer joy of that thought.

Somehow the words and tears had washed everything away, leaving her bright and shiny. She felt brand-new. A clean slate. The first day of the rest of her life.

Jake pulled back, breathing hard. "This isn't why I brought you here."

"I know." She stood on tiptoe and kissed him again.

He stopped her. "I just don't want you to get the wrong idea—"

"Every idea I have feels exactly right." She slid her fingers into the hair at his neck.

"You're sure about this?"

She smiled. "Very."

A heartbeat later they were devouring each other while closures, snaps and belts were feverishly undone. Jake pulled her sweater over her head and flung it somewhere. As soon as her arms were free, she went to work on the buttons marching up the front of his white dress shirt, but her hands were shaking and it was taking too long. He grabbed the bottom and dragged it over his head.

Then his gaze dropped to her breasts and the prim white bra holding them. He reached behind her to unhook it and the thin nylon dropped between them. "For Valentine's Day I'm buying you lace."

Her heart caught as she let herself look ahead and

anticipate the future, something she hadn't done for a very long time. The exhilaration made her feel bold and sassy. "That's a waste of money. It will just end up on the floor."

He grinned a whole lot of wicked. "But the vision of you wearing it will stay in my head forever. You can't put a price on that."

And then they came together, bare from the waist up. Soft to hard; skin to skin. The dusting of hair on his chest teased her breasts, sending liquid desire coursing through her. She tugged him toward the couch, desperate to be horizontal in his arms, but he held her fast, much stronger than she was.

He lifted his mouth from hers and dragged in a breath. "No. Bedroom."

She'd single-handedly rendered him incapable of anything but one-word sentences. How awesome was that? But his mouth on her neck produced the same result.

"Here. Now—"

"I want you in my bed." He brushed strands of hair from her face and met her gaze. "I've spent too many nights remembering you there with me. Too many dreams of you in my arms only to wake up empty and alone."

If anyone knew that feeling, it was her. It was awful. She'd been heading for this emotional cliff for a while, but the achingly sweet words sent her tumbling over.

"Okay," she whispered.

He swung her easily into his arms and carried her down the hall to his room. Light from the backyard illuminated the bed with sheets, blanket and comforter at the foot. She had the fleeting thought that just once she might like to see his bed made.

Possibilities.

It felt good to think about what could be.

He set her down and took his time removing her slacks and panties, trailing kisses over her breasts, belly and the inside of her thigh. She couldn't remember wanting the way she wanted him now and simply couldn't wait any longer.

She reached for his hand as she backed toward the bed. When their gazes locked, his eyes caught fire. Desire poured through her until there was no room for anything else, including fear.

As they tumbled to the sheets together, Hope was breathing so hard she could barely draw in air. "Now, Jake. Please—"

"I know." He was already pulling a condom out of the nightstand. "Me, too—"

He ripped open the packet and covered himself. Then he rolled over her and nudged her thighs apart with his knee. The gentle thrust belied the frenzy of movement moments ago. He entered her slowly, tenderly, as he framed her face with his hands and kissed her until she wanted to weep from the sweetness of it. When he traced her lips with his tongue, she opened to him and he plundered her until their breathing was ragged.

The tempo of his hips increased and he drove into her until the knot of need inside her tightened, then exploded in a fireball of heat and light. Tremors of pleasure rolled through her for what seemed like an eternity and Jake held her until it stopped. Then he started to move slowly again, but quickly picked up momentum until he groaned and went still. Hope held him until his body went lax and she felt his smile against her neck.

"Awesome," he mumbled.

"That goes double for me."

He chuckled as he rolled out of bed and disappeared into the bathroom. She drifted in a haze of happiness until the mattress dipped and he was back, pulling her into his arms.

"I'm sorry about the champagne and flowers." He kissed her temple.

"There weren't any," she reminded him.

"That's what I'm sorry about. Next time I'll take you to a fancy restaurant first for food, flowers and expensive bubbly. I owe you."

"It sounds lovely. Count me in. But you don't owe me. You've given me more than I could ever have imagined."

Joy welled up inside her because for the first time in a long time she wasn't looking back. And when the future stretched out in front of her, the past wasn't standing in her way.

Chapter Thirteen

After waking up beside Jake and a repeat of the night before, Hope's day had started the best possible way. After that, he'd given her his house key and told her to meet him there after work. It was nearly time to leave the hospital after a long day and just thinking about him made her want to hum. That felt like a miracle.

Condolence cards had told her that time would heal her heart. That one day she would wake up, remember Kevin and not hurt. She'd never believed that until today. Somehow she knew that her husband was happy because *she* was moving forward again.

Happiness was possible and nothing could stand in her way. But when she looked up from the computer and saw the beautiful woman standing in the doorway of her office, the urge to hum disappeared…

"I'm Blair Havens."

It was like someone poked a pin in her bliss balloon and let all the happy air out.

Hope stood behind her desk, then walked around it and held out her hand. "It's nice to meet you, Blair. I'm Hope Carmichael."

"I know who you are." The other woman ignored the outstretched hand.

Hope held her own in the hospital world with employees, administration and doctors who had a God complex. But this woman intimidated her and not just because she was stunningly gorgeous and incredibly sexy. She was a tall, slim, blue-eyed brunette. If she wasn't a fashion model, it was a loss for the advertising world. A face and body like that could sell anything.

None of that made Hope especially comfortable, but she could deal with it. What flustered her most was that Blair had a history with Jake.

Hope folded her arms over her chest and leaned a hip against the corner of her desk. "Since you know who I am, you probably didn't wander into my office because you're lost and looking for directions."

"Actually I'm here to give you some directions," she said with a sexy shake of her head that showed off all the high-priced highlights in her long brown hair. "Do you mind if I sit?"

Let me count the ways, Hope thought, watching the woman shimmy into the chair without waiting for an answer. She crossed one bare leg over the other as her black pencil skirt slid up her shapely thigh. Four-inch designer pumps covered her feet and a cashmere sweater the exact shade of her eyes completed the ensemble.

Hope had never felt quite so short, squat and insignificant in her life. "What can I do for you?"

"As I said, I'm actually going to do you a favor."

It might be small-minded and judgmental, but Hope was pretty sure this woman didn't do anything for anyone unless there was every chance of sizable personal gratification.

"Really? A favor?"

Good comeback, Carmichael. Way to go, she thought.

"I heard about your little thing with Jake Andrews, Hope."

Just the mention of his name had her heart racing. "Little thing?"

"I'm not judging," Blair said, in a tone that made it clear she was actually doing just that.

And if by some chance that was the truth, she's a bigger person than I am, Hope thought. In fact, she was bigger—taller and incredibly statuesque.

"What little thing are you talking about?" She wasn't proud about the stall tactic.

"Affair is such an unattractive word." Blair wrinkled her perfect nose in distaste.

Hope desperately wanted to ask the name of her plastic surgeon, but held back. "An affair? With Dr. Andrews?"

"Hospital gossip," Blair said, shrugging.

It wasn't gossip if Jake told her exactly what was going on with Hope. But she was right about the word *affair*. It was unflattering.

"Let me get this straight," Hope said. "Are you asking me if Jake and I are seeing each other?"

"Oh, sweetie—" Blair shook her head. "I'm saying that everyone knows you're Jake's flavor of the month."

"That implies he'll be moving on." Hope was seething and barely kept her tone level.

"Am I being too subtle?" She tapped a long, pink-lacquered nail against her lips, never letting her gaze wander. "As I said, I'm here to do you a favor. Warn you, really. Because you seem like a very nice woman. If you're looking for something permanent, Jake isn't your guy."

"Really?"

"Sad but true." Blair's pouty lips thinned. "A fling is all you'll get from him."

"Isn't that ironic?" Hope made herself laugh.

"What?"

"I was the one who told Jake that he was wasting his time because a long-term relationship wasn't something I wanted. And that didn't discourage him."

A glare heated Blair's ice-blue eyes. "Because you're a widow."

She froze. There was no way for Blair Havens to know that unless she'd been asking around. Hope would think about why she'd done that later. "My reasons are personal."

"So are mine. And you're playing games."

"It's called honesty," Hope said. "Maybe you've heard of it?"

Blair shot to her feet. "I tried to be nice."

If that was her being nice, Hope wanted body armor when Blair went into bitch mode. "Nice is always appreciated when sincere."

"Here's the advice," Blair snapped. "If you really care about him, end it. In the long run you'll just hold him back."

"Really?" Hope straightened to her full height away from the desk. She still had to look up. "Jake is a successful surgeon with an impeccable reputation. His services are in demand all over the valley. I don't see that who he socializes with can impact his career in a negative way."

"That's where you're wrong." Blair tossed her head and flipped her long hair over her shoulder. "I can help him go places."

"So can a travel agent."

"Aren't you clever." The beautiful mouth twisted. "People with power can do things for Jake that truly make the sky the limit. I can introduce him to those people. What can you do for him?"

Make him laugh, Hope wanted to say, but somehow it didn't seem to be enough. "That's something you'll have to ask Jake, isn't it?"

"He'll get bored. You're nothing more than a distraction."

"And you're not?"

"I'm his future," Blair affirmed.

What she wanted to retort was that Jake had broken it off with Blair because Hope had refused to see him otherwise. Instead she chose her words carefully. "Look, Blair, Jake's actions in no way support your statement."

"You don't believe me?" Blair rested her hands on slender hips. "Look in his armoire. Top drawer, right-hand side."

"And why would I do that, even if I didn't think it was a violation of his space?" she added.

"Oh, please. We both know you're sleeping with him. If you want proof that what I'm saying is true, look for the diamond engagement ring. He bought it for me. A big, square-cut diamond set in platinum. Just the one I wanted. And I know it cost him a bundle. But his intentions are crystal clear. He's going to ask me to marry him."

"Why would you want to? One of two things is going on. Either he's moved on or he's cheating on you. That doesn't sound like a successful relationship."

"Jake and I are two of a kind. We both want power. He wants to have it and I want to be with a man who does. We can help each other get there. He *needs* me." Blair was adamant.

Not once had this woman declared that she couldn't live without him. It was all about control and pushing him toward success. Not once had Blair mentioned the most important thing.

"What about love?" Hope asked.

"It doesn't buy dinner at exclusive, expensive restaurants. Or million-dollar homes in Vegas, Vail and the Hamptons." Blair laughed. "Jake doesn't talk about it, but he grew up poor. Marrying the right woman will guarantee a success-ful future and that's what he'll always care most about. I understand him. Money and success will always come first and I can make both of those things happen for him."

"Okay, then." Hope's hands were shaking. She'd had just about enough of Blair the bitch. "Thanks for stopping by. It's been fun. We'll have to do this again sometime."

Blair slid the strap of her pricey purse more securely on her slender shoulder and walked to the doorway before turning back. "If you care about him, you'll walk away and let him get what he wants most."

When she was gone, Hope dropped into the chair. Her legs were trembling and she was so mad she could spit. What had Jake ever seen in that woman, besides the obvious? Then she went cold inside as another thought slipped in.

What if Blair was telling the truth?

Was Jake just having a fling and Hope was handy? A challenge? When he got tired of her, would he drop her like a hot rock?

She glanced at the doorway where that woman had stood just moments ago. Hope disliked her with the same intensity with which she cared about Jake. Maybe more than care. The last time she'd felt like this she'd been in love.

Her gaze settled on the key he'd given her sitting on

her desk and the doubts crept in as she picked it up. She had to know whether or not Blair Havens was yanking her chain.

Hope pulled into Jake's driveway and was really upset when she didn't see his car. She needed answers only he could give her and the sooner he confirmed that Blair was lying through her beautiful, straight white teeth, the better.

He'd given her the code to the security system along with the key and said to make herself at home until he got there. She accomplished the first two steps without a problem, but number three was harder to pull off. She couldn't forget Blair's words.

If you don't believe me look in his armoire.

It was wrong to go snooping through someone's things, even someone you'd been intimate with. Was that how Blair had found the ring? After sleeping with Jake?

After a ten-minute argument with herself about what to do, Hope was no closer to getting answers because Jake still hadn't arrived. But on her own she could find out whether or not Blair would lie to hang on to Jake.

Hope walked into the master bedroom, turned on the light, then stopped in front of the armoire. Her hand was shaking as she grabbed the shiny gold circular knob and pulled out the top drawer. Reaching inside, her fingers closed around a small velvet jeweler's box, the kind that would hold a ring.

"I so wanted her to be lying," Hope whispered.

But when she lifted the lid on the black box, a very big diamond caught the light and winked at her. So, it was true. While he'd been with Blair, Jake had acquired an expensive ring that could signify a marriage proposal.

This hurt so much more than she wanted it to. As a

nurse, she knew pain was an indication of healing or a warning that something was wrong. Sometimes the problem couldn't be fixed. Or it was just a matter of changing a behavior. Like pulling your hand away from a hot stove to stop the burning.

She'd gotten too close to the flame this time. The searing in her chest was proof of that.

"Hope?"

She jumped at the sound of Jake's voice. "I didn't hear you."

"I saw your car, then couldn't find you. Don't take this the wrong way—" He'd moved closer, was standing behind her, his big hands curving around her upper arms. "But I sort of hoped you'd be in bed. Naked."

His warm breath tickled the back of her neck and Hope shivered. "I never thought of that."

It was the truth. The scene with Blair playing over and over in her mind didn't leave much room for seduction plans. Blair had told the truth about this engagement ring. Was it also the truth that Jake belonged to Blair?

Hope slid away from him and turned. He wasn't in a suit because he'd been in scrubs for surgery all day. He was wearing jeans and a long-sleeved navy cotton shirt. The effect was just as potent to her senses as his Dr. GQ look. The clothes didn't make the man. It was all about the man himself and she needed to find out who Jake Andrews really was.

"I need to talk to you."

"Okay." There was an uneasy look in his eyes when he said, "What about?"

She held out her hand with the open jewelry box resting on her palm. "This."

He looked down, then dragged his fingers through his

hair. "Isn't it a violation of something to go through a person's things?"

"I didn't go through anything. Blair told me exactly where it would be."

There was bitterness in the gaze he lifted to hers. "That was low even for her."

"She told me you're going to ask her to marry you and if I didn't believe that, I could find the ring here. Fifty percent of what she told me is true. What about the other half, Jake?"

"I don't plan on proposing to Blair," he said firmly, snapping the lid closed on the exquisite ring.

"All evidence to the contrary." Her voice was so empty and cold it made her shiver.

"The truth is I came close to asking her," he admitted.

The words pierced Hope's heart. "So you're in love with her."

"That's not what I said."

"I don't understand. Love is the only reason to get married."

"In a perfect romantic world," he said grimly. "Not in mine."

"That needs a little more explanation."

"Yeah." He met her gaze. "My partners were settling down. Mitch and Cal got married and started families—not necessarily in that order. I'm not getting any younger. It seemed like as good a time as any. Blair is beautiful and fun. We got along well. But there was something that drew me in deeper. Something bigger than all of that."

"What?" she asked, unable to look away from the intensity in his eyes.

"I came damn close to proposing to Blair, but it had nothing to do with love. It was all about my pride. My past."

"But you triumphed over adversity. Poverty doesn't define a man. You're a perfect example of that."

"It doesn't define me on the outside. I can afford the car, house and clothes." His voice was low, harsh. "But on the inside I'll always be the poor kid who doesn't have jeans without holes, shoes that aren't too small or too big, or a roof over his head. I'll never be good enough."

She wanted to put her arms around him but didn't dare. "That's not true, Jake."

"I was in love once. In college." His gaze burned into hers. "I'd never been happy like that. Ever. Graduation was coming up and I'd been accepted to medical school. I couldn't stand the thought of being separated from her, so I asked her to marry me. I knew better than anyone how to survive on practically nothing."

The hurt and anger twisting his mouth told her it hadn't ended well. "What did she say?"

"She talked to her father." Jake blew out a long breath. "Did I mention that her family had a lot of money?"

"No."

"My bad." He shook his head. "Actually *my bad* was being born poor. Her father told me I wasn't good enough. He asked how I'd feel in his place. Why he shouldn't believe that I was using his daughter for her money, looking for an easy way to finance my education. Women marry rich guys all the time. But he wouldn't stand by and let some penniless loser get to his little girl."

"But he was wrong about you," she protested.

"He was. But it didn't matter. He didn't care that I'd already secured enough in student loans to pay for med school."

"That's awful, Jake."

He dragged a hand through his hair. "Believe it or not, I can understand how he felt. What kicked me in the gut was that the woman I thought loved me really didn't. She sided with the family and cut me out of her life."

"I see."

"I'm glad someone does, because I sure as hell don't. But here's the thing." He pointed at her. "Blair's family encouraged our relationship right from the beginning. I thought they didn't know about my past, but found out her father does background checks on his daughter's 'friends.' The guy used to be a congressman and her mother is third-generation Las Vegas society. They accepted me. In spite of my past. And they couldn't be happier that Blair and I were together. For the first time the poor guy got the prom queen."

"So why did you break it off?"

He folded his arms over his chest and met her gaze. "Deep down I knew that Blair and I never would have worked."

Hope had expected him to say it was because she'd refused to be the other woman. "Then why did you buy a ring? A man only does that when he's seriously considering a lifetime commitment."

"Without love it's just jewelry." He took a step forward. "Without the proposal of marriage it means nothing. And I just couldn't make myself pop the question because I knew she'd say yes. Since ending it, I haven't had a chance to return the ring."

Hope studied his eyes, the earnestness on his face, but couldn't let herself believe.

"I need to go." She moved past him and down the hall, hurrying to the front door. Desperation to get away had her practically running because she wanted so badly to be by herself.

Jake caught her arm in the entryway and stopped her. "Wait."

"Please, just let me go." She couldn't look at him and risk destroying her resolve.

"Did you hear anything I said?"

"Everything," she confirmed. "Love didn't work out for you either."

"Yeah. But I got over it. A long time ago. I told you that story so you'd understand the ring was nothing more than a symbol of how far I'd come from being a penniless loser."

"Maybe it's more than that. What if you and Blair belong together?" she asked.

He dropped his hand from her arm. "Life threw me some curves and a lot of hard knocks. But it didn't make me a liar. Or an idiot."

"That's two of us," she said. This was a hard knock she'd fought tooth and nail to avoid. Why couldn't he have just taken no for an answer? "The truth is that I'm glad all this came out. You and Blair—"

"There is no me and Blair."

"That's not what she said." Hope chanced a look at him, then wished she hadn't.

"You're more willing to believe her than me?" Angry words died on his lips as a frustrated expression pushed through the pleading. "I get it. This is just one more thing to push me away. You've been looking for excuses to do that since the day we met. You're afraid to take a chance."

Hope wanted to tell him he was wrong about her being a coward, but that would be a lie. Pain was an indicator to make you change behavior and that's what she was doing. She'd just had a taste of how hard losing Jake would be. This was her last chance to get out before she couldn't get out at all.

She opened the door and walked out into the cold. With

a desperation that carved straight to her soul, she missed Jake's warmth. But a clean break was for the best.

Her survival instincts confirmed it was the right thing to do.

But when the door closed softly behind her, survival instincts didn't keep her heart from shattering.

Chapter Fourteen

Jake hadn't slept the night before. After Hope walked out on him, he'd paced for a while, then tried to sleep but tossed and turned, wondering what he could have said to get through to her. He was in a crappy mood when he got to the hospital and it didn't improve when the first thing he got was a message to go to see Ed Havens—stat.

The president of the board of directors had an office at Mercy Medical Center on the second floor, west wing. Seemed appropriate, Jake thought. It was rumored that the former congressman had flirted with presidential ambitions until his flirtatious reputation and an affair with a staffer plus hush money to keep her quiet had surfaced.

Jake wondered why Mrs. Havens hadn't kicked him to the curb. Some women were attracted by power and paid for it with their self-respect. Blair definitely took after her mother. He couldn't picture Hope putting up with that kind of crap and admired her for it.

He walked down the green-walled hall and turned right at the end, then stopped at the appropriate office. It was entirely possible that the man wanted to discuss hospital business, but Jake didn't really believe that. Blair had gone to see Hope to sabotage their budding relationship. Mission accomplished, he thought angrily. Her next stop had probably been this very office, to pout. Get Daddy to make it better.

Jake let out a long breath, then walked inside. A pricey floral-patterned sofa and two coordinating chairs made up the waiting area. The congressman's administrative assistant, Addie McBride, was at her desk. She was a curvy brunette and smart as a whip. In the months leading up to his appointment as the trauma medical director, he'd gotten to know her pretty well. He'd also gotten to like her.

Walking up to her desk, he gave her a big smile. "Hey, beautiful, are you ready to ditch this job and run away with me to Bora Bora?" It was a running joke.

"I'm still waiting for you to bring me the travel brochures. After all I've got my standards. Not to mention ten extra pounds that need to come off before this body goes public in a bikini."

He shook his head and said, "That excuse doesn't track with me. And if the boyfriend has any complaints, you should dump him for someone with an actual brain."

"Too late. He beat me to it." The tone was teasing, but there was no laughter in her blue eyes. Another relationship had gone south.

He didn't normally pick up on stuff like that, so it must have something to do with getting dumped himself. Made him more sensitive. And wasn't that ironic. Because sensitive felt pretty crappy.

"Sorry to hear that. Anything I can do?"

"Beat him up for me?"

"That goes without saying," he agreed.

"Just don't damage those magic hands."

"Okay."

"Or that pretty face." Then the teasing disappeared and she was all business. "Mr. Havens is waiting for you."

"Do you know what it's about?"

She shook her head. "But he's not happy."

"That makes two of us," he muttered as he walked past her desk.

The door was ajar, so he pushed it open and walked inside. The room was big, with a mahogany conference table to one side. Behind it was a wall of floor-to-ceiling windows with a sweeping view of the west valley, all the way to the mountains. The congressman's big, flat desk looked big enough to land Air Force One on. Prominently displayed was an eight-by-ten photo of Blair. There were no pictures of his wife or the three of them as a family. Expensive glassware and paintings were displayed throughout the office and Jake would love to know if the pieces were paid for out of the congressman's pocket or the hospital budget.

The man looked up from his computer monitor. "Hello, Jake."

"Sir."

Ed Havens was handsome in a John F. Kennedy way, with light blue eyes and sandy brown hair. In his fifties, he was still trim and fit. A chick magnet.

"Have a seat," he invited.

"Thanks."

There were two chrome-and-leather chairs in front of the desk and Jake took the one on the left. All the better not to see Blair's photo. Every time he thought about her talking to Hope he got pissed off all over again. But Blair was past history, thank you, God. This was business. He hoped.

"Well, the hospital opened its doors on time and everything went smoothly," Jake reported. "It's a little slow right now, but we expected that. In time we'll be able to—"

"That's not what I wanted to see you about."

The man leaned forward and rested his forearms on the desk. Anger simmered in his eyes. "What's going on with you and Blair, Jake?"

"Nothing, sir. Not anymore. I broke it off. It was the best thing for your daughter in the long run." Not that it was any of his business, Jake thought.

"She doesn't see it that way."

"Give it time."

"She's my daughter and she's not happy. I want to fix this."

"There's nothing to fix," Jake told him. "Nothing you can do."

On the one hand, he could see where the guy was coming from, trying to protect his child. On the other hand, she was a big girl and had to learn to stand on her own two feet. Welcome to the real world.

The truth was that things weren't working between him and Blair. Otherwise she wouldn't have slept with what's-his-name in Europe and he wouldn't have fallen for Hope. Clearly he'd fallen hard and somehow he was going to convince Hope that he wouldn't give up. She could run, but no way was he going to let her hide.

"There's nothing I can do?" The congressman glared at him. "I went to Washington and served the people of Nevada."

It was common knowledge that he'd practically bought the seat, but Jake figured there was no win in pointing that out. "Yes, sir."

"I'm a wealthy and powerful man and you really don't want to tell me there's nothing I can do."

"Blair and I don't want the same thing."

"Really?" Shrewd blue eyes narrowed. "It was my understanding that your job was important to you. And that being the trauma medical director at this facility was just what the doctor ordered to really make your career take off. Just the shot in the arm you needed to erase the stigma of being poor white trash."

The words were like pouring salt on an open wound. An angry rebuttal was on the tip of his tongue, but Jake held back. A vision of Hope jumped into his mind, that day she'd volunteered at the clinic. She'd told him he was a good man. Somehow, those words coming from her had made him believe. No one could make him less than he was unless he allowed it. And that was something he wouldn't do. Not ever again.

"My patients are my job and they're very important to me."

"Oh?" The man leaned back in his high-backed black swivel chair. "It's come to my attention that the nurse coordinator here at Mercy West is important to you."

"Yes, sir, she is."

"More than being trauma medical director?"

"The two have nothing to do with each other," Jake pointed out.

"That's where you're wrong, Doctor."

"What are you getting at?"

"Stop sleeping with the nurse or I'm rescinding the hospital's offer."

"I have a contract," Jake pointed out.

"It's not signed. Legal is holding it up."

"At your direction," Jake guessed.

"You know Legal." The man shrugged and looked smug.

"Don't be stupid, Jake. Do you really want to give up everything you've worked so hard for? Women are a dime a dozen."

"Including Blair?"

"Watch your step." The man stood slowly, then leaned forward, palms on his desk. "This is how it's going to be. Dump the woman and patch things up with my daughter or the appointment goes away."

Jake was seething, but the same willpower he'd used to get him through cruel taunts in school served him well now. He stood and coolly met the other man's angry gaze. "You don't get a say in my personal life."

"Don't bet on it, Doctor. I can do more than make the appointment disappear. I can ruin your practice."

Jake took a step forward. "Ed, you're the one who brought up my past. And here's the thing about surviving on the street. It's down and dirty, bare-knuckle, winner-take-all. You learn to be scrappy and come out on top. You really don't want to take me on."

"Are you threatening me?"

"I could ask you the same thing." Jake's eyes narrowed.

"I'll break you." The congressman pointed at him. "I'll have your job."

"No, Ed." Jake turned and walked to the half-open door, then turned back and glared. "This is an abuse of power and I'm not the one who will be out of work. You need me more than I need you. And for the record, you can go to hell."

Jake walked past a wide-eyed Addie who was still at her desk, then out into the hall. He couldn't ever remember being this angry in his life.

Give up Hope? Not while his heart was beating and there was breath in his body. For the first time in his life he was grateful for the tough breaks that had landed him on the streets. That had made him strong and stubborn. It's where he learned that you keep fighting and never give up on a dream. He knew how to get what he wanted.

And he wanted Hope.

"Hope? Have you heard?"

Hope looked up from the budget spreadsheet on her computer monitor and saw Stacy Porter. The green-eyed brunette wearing plum-colored scrubs was standing in the office doorway. She looked like she wanted to rip someone's head off.

Swiveling her chair to face the E.R. nurse, Hope said calmly, "I've heard lots of things. Which one are you talking about?"

"The one where Jake Andrews is no longer trauma medical director because Blair Havens's father is ticked off about her getting dumped."

Hope felt the color drain from her face. "I— Wow."

Stacy walked in and stopped in front of the desk. "I'll take that as a *no*."

"Is it true?" If so, it was fifty kinds of wrong.

"I was hoping you could tell me. There's been no official statement from the board president. But it's all over the hospital." Stacy folded her arms over her chest. "I can't believe you don't have any information. I'd really like you to tell me it ain't so."

"Why would you think I'd know anything?"

"Oh, please," Stacy scoffed. "Everyone knows you're the reason Jake finally came to his senses and broke it off with Blair Havens. She'd ruin his life. She'd make him miserable. We were all afraid he was going to ask her to marry him."

The night before last Hope had seen the ring and knew

how close Jake had come to doing just that. Then she, Hope, had walked out of his house after he'd accused her of being afraid to take a chance. The words had festered and burned inside her all night as she'd searched for a way to put them to rest. But she hadn't been able to do that because he was right. Even worse, she was an idiot.

How many people got a second chance at love? And how many threw it away, too scared of being hurt again? She'd made up her mind to tell Jake she loved him. Even though she'd completely destroyed any chance that he could return it.

She looked at the E.R. nurse. "Everyone knows about Jake and me?"

"Duh."

Except for that mind-numbing kiss here in her office, they'd been completely professional here at the hospital. "How?" she asked.

"For starters you couldn't stand him when you first got here. There were sparks every time you two talked. Then at his party, the conversation just before you walked out? Pretty intense." Stacy sat on the corner of the desk. "But when Blair showed up the other day and catwalked her way into this office, we were on 9-1-1 alert."

"For?"

"Chick fight." Stacy nodded emphatically.

"It didn't come to that."

But the other woman had succeeded in breaking them up because Hope had been looking for an excuse.

"There is no Jake and me." Not anymore, she thought sadly.

"Well, according to my source, you are a couple. And unless he dumps you and kisses up to daddy's little girl—" The nurse dragged the side of her hand across her throat. "He's out in the cold."

Hope knew that was his worst nightmare. All his life he'd struggled to put the poverty and homelessness behind him. Now he was in danger of losing the appointment he'd fought so hard for.

"I just thought you'd want to know." Stacy walked to the doorway, then stopped. "For what it's worth, everyone on the trauma team thinks you two make a fantastic couple."

Hope had finally come to that conclusion, but… There was always a but.

"I appreciate that," she said. For what it was worth.

"Hope?"

She met the other woman's gaze. "What?"

"He's the right doctor, in the right place, at the right time. There must be something we can do."

Hope knew there was something *she* could do, but first she had to separate fact from fiction. Rumor from reality. She had to find out if this particular rumor was true.

She stood. "I'm going to talk to him."

Stacy grinned. "My work here is done."

Hope turned off her computer, then marched from her office to the Emergency Department. Everything looked quiet, so she went into the doctor's break room and stopped in the doorway. Jake was sitting at the table drinking coffee and looking sexier than any man should in blue scrubs and a white lab coat. Her heart stuttered and sighed before normal sinus rhythm returned.

He glanced up from the newspaper and did a double take before a gleam stole into his eyes. "Hope."

"Jake, I need to talk to you."

"Okay." Wariness slid into his expression. "But I have something to say first."

He stood and walked over to her, then reached out and shut the door. When it was closed, he took her in his arms and kissed her. His mouth was warm, his lips soft and desire spontaneously erupted inside her. Her arms went around him as heat seared all the way to her soul.

Their tongues tangled in a dance of erotic yearning. He tasted of coffee and something uniquely his own—flavors that were impossible to resist. But she had to find a way; it was for his own good. She put her hands on his chest with every intention of pushing him away, but the solid contour of muscle felt too good. He kissed the corner of her mouth, then her jaw, and nibbled a path down her neck that made her skin tingle everywhere.

When he gently sucked on a spot just behind her ear, her brain turned to mush and she moaned.

"I'm so glad to see you," he whispered, sliding his arms around her. His deep sigh stirred her hair as he held her against his warm strength.

The feel of him distracted her, but she had to pull herself together. She hugged him hard because it was the last time she would hug him at all. Then she slipped out of his arms and dragged in a breath.

"I have to talk to you, Jake."

He nodded. "You came to tell me you were wrong and apologize for overreacting when Blair told you about the ring."

"No, I—"

"Because you kissed me back just now and you wouldn't have done that if you really believed I was a two-timing jerk."

"That's not why I came to see you."

"I'm grateful for whatever it is that brought you here." He cupped her cheek in his hand. "I've missed you."

"How can you say that?" she cried.

"Because it's true." That was more question than statement.

The good news was that he'd missed her. The bad news was that he was going to miss her even more. Why was it always good news, bad news?

She folded her arms at her waist. "I just heard that the president of the hospital board removed you as the trauma medical director."

"Wow." He didn't look upset, just bemused. "I don't know why it still surprises me that information travels at light speed in a hospital." His sexy, teasing expression disappeared, replaced by grim intensity.

"So, it's true."

"Ed Havens likes to throw his weight around. He talks big, but the reality is that I have a verbal contract."

Hope shook her head. "You've worked so hard for this job. Everything you ever wanted fell into place. The staff loves you."

"What about you?" There was an edge to his voice and his gray eyes turned dark and stormy.

She wanted to tell him she loved him, too, but that would just cloud the issue.

"I just wanted you to know that I'm going to turn in my resignation to Val Davis."

"That's crazy. Why would you do that?"

"It's for the best," she defended.

"Best for whom?"

"This was always a temporary job for me," she answered, without really answering at all.

"They offered you a permanent position, but you wouldn't accept it. Just say the word—"

"No. If I go away, leave Las Vegas, you'll get the appointment. You can go back to your regularly scheduled life with Blair and everything will be the way it was."

"What if I don't want to go back?" he argued. He stepped closer and curved his fingers around her upper arms. "I had nothing with Blair. There's no going back with her. I'd rather poke a stick in my eye—"

A high-pitched beep screeched from the pager at the waistband of his scrubs. He looked at the digital display and said, "E.R. Stat."

"You need to go," she said.

"Not until we've settled this."

As far as she was concerned, it was settled. She'd fallen in love with him. She wanted what was best for him. That meant leaving Las Vegas even though her heart would break.

She took a step back. "We'll talk later."

"No. Now."

"Someone might need the best surgeon in Las Vegas. Luckily for them, it's you." She smiled even though her chest ached and her eyes burned. "Go, Dr. GQ. And take those magic hands with you."

"Hope, I can't leave things like this—" The pager squealed again.

"It's okay. Really. Go take care of your patient."

He huffed out a breath, then brushed by her and opened the door. "I'm coming back."

And when he did, she'd be gone.

Her pain wasn't any less because she'd made the choice. But she felt better that at least this time the loss would mean something. It would give Jake what he wanted.

Chapter Fifteen

Jake had managed to remove the hot appendix before it ruptured. The emergency surgery was textbook-perfect and he expected the teenage patient to make a full recovery. That was the good news. The bad was having to leave Hope before he could say what was in his heart.

He was completely in love with her. He was certain of it.

No way would he let her leave Las Vegas. Ed Havens was abusing his position. Jake would contact his attorney and figure out how to stop the congressman, but he wouldn't roll over and let the jerk get away with using his power for personal reasons.

At the nurses' station outside the recovery room, he jotted some notes in the patient's chart. He had standing orders for pain medication and the staff would follow protocols. The kid was in good hands. If there were complications, which he didn't expect, they could page him.

Mary Pat McConnell, recovery room supervisor, sat in the chair behind the desk. She was wearing a green disposable gown over her scrubs. "Your patient is waking up, Doctor."

"Good. Dr. Wallace has a really good touch with the anesthesia. Not too heavy, not too light."

"Always just right." The fiftysomething nurse smiled. "Just like Goldilocks."

"I guess."

"She looks like Goldilocks, too. Dr. Wallace does," she added. "The blond hair, I mean."

Jake met her gaze. "I wouldn't know. When I see her, she's always wearing a scrub cap."

"She's new. We should get together any of the staff who can make it and have a bonding drink with her at the sports bar across the street."

He'd known Mary Pat for a couple of years and considered her a friend as well as a colleague. This wasn't the first time she'd tried to be his matchmaker. "Don't try to fix me up."

The expression in her brown eyes oozed innocence. "Me?"

"Yes, you. I'm off the market."

"But I thought you broke up with Blair Havens. Don't tell me she soured you on love forever."

"Excuse me?"

"It's all over the hospital that her father is ticked off because you dumped her and he's throwing his weight around. You're made of sterner stuff than that. Please tell me that you didn't knuckle to the pressure."

"Okay."

"Okay, you're not back together?"

"Okay I won't tell you that," he clarified.

"Exasperating man." She pushed her wire-rimmed

glasses more securely on her nose. All the better to glare at him.

"Why shouldn't I take her back?"

"So many reasons, so little time. Number one, she'd just make you miserable. Number two, we just wouldn't respect you in the morning. You're not that spineless."

"True." He grinned. "We're not back together."

"Thank you, God," she breathed. "So you are available."

"I didn't say that." This was just her way of getting information out of him and he wasn't going there. Hope would be the first to know and after that the news would spread like the flu virus on crack.

"So what *are* you saying?" she prodded.

He pointed a finger at her. "Stop trying to fix me up."

"Yes, sir." She saluted smartly.

"Wise guy. I'm leaving now."

"Bye, Doc. Have a good night."

From her mouth to God's ear. With luck Hope would still be in her office. It was time to finish the conversation they'd started earlier. If she still wanted to leave, that would be her choice, but he'd go with her. No way was he letting her walk out on him, give up without a fight. He'd convince her that they belonged together, even if it took him the rest of his life.

Jake left the surgery/recovery wing and walked down the quiet hall, then turned right to take a shortcut through the E.R. This was the quickest route to Hope's office. He pushed the double doors open and let them close behind him. About five people were in the waiting area, one of them an infant in a carrier.

He walked over to the information desk. "Hi, Sister Irene."

The Dominican nun was probably in her sixties. "Dr. Andrews. How are you?"

"Good. And you?"

"Fine." He was in a hurry, but it seemed rude to keep walking. He leaned an elbow on the desk and glanced out the automatic glass doors to the semicircular ambulance bay and the parking lot beyond. "How's business?"

"Not bad."

The doors he was watching whispered open and a man came inside. Something about him made the hair on Jake's neck stand up. He didn't look sick, wasn't bleeding or obviously impaired in any way. The guy was fortyish, with dark hair graying at his temples. He was dressed in jeans and a camouflage jacket and there was tension along with desperation in every line of his face. He scanned the waiting area as if trying to figure out how the system worked, which most people did. But most people didn't pull a pistol out of their pocket on their way to the information desk.

Jake snapped to attention and said in a low voice, "Sister, go call 9-1-1."

"What?"

"That guy has a gun. Hurry. Through the doors behind me. Find a phone. Call the cops."

"But—"

"Go. Now," he ordered.

Fear jumped into her eyes just before she slid off her chair and ducked behind him. The double doors clicked and bumped as she made it through just before the guy looked back in his direction.

The man was big, at least six feet. Anger burned in his blue eyes which is not what Jake expected. But when he stopped in front of the desk and raised the gun, all expectations went out the window. A woman screamed, "He's got a gun!"

"Don't move." The guy waved the weapon at everyone in the waiting area. "It's real. It's loaded."

"Calm down," Jake said as evenly as he could, what with his heart racing. "You don't want to hurt anyone."

Frail human flesh had no chance against bullets. Too many times to count Jake had fought to save the lives of violent crime victims and repair the damage guns did. But he'd never personally witnessed someone getting shot. A hospital was the last place he'd ever thought to see it and the whole situation felt surreal.

"I got nothin' to live for." The man swung the gun around the room again and one of the women screamed. Others ducked, an automatic reaction. "I got nothin' left to lose."

Jake couldn't say the same. A vision of Hope flashed through his mind. He'd finally found what he wanted and she was more precious than a job or money in the bank. He loved her and hadn't told her. Saying the words seemed like the most priceless gift in the world. Unlike the gunman, he had everything to lose.

"What's your name?" he asked.

The man's wild-eyed gaze locked on him. "Doesn't matter."

"It does to me. What's your name?" he repeated.

"Stevens."

"Okay, Mr. Stevens. Is there someone I can call for you?"

"I got nobody. My wife left me. Took my kid to Oregon. There's nothing—"

"Boy or girl?" Jake asked.

"What?"

"Your kid. A boy or girl?"

"What do you care?"

"I'd just like to know."

If asking questions would keep this guy from pulling the trigger, Jake cared a lot. He'd taken an oath and the first rule was to do no harm. He'd ask questions until hell wouldn't have it if he could keep someone from harm.

"Boy or girl?" he asked again.

"Girl."

"What's her name?"

He wasn't sure how or why the questions kept coming, but they did. Maybe he could establish a rapport. At least he could keep attention focused on himself and off the other people in the room.

"Alicia." The name on his lips was almost a groan of pain and bleakness mixed with the anger, frustration and despair in his eyes.

"Why don't you put the gun down?" Jake said.

"No."

Couldn't hurt to ask. More questions. He needed to keep him talking. "How old is she? Your daughter."

Distract him until the cops got here. It felt like a lifetime since he'd nudged Sister Irene into action and told her to call for help. It felt like he'd been standing here forever. He was ready to turn this situation over to the law enforcement professionals. He saved lives in the operating room, not the OK Corral.

Where were the damn cops?

Jake's gaze kept jumping to the ambulance bay outside, praying to see flashing red lights. When Stevens didn't answer, he asked again, "Alicia. How old is she?"

"It doesn't matter. I've lost her. I got nothin'." The man's gun hand was shaking.

Cold fear was like a stone in Jake's gut. He put up his hands, a gesture intended to calm. "We can talk about things. I'm sure it's not as bad as you think."

"You don't know. I'm never going to see her again."

The words were chilling. Clearly the man was suicidal. The question was whether or not he wanted to take other people with him.

"Stevens—" When the guy looked at him, Jake continued. "Put the gun down. You don't want to hurt anyone."

"You a doctor?"

"Yes. I can help you," he said.

"No." He shook his head, eyes filled with pain. Sweat dripped into his eyes and he brushed it away with the wrist of his gun hand. "I'm just so tired of hurting. I just don't want to hurt anymore. I have to make it stop—"

Jake racked his brain, trying to think of a way to side-track this guy and give the people a chance to get out. Find some cover. This guy was close to snapping, deteriorating right before his eyes.

Just then Jake heard the faint whine of sirens. Stevens glanced over his shoulder, looking more agitated. "Everybody against the wall. Move."

With hands raised, Jake moved past the gunman and joined the innocent bystanders all huddling together. He stood in front of the infant carrier and saw that the baby was mercifully asleep.

"Get down," he whispered to the people clustered around him. "On the floor."

If the guy lost it, they'd be smaller targets that way.

Jake had heard about your life flashing before your eyes when facing death, but not for him. He could only think about Hope. Sister Irene had gone for help and by now the whole hospital would know that the E.R. was under siege by a nut job with a gun. Hope would know that Jake was one of the hostages after she'd urged him to go do his job.

For her it would be like her husband all over again. Whatever happened, Jake couldn't stand for her to blame herself for something that was completely out of her control.

Suddenly the E.R. doors whispered open and the cops rushed inside dressed in black—with helmets, bulletproof vests and boots. Their guns were raised.

The first officer inside pointed his weapon and commanded, "Drop the gun."

Sweating profusely, the desperate man stared them down and lifted his arm with the gun extended toward the police. Almost instantly shots exploded and he fell. The officers advanced quickly and kicked the pistol away from his outstretched hand.

Jake looked at the terrified people around him. "Everyone okay?"

They nodded and he stood. The threat to their lives was over, and there would be lots of time to Monday morning quarterback about how this had gone down. But he was trained to save lives and hurried over to the fallen man. Pressing two fingers to the carotid artery in his neck, he felt the pulse—weak but still there.

"He's alive. Get the trauma team in here."

Hope paced the hallway near the recovery room where she knew Jake would come when he was finished with the gunman's surgery. Word of the E.R. hostage situation and shooting had spread like wildfire through the hospital. News vans and reporters from all the local stations were interviewing everyone except the guy they most wanted. The hero of the hour.

Jake Andrews, M.D.

She'd heard how he kept the man talking, to prevent him from shooting people who were just in the wrong place at the wrong time. Hospitals were in the business of making people better. It was the last place anyone would expect to be gunned down.

She thought of Kevin and felt the last tiny tug on her heart. He'd been a good and decent man she'd loved with all her heart. But now it was time to tuck away the feelings into a warm, safe place. It was time to move on.

And she desperately needed to see Jake. To make sure he was all right.

As if her prayer was answered, a door opened at the end of the hall and there he was. She started toward him but her legs trembled. It was like a bad dream where she needed to move but couldn't make herself go fast enough. But he met her halfway. She stared at him and her first thought was that he was alive. Her second was that he looked so tired.

Then she burst into tears.

He pulled her into his arms. "Don't, Hope. Please, don't cry."

But she couldn't seem to stop. She'd stuffed the fear down for hours and it was all coming out now. And there was an awful lot of terror.

"Come on."

He wrapped an arm around her shoulders and guided her down the hall. She had no idea where they were going and couldn't find the will to care. Jake was here. He was warm and solid and most important—he was here. That was all that mattered to her.

He took her inside a room and let the door close behind them. They were alone and he held her. She rested her cheek against his chest, listening to the strong steady beat of his heart while the sobs slowly tapered off.

Finally she lifted her head and brushed the tears away with the palms of her hands. He'd brought her to the doctor's break room which seemed an ironic setting for her breakdown.

She blew out a long breath and said, "I'm sorry. I didn't mean for that to happen."

He studied her, his gaze intense, assessing. "For the record, I hate it when you cry. Don't ever do that."

"Okay. As long as you promise not to ever be held hostage by a gun-wielding wacko again."

"Deal. So…" He brushed a hand over the back of his neck. "Why did you? Cry, I mean."

"Because you're okay."

"You knew I was." He looked puzzled. "The cops had everything locked down in minutes. You'd have heard if there were any other casualties."

She'd seen the yellow crime-scene tape closing off the area. The bullet holes in the wall. The blood still on the floor where the only victim had been before Jake had gotten him into surgery.

"I knew," she said. "But I needed to see with my own eyes that you weren't hurt."

"Dammit. I was afraid of that." The angry words were spoken through clenched teeth. "I couldn't get to you. The guy was losing a lot of blood and we had to get him into the O.R. right away."

"I know." How could she not be in love with this man?

"He caught a couple of bullets, but the one in his abdomen nicked a couple of organs. It was touch and go, but we stopped the bleeding and repaired the damage. The next twenty-four hours are crucial."

"You went from hostage to hero in a heartbeat. Most people wouldn't understand how you could be held at gunpoint one minute, and the next be in surgery battling for the life of the man who threatened you and a lot of other people."

"Crazy, huh?"

"He could have just as easily shot you." Her mouth trembled and she caught her top lip between her teeth.

"I don't think he's a bad guy." Sympathy swirled in his gray eyes. "His wife left him and took his daughter. To Oregon. He snapped. The working theory is that he wanted to commit suicide by cop. I really don't think it was his intention to harm anyone else."

"You saved him," Hope said, in awe of what he'd done.

"Now he has a chance to get the mental health care he needs and straighten things out. Life is precious."

"You're preaching to the choir. I know that better than anyone."

He got her drift and shook his head, clearly angry at himself. "I'm sorry, Hope. I was afraid you'd blame yourself for sending me off to a dangerous situation."

"Don't be sorry. You did what you had to do, what you do best."

"Still, I—"

"And just so you know? I didn't blame myself. Not even close. The only thing I blamed myself for is not telling you I love you when I had the chance."

Jake looked surprised. "You do?"

No more running. No more hiding. If she'd blown everything with him, so be it. But not having a chance to tell him how much she loved him was the worst mistake she could make. She met his gaze and nodded. "Yes, I'm in love with you."

"Well, you're not the only one who had an epiphany. Looking death in the eye makes you think."

"About regrets?" she asked.

He nodded. "You know what they say about your life flashing before your eyes when in a dangerous situation?"

"Yeah."

"Well, it's not true."

"No?"

"At least not for me."

"What were you thinking about?" she asked softly.

"You." He drew in a shuddering breath. "All I could think was that I love you more than life and I might never have the chance to tell you."

"Oh, Jake—" Her voice caught as emotion grew thick in her throat.

"Since I was a kid, homeless and hungry, all I could focus on was security. To me that meant wealth. I forgot that money can't buy happiness. That the best things in life are free."

She took a step forward, close enough to feel the heat from his body. His breath stirred the wisps of hair on her forehead.

"I couldn't agree more," she said.

"For so long I've been putting all my energy into work and getting appointed medical director. Now that it could be off the table—"

"Oh, please," she interrupted. "Havens wouldn't dare fire the hero of the hour, the man who got between a crazed gunman and innocent bystanders."

He grinned. "There is that."

"The press would crucify him. I think he'll be eating crow. The only question is how he'll grovel when he has to get you back."

"More important than that…" The honest intensity in his eyes was incredibly compelling. "The thing is… What I'm trying to say…" He thought for a moment, his gaze locked on hers. "Rich, poor or somewhere in between, whatever time I have on this earth, I want to spend in your arms. I'm completely in love with you. Marry me, Hope."

Her heart filled to the rim and overflowed with happiness.

She smiled and touched his face. The scruff on his jaw scraped her palm and it was the best feeling in the world.

"I so wasn't looking for love, but it managed to find me. And I learned the best lesson of all. Life is full of surprises—both good and bad. Love gets you through the rough patches."

"Is that a yes to my proposal?" he asked impatiently.

"That's a big, fat, try-and-stop-me yes." His wonderful grin made her heart beat faster. "Thanks to my favorite doctor, I learned that every day is precious and every second of every day should be lived to the fullest."

She stood on tiptoe, her mouth almost touching his. Before kissing the daylights out of him, she whispered, "My hero."

* * * * *

Cherish™

ROMANCE TO MELT THE HEART EVERY TIME

My wish list for next month's titles...

In stores from 18th January 2013:

☐ The Heir's Proposal — Raye Morgan

& The Secret That Changed Everything — Lucy Gordon

☐ Mendoza's Miracle — Judy Duarte

& Fortune's Hero — Susan Crosby

In stores from 1st February 2013:

☐ The Texas Ranger's Reward — Rebecca Winters

& The Ranger's Secret — Rebecca Winters

☐ A Bride for the Maverick Millionaire — Marion Lennox

& The Billionaire's Fair Lady — Barbara Wallace

Available at WHSmith, Tesco, Asda, Eason, Amazon and Apple

Just can't wait?

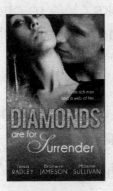
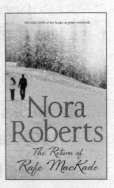